THE RUGS HAD been moved aside, and Chokolade heard the satisfying click of her shoes against the hard wooden floor. Once she moved into the dance it was as though she was possessed. The music, and Gyuri's strong arm about her waist, made her drunk. He swayed above her, and her body moved to the rhythm that he imposed upon her. Chokolade's mind exulted at being conquered in the dance, and then her mind was no more, her body was imbued with its own spirit. She had no will. The music, and the movement of the man who spun her away from him and then gathered her back into his arms, ruled her completely. Did he move away from her? Her heels rat-a-tapped their anguish on the hard floor. Did he desire her again? Her eyes shut with pleasure. A pleasure that actually made her moan as he leaned so close that their bodies brushed against each other.

Romany Passions

ALEXANDRA ELLIS

A BERKLEY BOOK
published by
BERKLEY PUBLISHING CORPORATION

Berkley Publishing Corporation
200 Madison Avenue
New York, New York 10016

SBN 425-03672-3

*BERKLEY MEDALLION BOOKS are published by
Berkley Publishing Corporation
200 Madison Avenue
New York, N.Y. 10016*

BERKLEY MEDALLION BOOK ® TM 757,375

Printed in the United States of America

Berkley Edition, APRIL, 1978

PART ONE

The Great Plains of Hungary

Chapter I

IT WAS COLD on the Great Hungarian Plains, too cold for early November. The peasants cut more firewood, and predicted a bad winter. The landowners living in the great houses gave orders to their overseers about stockpiling more corn, more feed for the animals. The nobility who lived behind the thick walls of their stone castles talked about leaving the Hungarian countryside for their homes in Vienna and Budapest.

All the people living on the Puszta, which was just one part of the Great Plains, looked warily at the gray sky that stretched above them. But the people who lived in huts, houses, and castles were not as frightened by those skies as the Gypsies who camped beneath them.

Most of the Romanys had moved south to Spain, or to the warm pine forests of Austria, but the Tura Tribe was still on the Puszta. Still there in November of God's—or maybe it was the devil's—year of 1887. They camped in northern Hungary as though it were the middle of May, surrounded by cornflowers and sunflowers in bloom.

Lying between two feather quilts in her caravan, Chokolade Tura could hear the complaining voices of some of the other Turas huddled around a crackling fire.

"He's crazy—crazy. We should have been gone from the Puszta a month ago. We should be in Austria by now."

"A fine Gypsy chief—Gyuri Tura—a disgrace to all Romanys."

Chokolade buried her head in a pillow, but even though she could no longer hear them, she knew that what the Turas were saying about her brother Gyuri was true. When their father, Chief Bela, was dying he named Gyuri as the next chief. But a chief was responsible for the well-being of the entire tribe, and while Chokolade loved her brother, she knew that Gyuri wasn't a proper chief. When she raised her head from the pillow a few minutes later she realized that the complaining voices were down to a murmur; that meant her brother had returned to camp.

Chokolade sat up halfway in her feathery bed and pulled aside the curtain that hid the entrance to the caravan. Yes, there was Gyuri. He was older than she, but she had to smile at his boyishness. He was doing his best to pretend that he wasn't cold. He, too, had built a small fire, but he stretched out on the cold ground, leaning back from the fire as though it were a spring day. And instead of donning a warm, sheepskin cape, he still wore his black, flower-embroidered felt vest which Chokolade knew wasn't warm at all.

The dark-haired Gypsy girl pulled the feather

4

quilt more closely about her. She knew what it was that made Gyuri play the fool; it was his romance with Countess Magda Meleki that kept them on the plains. The Countess's castle commanded the entire section of the Puszta where they were camped, and day after day they remained on the cold, open plain while Gyuri waited for a summons to the castle and to the Countess's bed.

It was all done with a certain amount of fine pretense, of course. The Countess invited both Gyuri and Chokolade to dance for her guests, but Chokolade knew that it wasn't the dancing that interested the Countess.

What was it like to have a man eager to obey your every command, Chokolade wondered. As a Romany she had heard of love potions and spells that drove a man wild, but as she hugged her knees beneath the feather quilt Chokolade knew that the Countess used a different kind of enchantment. Gyuri, she shook her head at the idea of her brother's foolishness. She tried to be understanding, but the understanding that could only be supplied by her heart was completely missing.

Chokolade had danced before many men; she had seen the way they looked at her, and she knew what their looks meant, but never, never had she been interested enough to return a glance, or respond to a touch. Gyuri talked frequently of finding her a man—a husband—among one of the other Gypsy tribes, but she shied away from such talk. Chokolade knew that she would have to marry another Gypsy, because to marry a *gajo*—a non-Gypsy—was unthinkable. But she also knew what happened to Romany women once they did get married. They lived quietly behind caravan curtains, cooked endless meals, bore a child a year, and were old by thirty.

More, she thought restlessly, *I want more.* But the thought was incomplete, because not even to herself could she define that longing for something more, something else. If only she had someone to talk to, someone to whom she could express her feelings. Once, and only once, she had tried to talk to her brother, but Gyuri's quick answer infuriated her.

"You need a man," he had said, "someone to take you to bed. That would quiet you down."

But Chokolade didn't want just any man; she needed more than that. She had lived all her nineteen years among Gypsy caravans, but she glimpsed other lives when she danced in such elegant places as Meleki Castle, and wondered what it would be like to live with a roof over head and thick rugs beneath her feet. Just once, she thought, just once it would be wonderful to have a dinner served to me on delicate china, and to wear fine clothes.

The other members of the tribe seemed satisfied with their lives. Chokolade had never heard anyone complain, even though they were always on the move. None of them had ever lived in a house, or had warm water to wash with. Their meals were cooked over an open fire, and the meat was usually burned on the outside and cold on the inside, unless, of course, they ate the familiar *gulyas* stew. Why was she the only one to be restless, to want that indefinable more?

She thought rebelliously about her brother; he would be happy to hand her over to any man—as long as he was a Romany. Gyuri wouldn't care if the man beat her, or wore her out bearing children. That was the way of life for Gypsy women, but for a Gypsy man, things were very different.

Chokolade kicked the feather quilt. A Gypsy man was a free spirit. As he ranged about the world he enjoyed life and *gajo* women. No one expected him to live quietly behind caravan curtains after he got married.

Chokolade peered out at her brother once again. Oh the fool! She watched him take a wedge of *paprikas szalonna*, the smoked bacon that she also loved, from his leather bag. She laughed to herself. It was clear that Gyuri was doing all this to show the Turas how relaxed he was, how little he felt the cold. He would sit by the fire and calmly roast bacon when he should have been busy getting the caravans packed and moving away from the Plains.

As she watched, he pulled an unsheathed knife from his boot top and cut a wide strip from the *szalonna* and pierced it with a sharp stick. Rummaging again in the leather pouch, he pulled out an even larger wedge of potato bread. His sharp knife cut a slice of bread three times as wide as a man's palm and twice as thick.

Gyuri sat up and held the stick with the *szalonna* over the fire. When the bacon began to sputter and crackle, he pulled the stick back from the flames, and let the bacon fat drip on the slice of bread.

"Look at him!" Chokolade heard a woman's enraged scream, and she knew that it was Aunt Haradi, the oldest woman of the Tura Tribe. "He sits there roasting *szalonna* as though he had nothing else in the world to do! *Szalonna*—when the snows may come any moment, and we'll be trapped without shelter on this Godforsaken plain. We should have been on our way many good weeks ago.

"But this—this fine gentleman—he just sits here as though we were nothing to him. Our Chief, hah!" Haradi Neni spat into the fire, barely missing the roasting bacon.

Gyuri was on his feet in an instant. His meal was lost among the ashes of the fire.

"Another word," he shouted, "just one word more and I will tell every peasant on the Puszta that you are a witch. *Ap i mulende*—I will."

Ap i mulende—by death—the strongest of all Romany oaths.

Chokolade shuddered when she heard those words, and she saw Aunt Haradi back away from Gyuri. The old woman twitched her long, black skirt out of his way, as though afraid of being touched by him. Her hand, with rings on each finger, covered her mouth, and Gyuri saw her eyes, black in the firelight, fill with fear.

Both Chokolade and Gyuri knew what she was afraid of. The peasants in the nearby village of Sárospatak had long been muttering that the Tura Tribe had a real witch among them. Oh, they didn't mind crossing her palm with a small silver piece to hear her predict a good fortune, but they knew all about witches. Fortune-telling didn't bother them. But a witch could do other things as well. She could lay spells, she could invite the devil to pay them a visit. Yes! The Turas had been aware of the way the peasants had looked at Haradi Neni during recent weeks. The mellowness that they seemed to feel during the warm summer months disappeared as the weather grew colder, and they withdrew into their suspicious, sour selves. The Turas had heard of another old woman whose cottage had been burned to the ground, with her in it. Supposedly, it was an accident, but the Gypsies were wise to the ways of such accidents, and they were sure that the peasants had crept up on the cottage in the middle of the night to destroy a harmless old woman whom they believed to be a witch.

Gyuri felt a twinge of shame when he looked at the frightened old woman, still staring at him. Well, so be it. He was the Chief, it was good for the tribe to be a little afraid of him. But now, Uncle Miklos came forward and put his arm around Aunt Haradi.

"*Ap i mulende*," he repeated his nephew's words with anger, "by death—we don't use those words against each other, only against the *gajo*. You know you may say anything to a *gajo*—they say plenty to us. But *ap i mulende*—an oath to call the devil or death. Watch that they both do not arrive to do your bidding." He led Haradi Neni back to her own caravan.

Gyuri turned back to the fire. He no longer had appetite for another wedge of roast bacon. Even though his back was to the circle of caravans, he knew what Aunt Haradi was doing.

She was sitting on a fringed and striped blanket laying out the *maryas* cards. Over and over she would shuffle the deck and lay out the cards that pictured knights, kings, queens, peasants, and jesters. And over and over again the same card turned up to lead the pack: the black knight, the sign of danger, maybe even the sign of death.

Gyuri could hear her mumbling, and he knew she was afraid of what the cards told her. Was the danger and death meant for him? He leaned back from the fire, stretched out his long legs, and laughed. Perhaps that was his fate—to die because of a woman. He laughed again, because even he could see the humor of it.

He, Gyuri Tura, who had all the women he had wanted ever since he was sixteen, to be finally threatened by an unknown danger because of a blonde, blue-eyed witch! Oh yes, Countess Meleki was the true witch in Gyuri Tura's life—he had no doubt of that. Aunt Haradi's so-called witchcraft was child's play compared to what the Countess could make him do and feel.

All the Turas knew that she was the real reason they hadn't moved from the cold, wind-swept plain. Each morning Gyuri determined that they would start out toward Austria, but each noon he knew that he couldn't leave. Not without seeing her one more time, not without spending one more night in the witch's bed.

The Puszta was famous for *delibab*—its mirages. Travelers spoke of them, and the cowboys who tended the horses on the Puszta never grew tired of describing them. The cowboys told how they would ride along the broad reaches of the plain herding the shaggy-maned wild horses. They knew that the land was flat and empty, but then in the distance castles rose suddenly from the tall grass, beautiful lakes appeared, surrounded by groves of trees. They saw magical forests, and even snow-capped mountains. Gyuri, too, had seen some of these *delibab*, but they were nothing compared to his Countess; even when he possessed her he wasn't sure if he was possessing a real woman. She was his dream, his mirage. He touched her, but yet he didn't touch her. He spoke to her and she answered, but what did her words really mean?

He pulled his knife from his boot top and plunged it hard into the ground. This mirage of a woman, this enchantress, this witch. Each evening he sat by the fire like a love-sick boy waiting for her to call him to her bed.

He would stay with her until three or four or maybe even five in the morning—she never tired, the witch—and he would say, "I will see you tonight, yes?" and she would laugh and answer, "We shall see!"

God! He pulled the knife out and plunged it viciously into the ground once again. He had pleaded with her—as a woman pleads—and he was a man! Wherever he danced, women who saw him wanted to climb into his bed. The way he moved on the dance floor let them know just how he would move once he had them in his bed.

And the Countess knew, too—yet she made him wait—teased him. Each day he was unsure whether he would be with her that night. And here he was, waiting by the fire, waiting for her to summon him to her castle, to her room, to her bed.

Gyuri stretched out on the ground full length.

The hell with the cold! It would cool his fever. It was while he lay there that he heard, or rather felt, the throbbing in the earth beneath him. He sat up eagerly, and in the distance he could see the coach and horses riding acrossing the Puszta toward the Gypsy camp.

In her caravan, Chokolade, too, heard the sound of horses hooves and metal-rimmed wheels on the hard ground. She looked out, and saw that it was the Meleki coach with the gold coronet painted on the door; the Meleki coach was coming for Gyuri. It was either that, or one of the Puszta's famous mirages—but no, the coach came closer, something that never happens with a mirage. Chokolade knew that the harder you try to reach a *delibab*, the more quickly it disappears.

This coach was real; sent out by a woman who wanted her brother every bit as much as he wanted her.

Why, Chokolade wondered, why did the Countess want him so very much? How was her brother different from all the other men that the Countess had known? She shook her head. She didn't understand, she probably never would understand.

Chokolade saw the coach pull up to the camp, and she also saw that her brother remained casually seated by the fire. Chokolade was pleased by his control. It was enough to play the fool for the Countess; he didn't have to show his eagerness to the entire *gajo* world.

The coachman pulled the horses to a halt, and Janos, a servant from Meleki Castle, came toward Gyuri, who still hadn't moved from the fire.

There was no "Good evening" from Janos, no politeness. It was clear to Chokolade how Janos felt about her brother—how all the servants at Meleki Castle felt about him. They despised him, even as they feared him. They all saw the way their women looked at the tall, dark Gypsy—seen the way they bit their lips as Gyuri danced, his golden earring flashing. Gyuri knew that he could have any of those girls, and Janos and the others knew it, too.

"The Countess wants you to dance at the castle tonight," Chokolade heard Janos say to her brother lounging so casually beside the fire. "There is to be a party. She wants you, and she wants *her*, too." He jerked his thumb at the closed curtains of Chokolade's caravan. "You are both to dance tonight, that is why the Countess sent the coach."

Gyuri's heart and blood were pounding, but he would never let this peasant see that. "I don't know," he said slowly, his words coming out almost in a drawl, "perhaps we shall come." He shrugged. "I shall ask my sister, but then, she may not feel like dancing tonight. We shall see."

Chokolade, still hidden in the caravan, could imagine Janos's fury. The servant would be raging; how dare a common Gypsy be so disdainful of a summons from Magda, Countess Meleki? Janos would have been happy to beat up Gyuri, but it would have taken three like him to do it, and by himself he was afraid. He knew that Gyuri was quick—quick on his feet, and quick with his knife.

"Chokolade"—Gyuri deliberately lounged over to the closed caravan—"Chokolade, little sister, are you asleep in there?"

"Not asleep, no." Chokolade tried to sound as casual as her brother. "Just trying to keep warm beneath the covers."

Janos shut his eyes. He could picture the beautiful, dark-haired, green-eyed girl nestled under the mound of a goosedown quilt.

"Chokolade." She could hear the hint of laughter in his voice. And she could imagine that pig of a servant, standing there with his eyes shut. She knew what he was dreaming about, all right. "Chokolade, come out, I must talk to you."

Janos continued to keep his eyes shut. He pictured Chokolade pushing the feathery *dunyha* aside, imagining her nude body. But then he heard her voice, and opened his eyes to see her standing on the top step of her caravan. Obviously, she had been lying under the quilt fully clothed. No one could have dressed that quickly.

It didn't matter, Janos thought. Even fully dressed she was the most enticing girl he had ever seen. A shawl slipped back from her shoulders, and he could see the sweet, high breasts outlined beneath her thin white, low-necked blouse. To have her—to have her just once! Chokolade—the word for chocolate—she was well-named. Janos was sure that in bed she would be as sweet as her name implied.

Gyuri put one foot up on the caravan steps, and looked up at her. "Chokolade, the Countess Meleki is having a fete at the castle tonight. She has sent a coach especially for you. She would like you to dance for her guests."

Chokolade leaned down toward her brother. "To

dance—yes. But just to dance—nothing more. Does the Countess understand that? And the Count, will he understand that, too?"

Gyuri pulled his knife out and rubbed it against his boot top.

"I go with you, my sister. You know I will not allow anything to happen to you. We go to dance, nothing more."

Chokolade looked beyond her brother to where Janos was waiting. She wouldn't speak out in front of that *gajo*, what she had to say was only for her brother's ears. She wanted him to tell him she knew that he didn't go for the dancing, or the gold he earned for it. But that was Gyuri's business. He was a man, and he could do as he wished. But the *leis prala* were different for Romany girls. A Romany girl was expected to be a virgin until her husband took her to their wedding bed. The law was strict about that. Without virginity, a Gypsy girl would have trouble finding a man to marry her, and even if she did marry, her man would make her life miserable, accusing her of faithlessness if she even smiled at a man.

She saw Janos staring at her, and watched as he licked his lips, his eyes never moving. *Gajos*, she thought with contempt, she knew what they thought about Gypsy girls. They believed that a piece of silver and any Romany girl would happily fall into bed with them.

Chokolade pulled her shawl more closely about her, and leaned forward again to speak to her brother. "I go only to dance," she repeated softly, "no matter what you do, I go only to dance."

15

Gyuri gripped his sister's hand. He knew that she was going for his sake. They had never spoken of it, but Chokolade understood his need for the Countess, understood the way she fevered his blood.

He left Chokolade at her caravan and went back to talk to Janos.

"We will come," he said, assuming his careless air once again. "You may return to the Countess and tell her that she can expect us when the moon rises high over the Puszta. We will ride to the castle then."

"The Countess sent the coach," Janos said sullenly. "She said you were to ride back in it."

Gyuri threw his head back and laughed, and his white teeth flashed against the brown of his face. "She's in such a hurry to see us dance, is she? Well, tell her she must wait. We will come in our own good time—but tell her not to worry, we will not disappoint her guests—or her."

The double meaning of Gyuri's words were not lost on Janos, who longed to beat that smirk off the Gypsy's face. Yes, to see Gyuri Tura rolling in the dust at his feet would give him great pleasure. To do that, and then to take the Gypsy whore to bed. He looked to where she was still standing. Her shawl had slipped back from her shoulders, and he could swear that she had pulled her low-cut blouse even lower, so that her breasts seemed to beckon to him. He could actually feel the blood mount in his face, and he was breathing hard. There stood Chokolade, but between them stood her brother which meant he could do nothing.

16

Janos's fists clenched and unclenched before he was able to get the words out. "I will tell Countess Meleki that she may expect you later tonight."

"Yes," Gyuri said softly, and there was menace in his eyes as he looked at the servant, "you tell her that. Perhaps you had better start back now, my friend, you have a long way to ride. Our horses are fast, we might even arrive at the castle before you."

Janos climbed back in the coach, and only once he was inside the vehicle did he dare stick his head out and shout, "I'm not a friend to you—cursed Gypsy—no one is a friend to you haters of Christ."

The driver raised his whip above the four matched grays that pulled the lumbering coach and started off, with Gyuri and Chokolade looking after them.

Haters of Christ. Gyuri shook his head. Another false legend about the Gypsies; but some people really believed that the Romanys were descendants of the man who refused to help Jesus Christ carry his cross, and therefore were condemned to wander the earth forever.

Gyuri walked back to his sister. "What do you think, Chokolade? Did one of us truly refuse to help carry the cross, or did we come from India, the way other people say?"

"Or did we come from Persia," Chokolade said, "or perhaps we are Turkish or Mongolian?" She shrugged, "Who cares what the *gajos* believe? I've seen people cross themselves when our caravan goes by. Do you care, Gyuri? Does it bother you what the *gajos* think of us?"

"No," he said, looking down at the dirt at his feet.

"I don't care about the *gajos*—"

"No," Chokolade taunted him, "just about one *gajo* lady. Isn't that right, my brother?"

"I can't help it, Chokolade. This woman—there is something about this woman—"

"There was something about that woman last year in Debreczen, and then there was something about still another woman the year before in Abazzia, and—"

Gyuri smiled up at his sister. "You cannot understand me, little sister. Wait until you are married, then you will see."

"Yes," Chokolade mocked, "a woman can only understand this magical feeling if she is married, but a man can understand it all of his life, isn't that so?"

Gyuri shrugged. "That is the difference between men and women."

"But once she is married," Chokolade continued sweetly, "then a woman suddenly becomes so filled with understanding that she can enjoy man after man—just as men enjoy woman after woman, is that right, my brother?"

Chokolade could see the red flush beneath her brother's dark skin.

"That will never be right for you," he said, the smile gone from his face.

"But it is right and fine for your Countess?" she taunted.

Gyuri understood that his sister was teasing him, and he took a step back and looked up at her.

"She is a countess," he answered her lightly. "You know the Hungarian saying: 'Nobility can do no wrong.'"

"I will remember that," Chokolade said before she retreated into her caravan. "Our father used to say I was a Romany princess, and I shall remember that should I want to do something wicked."

Once inside her caravan, Chokolade brooded on the legends surrounding the Romanys. The ones she hated most emphasized the cruelty of the Gypsies. If some people believed it was a Gypsy who refused to help Jesus Christ carry His cross, others believed that it was a Gypsy who forged the nails that pierced His hands and feet. It was because of this, the legend claimed, that Gypsies were doomed to wander, because wherever they went the image of those nails appeared before them, and they traveled on, hoping to escape that bitter vision.

From time to time, Chokolade too wondered about her people. She preferred to think that they were descendants of Egyptians, who had come to Europe some time during the fourteenth century. Supposedly, these Egyptian ancestors were the most marvelous magicians and alchemists ever known, and in time other Egyptians feared their powers and drove them out of Egypt. They traveled far, and arrived in Europe, where they were said to follow the armies of the conqueror, Charlemagne.

What was the truth and what was legend? Chokolade knew that no one could do more than guess. Haradi Neni seemed to have second sight when it came to looking into the future, but she herself admitted that all that had happened before was a door closed tightly behind her.

"We can scratch at it with our fingernails," she had once said to Chokolade, "or we can hammer at it with our fists, but that is one door that will not open. Who knows? Perhaps when we get to the other side of the Blue Lake it will all become clear to us."

"What Blue Lake?" Chokolade had asked.

"The Blue Lake between life and death," Haradi Neni explained. "The lake that separates this world from the next—the lake we come to when we die."

Chokolade was a child when she first heard that story, and her questions were the persistent ones of a child.

"But how can it be a lake?" she had wanted to know. "A lake has land all around it, you can see the other side. You mean a river."

"It is a lake," the old Gypsy woman said, "a round lake, just as the world is round, and life is round—"

"Life is round?"

"Of course. We tread a wheel from birth to life to death, and everyone born treads that same wheel. And some say we come back to take our places upon the wheel over and over again."

"Do we?" Chokolade had asked.

"Who knows?" Haradi Neni answered. "No one has come back to tell us what they have found on the other shore of the Blue Lake."

Chokolade sighed whenever she remembered those conversations with Aunt Haradi. In those days the old woman had been loving and had cared for Chokolade as though she had been her own grandchild. But things had changed when Chokolade's father had died. The old woman was resentful that young Gyuri Tura had been named as the next chief, and that resentment included Chokolade as well.

When she got truly angry she would scream at Chokolade and insist that she was no true Romany.

"Look at her hair, look at her eyes," she would shout. "This is no Gypsy—this is a devil's child!"

Chokolade examined herself as best as she could in the fragment of mirror that hung from one of the caravan's curved hoops. It was true that her hair was a rich, chocolate brown—one of the reasons for her name—while her brother's hair, and the hair of the other Gypsies, was a blue-black. And while their eyes were a dark brown, so dark that they seemed almost black, her eyes were the green of a fine piece of Chinese emerald jade—the same color as the jade ring her father had given her shortly before he died. And Chokolade could see that her skin was lighter—the color of rich, heavy cream—rather than the burnished brown of her brother's skin. But still, it took more than dark coloring to make a Gypsy. Her mother had died when she was born, but her father, Chief Bela, was every inch a Gypsy— even better-looking than his handsome son. If Chokolade hadn't inherited his coloring, she certainly had his features: the aquiline nose, the full mouth, the broad shoulders and slim hips.

What difference did it all make? She was a Tura. Born in a caravan, living among Gypsies, and it was here that she would spend her life until she died. Haradi Neni was getting old, that's all, and old people often turned on the people they loved.

Chokolade bent over the wooden trunk that held her dancing clothes. She pawed through them

21

impatiently. She knew that they looked fine on her when she danced, and she also knew that the men didn't look at her clothes when she whirled and twisted. Her skirts would rise higher and higher, and that was all they cared about, but it bothered her that the fabrics were cheap and the workmanship shoddy.

"Why should you care?" her brother had said when she told him of her desire to own fine clothes like some of the *gajo* women she saw. "It's not your clothes they're interested in. I watch the men—they undress you with their eyes."

Chokolade had flared up at him. "Is this the way a brother talks?"

"I am your brother, true—but first, I am a man— and I can't help noticing how you look, or how other men look at you."

Chokolade had looked at him resentfully. "But you enjoy fine clothes."

Gyuri had preened like a peacock. "My women like to see me in fine things—I do it to please them. They enjoy unbuttoning a silk shirt more than a cotton one."

That time Chokolade had thrown a pitcher of water at her brother's head, but he had ducked, and the brown pitcher splintered on the ground.

Of course Gyuri had nice clothes, Chokolade thought, as she shook out her sleazy black taffeta skirt and a shiny, but cheap, satin blouse. He wore a cream-colored silk shirt given to him by Countess Meleki. And before they started out for the castle, he would change into fawn riding pants that tucked tightly into his supple boots.

Chokolade had to admit that those pants showed Gyuri's lean figure to good advantage. Both brother and sister were slim-hipped and broad-shouldered, and both moved so lightly that they seemed to be above the earth rather than part of it.

Chokolade packed her dancing clothes into a flat leather case that she could throw easily across her saddle. She knew why Gyuri insisted they ride their own horses rather than ride in the Countess's carriage. If the Count, for some unfortunate reason, should find out about her brother and the Countess, they could get away much more quickly if their own horses were waiting and saddled outside.

In any event, Chokolade was pleased with her brother's decision that they should ride because she felt freer when she was riding her gray mare, Kichi, than at any other time in her life. For reasons she did not understand, some days she felt like getting on Kichi's back and riding and riding without ever stopping. Certainly she was free even when she was in her caravan. Nobody ordered her about, nobody told her what to do—but yet, she felt this faint disquiet—felt that there should be more to her life.

She had once tried to explain her feelings to Gyuri, but he had only laughed and said, "That's because you're almost twenty and not married. All women feel like that when they're ready to have a man take them—"

"No man will take me," Chokolade lashed out at him. "I'm not here to be taken!"

"No?" Gyuri looked over at his sister, his eyes examining her frankly and insolently. He saw the curves of her breasts, her body tapering to a waist so

23

narrow a man could span it with his hands. He had seen Chokolade's fine, slim legs when she had danced, and he had watched her skirts whirl up higher than her sweetly curving hips. Any man would like what he saw, and it was clear to him that his sister was ready for a man—needed a man.

"Perhaps when we get to Austria," he offered, "and we meet with the other tribes. I will talk to them. You will have a fine dowry—"

"I'm not a horse to be traded—"

Gyuri shook his head. He loved his sister, but he didn't understand her. "But don't you want to get married?"

"In my own way and my own time," Chokolade said, "and to a man I choose."

"A man you choose." Gyuri laughed softly. "A woman doesn't choose—she is chosen."

"Sometimes a woman chooses," Chokolade retorted. "Look at the Countess Meleki, didn't she choose you?"

Gyuri's handsome face darkened. "It's too bad you're my sister. If you weren't, I could show you what happens to a woman who talks that way to a man."

"Show your Countess," Chokolade had taunted, but she was already on her feet and running when she said those words.

What could he show her, she wondered. Would he use his strength to hurt her, or to teach her other lessons? It was better not to think about some things, and to clear her mind, Chokolade had mounted Kichi and had ridden her hard across the Puszta.

Now she was getting ready to ride again, and she changed into her favorite riding clothes. She knew the *gajo* women rode sidesaddle, covered by their black habits, but she rode astride, and she wore pants—the wide pants worn by the *csikos*, the Hungarian cowboys who tended the herds of horses on the Puszta. And as the *csikos* did, she tucked the pants into wide-topped, soft leather boots.

After she had donned her pants, she pulled a man's shirt over her head. The full, long white sleeves flowed over her narrow hands and tapering fingers. Finally, she put on a sheepskin vest. The cowboys of the Puszta wore vests of sheepskin, the shepherds, long coats made of the same material all year long. During the cold months the fur side was turned inward for maximum warmth, and during the summer the vests and coats were turned the other way.

"Are you ready?" Gyuri called from outside her caravan. "The horses are saddled, and they're getting restless."

Chokolade laughed to herself. She knew who was getting restless. It wasn't Gyuri's stallion pawing the ground, eager to be off. It was Gyuri, eager to get into his Countess's bed.

"One more minute," Chokolade called, as she leisurely examined herself in the mirror.

"Hurry up!"

"I am hurrying."

There was something in her tone that made Gyuri say, "I'm coming in to get you."

"I'm all ready," Chokolade said hastily, and she pulled open the heavy fabric that curtained the entrance to her caravan and stepped outside. "There, I told you I'd only be another minute."

"Do you have everything?" Gyuri asked. "Your costume—"

"Yes, yes, you were in such a hurry a minute ago—now let us ride."

Chapter II

CHOKOLADE LOVED RIDING across the Puszta. Ever since she was a little girl, riding had always made her feel happy and wild and free. Thanks to her father, she had been riding since he had put her bareback on a shaggy pony when she was barely five.

"Horses are for men to ride," the other Gypsies had said. "Women sit up in the caravan. They take care of the belongings, the bedding, while men ride ahead. That is how it has always been."

"My daughter will ride," Chief Bela had answered. "She will ride like the *gajo* Queen, the Empress Elizabeth."

The Gypsies had jeered at the idea of a Gypsy girl riding like the Austro-Hungarian Empress. Who did Bela think this child was?

"She is my daughter," he had said, "and that is enough."

They said no more. He was the Chief, even though they were sure he had gone mad, especially when he brought a *csikos* into camp to instruct Chokolade in horsemanship.

The *csikos*, Uncle Matyas, who taught Chokolade how to ride, explained to the child that the *csikos* were the aristocrats of the Great Plains. So respected were they that once when Empress Elizabeth was vacationing nearby, she came out to race with them.

"Do not forget, little lady," Uncle Matyas had told Chokolade, "that it is the *csikos* who rule the Great Alföld, no one else." He told Chokolade the many facts and legends about the Great Plains. The herds of cattle with the long, white horns were descended from herds that had originally come from the south of Russia. They had been driven into Hungary by nomadic tribes, where they had thrived. The Puszta on which they rode looked huge to the little girl, but Uncle Matyas said that it was even larger than she knew.

"This Puszta is only a corner of the Great Alföld; the plains go on for many miles—as many as two thousand, I have been told."

When Uncle Matyas described the plains to Chokolade, he compared it to the Garden of Eden before the Fall.

"There are rivers like the Danube and the Tisza, keeping the soil green," he said. Parts of the Great Plains contained great orchards where millions of apricot trees, purple plum trees, and cherry trees bloomed and blossomed. Vineyards flourished in the Great Alföld, too, providing the country with wines, both red and white.

"That isn't all," Uncle Matyas said. "On some parts of the Great Alföld there are fields of corn so large, that, from a distance, it looks like a green sea on a summer's day. And there is wheat, too, and barley, and watermelon growing between the rows of corn."

Chokolade had looked round-eyed at the *csikos* who rode beside her. "Is the Great Alföld the world?"

"It is the best part of the world," Uncle Matyas had told her. "It is a sign that God loves Hungary."

Chokolade learned to love the Puszta, and even as a child she began to understand that it symbolized freedom to the men who lived and rode there. Uncle Matyas told her tales of the War of Liberation in 1848, when the Hungarians had fought for freedom against the Austrians, only to be finally conquered by a foreign troop of Russians.

"And did you fight, too?" Chokolade had asked the lean and weathered *csikos*.

"I fought with General Rosza for Kossuth and my country," he said.

Chokolade didn't understand all Uncle Matyas said, but she asked, "And did you win?"

"No," Uncle Matyas said shortly, "but I would make the fight again."

"Is it worth fighting, even if you lose?" Chokolade had asked him.

"Yes," he said.

As much as Chokolade loved the plains, she was also occasionally frightened and perplexed by the magical *delibab* which could not be explained. How could there be a castle on the horizon that disappeared as they rode closer to it? Uncle Matyas didn't know the answer to that.

Nor could he tell her where the fog came from. They would be out riding, the day clear and sunny, and suddenly they were surrounded by a rolling, muffling, white mist that obscured everything around them. There was nothing to do but dismount, stake the horses, build a small fire, and wait.

"But where does it come from?" Chokolade had asked fearfully.

"No one knows," Uncle Matyas had said. "The Great Plains is like a great sea. They both have fog. God must send it."

Chokolade had to be satisfied with that explanation, and for the most part she enjoyed her riding expeditions with the old *csikos*. Because Chief Bela had decided that his daughter was to ride well, she spent less time among the caravans than other girls her age. She couldn't do many of the things that Gypsy girls were taught from childhood. She didn't know how to tell fortunes, or read the *maryas* cards, or even cook a decent pot of stew.

"He treats her more like a son than a daughter," the other Turas complained, but Chief Bela didn't care what anyone said; and when Chokolade was in her early teens, the tribe discovered that the girl had a great talent—greater than they had ever seen.

Chokolade could dance—she could dance even more magnificently than the finest Gypsy flamenco dancer in Spain.

Chokolade's dancing had elements of the Hungarian *csardas* and the Gypsy *zambra*, but it also told of flamenco danced in a cave in Seville, and of an oriental nautch dance performed before the most exacting Pasha of Turkey. She brought something to her dancing that made the most cynical and experienced Romany look at her wide-eyed. Where had the girl learned about these dances? No one knew.

"It is in her blood," some of the Turas said.

"She dances as though possessed by spirits—by the spirits of all our people who came before us. The ones from Egypt..."

"And the ones from Persia and Spain..."

"And the ones who lived in Turkey."

All that, plus fire and flame, was in Chokolade when she danced. Yet coupled with her passion was innocence. Men saw an unsatisfied desire when Chokolade danced, and that was the reason Gyuri was so happy to have his sister with him as they rode toward Meleki Castle.

He let her ride ahead of him, and even in her wide pants and clumsy boots he could see the fine curves and outline of her flanks and backside. He knew that it was up to him to find a proper husband for his sister, a good Romany *pral* who would subdue her wildness, but now it suited him to have her unmarried. She was the distraction he needed if he was to get into the Countess's bed.

Luckily, Count Meleki liked to consume enormous quantities of honey-colored Tokay wine. And when that failed to quench his thirst, he would go on to apricot brandy. The alcohol made him unaware of what was happening in his own home, but it was Chokolade who made the Count completely drunk. When she danced, he saw nothing else, and it was during Chokolade's dance that Gyuri and the Countess could slip upstairs.

* * *

"It looks like a *delibab*," Chokolade called to her brother as they neared the castle.

He saw what she meant. Meleki Castle seemed to appear suddenly on the horizon, as though it were a mirage. The old, gray stone walls gleamed with light from the hundreds of ten-foot-tall candelabrum that the Countess had placed on the castle grounds and gardens.

Meleki Castle had been old in the Sixteenth Century, when the Turks conquered Hungary. The Ottoman Empire had used the castle as a fortress for more than a hundred years, but it had been returned to the Meleki family when the Turks were driven back to the east.

Some aristocratic families had left their old castles in ruins, but the Melekis were different. They reclaimed their old home, rebuilt parts of it, and used it as a hunting lodge in the winter and a place to escape from the city's heat during the months of July and August.

It was true that Magdalena Meleki, the present Countess, was less than happy with the idea of spending very much time on the desolate Hungarian plains. She went there only when her husband became dangerously aware of her liaisons in Budapest and Vienna, or when her dressmaker's and jeweler's bills became too pressing.

"But you cannot expect me to live like one of the peasants," she had told the Count. "If we are to stay at Meleki Castle, it must be properly furnished."

The Count had looked at the rooms of the castle crammed with the heavy, black, carved mahogany furniture his great-great-grandmother had brought from Bavaria and then he looked at his blonde, Dresden-figured wife. He wanted to say that the castle was properly furnished—that, indeed, there was more furniture than they could use—but he knew it would be better to let her do as she wished.

He was unable to control his wife's spending sprees. It would be cheaper, he thought, to let her refurnish the castle than to continually buy her new clothes and bijous. Furniture, would surely last longer and couldn't go out of fashion as quickly.

He remembered the one time when he assumed he could control his wife's profligacy by sending her to Venice for a vacation instead of to her beloved Paris. He had reasoned there were no great couturiers in Venice, and the Countess would be able to spend little money there. He hadn't counted on her inventiveness. When the Countess returned to his side in Budapest, she informed him that they now owned a charming palazzo on the Grand Canal.

The Count knew that his wife was as abandoned with men as she was with money. He only asked that she be discreet, and not embarrass him at court or among their friends; he trusted her to choose her lovers from their own class. Anything else would be unforgivable. As for his own affairs, he took his pleasure among women of all classes; indeed, he found women of the lower classes far more intriguing. They were more obedient, and more grateful for anything he gave them.

Count Meleki knew that his wife longed to be back at the glittering court of Franz Josef, but he had decided that they would stay at the castle through the fall. There was a certain Italian count—ambassador to Austria—he was hoping the man would be recalled to Rome. Then he would feel safe to return to Vienna with his wife.

It surprised him that his wife made very little fuss about their extended stay at Meleki Castle. He was no fool, Count Meleki told himself. He knew that Magda had her eye on a certain Hussar captain; she invited him to the castle often enough.

Never mind, better to have him at the castle, where he could keep an eye on him. The Count knew his wife's little games and tricks, and it amused him to think that he was thwarting at least one of her love affairs. Let her enjoy all the delicate gilt bergère chairs upholstered in white silk, and the Louis Quinze loveseats upholstered in cream satin. She could play Marie Antoinette, and pretend she had her own Petit Trianon, and be a royal milkmaid amidst her expensive toys. He knew that the Hungarian magnates, the country landowners who held seats in parliament and who controlled much of the wealth of the area, laughed at Meleki profligacy. But the magnates weren't true aristocrats, and what they thought could never matter to a Meleki. He did notice, however, that whenever Magdalena invited them to one of her parties, they were eager to come.

Everyone came eagerly to a Meleki party, especially the Hussar officers whose regiment was garrisoned in nearby Sárospatak. Without those parties, the officers were bored and miserable in the small town where they were quartered. A party at the castle meant an exciting evening, especially when the Countess so thoughtfully provided the entertainment of the Gypsy dancers, Gyuri and Chokolade Tura.

When Gyuri and Chokolade arrived at the castle, they dismounted from their horses and threw the reins to a waiting groom.

"I'll unsaddle them," the groom offered.

"Yes," Gyuri instructed, "and then walk them and give them a rub."

The groom nodded.

"And then," Gyuri further instructed, "saddle them once again, and tie them to the iron gate at the back of the garden."

The groom grinned. "Just in case you have to ride out of here fast, is that it?"

Gyuri looked at the servant deciding whether he should behave with indignant rage or give this peasant his "we are all men together" act. The groom seemed sympathetic, unlike that fool Janos.

Gyuri considered it safe to clap him on the back, grin, and say, "If you wait with the horses, there'll be a bottle of *barack* for you."

The groom shared the Gypsy's leer and sly smile. What did he care about his master's wife, or who was taking her to bed? Besides, it served the Count right; he still remembered the time the Count had taken a riding crop to him because he claimed his favorite horse wasn't groomed properly. Let the Gypsy take the Countess to bed. He just wished he could climb into that bed after him.

A footman with a torch led Chokolade and Gyuri into the large entrance hallway with the high, vaulted ceilings and the marble pillars.

"Wait here," he said, and he went into the large salon on the right to announce their arrival to the Count and Countess.

"Bring them in! Bring them in here." Chokolade heard the booming voice of Count Meleki.

The footman was at their side once again, and they followed him into the salon. The room amazed Chokolade each time she saw it. The first time she had been there she had rubbed her fingers against one of the walls only to discover that it was covered in silk. And such floors! Inlaid squares of wood, overlaid with blue and gold carpets her brother said came from Persia. And the unbelievable furniture! Couches and chaises were puffed with down-filled pillows that were covered in gleaming silks and shining satins. What must it be like to live in a room such as this, Chokolade wondered, a room that was always warm in winter thanks to the huge fireplaces, and always cool in summer because of the old castle's stone walls.

If the rooms seemed wonderfully exotic to Chokolade, she and her brother seemed equally wonderful to the young Hussars who now gathered around them.

"Leave it to the Countess," a tall blond officer said, as he held Chokolade's hand to his lips.

Another young officer jostled him out of the way to take Chokolade's hand. His lips sought her soft palm, while his eyes devoured her.

"I was giving up hope," he said, speaking Hungarian with a heavy Viennese accent. "I thought all this town had to offer were girls plump as pigeons today, fat as cows tomorrow." His eyes raked Chokolade's slim body and voluptuous bosom. "But now—"

Countess Magda laughingly removed Chokolade's hand from his.

"Let the poor girl alone—at least for the moment. She must change so that she can dance for you." She smiled at Chokolade. "Come! You shall change in my boudoir. And you," she said offhandedly to Gyuri, "the butler will show you where to change."

Gyuri bowed slightly and followed Janos out of the room, while Chokolade went up the curving staircase with the Countess.

"Letting a Gypsy above stairs," Janos muttered as he led Gyuri away. "The servants' hall would have been good enough for her, too."

The Countess smiled. Of course Chokolade could have changed below stairs, but she wanted to talk to the girl. She wanted to learn more about her, and more about Gyuri. Were they really brother and sister? When they danced together it certainly seemed as though there was more than mere family feelings between them. The way Chokolade moved her hips, and thrust her pelvis toward Gyuri, and the way he leaned over her. Not exactly touching but only a few centimeters apart. It had made the Countess gasp the first time she had seen them dance together, and it had also made her decide to take Gyuri to her bed.

Now, as she watched Chokolade change from her riding clothes into her dancer's costume, she was sure that the girl must have shared her brother's bed.

Who could resist a body like that, even a sister's? Chokolade had pulled off her shirt, and bare-breasted was tugging at her boots.

"Help her, Mariska," the Countess ordered her maid.

Mariska glared, but bent down to obey. After her boots were off, Chokolade slipped off her wide riding pants and stood in a pair of brief, tight shorts that were cut high on her thighs.

Outrageous, Countess Magda thought to herself, laughing inwardly. *Whoever saw such underwear?* It was like a man's! Still, she was tempted to have a discreet seamstress make something similar for her. Imagine disrobing before her next lover and having him see her in something like that. The underwear of a young man on a woman's body would lend a certain spice.

"Interesting," was her only comment to Choko-lade.

Chokolade shrugged, she stood practically naked before the Countess and her maid, yet she didn't feel one bit shy. She knew she had a good body, and that was nothing to be ashamed of.

"Gyuri had Aunt Haradi make them for me," she said, explaining her undergarments. "He said it was silly to wear ruffled pantaloons to ride astride."

"Very interesting," murmured Countess Magda, more sure than ever that Chokolade and her brother were lovers. How else would a man concern himself about what his sister wore under her riding clothes?

"Your life must be interesting," she said, perching on a white satin chaise as she watched

Chokolade ready herself. "It must be marvelous to be a Gypsy!"

Chokolade was sitting before the mirror, brushing her dark hair, and securing it in a knot with a tortoiseshell comb.

"Interesting?" She could see the Countess's reflection in the mirror. "Why do you think so? It is quite an ordinary life—the life of a Romany."

"Ordinary! I can't believe that! You travel, you never stay in any one place for long. You move like the wind. So free." The Countess moved restlessly about her large boudoir, her high-heeled slippers leaving marks on the thick, fluffy carpet. "This—this is so ordinary, so dull. I feel as though I am in a cage. I would love to be free—like you. To travel with the Gypsies, to camp beneath the stars, eat food cooked over an open fire. Wonderful!"

Chokolade smiled, but said nothing. How would the delicate blonde Countess manage, she wondered, without a lady's maid, without the comfortable warmth of this very lovely room? Would she really like to wash in icy water, to sleep inside a caravan, and to dress hunched over in that same caravan? She thought not.

"And the way you and your brother dance!" the Countess continued. "Marvelous. He is your brother, is he not?"

"Gyuri?" Chokolade turned to look at her, and her green eyes opened wide in mock innocence. "Of course he is my brother, why do you ask?"

The Countess's laughter rippled across the room. The sound was every bit as mocking as Chokolade's question. *Oh, we understand each other,* the Countess thought.

"I ask," she said, "because when you dance—there is an intimacy—not usually seen between a brother and sister."

Chokolade stepped into a white petticoat with a whipped-cream border of ruffled lace. This time she didn't answer the Countess. Oh, she knew what this blonde aristocrat was thinking. She had heard similar murmurs, had seen raised eyebrows when she and Gyuri had danced in various cafés around Hungary and Austria. If it pleased the *gajos* to think that she and her brother slept together, so be it. When she had first realized what they believed, she had been upset, but her brother had only laughed at her.

"Don't be a goose," he said, "what do you care? All we want is their money. If it excites them to think that you and I make love every night after we finish dancing, fine! They'll whisper it to their friends, and that will mean still more money for us. *Gajos,*" he had said with fine Gypsy contempt. "Who cares what they think?"

After awhile, Chokolade had learned to be as contemptuous of *gajo* opinion as her brother. And the Countess, watching the Gypsy girl dress, decided that her very silence was an admission of incestuous passion.

I will have something to talk to Gyuri about tonight, she thought. *Most interesting. I will ask him to show me what he and Chokolade do when they're in bed.*

The petticoat lay smooth around Chokolade's

hips, and she gave an experimental twirl before the long, gilt-edged mirror before she let the maid help her into a black skirt that was two or three inches shorter than the petticoat. The white ruffle seemed to peep demurely from beneath the heavier, clinging skirt. After that, Chokolade put on a sheer blouse that was laced so low that half her creamy breasts were exposed. The fabric was so sheer that a hint of darker nipples were visible through the thin white fabric.

"The fabric is too sheer," Chokolade had complained to Gyuri when she first saw the blouse he had had made for her.

"It can't be *too* sheer," he had said, and he had laughed when she had suggested wearing a camisole beneath it.

Now, when the Countess saw it, she thought she would have the design copied in a similarly sheer fabric. Not for Gyuri, of course, but for the more sophisticated lovers who would follow him. They would appreciate seeing her dressed as a Gypsy, she was sure.

The last thing Chokolade took from her leather pouch were her red satin dancing slippers. They were decorated with scarlet satin bows, and there were small metal strips attached to the tip of the soles and the high heels.

The Countess held her hand out for one of the slippers. It amused her to kick off a shoe and to try the slipper on, but to her surprise, the Gypsy girl's foot was smaller than her own.

"Quite an aristocratic foot." The Countess laughed. "Smaller and slimmer than mine."

Chokolade put on her dancing shoes and sat before the dressing-table mirror again. She deftly applied a dark pencil to her eyebrows, and outlined her green eyes with a glass wand dipped into kohl. A small pot of a red cream came out of her leather pouch next, and first she applied it to her cheeks and then to her lips.

"Delicious!" the Countess said. "How I would like to try that!"

Chokolade held out the little pot of red cream to the Countess, laughing as she did so. They both knew that only a dancer was permitted the use of this daring, new French *maquillage*.

"We are so primitive, so—so Eastern," the Countess pouted. "You would think we are still being ruled by the Turks. What is being used in Paris this very day won't arrive here for another five years."

The two women left the boudoir and walked down the curving staircase together. When they reached the hallways, the Countess signaled Janos, who preceded them into the salon. As they walked through the door, the Gypsy musicians began to play, and Gyuri came forward to lead his sister to the floor.

The rugs had been moved aside, and Chokolade heard the satisfying click of her shoes against the hard wooden floor. Once she moved into the dance it was as though she were possessed. The music, and Gyuri's strong arm about her waist, made her drunk. He swayed above her, and her body moved to the rhythm that he imposed upon her. Chokolade's mind exulted at being conquered in the dance, and then her mind was no more, her body was imbued with its own spirit. She had no will. The music, and the movement of the man who spun her away from him and then gathered her back into his arms, ruled her completely. Did he move away from her? Her heels rat-a-tapped their anguish on the hard floor. Did he desire her again? Her eyes shut with pleasure. A pleasure that actually made her moan as he leaned so close that their bodies brushed against each other.

"My God," one of the Hussar officers groaned, "if she does that on a dance floor, what must she do in bed?"

The other men hushed him, but under the cover of the music Count Meleki said, "Her brother, eh? I wager one hundred *pengö* that they are more to each other than brother and sister!"

The officer beside him laughed, but no one took the Count's bet. It was plain what Chokolade and Gyuri were to each other. Quite plain. Well, that was a Gypsy for you. Everyone knew that the girls started sleeping with every man around when they were only twelve or thirteen.

"Again, again!" the men shouted when Gyuri and Chokolade came to the end of their dance.

As usual, Chokolade felt as though she had been awakened from a drugged sleep. Her sheer blouse clung to her damp body, making everything even more visible beneath it. What had she been doing, she wondered, how had she gotten into this state? She was never quite sure, just as she was never in control of her emotions when she danced.

Both she and Gyuri were breathless, but then, all

the men in the room were breathing hard, too.

"More—" the Count came over to them—"you will dance some more?"

Gyuri pretended to be more breathless than he was. "I must be excused—a few minutes to catch my breath. But I think it is mỹ sister you wish to see dance again. Perhaps you would like to see her do a solo?"

The men applauded, and before Chokolade could speak or demur, Gyuri had signaled the musicians to play a slow, sad melody. Chokolade began to sway in sympathy. The Gypsy *primas*, the leader of the small band, stood close to Chokolade, and his violin sobbed in her ear.

Hearing the plaintive music, the Count shouted, "It is true, it is true, give a Magyar a Gypsy violinist and a glass of water, and he'll get drunk!"

The Hussars laughed appreciatively, and one of them said, "It isn't only the music that makes Meleki drunk, the Tokay wine he's been drinking all night helps, too."

Chokolade raised her arms above her head, and the *primas* stepped back and signaled the cimbalom player, who took up his mallets and repeated the melody with a faster rhythm on his xylophone-like instrument. Soon a second violinist joined in, and then a flute took up the melody.

Now Chokolade was deep into a flamenco-like dance. She wanted to dance—the dance was her life! The high cry of the *primas*'s violin inspired her. She gave a little cry, and kicked off her shoes. Another minute later she pulled the tortoiseshell comb out of her hair, letting her thick brown hair cascade over her shoulders.

Chokolade's head went back, her eyes shut. What past lover was she remembering, the men wondered? And then her head went forward, and her hair covered her face; but a minute later, her hair was tossed back again, and the men saw the emerald green eyes that laughed and mocked them, and told them as clearly as words that while many men might know her body, no one had ever conquered her soul.

"Damn," a Hussar exploded in anger, the girl was taunting him—taunting him personally. That was how he felt—and he tried to reach the floor where she was dancing. He would take her, he would show her! Other men pulled him back, they knew what he felt—they understood—but the time was not right, not now. They wouldn't let anyone stop Chokolade's teasing, enticing dance.

And then—then—when they thought they could stand no more, Chokolade climaxed the dance by starting to whirl. She moved so fast that their eyes had trouble following her. But they had to follow her—had to see—her skirt whirled around her ankles at first, and then around her knees, and then her white petticoat went higher and higher, and they saw slim calves, tawny curved thighs. And to each man who watched, Chokolade's body made a promise.

She will be mine, each of them thought, *mine*.

Count Meleki's words expressed out loud what every man in the room felt. "I will have her—I must have her—" and the fragile stem of the glass he was holding snapped.

Chokolade's face was flushed when she finished her dance. She looked like a woman who had just made love, and who had enjoyed it immensely. The color in her cheeks, her hair in disarray about her, the slight line of perspiration that made the hair at her forehead damp, all this made her seem even more desirable and available.

Chokolade looked dazed and bewildered. She always felt dazed and bewildered once she finished dancing. It took her a few minutes to collect herself, but meanwhile, Count Meleki was at her side, forcing a glass of Tokay to her lips. Chokolade turned her head to one side, and tried to pull away from the Count. Where was her brother? He was usually by her side when she finished her dance and the men began to crowd her.

Gyuri... but then she remembered. Of course, Gyuri had used those moments when everyone was watching her to escape to a quiet bedroom with Countess Meleki.

Chokolade did her best to smile at the Count, while at the same time trying to loosen his arm from her waist. She would not only have to take care of herself this evening, she would also have to make sure that the Count didn't realize what was happening in his own home.

"Forgive me, Count Meleki, I am so hot—"

"Hot, yes!" Count Meleki chose to give her words a meaning she had never intended.

"A glass of wine"—a Hussar officer stood at her other elbow—"with a great deal of soda water. I think this might help."

Chokolade turned and saw the tall officer. His face was flushed from drinking, but the short, tight jacket of his uniform was still decorously fastened with the gold frogs that made the jacket fit tightly to his body.

She saw the admiration in his eyes, but she believed that it was an admiration she could control better than the naked lust of the Count, who was still tugging at her.

"The entertainment was splendid," the Hussar said over her head to the Count. "Gentlemen!" He addressed the men lounging about the salon. "A toast to our host."

The Count reluctantly released Chokolade while he took a fresh wine glass from a servant.

"Thank you, St. Pal," he said, raising his glass, and then he drained the contents in one swift moment and turned again to Chokolade.

But Captain Sandor St. Pal was determined to keep the Count drinking. He wanted the Gypsy girl for himself, and he felt sure that he could drink the Count under the table. He had no worries about Chokolade; he was sure that she would prefer him to the Count, who had a figure like a pouter pigeon. Besides, what did it matter what she preferred? A captain of the Hussars didn't negotiate with a Gypsy dancer. If he wanted her, he took her, and that was that.

Chokolade was grateful to the young Hussar for distracting the Count, and she wondered how soon she could slip away, find her brother, and leave.

Unfortunately, when the Count stopped thinking about Chokolade, he began to think about his wife. "Magda,"—he looked around the room—"where is my Magda?"

St. Pal and Chokolade looked at each other over the head of the Count, and it was clear to Chokolade that the Hussar knew exactly where the Countess was, and what she was doing.

She turned her full attention to the Count. "More wine, Count Meleki," she said, leaning as close to him as she dared. "Do you like my dancing? Perhaps you would like me to dance for you again?"

"Yes!" The Count's voice was thick with wine and desire. "Yes—will you—will you dance again?"

"Of course. Tomorrow night, if I am asked to come back, I shall dance the *zambra* for you. Have you ever seen the *zambra*, Count Meleki, the way I dance it?"

The Count's hands traveled up and down Chokolade's arms, pulling her low-cut blouse even lower, exposing her breasts to the nipples.

"I have never seen you dance the *zambra*." His voice was becoming more and more slurred. "Ah, how I want to see you dance again—"

"Let us drink to that," Sándor St. Pal was saying, "let us drink to that in apricot brandy. A toast to the dance of tomorrow night—and a toast to Chokolade—"

He raised his glass, and the other Hussars followed suit. It amused them to toast the Gypsy girl, to treat her almost—but not quite—like a lady.

"To Chokolade," St. Pal said just before he drank his *barack palinka* down in three fast swallows. When the glass was empty he flung it into the fireplace, and the fine crystal shattered, while the few remaining drops of alcohol made the flames burst a little higher.

The other men followed his example, and shards of crystal lay all round the fireplace. Everyone had thrown a glass except the Count. His had dropped from his fingers onto the blue and gold carpet, and the Count slumped dozing in a deep chair.

This was the time to make her escape. If necessary, she would go upstairs and pull her brother from the Countess's bed.

"I must go," she murmured, but now it was Sandor St. Pal who held her arm tightly.

"I will let you go tonight," he said, "with the promise that you return tomorrow to dance."

"Of course," Chokolade said impatiently, "tomorrow—to dance."

The Captain let go of her. At first she will dance for me, he thought, and then we will go on to other things. Without this fool of a Count.

Chokolade ran from the room, and without her shoes she dashed upstairs to the Countess's boudoir where she had left her riding clothes. She was changing quickly when Gyuri came into the room from the adjoining bedroom.

He was calm and smiling, and his nonchalance infuriated his sister.

"You fool," she snapped, "the Count was looking for you—and for her—he might have killed you."

Gyuri smiled. "I relied on you to distract him, and I was right."

"I will only go so far," Chokolade said, "even for you."

Chokolade and Gyuri moved quietly to the back stairs, and left the castle without anyone seeing them. The groom who was guarding their horses was waiting, and he enjoyed Gyuri's man-to-man wink and leer even more than the promised bottle of *barack* Gyuri handed him.

It was cold, riding back to the caravans, and

Chokolade pulled her sheepskin jacket closer about her. The sudden change from the warm, fire-filled room to the windy Puszta made her shiver, but her brother rode along as though it were a summer's evening. His vest was open, and his shirt was unbuttoned at the throat.

Countess Magda had been more exciting than ever. She had asked him questions about his relationship to Chokolade, and when he had only smiled without answering, she had become fantastically excited.

She made Gyuri lie back on her wide, canopied bed, and she insisted on undressing him. Her hands had moved with agonizing slowness over his body. First her fingers had caressed him, and then her hands, and then her mouth.

"Does she do this to you," she had whispered hoarsely, as her tongue caressed his ear lobe, "and does she do this . . . ?" Her mouth moved all over his body. And when he had tried to reach over to take her, she said, "No, not yet!" Her hands, her mouth tantalized him, until he could stand no more. He pushed her back down on the bed, and with hands made still stronger by desire, he forced her thighs open and entered her even while she tried to squirm away from him.

He had no tender caresses for the Countess, knowing tenderness was not what she enjoyed. Each time he made love to her it was close to rape. She never willingly let him take her, but fought him each time. He didn't understand this strange, high-strung woman, but he knew how to please her. She wanted force, not gentleness, and he was happy to take her just as she wanted to be taken. This time it had happened on her bed, but he had had her on the thick rug of her bedroom, and once he had forced her back against a marble table, and pinning her down against the hard surface, he had made her accept him without the comfort of a bed or even the comparative softness of a rug.

He didn't understand it, but he knew that as long as he could master her, she would want him in her bed. Gyuri thought of the Count with contempt. That soft fool, he probably said "Please."

Chapter III

"I WILL NOT go back to the castle with you," Chokolade told her brother the following morning.

Gyuri pushed a mound of quilts away, and sat up in his caravan. "You woke me at this ungodly hour to tell me that?"

"It is almost noon," Chokolade said. "I have told the others that we will be starting for Austria as soon as you have awakened."

"You told the others? Who are you to give such orders?"

"It is not safe here," Chokolade persisted.

"The snow storms are still weeks away."

"I am not talking about the snow," Chokolade said. "I am talking about you and the Countess. The Count came close to finding out about the two of you last night. One more night and I'm sure he will find out. Gyuri"—she put her slim hand on her brother's arm—"the Count will kill you. He will shoot you down."

"Nonsense." Gyuri said airily. "At most maybe he will challenge me to a duel—"

"Aristocrats don't duel with Gypsies," Chokolade reminded him.

"Wonderful." Gyuri burrowed beneath the warm feather quilts again. "Then there is nothing to worry about."

"But there is. I have a terrible feeling that if we stay on here we'll be in danger."

Gyuri laughed. "Have you taken over the fortune-telling from Aunt Haradi? If you think you're so good, why not go into town this afternoon and made a few extra *pengö* reading palms?"

"Gyuri, please," Chokolade insisted. "You should have seen the Count last night—"

"No," Gyuri said with a little sigh, "you should have seen the Countess last night, that was worth seeing!"

There was no talking to him! Chokolade climbed out of his caravan and walked over to the small fire where Aunt Haradi sat, huddling close to the warmth of the flames. If only the old woman would help her. Chokolade never did understand why the old woman had turned against her. She just knew that now she needed her help.

"We are to go back to the castle tonight," she told Haradi Neni.

The old woman looked up and pulled her shawl more closely about her shoulders. "You mean we do not leave for Austria after all? That is the decision of that great Romany chief, Gyuri Tura, I suppose."

Chokolade hated the spite she heard in the woman's voice, but she couldn't blame her. Gyuri's actions were endangering them all, and he was so enchanted by that bitch of a Countess, no one could persuade him to leave the Puszta.

Chokolade sat down beside Haradi Neni. "It is the Count who frightens me. If he finds out about Gyuri—"

"He will kill him," the old woman finished. She shrugged. "Why not distract him?"

"Distract him? How? I dance for him, but then after the dance is over—"

"He wants more than dancing." The old woman's laugh was a dirty cackle. "He wants to see you in his bed. You, stripped of your dancing clothes, lying on his soft bed, just waiting for him to take his pleasure. Oh, that's what he wants all right. Well, why not?" She rubbed her thumb and middle finger together. "You could make much gold *parne*."

"Haradi Neni," Chokolade exclaimed, "that fat little man with his thick fingers. I couldn't! And besides, what about the *leis prala?* Our own law says I must remain a virgin until I marry."

"The *leis prala!*" Aunt Haradi spat into the fire. "That law is for girls who are of true Romany blood. Look at you! The devil alone knows where you really come from—yes, the devil; because you're a devil's child."

"Why do you say such things to me?" Chokolade was close to weeping. She could stand up to anything that might be said of her by a *gajo*, but this sudden attack by one of her own family made her want to cry.

She swallowed back her tears and said, "I am truly Romany—you know that—just as true as you or anyone here."

"A true Romany with green eyes," Aunt Haradi scoffed.

"My father was Chief Bela Tura," Chokolade insisted.

"Oh, your father," Aunt Haradi said slyly. "That is all very well. But your mother? Tell me about her, why don't you?"

"My mother died when I was born," Chokolade blazed, "everyone knows that—just as they know she was a Romany princess from another tribe—"

"Does everyone know that?" Aunt Haradi cackled. "I don't know that. That is why you might as well sleep with the *gajo* and take his gold. That's all you're good for. Look"—she put her hand on the girl's arm in pretended friendliness—"suppose I go to the castle for you? I could tell the Count what you are willing to do for ten *pengö*, and how much more you will do for twenty—"

That was too much for Chokolade. She took the old woman by the shoulders and began to shake her, while Haradi Neni tried to free her hands so that she could claw at Chokolade's face and eyes.

"Enough!" It was Uncle Miklos who had come running, and who was now doing his best to separate the two women. "No more of this— Romanys fight with *gajos*, not with each other."

Chokolade and the old woman backed away from each other.

"How did this stupidity begin?" Uncle Miklos asked.

Chokolade couldn't bear to repeat all the

insinuations, and the bawdy suggestions she had heard. She only said. "Gyuri and I go to the castle tonight. I am afraid of the Count—afraid that he will find Gyuri with his wife and kill him. And if he doesn't do that, then I am afraid of what he will try to do to me. I was going to ask Aunt Haradi to help me. I know she can make a sleeping potion. The Count gets so drunk, I thought maybe I could slip the potion into his drink. Just something to make him a little groggy, so that Gyuri and I could get safely away—"

Uncle Miklos looked at her with admiration. "Aunt Haradi will prepare your potion. Just a little something to give the Count a good night's sleep. Nothing dangerous, mind," he cautioned the old woman.

Aunt Haradi turned and started toward her own caravan.

"Haradi Neni," Uncle Miklos called after her. "Did you hear me?"

"I heard, I heard," she said gruffly. "That is all I hear in this misery of a camp—people telling me what to do."

That night when Chokolade and Gyuri rode across the Puszta, Chokolade carried a small vial of a colorless liquid in her leather pouch. She only wondered where she would keep the sleeping potion when she danced. Her clothes were so tight-fitting, even the small vial would create a bulge. But she could knot it in one corner of a silver and green scarf she sometimes used when dancing. No one would notice it there.

Meleki Castle was even brighter than it had been the night before. Countess Magdalena Meleki had outdone herself. This time she planned to keep Gyuri in her bed until early morning, and the only way she would be able to do that was to present the Count with more than one distraction.

Chokolade was wonderful, of course, but the Count found it more interesting to be surrounded by a bevy of girls in his bed. That way all of his varied demands and desires could be fulfilled. He liked to see two women making love to each other, though he was never sure whether what he saw was true passion or play-acting for his benefit. But no matter, it amused him, just as it amused him to have the girls watch while he made love to one of them. And sometimes they could supply the excitement that he was finding increasingly hard to marshal by himself.

The Countess wondered how Chokolade would feel about being one among such a group. No doubt she was used to being the star in bed just as she was the star on the dance floor. Well, it would be a new experience for the girl—an experience that the Countess had every intention of describing to Gyuri once she had him alone. How would he feel about his sister being the center of such a party? That is, if she was his sister.

Once inside the castle, Chokolade was happier than ever that she carried the small vial of potion with her. The party had been going on for quite a while, that was clear. When she went upstairs to change her clothes, she met a young Hussar officer coming down, two half-dressed, barefoot girls on either side. They had long shed the seven full petticoats that peasant girls loved to wear under their brightly colored skirts. Each was down to one petticoat, and a half-buttoned white camisole top.

"I'll take that one," another officer called from the bottom of the stairs. He grabbed one of the girls, and turned her around. Obediently the girl started up the stairs again, the Hussar a step behind her, cupping his hand beneath her swaying buttocks.

No wonder that the girls didn't bother getting fully dressed, Chokolade thought. This time the Countess did not watch her as she changed her clothes, and when Chokolade made her way downstairs again, she saw that the Countess had provided her male guests with plenty of entertainment. There were girls, half-dressed as the ones she had seen on the stairs, tumbled over arms of chairs, sitting in the laps of the officers. Their legs were bare, and as the men caressed them, they would shriek, their legs would scissor the air, and the triangle of hair where their thighs met was visible to all.

Or would have been visible, if anyone had cared to look. But most of the men were so drunk that Chokolade doubted that they saw much of what was going on. All except for Captain Sandor St. Pal and Count Meleki. These two men were either able to hold their liquor better than most, or for some reason they had refrained from drinking as much as the others.

"We have been waiting for you." Count Meleki

kissed Chokolade's hand, and led her to the floor.

"Indeed, waiting," the Captain echoed, and Chokolade shivered a little at the way his eyes raked her body.

Count Meleki noticed it, too. "Now, Captain," he slurred, "it is true you are my guest. But there are certain prizes I reserve for myself in this house. There are little partridges that I believe in tasting first, *before* I share them with my guests, you understand."

He winked, and the Captain answered with an almost formal bow.

"Certainly, Count, but Meleki hospitality has always been famous—I cannot believe that the Count would deny a guest anything. Especially not a favorite dish—that is, if there was only enough for one."

The Count clapped his guest on the shoulder. "Don't worry, my dear fellow, don't you worry. I am a connoisseur—a gourmet, you understand—never a gourmand. Have no fear, I willingly share—after I enjoy, that is."

The Captain bowed, and said nothing more. He would be willing to share Chokolade, too—after a few days, or possibly even as long as a week. He felt sure that the Gypsy girl could amuse him for that long. After that, the Count could have her and welcome. But this night she was his. He had drunk moderately, while making sure that the Count's glass was always brimming with wine or brandy. It would be an amusing evening, he decided, it presented a double challenge. First, the Count had to be distracted, or made so drunk he couldn't perform with a woman. Then he had to snare the girl. Looking over at the Gypsy dancer, he decided that Chokolade would give him far less trouble than the Count.

Chokolade had only vaguely been listening to the two men. She caught the word "partridge" and decided that they were probably discussing a hunting expedition. Nobles liked to do that, go out with elaborate firearms and with dogs and servants merely to kill a few brightly plumaged birds, or to bring down a wide-eyed deer. Gyuri and the other Gypsies hunted, too, but only during the winter if they were hungry, and food could not be cadged, stolen, or exchanged for other goods with the local peasantry.

She glanced back over her shoulder as she went to talk to the Gypsy *primas* and she saw the tall Hussar captain looking at her. He reminded her of a Gypsy with his dark hair, though his skin was nowhere as dark as her brother's. And then he had light eyes. Not green like hers, but a startling gray that seemed even lighter in his tanned face.

Chokolade didn't like *gajos*, but she couldn't help noticing that this man's shoulders were so broad they pulled his jacket taut across his back. The Hussar's uniform of tight breeches and high boots accentuated his slim hips and long legs. Oh, he cut a fine figure, all right, and when she saw his bold stare she could see that he knew it, and was sure of his appeal to women. Fine! Let this rooster crow all he liked, she was sure that the blonde, blue-eyed peasant girls adored him. Peasant fathers tried to guard their daughter's virginity, but that was only as far as other peasants were concerned. Let a troop of Hussars be stationed in their village, and they were happy enough to hand over their daughters—only to the officers, of course. The same was true if aristocrats such as the Count made demands. The peasants cared for their daughters, but they cared for silver *pengö* even more.

It was hard being a Gypsy, Chokolade decided, but better a Gypsy who had pride than a peasant who fawned before his masters one minute, and cursed them behind their backs the next.

She looked away from the Captain, and looked around the room for her brother. Neither he nor the Countess were anywhere to be seen. Gyuri was impossible. He had already disappeared with Countess Magda, leaving Chokolade to do all the dancing by herself. She knew they were expecting her spectacular *zambra*, but she had thought she would dance first with her brother. Now it was completely up to her to keep the Count distracted and unaware that in her bedroom upstairs the Countess was enjoying the attentions of Gyuri Tura.

Very well—her green eyes narrowed with contempt—she could control these *gajos*. Most of them were half-drunk, and her dancing would dizzy them completely. She nodded to the *primas*, and began to tap her right foot very slowly against the hard wood floor. The clicking sound was soft at first, and only gradually did it grow louder. When she saw she had their attention, Chokolade's heels made a loud rat-a-tat sound against the floor. Her head went back, and her arms went up, and her fingers snapped in unison with her clicking feet.

"Aha, flamenco," the Captain said. "I've seen it in Seville—wonderful dance."

But Chokolade's *zambra* was no flamenco. True, it had elements of flamenco in it, but while the flamenco evokes passion because of its very control, the *zambra* went past the flamenco in losing that control. The flamenco hinted at what could happen between a man and a woman, while the *zambra* illustrated it.

Chokolade looked as though she were dancing with an invisible demon lover. Surely no woman could move that way without having a man making the counter moves. The men who had been fondling the peasant girls pushed them away for the moment. Chokolade wasn't just dancing, she was making love. First she moved slowly, then she accentuated her hip gyrations, just as a woman will move faster when she comes closer to the peak of her desire, and then her movements were slow once again, the sweet, slow movement of a woman fulfilled, but yet insisting upon the last drops of pleasure.

One of the men groaned, and each man wanted to be on the dance floor with her, his body pressed into hers. The shrewd peasant girls knew that after such an exhibition, the Hussars would hurry them into beds, while some of them wouldn't even wait to get to the privacy of a bedroom, but would take them right there, not caring how many others were in the same room.

The Captain licked his dry lips. No woman had ever made him feel this way. He glanced over at the Count, and he could see that the man was breathing hard. *Control,* the Captain told himself. *I must exercise control for the moment.*

The Count had no thought about control. He wanted Chokolade and he wanted her that very minute. His face was flushed, and he was so breathless he looked like a man who had run a three-mile race.

"Chokolade—" He pawed at the girl, trying to pull her blouse down, his fingers eager to touch the high mounds of her breasts. "Chokolade—you're wonderful—wonderful!"

Chokolade did her best to pull away. "Thank you, Count. I'm glad you enjoyed my dancing."

"Dancing, yes! I enjoyed that—and now I want to enjoy you."

Chokolade struggled in his grasp, and looked appealingly at the Hussar captain, who looked back at her with amusement. Let the Count tire the girl. She would be grateful when she discovered that she was meant for the bed of a tall, young Hussar captain this night, rather than the grapplings and heavy breathing of this pudgy, middle-aged man.

When Chokolade saw that the Captain was not going to help her, she decided to help herself.

"Count Meleki," she said with a little laugh. "Dancing is hot and thirsty work. Surely I may have a drink—first?"

"Of course, my dear girl." The Count let go of Chokolade, and signaled to a servant. "Tokay for this lovely child."

Chokolade took the fine crystal glass, and the Captain noticed that her hand trembled slightly.

She raised the glass to her lips, and then her green eyes looked langorously at the Count over the rim of the glass.

"You are not drinking with me, Count Meleki? No toast for my dancing?"

"Of course," the Count said eagerly, "of course—a toast to the most exciting dancer I have ever seen." He looked around for a servant. "Where is he? A glass of Tokay, fool."

During those few seconds in which the Count's head was turned, Chokolade was able to empty the tiny vial of sleeping potion into her own wine glass. When the Count turned to her holding his own wine glass, she held her glass out to him.

"Perhaps the Count would like to drink from my glass while I drink from his. My lips have touched this glass," she said softly. "Gypsies exchange glasses as a pledge of love.'

"Certainly." Count Meleki eagerly handed his glass to Chokolade and took hers. "A pledge—yes—of love. And of much more."

He drank the wine laced with the potion in a few swallows, and then turned to hurl the glass against the fireplace. But suddenly he had no strength in his arm. The glass slipped from his fingers and fell quietly on the rug.

The Count clutched his throat and staggered. "My God, I've been poisoned."

Chokolade gasped. She knew immediately what had happened. Haradi Neni had concocted poison. Chokolade would be arrested, and the Turas would

65

be rid of her forever. That was Haradi Neni's plan. Chokolade was sure that was what happened, because no proper sleeping potion worked so quickly. The best ones worked so gradually that the person who took one just became drowsy, and thought he was falling into a normal sleep.

Just as Chokolade realized what had happened, so did the Captain. He saw the tiny glass vial lying on the carpet beside the fallen glass, and he pocketed it quickly.

"A doctor," he yelled to a staring servant. "Ride for the doctor! The Countess—" He looked around the salon full of drunken officers and their half-dressed girls, but the Countess was nowhere to be seen. He hated to disturb her, but this was an emergency. "You," he said to another servant, "summon the Countess."

"But—" the servant began, and then was afraid to continue.

"I know," Captain St. Pal said, "but never mind that—go get her!"

He turned to where Chokolade had been standing just a minute before, but the girl was gone.

"Damn," the Captain swore. He had let her get away, and she had probably murdered the Count.

Chokolade had run from the salon. Everyone had gathered around the Count, and no one had stopped her. She looked up at the wide staircase— Gyuri! But she had no time for him. They would be after her, and she would die in jail. The heavy bars on the window, the locked door, the stone walls closing in—Gypsies died without their freedom.

She ran outside to where her mare waited, saddled and ready. There was no time to think about changing into other clothes. Chokolade put one foot into a stirrup, rucked up her skirts and petticoat, and swung her other leg over the saddle. She stood in the stirrups for a second, so that she could adjust the bunched-up fabric beneath her, and then she bent over her horse's head and clicked a soft signal into the mare's ear. The animal's ears went back, and she stretched out immediately into a long, galloping stride.

Free, Chokolade thought, though her heart pounded with fear. I'm free. But I've killed a man. She was shaking, and her trembling imparted itself to her mare, who danced and shied, sensing the sudden lack of sureness in her mistress' hands on the reins.

How long would she remain free, Chokolade wondered. A dancing girl couldn't kill a Magyar Count and hope to get away with it. A Gypsy couldn't even steal a chicken or poach a pheasant and hope to escape punishment. Oh, God, what would they do to her for murder? It would be jail and execution, and it wouldn't matter to the *gajo* police how hard she tried to explain that she hadn't killed the Count intentionally. They wouldn't care about that.

Chokolade was trembling so desperately that she couldn't ride. She reined her horse to a stop, and sat for a minute, taking deep breaths, trying to calm her pounding heart. She signaled to her horse again, and this time the animal went at a canter. Moving more slowly, Chokolade tried to think, to plan, to come up with a way she could escape. Haradi Neni, she thought furiously, she would kill that old witch!

Had Chokolade stayed at the castle a few minutes longer she would have seen that the Count was not dead. The doctor had come quickly, and he confirmed that the man had been very heavily drugged—too heavily for his heart's sake—but other men had lived from such doses of drugs, and there was hope for the Count's life.

Captain St. Pal had waited only long enough to hear that Count Meleki was not dead, and would probably recover. He shouted for a groom to bring him his horse and then he rode after the Gypsy dancing girl. Tomorrow morning he would send the local police to arrest her for trying to poison the Count. He and some of his men would probably ride with them, as the police were none too brave about entering a Gypsy camp. But tonight he had other plans for the girl, and what had happened to the Count was a spur to his desire. A girl who was willing to kill rather than be taken was a girl worth conquering. He urged his stallion into the night. Chokolade's horse might be fast, but his horse had won a cross-country race against another Hussar regiment. Sandor St. Pal was not worried; he could catch up with Chokolade, and his mind filled with vivid images of what he would do once he tumbled the Gypsy girl on the ground.

Chokolade had reached the Tisza River, but rather than ride for the bridge which was miles downstream, she was doing her best to ford the water on horseback. It was the shortest way to the Gypsy camp, the shortest way to escape, but the trembling mare raised her head, her nostrils wide with fear at the idea of entering the cold, dark river.

Chokolade leaned forward, whispered in her horse's ear, and tried to soothe the frightened animal. Her own fear of what she had done and what might happen to her had been transmitted to the sensitive animal, and the horse backed away from the water again and again, taking a few dancing steps sideways.

"Come, my lovely," Chokolade murmured trying to keep panic from her voice, "come my beauty—we can do it—you and I."

But the horse heard no confidence in her mistress's voice, and she whinnied and neighed, and tossed her head.

Chokolade was in a fury. She pulled the horse's head up with a hard jerk of the reins, and then she dug her shoes with their sharp, metal-tipped heels into the animal's flanks. That was too much for the gentle horse. In its rage, the animal reared back on its hind legs. Chokolade had never seen her mare act this way, and she was completely unprepared. Her high-heeled slippers couldn't keep their hold on the stirrups, and her thighs, encumbered by yards of petticoat and skirt fabric, couldn't grip the horse properly. She lost control of the animal and fell to the ground.

Once Chokolade was off her back, the mare stood quietly by. The animal's eyes were white and rolling, and she was snorting, but she made no move to gallop away.

Chokolade approached the horse gingerly, talking softly. She had decided that if the mare let her mount again, she would ride for the bridge. It was clear that the animal would never enter the river. Chokolade pushed her hair away from her forehead. God, she was so tired—so frightened. She leaned her hot forehead against the animal's mane for just a minute, one arm thrown across the animal's neck.

The mare twitched, stood still, and then her ears went back. A few seconds later, Chokolade heard the sound that had made the horse restive once again. She could feel it in the earth beneath her feet, the sound of hooves. Another horseman was coming, riding hard and fast, pushing his horse to the limit. Chokolade looked back at the flat Puszta. So far she could see nothing, but the sound told her that it was just one horse, which meant that a troop of police had not yet been sent out after her. Besides, the police didn't ride after dark on the Puszta. They waited till daylight to make their arrests. Gyuri—it had to be her brother Gyuri riding after her. Thank God!

Chokolade stopped trying to mount her horse. Instead, she stood quietly beside the animal, murmuring soft words, trying to calm herself as well as the horse.

She saw the rider coming across the plain, and she called out, "Gyuri—over here."

Chokolade could not make out the man until he

was close to her. It was then that she saw that it wasn't her brother, but Captain Sandor St. Pal who had ridden after her. She gasped, and quickly tried to mount her horse. Again she imparted her own fear to the animal, and the mare turned and pranced. Chokolade had managed to get one foot into a stirrup, but she was hampered by her skirts and the mare wouldn't stand quietly enough to allow her to throw her other leg across the saddle.

Captain St. Pal was off his horse in a second, and he pulled Chokolade away from the horse. Her one slipper was left dangling in the stirrup as he half-carried, half-dragged her to the bank of the Tisza, where the grass was still thick and green.

With one hand he grasped Chokolade's wrists together tightly, while with his other hand he loosened his dolman cape and threw it on the ground. He kicked the fine white wool dolman with its wide sleeves so that it spread more completely upon the ground.

"Now," he said, his gray eyes black in the moonlight, "now," and with his free hand he ripped Chokolade's blouse down so that her breasts were completely exposed.

"No," Chokolade screamed as he threw her down on the spread dolman. She tried to get to her feet again, but a back-handed slap across her face sent her reeling. For a few seconds she lay stunned at the Captain's feet, her skirt and petticoat high around her hips. When she tried to get to her feet again, the Captain took a step so that her body was contained between his black-booted legs.

"I didn't ride all this way to hear you say no," the Captain snarled. "You've probably said yes to a hundred men by now, you green-eyed witch. How dare you say no to me?"

He pulled off his jacket, and threw himself down beside Chokolade. Again one free hand gripped her wrists, and pinned them down above her head. One booted leg forced her two legs apart, and with his other hand he reached beneath Chokolade's petticoat and ripped off her tiny white silk underwear. He had caught glimpses of that silk when she had danced. It had barely covered what he had wanted to see, but now Chokolade had writhed so much that her skirt and petticoat were waist-high. Yes, he could see it all. The flat stomach, the curving hips, the brown triangle of hair just above ivory-toned thighs she was trying so desperately to close, but that she was prevented from doing by his own leg between them.

The Captain would have liked to make love to the girl, but it was she who prevented it—she, with her head tossing from side to side so that he couldn't get his mouth down on those full lips, and with her body that tried to squirm away from beneath his.

He wanted to make love—but some women didn't want love—the Captain knew that. Some women were so perverted that only rape would satisfy them. Very well, if that was what she wanted. He fumbled at his trousers, and then let his whole body come down heavily upon the girl's. He wanted to tell her that it would be easier for her if she let him do what he wanted. But if she preferred it this way—

besides, it was too late for long, enticing, lovemaking. He could feel the blood behind his eyes, and he knew that he had to enter her—had to have her right then. He forced her legs open even wider, and with a plunging movement he was inside.

Chokolade never stopped writhing—never stopped trying to escape. These were not the movements the Captain had been expecting. He had wanted the eager submissiveness and the desire he had glimpsed when Chokolade had danced; but never mind, that would be for the next time. Right now he was content to master her, to overpower her. God, he had never realized just how much pleasure a man could get from imposing his sexual will on a woman.

Oh, but this Gypsy girl knew! Her struggles probably increased her own pleasure, that was why she went on with them. These Gypsy whores knew what pleased a man—knew what was going on in a man's imagination even when a man didn't know it himself.

It was only when his passion had ebbed that he understood what had happened during his assault on Chokolade. There had been a scream—a cry of pain—a scream and a cry that would stop no man when he was so far carried by passion. Slowly, ever so slowly, the Captain's fever abated. Still gripping the girl's hands, he swung his body off hers, and he heard her gasp of relief. The Captain looked down at what he had so recently enjoyed. Chokolade's legs were still spraddled, again the image of an experienced whore crossed the Captain's mind. He saw her thighs wet and gleaming in the moonlight. Wet from him, he knew, but there was more. With his free hand he took the edge of Chokolade's petticoat and touched it to her thigh. She winced, as though she feared what he would do next, but the Captain looked at the white fabric and saw that it was now stained with red. Again he remembered her scream and her cry of pain. That, and the blood on the petticoat, proved something that stunned him. The Gypsy girl had been a virgin! And after all he had heard about Gypsies!

He let go of Chokolade's hands finally, and sat up. His smile of satisfaction infuriated the girl. It was obvious that virgin or not, he would have taken her.

The Captain laughed softly. "Well, that certainly steals a march on old Meleki."

Chokolade turned on him with fury. Her fists flailed at his chest, but again she was helpless when he gripped her wrists.

"Go on," the Captain said, his eyes gleaming, "just go on—if you want more of the same. I'm ready, if you are."

Chokolade became quiet. "That's better," the Captain said softly, and once again he let go of her wrists.

Chokolade scrambled quickly to her feet, and ran to her horse. Captain St. Pal followed more leisurely behind her. He doubted that the girl was in any shape to get quickly on that horse. Hell, he laughed to himself, he had ridden her well—she'd probably ache for a week!

But Chokolade had pulled out a knife from a leather sheath below her saddle. The five-inch blade gleamed in the moonlight. The Captain could see its razor edge, but he was sure he could take it away from the slender, weakened girl if he wanted to.

"Don't come any closer." Chokolade clutched the knife, and it was plain she knew how to use it.

The Captain held his hands up, and didn't move toward the girl.

"Don't worry. I've had enough for tonight. Besides, it's cold here. Next time I take you, it will be on a bed. I like my comfort."

Chokolade screamed with rage, and her hand with the knife darted toward him. The Captain stepped back quickly, and then he beckoned to her.

"Of course, if you want it again—here and now— I'll be happy to oblige. Just come ahead."

Chokolade retreated, her back against the horse's saddle. Her whole body felt bruised and aching. She couldn't fight this *gajo* devil of a man, she had all she could do to keep the knife in her trembling fingers. And her knees, her knees kept buckling. She only managed to stand upright because with one hand she gripped the saddle for support. Damn him! She blinked, trying to clear her eyes of sudden tears. She would never cry before this man—never. It was bad enough that he had overpowered her—damaged her—destroyed her life—she wouldn't give him the further joy of seeing her weep. Her virginity was destroyed, and her pride was gone—but he would never know that.

She did her best to straighten up, gripping the

knife with more determination. She wouldn't try to mount her horse while he stood there, hands on his hips, sneering at her. She felt a surge of pain, and she wasn't sure whether her sore thigh muscles would enable her to climb into the stirrups and onto her horse's back. She would try to mount—but not while he stood there laughing at her!

But Captain St. Pal seemed to have lost interest in her. He picked up his dolman, put on his jacket, and straightened his clothes. His very nonchalance infuriated Chokolade. By his actions he was showing her that what he had done meant nothing to him. A Gypsy girl, a peasant, or a Countess, women were just there to be used.

Chokolade couldn't help her cry of rage, and the Captain laughed to hear it. By Saint Istvan, he had gotten to the girl. She wouldn't forget this night. He turned and looked at her once more, a good-looking piece. It might be interesting to have her again, in a warm room, and on a comfortable bed, and with a good bottle of wine shared between them. Well, he would have no trouble finding her if he wanted her. He mounted his horse, let his dolman swing behind him, and raised his gold-braided hat in a mock salute. A soft click to his horse, and Chokolade saw him ride off across the Puszta, an echo of his laughter drifting back across the Plains, just as though he were an evil *delibab* which had come and gone.

Painfully, Chokolade mounted her horse. It took her three tries to do it, and she was wondering if it wouldn't have been better to walk, so achingly did her body respond to the horse's movement. This time she turned her horse's head toward the bridge. No need now to try and ford the Tisza, she could take the long way back to camp.

When she arrived at the caravan, she sat in the saddle for another few seconds, gathering the courage to dismount. She finally managed to do so, but with every movement, she ached down to her bones. Chokolade rested her face against the saddle for a minute, bewildered and exhausted. Where was Gyuri, she wondered, and how much should she reveal to the Turas of what had happened to her?

Chapter IV

SHE WAS STILL standing there when Gyuri rode up on his horse. The stallion was lathered and snorting, and Gyuri slipped off the horse's back with a shout.

"Where the hell have you been? I searched for you—I almost didn't make it out of there because I searched for you! Where is everyone? Why haven't you gotten them together? We have to ride out of here at once!"

Chokolade stared at him dully. He didn't even want to know what had happened to her—he was just shouting, shouting. But why was Gyuri carrying on so? He couldn't possibly know. And yet the way he was shouting made her think that he might know; the idea that he had seen the Captain's obscene performance made her shake.

But that wasn't what made her shake. No, it was Gyuri's hands on her shoulders—he was shaking her—and hard. And then through her sense of shock, his words began to penetrate. He was saying something about the Count—something about the potion.

"He's dead," Chokolade whispered, "the Count is dead—and I killed him."

"No, no," Gyuri was impatient, "he's not dead, though he's still unconscious. That potion that Aunt Haradi gave you—"

"It was poison?"

"No, but five times as strong as a sleeping potion should be. That old woman. She did it deliberately."

"Because she hates me, and she wanted them to arrest me, execute me," Chokolade said.

"Don't be a fool." Gyuri's hands on her shoulders were rough and painful once again. "She did it because she knew that all the excitement would give her the time she needed to slip into the castle and take some of the Countess's jewels."

"The Countess's jewels?" Chokolade repeated the words, but they meant nothing to her.

"The jewels. I suppose she took one or two of the famous Meleki diamonds. Nobody saw Aunt Haradi slip into the castle—she's too skillful—the old witch. So they think it was either you or me who stole the jewels—or better, you and me. We're a team of jewel thieves now, as well as a team of dancers. I'll kill that old woman! Where is she?"

"Not back yet." Uncle Miklos and the other Turas gathered around the brother and sister.

Gyuri turned on the old man. "You knew—you knew she was going to do this!"

The old man backed away. "I did not—I swear! *Ap i mulende*—by death—I swear it."

Gyuri nodded, not because the oath satisfied him, but because they had no time to waste in discussion. He was sure that the troop of Hussars

80

and the police were probably not far behind them on the Puszta.

"We ride out tonight," he ordered, "everyone—now!"

The Turas ran for their caravans. It wouldn't take them ten minutes to get ready. Their belongings were in their wagons, and it was just a matter of settling some of the horses between the wagon traces and saddling the others. They were used to breaking camp on a minute's notice.

"But Haradi Neni," Uncle Miklos implored.

"We leave her," Gyuri said abruptly. "Let the soldiers find her and do what they want with her."

"No," Uncle Miklos cried out, "*leis prala* says we cannot do that—we cannot leave one of our own to the *gajos*."

"*Leis prala*"—the men were surprised at Chokolade's angry shout—"*leis prala* means nothing—do what Gyuri says! We go now."

Gyuri looked at his sister with surprise. He didn't need Chokolade's help to make the others follow him. What was happening to the Tura women? He would have a talk with her after they arrived at some hidden, safe place, but the important thing now was to start traveling.

"Won't someone help me?" he heard whimpered a few minutes later.

It was Haradi Neni! If he hadn't been so furious at the old woman he would have swung her up in his arms and danced her around the camp. She had done something amazing. Old as she was, she had ridden through the night on her horse to the Meleki Castle. She had crept inside, stolen a few jewels, and then ridden back again. Gyuri shook his head, you had to admire an old woman like that. Romany women were stronger than *gajo* men, that was sure.

But he would never let her know that he was proud of her.

"Where have you been?" he demanded, pretending he knew nothing of her activities. "We were going to leave without you."

The old woman crept close to him, and she unwrapped a large paisley kerchief.

"Here, Chief Gyuri," she whispered, "enough for the Turas for a lifetime."

It was only when he looked down at the kerchief that Gyuri appreciated completely what Haradi Neni had done, and he began to sweat. She had not been satisfied to take a ring, an earring or two, perhaps a necklace. Oh, no, the stupid old woman had taken Countess Meleki's entire jewel collection. No one—not even his Countess—could save them from the law after this.

"You stupid old woman," he said furiously, "and where can we go with all that? How far will we get?"

"We can slip across the border," she said with a small cackle.

"We can cross ten borders," Gyuri said, "and it still wouldn't be far enough. The Emperor who sits on the throne in Vienna has a cousin who sits on a throne in Russia, and his cousin sits on a throne in Germany! The police of the world will be after us." His hands gripped the old woman's shoulders. "One ring—one bracelet—and we might have been able to talk our way out of it. But this!" He let go of the old woman. "You stay here and face the soldiers. You did this without consulting any of us, now you face the Emperor's men alone!"

"No," said one of the Turas, who again had gathered around, and stood massed behind the old woman. "We do not leave her, it is not according to Romany law."

"And was it according to our law that she gave the Count poison when Chokolade asked for a sleeping potion?" Gyuri asked.

"It was not!" Aunt Haradi protested. "It was a good, strong sleeping potion. How could I know that the Count is so weak that it would affect him like poison?"

"Poison and stealing," Gyuri persisted. "If the Count is dead they will decide we are murderers and hang us, everyone. And if they don't hang us for that, they will certainly hang us for being thieves. And all because of this foolish old woman! Leave her for the Hussars, I say."

But the other Turas didn't move. One Gypsy didn't leave another to *gajo* law. Gyuri yearned to leave them all, but there they stood. In every face he saw the ties of blood, of family, of the tribe.

"All right, all right," he said hoarsely. "You— Laci—help Haradi Neni with her caravan. The rest of you, are you ready to go? Or do we stand here talking like old women until we are caught?"

Everyone ran for their caravans and their horses. Fires were kicked out. Gyuri tied his lathered horse and Chokolade's mare behind her caravan, and chose a fresh horse to ride. But where were they riding to? Even as he shouted orders, and saddled his horse, Gyuri wondered just where he would lead the Turas.

"We can start for Austria," his cousin Laci suggested.

Gyuri shook his head. "We wouldn't get far enough."

"The other way then—Galicia."

"Among the Polish peasants? They hate us more than the Hungarians."

Laci shrugged. "Where, then?"

Gyuri realized that trying to put too much distance between themselves and the Hussars and police of Sárospatak was a mistake. Horses pulling caravans that carried women and children could never move as fast as a troop of armed men. They would do better staying nearby. If they could find a place to hide, it would be better than being trapped on the open Puszta. Gyuri smiled, pleased at his cleverness.

Laci stared at his cousin. "Well?"

"Just follow me. You will see."

The Turas started out across the Puszta. Gyuri rode ahead, and Chokolade was in the first caravan behind him. "He doesn't care about me," she thought, "he never even asked if I was all right. He doesn't care. None of them do." But perhaps it was better that way. Perhaps no one need know about the shameful thing that had happened to her.

The Turas moved as quietly as possible across the plains. The sky was growing light, and toward dawn shepherds came out of their round straw lean-to's to watch the Gypsies go by.

Gyuri led the Turas across one small section of the Puszta until he could see cultivated fields of corn on the horizon. It took another half-hour's riding before they could see the outline of a low wall on the horizon, and then a few minutes later, the large sprawling villa that lay beyond the carefully gated wall.

"It's Gorshö."

Chokolade heard the cry as it echoed through the Gypsy caravan, but she was too exhausted, too bruised in body and spirit to wonder why her brother had chosen the wealthy estate of Gorshö. But some of the other Turas did question Gyuri's decision among themselves. Why had Gyuri chosen an estate located only a few miles from Meleki Castle?

Gyuri had his reasons, but he felt no need to explain them to the docile tribe that followed him. Magda Meleki had regaled him one night when they were in bed about the feud between Imre Balog, who owned Gorshö, and the Count.

"They're such fools," she had said to Gyuri, "such boring, old fools. I keep hoping there will be a duel, and that they'll both be killed, and I'll be rid of both of them."

"Both of them?" Gyuri had asked.

The Countess shrugged. "Balog interested me for a little while. He's not an aristocrat, but he's frightfully rich, and he was so timid—so impressed with me. I wondered how a man like that would perform with a Countess. Every time he breathed my name or kissed my hand, I thought he would faint."

"And?"

"And what?"

"And how did he perform?"

The Countess laughed. "Like a timid man." She leaned over and pressed her cheek against Gyuri's chest. "Not at all like you, my love."

Gyuri had laughed with her, and he had gripped her shoulders and pressed her back against the mattress. He remembered that now, even as they rode toward Gorshö estate, and he also remembered that while the Count suspected Balog of sleeping with his wife, Balog was just as sure the Count had seduced Madame Balog, and he further suspected the Count of trying to steal some of his land. There had been an old dispute—hundreds of years old— between the two families about boundary rights.

Wonderful, Gyuri thought. While the Balogs and the Melekis fight over land and women, the Turas will have a chance to escape. He was sure that the landowner would hide them, especially if Gyuri once regaled him with stories of the Countess's wanton behavior. That would make him feel at least partially revenged on the Count.

The undercurrent of enmity between *gajos* always interested Gyuri. He could see how the peasants would resent the men who lorded over them, but it was hard to understand why the landowners and the aristocrats despised each other. Gyuri saw the contempt clearly, and he couldn't know that the aristocrats considered the large landowners vulgar, new rich, who had probably come by their large tracts of land dishonestly. The landowners, on the other hand, who had no titles but who now held seats in parliament, were well on their way toward ruling the country. They despised the aristocrats because of their prodigal ways. They couldn't understand their love of travel and elaborate, imported furniture. Though the landowners were now rich in money as well as in land, they held their money closely, and were loath to waste it on decorating their homes, or their women. The only time they put on a show was once a year when whole families attended the opening of the parliament in Hungary.

It was Imre Balog's love of money as well as his hate for Count Meleki that Gyuri was now counting on. Landowner Balog differed in one important way from his fellows: he loved to gamble. And like most gamblers, he never had quite enough money to fulfill his passion for cards.

It was barely dawn when the entire caravan arrived before the large gate that led to Gorshö. The Turas stopped, while Gyuri rode up to the gate, and banged a heavy iron ring against stout wood.

The dogs within howled and threw themselves against the wooden gate. Gyuri chirruped and whistled to the dogs, trying to soothe them, but the animals continued their howling and barking, until a sleepy voice demanded to know who had come to Gorshö.

Gyuri recognized the voice of Tomas, Balog's overseer, and he called out, "Gyuri Tura, good morning to you. I wish to see Landowner Balog."

"Now? You wish to see him now, you fool of a cheating Gypsy? You come back around noon. Perhaps the Landowner will see you then."

"I can't wait until noon," Gyuri said, trying to sound cheerful.

"You will wait," Tomas called over the wall to him. "I'm not waking the Landowner because of some stupid Gypsy trick."

Gyuri reached into his pocket, and pulled out a handful of coins. He considered a small silver piece regretfully, decided against it, and chose a larger coin.

"Here, Tomas," he said, "catch! And no more words about cheating Gypsies. We're all honest men here."

Gyuri could hear the overseer scrambling for the coin, and then the man opened the gate a small crack. "All? What do you mean—all?" He peered out. "Jesus and Maria, now it's an invasion of Gypsies, far worse than when the whoring Turks conquered us at Mohacs. What do you want here? No, no"—he started to close the gate—"you can't come in here—not all of you. I know you Gypsies— let you all in and there wouldn't be a horse, or a chicken, or a decent girl left on the place."

"Just let me in," Gyuri called out, while he cursed Tomas under his breath, "just me, good friend, no one else. I must see Landowner Balog—I promise, he will bless you for it. And here"—another coin went sailing over the gate. "That first *pengö* must be lonely by now."

Tomas scrambled for the coin. "Wait here," he grumbled. "I'll wake the Landowner, though he'll probably kick me for it."

It was a good twenty minutes before Tomas reappeared at the gate, but this time Landowner

Balog was with him. That's the *gajo*, Gyuri thought. They wouldn't invite a Gypsy into their homes, oh no, they think we can charm the silver right out of sideboard drawers, just as they believe we charm the horses out of their fields. Well, Gyuri had to admit to himself, there was some small truth about the horses.

"Tura"—Landowner Balog stepped outside— "what do you want? What are you doing here?"

The Gypsies in the caravans exchanged glances. Gyuri was a chief after all. How did this rich landowner come to know him, and to know him by name? Gyuri had never told them of the one night when he and Chokolade had performed at a local *csarda*, or inn, and the Landowner was there. So desperate was the man to gamble, that he even went to the simplest inns, frequented by small farmers and peasants. As the hours passed, there was no one left to sit at the card table with him.

"Please, sir,"—Gyuri had stepped forth—"if the kind sir would care to continue playing. I know a little about cards."

It was beneath him to do so, Balog knew that, and God give him strength if his wife ever found out, but there was no one else, and his appetite for the game was just whetted when all the other men in the place left the table.

He wasn't taken in by Gyuri's wheedling "kind sirs" and "good sirs," but when the passion was in him, he would play cards with the devil even though it meant losing his soul. Chokolade had sat at a nearby table and watched the two men play. To her surprise, by the end of the evening Balog had won.

Not much, to be sure, but he had won, something that filled the man with pride as he left the table with the Gypsy's *pengö* as well as everyone else's.

"Why?" Chokolade had asked her brother.

"Because we may need him someday," Gyuri said.

"Need him? For what?"

"Only God or the devil knows."

And now here was Gyuri talking to Landowner Balog. Maybe her brother was the devil who knew that someday they would need the Landowner.

"Take you in?" The entire caravan heard the man roar. "Let a bunch of thieving Gypsies camp on my land? You must think I'm a fool."

The Turas didn't hear Gyuri's answer, but they saw him reach into the leather pouch tucked beneath his saddle. He drew forth from it the red paisley kerchief Haradi Neni had brought from Meleki Castle.

Balog's eyes gleamed as Gyuri held the handkerchief open.

"We can pay," Gyuri said.

Balog put his hand out toward the contents of the handkerchief, and Gyuri stepped back. "Perhaps we can discuss the price," he said smoothly.

"All," Balog said hoarsely, "all of that—for one day. You can camp out beyond the wheat and corn fields. No one will see you there. But just for one day—and I want all."

"Not all, kind sir. Surely the kind sir wouldn't take all from my poor people."

"Poor?" Balog snorted. "Gypsies poor? Not while a horse runs or a chicken scratches. You can always get more where that came from."

"But that—that came from—" Gyuri began.

"No—no." Imre Balog understood the Gypsy's desire to involve him as an accomplice. "I don't want to know where it came from, you hear? You pay me for the privilege of camping on my good land instead of on the open Puszta, very well. There is no need for me to know where the payment comes from. And now—" He reached toward the glittering kerchief once again, and once again Gyuri backed away.

"Open the gates," the Landowner shouted to his overseer. The wooden gates swung back with a groan and a creak, and the Tura tribe followed their chief into Gorshö. The men riding behind Gyuri winked at each other at the way the Landowner now had his arm companionably around Gyuri's shoulders.

"We will talk, my friend," Balog said. "We will sit outside under the shade of a tree, and we will talk. We will drink a little *barack* together, and discuss business, isn't that right?"

"That is right," Gyuri said, "but first, I want to get my people far away from the house. That field beyond the wheat and the corn seems best. Because the police from Sárospatak—"

"Do not worry about them," Imre Balog said with contempt. "I rule on Gorshö. They cannot come through the gates if I do not permit it."

Gyuri knew that to be true. The large landowners of Hungary ruled their many acres as though they were feudal kingdoms. The local constabulary was chosen and appointed by the landowners, and their job was to protect them. He had come to Gorshö because he had relied on the Landowner's power to keep the police out. A few day's breathing space, a temporary hiding place, was all Gyuri hoped for. Just enough time to make the police think that the Gypsies were far away, that was what he was counting on.

The caravans rode past, and the Landowner shouted for one of his servants to bring a bottle of *barack* from the house. It was just what Gyuri had expected. The Landowner, unlike a true aristocrat like Count Meleki, would never allow a Gypsy inside his house.

The servant poured small glasses of *barack* for Gyuri and Belog. Gyuri thought of the delicate crystal he had been drinking from just a few short hours before. Each of the Landowner's glasses was as heavy as lead. But no matter, one or two drinks of *barack* first thing in the morning was the real Magyar way of starting the day. That, followed by slices of cold *szalonna*, with green pepper and potato bread, gave a man the strength he needed to get through the day. So said all good Hungarians.

"The jewels," Imre Balog was saying. "The jewels."

Gyuri unwrapped the handkerchief once again. The hoard glittered before his eyes. Too much, he thought, Haradi Neni took too much. A few pieces could be hidden, disposed of. But this! Too much gold, too many diamonds. The sapphires gleamed like all the stars in heaven, and there were enough emeralds and rubies to construct a rainbow.

Gyuri held up a necklace of graduated sapphire

pendants, the largest the size of a healthy Comice pear. He held it in such a way that the sun struck the facets, and the rays of light seemed caught in the heart of the jewel.

Gyuri heard Imre Balog's gasp, and he saw the man's hand reach out for the necklace. He moved the necklace away from the grasping fingers.

"How long can we stay at Gorshö for this? And how long for this?" And he held up a bracelet as wide as a man's shirt cuff, only this cuff of gold was pavéed with rubies.

"A day," Balog said hoarsely, "perhaps two."

"Two days? For a fortune in jewels?"

"A fortune, yes," the Landowner said, "if I could sell them. But that won't be easy. Jewels such as these, others will be looking for them."

"There are ways," Gyuri said, sure that the Landowner knew what to do with the jewels. He only had to get them across the border into the Hungarian province of Galicia. From there they would be carried into Poland.

The jewels could be sold in Poland, and would eventually find their way into Imperial Russia, where they would be welcomed by the members of the Czar's Court. The only spark of light and color among the somber and grim Russians was their love of jewels. They enjoyed cultivating depression, but at the same time they dressed in the most elaborate French silks, and they loved the jeweled creations of their own Fabergé. Most of the fantasies of Fabergé went directly to the Czar and Czarina and to other members of the royal family. The lesser dukes and duchesses had to be satisfied with jewels brought to them from countries to the west. When the discreet men carrying a fortune in jewels on their persons arrived at the large gray houses in St. Petersburg or Tsarskao Selo, they were welcomed. No questions were asked as to where their cache of jewels came from, and eventually, many of the jewels that once belonged to French, Hungarian, and Austrian royal families added their light to the Russians. From there, they would never find their way back to Hungary.

Imre Balog's large hand closed on the jewel-filled cotton kerchief. "All these, and you'll be safe. A sanctuary—Gorshö can be your sanctuary."

"For how long?" Gyuri wanted to know.

"Two days."

"Two weeks."

"One week."

"Done!" Gyuri let the Landowner take the jewels from him.

As they drank another glass of *barack* to seal the bargain, the Landowner couldn't stop touching the lump of jewelry that now pulled down his jacket pocket. He knew he would get a fortune for the brightly colored gems. A sum he would turn into an even greater fortune at the gaming tables. He wouldn't waste this money at small card games, oh no! With this wealth he could play roulette at Monte Carlo's gold salon, and be welcomed by other chemin-de-fer players at Deauville.

Finishing his brandy, Gyuri rode after the Turas. Gorshö was big, but he wondered if it was big enough to hide the Turas from the local police. True, they would be camped far from the main house, but they were not so far that the long arm of the Melekis couldn't reach them.

Gyuri had bargained for a week's stay with Landowner Balog, but he had no intention of staying on Gorshö for a whole week. By the end of a week, the Count would either be well enough to come after them, or he would be dead, and they would be hunted down by the Hussars.

They would camp at Gorshö for two days, Gyuri decided, and leave in the middle of the second night. Gypsies could move quietly when they had to, and they almost always had to. They would stay off the main road once they left the Puszta, and travel through the Erdely Forest. He knew that Erdely was honeycombed by brigands and thieves, but they could be dealt with more easily than police or soldiers.

Gyuri felt satisfied when he reached the small grove of trees where the Turas had camped. There were one or two fires burning, and he smelled *szalonna* roasting. Dogs and children ran about, and in a short time one corner of Gorshö looked like a Gypsy camp.

Only at Chokolade's caravan was there silence. The curtains in the front and the rear of the wagon were pulled together, and there was no sound from within. His horse pranced and snorted as Gyuri reined the animal in before his sister's caravan. He heard nothing, and decided that Chokolade must be sleeping. That's what he would be doing, too, after some breakfast. The *barack* and the excitement of the night had made him hungry. He remembered how Landowner Balog's eyes had narrowed when he had seen the hoard of jewels, as though he were gazing at the naked body of a beautiful woman. Gyuri touched the inner top pocket of his sheepskin vest. He could feel his wide leather wallet bulging slightly with the few pieces of jewelry he had put aside for himself. Haradi Neni hadn't risked everything just to make Landowner Balog rich. Gyuri debated about the best place for the wallet, and he decided to hide it even before he helped himself to breakfast at his cousin Laci's fireside.

Chokolade was lying rigidly and quietly in her own caravan, and she didn't stir until she was sure her brother had ridden away. Only then did she sit up wearily. She was naked between two thick quilts filled with down and feathers, her soiled clothes were crumpled in a corner. The morning was warm for November, yet she lay there shivering, the memory of the night before still vividly before her.

Gyuri didn't know. He hadn't even guessed that anything might have happened to her when she rode from the castle to their camp. Chokolade shivered. She would never tell him—she would never tell anyone. She turned, and burrowed into a soft, down pillow; even if she told no one, she would never forget! The vivid memory screamed through her mind.

She shut her eyes, and tried to shut out her thoughts, but she kept reliving that wild ride of the night before. She heard her horse's hooves pounding the earth, and then she heard the hooves of a horse behind her. Gaining, gaining—coming closer with every moment. Chokolade sat up in the caravan, and pulled the feather quilts about her.

It wasn't just her vivid memory or imagination. She did hear horses, and they *were* coming closer. She quickly buried the clothes she had taken off beneath a mound of bedclothes, and slipped a shirt over her head. Rummaging in the wooden trunk, she found a pair of riding pants and pulled them on. She found her second pair of boots, and put them on, tucking the pants legs into her boot tops. As she pulled on her sheepskin vest, she realized she was perspiring with fear. She had put on her least feminine clothes, the clothes that hid her lithe and shapely body best. But what did that matter if *he* came riding into camp? She knew now that he was strong enough to strip her and shame her no matter how she covered her body.

She lay under the bedclothes. She was fully dressed, the quilt was pulled up to her neck, yet she shivered. And then she heard *his* voice. There was no mistaking it. Once again, she buried her face in the pillow, and bit the knuckle of her hand to keep from screaming out. She heard *his* voice, and the voice of Landowner Balog, as well as her brother's shouts.

"You have no right to be on Gorshö without my permission," the Landowner whined.

"No right? The Emperor's Hussars? We have the right to go anywhere and everywhere. You know that."

"We have done nothing—" Gyuri's voice was loud, but Chokolade could hear the lack of conviction in his words.

"Nothing?" That was Captain St. Pal once again. "Only tried to poison the Count, and stolen the Countess's jewels."

"Poison," Gyuri tried to laugh. "Not poison. The kind officer knows it wasn't poison. It was just—just a little something. You know the Countess"—he tried to adopt a man-to-man demeanor—"well, sometimes the Countess prefers to be unobserved—"

He couldn't have said anything more infuriating to the Hussar captain.

"Don't you dare dirty the Countess's name by pronouncing it," he roared. "Now, where are the jewels, you Gypsy swine?"

Again, Chokolade heard the babble of voices, the sound of horses' hooves as the Hussars milled around, the cries of the women, the wailing of their babies.

"Jail," Captain St. Pal's voice roared above the rest. "We'll take you to the jail at Sárospatak, Tura, then perhaps you'll remember where you put the jewels. Yes, you! Get him, ride him down," the Captain shouted to his men. "Don't let him reach his horse."

Through the shouting, Chokolade heard Gyuri's voice, and she knew that he hadn't been able to escape the Hussars who surrounded him.

"No," she heard Gyuri's choked cry, "no—I won't go to jail. You want the jewels? Ask Landowner Balog about them."

Chokolade knew that her brother would never have admitted to knowing who had the jewels except for his fear of prison. Chokolade shivered at the very idea of it; jail, being locked up, behind bars, not being able to see the sky. Many Gypsies had killed themselves rather than stay in prison.

It didn't take long for Captain St. Pal to get the jewels away from Landowner Balog. Balog whined, and insisted that he knew nothing about the origin of the jewels.

"That lying bastard of a Gypsy," he said to the Hussar captain, "he gave them to me—how was I to know where they came from?"

The Captain scoffed. "What would a Gypsy be doing with jewels as valuable as these? You must have known they were stolen."

"Everything a Gypsy has is stolen," Balog responded. "But how could I know they were stolen from the Melekis? Besides, it was only from the goodness of my heart that I let them camp here. Valuable jewels? How could I know that? Did I have time to take them to a jeweler? For all I knew they were bits of colored glass. I've never known a Gypsy before to give away anything valuable."

Captain St. Pal didn't argue any further with the Landowner. The man wasn't as powerful as Count Meleki, but the landowners did control their own districts to a large degree, and the Captain was a long way from the court of the Emperor Franz Josef, the only place where he could have successfully lodged a complaint against the man.

He looked at the jewels still wrapped in the kerchief. He poked among the pile of bright gems, and then he looked at the Landowner.

"Very well. The Gypsy gave them to you, and you thought they were bits of glass. Fine! Now, where are the rest?"

Imre Balog's face became scarlet. He lunged toward Gyuri. "Where are the rest of them? You lying bastard, you said these were all!"

Gyuri's arms were pinioned behind him by two Hussars. He looked at the Landowner, took a deep breath, and then spat in his face.

Balog roared with rage. Captain St. Pal signaled his men, and two of them held the man back from attacking Gyuri.

"Bits of glass," the Captain repeated. "All right"—he turned to Gyuri—"where are the rest of the jewels? Countess Magdalena described the pieces to me, there are still some missing."

Gyuri shrugged. He knew they would drag him off to jail. The jewels were well-hidden, they could be used to bribe a jailer to look the other way.

"Into the caravans," the Captain shouted to his men. "Let's see what they've got hidden behind those filthy curtains."

The Hussars pulled dress swords from sheaths, and pulled the caravan curtains back by piercing them with swords' points. Children and women tumbled from within the caravans shrieking. The Captain, still astride his horse, looked at the melee of crying, yelling people with disgust.

"God," he thought, "the way they live. All jumbled together. Sleeping one on top of another. No privacy. They probably lend their wives to each other without a second thought."

"Captain," one of his men shouted, "look what I found."

It was Chokolade. The Hussar was dragging her out from beneath a mound of bedclothes. She was

100

kicking and clawing, but he pinned her arms behind her, and pulled her out of the caravan and down to the ground.

A lieutenant, the Captain's second-in-command, rode up beside him. "By God," he said, "the dancer—you know, St. Pal—from last night."

Captain St. Pal grinned at the girl who was in a heap on the ground. Oh yes, he knew. Last night's dancer and last night's conquest. Again he felt that strange wild pounding in his head. To hell with the Meleki jewels, he decided.

He wheeled his horse about so sharply that the animal reared.

"Let go of him," he ordered the men who were holding Gyuri, "we'll take the girl instead."

"But the rest of the jewels," the lieutenant said.

"We'll never find them," St. Pal answered. "You know Gypsies. They whisper horses from a meadow—casting the glamor, they call it—and then they hide the horses so well we can never find them. How do you suppose we can find something as small as a jewel if we can't find a horse?

"It's better this way. We'll take the girl as hostage. When they return the jewels, we'll return the girl. Let him go," he said to his men, who reluctantly released Gyuri.

"Captain"—Gyuri reached up to St. Pal's saddle—"that's my sister—you can't take her."

Captain St. Pal looked down at him. "Where are the rest of the jewels?"

Gyuri took a backward step. If he admitted that he had the rest of the jewels, he was also admitting to have stolen them, and that meant they would take

101

him off to jail—keep him there—maybe forever. Not even for Chokolade would he risk that. He stepped away from the Captain's horse.

Again St. Pal signaled to his men, and two of them yanked Chokolade to her feet. Chokolade stood there for a minute facing the Captain, and then with strength born of desperation she pulled away from the two men who were holding her and began to race across the meadow.

The Hussars, on foot and horseback, gave a shout, and started after her.

"Halt!" Captain St. Pal commanded, and as the men separated for their Captain, he spurred his horse lightly and set after the fleeing girl, the men laughing at the chase.

"Go get her, St. Pal," the lieutenant yelled.

"After her, Captain," the men shouted.

"Get the little partridge," one of the Captain's hunting friends shouted after him.

Chokolade heard the laughter and the jeers but she kept on running. She ran even when she knew that the Captain was riding beside her, his horse keeping up easily with her frantically racing feet.

It was the Captain who tired of the game first. He bent down from his saddle, and his strong arm went around Chokolade's waist. Without reining his horse to a halt, he pulled the girl up from the ground, and then just as easily he seated her on his saddle in front of him. Chokolade squirmed, and his grip tightened. His forearm cut into her rib cage until she couldn't breathe.

"You're hurting me," she gasped.

"Stop fighting," he ordered.

Chokolade went limp, and holding her tightly before him like a prize of war, he rode back to the Gypsy camp. "Give the order to ride out," he called to his lieutenant.

"Captain"—Gyuri ran frantically forward—"my sister—please."

"Your sister for the jewels," the Captain said shortly.

"Chokolade—" Gyuri looked up at her, pleadingly, and she looked down at him, her eyes wide with fear.

The Hussars rode out of Gorshö, past the bewildered Gypsies and the furious Landowner, their horses' hooves kicking up a cloud of dust that left everyone coughing.

"Get out," Balog shouted after the Hussars were gone, "all of you—out—out of here—now! Tomas, get the men—the dogs—I want these Gypsies out of Gorshö now!"

The soldiers had gone through the caravans like the wind, dumping everything they could find on the ground. Bedding, clothing, dishes, food—all were lying in jumbled heaps on the hard earth. The Gypsies ran about quickly, picking up their belongings and throwing them back into the caravans. Later—later they could smooth the bedding, pack the clothing in the wooden trunks, hang the good-luck charms and beads in proper places. But there was no time now—no time. Quickly, they formed a line and rode out of Gorshö. At last the Turas were leaving the Puszta, and as they rode, they left Chokolade behind them, too.

Chapter V

SÁROSPATAK WAS A small town, but the garrison wasn't as bad as some Captain St. Pal had seen. At least it was in Hungary, and not in that hated Polish province, Galicia. All soldiers dreaded the time when they would be posted to Galicia, as eventually, all of them were.

In the Sárospatak garrison, Captain St. Pal had a suite of rooms which his orderly was able to make fairly comfortable for him. Of course, it wasn't Budapest or Vienna, but it wasn't completely impossible—for the provinces.

Whenever he was stationed away from one of the two capital cities, Captain St. Pal sent his orderly, Kemeny, on ahead. Kemeny introduced himself to the local tradesmen, and explained that he represented the captain of the Corvinius Hussars. The local shopkeepers were happy to extend him credit, and Kemeny hurried to furnish the Captain's rooms as best he could.

In Sárospatak he took advantage of the local peasant handicraft, and when the Captain arrived two weeks later he found his rooms furnished with lace curtains, hand-stitched pillows, and needle-point throws meant for the bed, but which Kemeny threw on the floor, and which St. Pal's boots quickly shredded.

The chairs were overstuffed, and the tables and wardrobes were heavy and dark, but combined with the best Herend porcelain, and some halfway decent crystal, Kemeny was able to keep his Captain reasonably content.

"Naturally," he told the impressed local tradespeople, "it is not what we are used to when the Captain is in his apartments in Budapest or Vienna, but we shall manage."

His listeners wanted the Captain to do better than merely manage. They had experienced irritated garrison commanders before, men who had ridden drunkenly through their small town, burning houses, arresting the innocent. They wanted the Captain to be as happy as possible in his provincial outpost. So the wine merchant sent a weekly gift of a case of Little Grey Friar's Wine, while the meat purveyor always made sure that a haunch of well-hung venison or a brace of pheasants graced the Captain's table. Hopeful ladies who had seen the tall, elegant Captain ride into town sent over platters of home-baked cherry *retes*, the fruit encased in paper-thin, flaky pastry. The cakes came on the sender's finest china, covered with hand-embroidered linen napkins that might have been in the family for generations. And with these little gifts were flowery invitations.

"Any day between four and six, dear Captain," the notes were simperingly written, "we would be most pleased to receive the honorable Captain for coffee."

St. Pal always laughed when he read these notes.

"Any pretty girls at home?" he would ask Kemeny.

"A face like a horse," Kemeny said of one writer, or "A pretty, little blonde daughter at that house, Captain. I'm sure her mother sees her married to the Captain and living in great style in Budapest."

St. Pal tore all the notes into shreds, and threw the pieces into the air. He never visited these middle-class homes, and he was careful to stay away from the daughters of such households—no matter how pretty they might be.

He much preferred the daughters of the local peasants. The girls were freer and so impressed with the Hussar captain that he had no trouble getting them into his bed after a few glasses of wine. And when it was over—it was over. They had no illusions that they might one day bear his name, grace his home, or preside at his table, once he left Sárospatak.

Until he saw Chokolade, Captain St. Pal was managing very well with Ilonka, whose father owned the local *csarda*, a combination tavern and inn. It had started the night Ilonka delivered the Captain's dinner.

St. Pal had watched the girl as she moved about his table, setting out the platter of roast goose, deftly arranging the red cabbage beside it. He looked up to see Kemeny grinning at the doorway, and the orderly allowed himself a most informal nod to the

Captain. Kemeny could not indulge in such informality often, for the Captain would have him whipped and demoted to the stables. But St. Pal understood the meaning of the nod. The girl had undoubtedly given Kemeny a small bribe, and asked him to let her set the table for the Captain in the hope that St. Pal would notice her.

Well, he was noticing her, all right. Her full skirt stood away from her knees, and that made it clear to the Captain that when he undressed her, he'd have to strip off the peasant girl's favorite fancy dress: seven petticoats beneath a full skirt. Her red boots fitted snugly about rounded calves, and her white, embroidered blouse came down lower than necessary, revealing lovely shoulders and the tops of high, curving breasts.

The Captain looked at her with a connoisseur's eyes. She had the blonde, blue-eyed prettiness of many young Hungarian girls, with the full mouth and fleshy, upturned nose of the peasant.

She was probably somewhere between nineteen and twenty-one. Just the right age, he decided, because he knew that those blonde looks would fade after twenty-five, and the beguiling soft features would relax into fat after thirty. No matter, the girl was far from twenty-five or thirty, and the Captain was not going to be in Sárospatak when she did arrive at that advanced age, so he might as well take advantage of what was being offered to him at the moment.

He frowned at Kemeny. "A chair for the lady," he said, "move!"

Kemeny jumped forward, and pulled a chair

back for Ilonka. He held it respectfully while the girl seated herself, smoothing down her skirt and endless petticoats. Kemeny had been through this same charade with his Captain in many other garrison towns, and he knew what to expect next.

"A glass for Miss Ilonka," the Captain said severely, "hurry. And another plate. Will you join me, my dear?"

Ilonka looked at the intimidating array of forks and knives beside the Captain's plate and decided that she wasn't all that hungry.

"Just a glass of wine," she said, trying to match the Captain's haughty look at Kemeny with one of her own.

The orderly swallowed back his laughter, and managed to look polite and serious. "Oh, God," he thought, "the little fool. Putting on airs with me. I'd like to see what airs she puts on when the Captain gets her into his bed and strips her down to her bare ass."

But no matter what he thought, he politely poured the girl a glass of her own father's best wine, and he stood respectfully behind her chair, a white linen napkin folded over his arm.

The Captain waited for Ilonka to take her first sip of wine.

"Is it all right, my dear?" he asked.

She was so enchanted by the way the Captain talked to her—he actually spoke to her as though she were a lady—that she just managed to breathe out, "Oh, yes, it's wonderful."

He nodded to Kemeny. "You may go," he said, "and see that I'm not disturbed."

Kemeny bowed, and backed out of the room. He knew that these added touches of servility impressed peasant girls like Ilonka, and he, too, wanted his Captain to be happy. That made life much easier for him.

The Captain relaxed and ate his roast goose in a leisurely way. No need to rush, this little blonde wasn't going to leave him, he was sure of that. The only boring part of the entire evening was the act he would have to put on before he took her to his bed.

He wished he could just say, "You—strip down—and get into that bed—now." But a man couldn't do that—especially not with a peasant wench. Women were strange. An aristocrat like Magda Meleki liked to be ordered about, while a peasant like Ilonka wanted to be treated like a lady—or at least the way she thought a lady should be treated.

The Captain finished his roast goose and leaned back, a glass of brandy in his hand. Never mind, this girl looked as though she would be worth a little of the necessary pretense. He went through the motions, mechanically, but his behavior seemed inspired to Ilonka.

First, he handed the girl a glass of brandy. Their fingertips touched. He kissed her hand, first asking her permission to do so. From there he moved to small nibbling kisses on the palm of her hand and her wrist. His tongue then glided up her forearm. Just before he began nibbling on the lobe of her ear, the Captain looked at the girl. Her eyes were half shut, and her breath came in short gasps.

"My God," the Captain thought, "she's like a

rabbit paralyzed by a hunter. Enough of this."

The mask of a gentleman wooing a lady dropped from him. He stood and picked the girl up in his arms. In a few swift steps he was in his bedroom, and none too gently, he dropped the girl on his bed. She didn't give him any trouble—nor much help, either, as he loosened her skirt and pulled it down over her feet. Each of the petticoats quickly followed the skirt. By God, there *were* seven of them. The Captain grinned. Oh, it was clear why she had come to his rooms. The girl—what the devil was her name—wore no undergarments.

After the petticoats, he unloosed the tie of her blouse, and pulled it over her head. There she was. He enjoyed looking at her sprawled on his bed while he undressed. A good, firm body—a little fleshy— but that just meant a little more to enjoy. She still had her boots on, and that gave her a marvelous sluttish look—bare breasts, curve of belly, a triangle of hair, thighs spread, and wearing nothing but her boots.

He was tempted to take her, boots and all, but he remembered when he had done something similar, and he still had heel marks in his back to remind him of that experience. No, he decided regretfully, the boots would have to come off, too.

Again, she did nothing to help him. Nor did she do much after the boots were off. The Captain enjoyed the girl, but he would have enjoyed her even more if she had shown some emotion. He wouldn't have believed her if she had struggled, and said a few token "no's," but that might have been more amusing than having her just lie there.

And he would also have appreciated hearing a few sighs, perhaps even a gasp of enjoyment. Never mind, in time he would teach her how to please him. That first time with Ilonka went quickly, and afterwards the Captain lay back in bed and lit one of his long black cheroots. He made a mental bet with himself as to what Ilonka would say when she finally did open those big blue eyes.

"A hundred *pengö* she'll say something like— 'Where am I'—or 'What have you done to me?"

It took another few minutes before Ilonka did stir, pretending to come to from a long sleep, or an unconscious state. And then: "Where am I?" she murmured, her voice soft and weak. "What has happened to me?"

The Captain was cheered by the accuracy of his prediction, and that made him behave more kindly toward the girl than he might have. He was polite enough to continue the charade which he knew would please her.

"Do not be afraid, little bird, you're here with me—in our bed of love."

Ilonka responded joyfully to the word "love"— most women did, the Captain knew—and after that first time, she came to his rooms whenever he wanted her.

The Captain knew that if he had asked her to, she would have moved in with him, but he also knew how important it was to keep up the pretense that she came to his rooms only to deliver the meals from her father's *csarda*. He was sure that the girl's father knew that his daughter was the Captain's very pleasant bedmate. But as long as it wasn't admitted openly, the tavern-keeper could keep his head high in the little town. Meanwhile, he didn't mind sharing in those extra *pengö* Ilonka brought home from the Captain.

The girl also knew the importance of playing the game, and when she gave her father the extra money, it was always with, "The Captain sends this to you for an especially delicious dinner," or, "Captain St. Pal asks you to buy him a case of Egri Bikaver wine, father. A whole case," and she poured the coins liberally into her father's hand.

If Ilonka was unusually generous with the Captain's money, instead of hoarding it all for herself, she had a very special reason. She was sure that the supply of money from the Captain was endless, because she was sure that their relationship would never end.

She had no thoughts that the Captain would ever marry her—that was too much to hope for—but she was satisfied being his mistress, especially as she knew that he wouldn't remain in Sárospatak forever. Ilonka didn't want to stay in that small town for the rest of her life, she wanted to live in Budapest. She believed that if she pleased the Captain, he would take her with him when his troop moved back to the capital.

Why not? It wouldn't be the first time something like that had happened. She had seen it happen—well, at least once. That was when her friend Manci went to Budapest with a tax collector who had come to town. Of course, Manci first had to go the angel-maker to rid herself of the unwanted baby in her belly, but once that was out of the way, the tax

113

collector seemed happy enough to take her along with him.

Manci had only come back to Sárospatak once after that. A year or so later she had returned wearing beautiful clothes, and bringing elegant presents to everyone in her family. She didn't have much to say about the tax collector, except to admit that she was no longer with him.

But it didn't mater, she had assured Ilonka, there were plenty of lovely men in Budapest just waiting to take care of a pretty girl. The tax collector had done the right thing for her. He had set her up in an apartment in a section of old Buda called the Magyar Körút. It was a fine place, she had assured Ilonka, and after the tax collector had said his last goodbye, one of his very close friends had become her benefactor.

Was she with that man, Ilonka had asked?

Manci had admitted that the relationship had come to an end, but that nice man had introduced her to still another nice man, and so it went.

"It's better than staying here in Sárospatak," Manci had said, taking Ilonka's silence for criticism.

But Ilonka wasn't being critical at all. And if she was silent, it was only because she was busily trying to think how she, too, could find someone to take her to Budapest and the wonderful life that Manci had described.

The Captain was the answer. It was true that he wouldn't marry her, and he wouldn't stay with her forever, but he could take her to Budapest, and settle her in one of those fabled apartments. And she wouldn't be sorry to lose him as long as he introduced her to some of his friends. One aristocratic gentleman was as good as another, as long as she could live in Budapest. She realized that the Captain was only pretending to care for her, but then, she only pretended to care for him.

Did he use her? Well, she used him. He was her escape route from the life in a small country town. If she stayed, she would eventually marry a peasant who owned a small piece of land, and who would work her as hard as he worked his oxen. That's what all those farmers did, she knew. Treated their women not quite as generously as they treated their cattle. The Captain was her way out of a life of drudgery, hard work, and a baby a year. A life with a man who would slap her as often as he kissed her.

Every night Ilonka heard the Gypsies in her father's tavern play a popular folk tune that the men in the *csarda* enjoyed. They would all sing with the Gypsies: "I want the kind of woman, who even if she's sick, will get up and bring me my dinner...."

The peasants would roar out every verse of the *csardas*, and even when she was a little girl, Ilonka would wince when she heard it.

"It's only a song," her mother had said to the child.

But Ilonka, looking at her mother, worn and old at thirty, knew that it was more than a song—it was the gospel truth according to the Hungarian peasants.

Her mother had died just before her thirty-fifth birthday, and it was from this fate that Ilonka wanted to be saved. The Captain alone could help her, and she did her best to please him. She was available whenever he wanted her, and she tried to satisfy him in bed, though she thought that some of the acts he made her perform in bed were strange and unnatural.

If she didn't enjoy being in bed with the Captain, she at least knew enough to be obedient. She had even learned how to pretend enjoyment, because that seemed important to him. Every day she learned a little more from Captain St. Pal, and she stored the little nuggets away as carefully as a miser hoards gold. She knew now that she should sip wine, and not gulp it down. When she wiped her mouth, it was with a napkin, and not with the back of her hand. Aristocrats had strange habits, they broke a good roll into pieces before buttering it, and did the same thing with a large piece of bread. That was all amazing, and most amazing of all was their idea that a woman should enjoy herself in bed. Peasants knew that such enjoyment was meant for men, or for bad women, but if that was what the Captain wanted—well, she could act the part of a whore.

Ilonka guarded the Captain jealously. He never knew that there were other girls in the village eager to come to him, other girls who were willing to bribe Kemeny for the privilege of climbing into bed with the handsome Hussar. But the other girls were afraid of Ilonka's rage. She had let them know that she had a knife ready for anyone who tried to get between her and the Captain. They weren't sure if Ilonka really meant those words, but it hardly seemed worthwhile taking a chance, especially when there were other Hussar officers eager to kiss their hands, nibble on their earlobes, and promise undying love.

Captain St. Pal didn't concern himself with Ilonka's feelings or with her plans for the future. If he thought of her at all, it was the way he would think of a pet animal, a small cat that it pleased him to pet from time to time. She was no more than that to him, a pet that he could abandon without a second thought after she had ceased to amuse him, or after he had found someone else he believed would be more entertaining.

Now, it was Chokolade to whom he looked for his amusement and pleasure. He had been getting a little bored with Ilonka for awhile now, but until something better came along, he saw no reason to dismiss her from his bed. But now he had the Gypsy girl, and he knew from that first night he had taken her on the river bank that she would offer a challenge. This one wouldn't lie quietly on his bed, not moving, pretending to enjoy him when she was probably counting the *pengö* he would give her. No, that was Ilonka's way. This one would fight him— fight him until he conquered her. And if she moaned with pleasure beneath him, he would know that it was a moan wrested against her will, and the pleasure she felt was real.

Chokolade had been expecting the garrison jail, instead she found herself in Captain St. Pal's apartment. But this was worse, she realized. Better a cold jail with stone floors and iron bars than this apartment where she was a prisoner of the man she hated most in the world. She would rather trust herself to the mercy of a jailer than to this conceited Hussar captain.

The Captain pushed her into a plush, overstuffed chair, and shouted for his orderly: "Kemeny, where the devil are you? Wine! I'm parched."

To Chokolade, the orderly seemed to materialize from thin air. At first, he wasn't there, but at his master's call he appeared like a genie from a bottle.

"Wine, sir?" Kemeny ventured. "It is not yet noon. Perhaps the Captain would like coffee first? A buttered crescent roll?"

"Wine!" And both Chokolade and Kemeny jumped at his roar. "Cold wine—white. I'm parched. I've had a busy morning. And then coffee and buttered rolls for the young lady."

Kemeny looked at Chokolade, and his eyes grew round. Young lady? Not this one. But no peasant, either, by the look of her. He couldn't believe it, but it looked as though the Captain had brought home a Gypsy—and a wild one at that.

"I don't want your coffee," Chokolade spit out. "What am I doing here? You wanted to put me in jail. Very well, then. Put me in jail."

The Captain sat down and stretched out his long, booted legs. He unbuttoned the high collar of his jacket, and then removed the jacket's leather belt. He wrapped the end with the buckle around one hand, and he lashed out at the dark mahogany table with the strip of leather.

"You will stay here as long as it pleases me." His voice was low, and the quieter tones were more frightening to Chokolade than his shouts. "You are my prisoner, and if I wish to keep you in my rooms instead of in that filthy, rat-infested garrison jail, consider yourself lucky."

He emphasized his words by hitting the table once again with the end of his belt.

Chokolade was afraid, but something told her that the way to control this man, if he could be controlled, was not to admit her fear to him.

"How long do you intend to keep me here?"

Sandor St. Pal leaned back against the chair. His smile, Chokolade decided, was like the devil's, both winning and wicked.

"Until your brother returns the jewels," he said mockingly, "or until I find you tiresome. Which do you think will come first?"

Gyuri, Chokolade thought, Gyuri will come for me. He won't bring the jewels, but he will come for me. But when?

"I know nothing about jewels," she said coldly, "I'm a dancer, not a thief."

"Oh, yes"—the Captain's eyes gleamed—"you are a dancer. The best I've ever seen, and I've been many places. Now, if you only made love as well as you danced—you would be perfection."

A flush of pink rose beneath Chokolade's olive skin. "You have no right—"

"Right?" the Captain laughed. "You're going to have to learn not to use that word to me. Don't you know that little Gypsy dancers have no rights, and that soldiers have them all?"

Before Chokolade could answer, Kemeny was back in the room. His hands, she noticed, were trembling slightly as he placed the wine and wine glass before the Captain, and the coffee cup and small silver pot in front of her. Even this man was afraid of the Captain. It was true, Kemeny was afraid; he had never seen the Captain quite like this before. He had seen him with many women, but this was the first time the Captain seemed uncontrolled.

Kemeny waited until the Captain had drunk half a glass of wine, and then he suggested, "Some clothes for the young lady, sir? She seems to have come only with her riding outfit." This wouldn't be the first time that the Captain had wooed a girl with a new wardrobe.

"Clothes?" The Captain's voice was harsh again. "Why? Chokolade isn't going anywhere. No. She won't need any clothes, except perhaps one of my silk robes should I want her to be dressed for dinner. Yes, that's it, Kemeny, lay out two robes. The velvet for me, the silk foulard for Miss Chokolade. And then get the hell out of here, and don't come back until you hear me call. And make sure that I have called before you walk into this room again."

Kemeny hurriedly laid both of the Captain's robes on the chaise beside the bed, and then scurried out of the room, pulling the door shut behind him.

With a cry, Chokolade made a dash for the door, but the Captain had anticipated her move, and had locked the door before she could put her hand on the doorknob.

"Now," the Captain said, "now, we will finish what was started the other night."

"No!" Chokolade retreated behind the table. The Captain circled one way, and she moved the other. He pretended to move toward the right, and she ran toward the left, only to find him even closer. After that, she reached out for the wine decanter, and threw the cut glass at the Captain's head. Her aim was good, but his reflexes were better. He ducked, and the wine bottle crashed and spilled against the far wall.

"Come on," the Captain urged, laughing at what was a game to him. "Come on, you little wildcat, you must have more fight than that in you."

Chokolade screamed with rage, and the wine decanter was followed by the wine glass, and then by the little silver coffeepot. She kept missing, and the Captain kept coming closer—and closer.

"That's it," he said finally, capturing her in his arms. "Nothing left to throw, you Gypsy witch?"

His hands held her arms tightly to her sides, and his mouth came down hard over hers. Chokolade tried to twist her head away, but then one arm went around her body, while another held her head close to his. His kiss scorched her, she couldn't breathe.

And then she was in his arms, and he was carrying her into his bedroom. He dropped her in the middle of the bed, and she turned over quickly, trying to scramble out on the other side.

"Oh, no, you don't." He was on top of her, pulling her back to the center of the bed.

"Let me go," she screamed.

"Not yet, not just yet."

She tried to get away from his hands, but he pinned her to the bed. He knelt on the bed, her body imprisoned between his knees.

He reached for the top of her shirt, and ignoring the buttons, he ripped it down. He hesitated for a moment, taking pleasure in the sight of Chokolade's small, high breasts with their fawn-colored nipples, and in that second Chokolade was able to get one hand free. Her nails scratched a path down the Captain's right cheek.

He shouted with pain and rage, and didn't hesitate to pull her heavy riding pants down. He threw them across the floor, and while he did that Chokolade managed to get up on one knee, and again she tried to roll off the bed.

St. Pal captured her again, but he wasn't quick enough to dodge a kick from Chokolade's boot heel. The blow landed on his hip, not on the delicate spot she had intended it for.

"That's enough of that," St. Pal roared, now truly angered. He dealt Chokolade a back-handed slap, and while she lay back dazed, he managed to pull her boots off. It didn't take him long to get out of his clothes, and then he was on top of her, forcing his body's will upon hers.

The pain, Chokolade thrashed about, *the pain*. His rough treatment of her less than a day after her first experience of him was more than she could bear. She struggled for control, but she couldn't stop the sob that tore from her throat.

St. Pal heard it, but he was too far gone to stop and consider her feelings or her pain, he thought only of taming her, of forcing her into submission.

Sandor St. Pal got out of bed, and put on his robe. He tied the sash and poured a glass of wine. He felt strange. Usually, after he made love he felt both satiated and self-satisfied. For the first time in his male life, the feeling of self-satisfaction was missing. He swallowed the wine, but that, too, left a bad taste. He was bewildered by a sensation he had never experienced before. He actually felt badly about the girl crying on the bed.

He put the wine glass down and went back to the bedroom. He sat down on the edge of the bed. His movements were awkward, as were his words, because he had never acted or spoken this way before.

He tried to stroke Chokolade's tousled hair, and he said, "Now, look—I didn't mean to hurt you—"

That was as far as he got, because Chokolade was upon him in an instant, her fingers determined to scratch out his eyes.

"Damn"—St. Pal had to pin her back on the bed again—"I must be crazy—trying to say 'sorry' to a Gypsy bitch! Now, you listen to me: I rule here! I'll decide whether you live or die, or whether or not you go to jail. Get used to the idea. Learn to please me, and things will go a lot easier for you—"

"Please you!" Chokolade spat the words at him. "I will kill you."

"Not much chance of that. How many times do I have to prove that I'm stronger than you?"

"I hate you."

St. Pal shrugged. "Keep on hating me and you'll keep on causing yourself pain. Once you understand that I'm your master—"

"No one is my master," Chokolade said furiously. "Do you think I am your horse? A pet dog, or perhaps your orderly? I am none of those things, and no *kek kushti gajo* is going to make me his slave."

"'*Kek kushti gajo*,'" St. Pal repeated. "Are you

cursing me, you Gypsy tramp?"

"I am calling you just what you are—a no-good non-Gypsy—"

That made St. Pal laugh. "Is that all? I've been called worse than that in my life.

Chokolade was silent, but she swore to herself, "By the devil and Saint Sara, I'll make him sorry for what he's done to me."

That was the strongest vow that Chokolade knew, because it coupled the devil with the patron saint of the Gypsies who had traveled with the three Marys to Europe after the crucifixion.

Chokolade had been taught as a child not to call upon the devil unless she really wanted to see him. "The devil is always waiting for you," her father had cautioned, "and he will come if you really want him. Remember that."

Chokolade remembered it, but she also knew that no human could best the Captain, only the devil could beat him. Let the devil take care of the Hussar and she had faith that Saint Sara would take care of her. The Captain was talking on, not realizing that Chokolade had called upon some of the strongest powers in her universe to destroy him.

"We won't be staying in Sárospatak forever, my love. I'm bound to be sent back to Budapest very soon—oh, a month or two. And by that time I will have taught you what you must do to please me. Taught you some of it," he amended, "and we shall continue the lessons in Budapest. You'll like that, I imagine," St. Pal said, remembering how Ilonka's eyes had sparkled whenever he mentioned the capital city.

Did Chokolade's silence mean that she was becoming more agreeable? He didn't know, but he continued talking, thinking he was soothing her with his promises. "Don't worry, I won't leave you behind. And when we get to Budapest, I'll set you up in a fine apartment. You'll never have to worry after that. Naturally, you can't expect us to be together forever, but later on—and I'm sure it will be much later on, my love—there will be my friends—"

Chokolade seethed in silence. He was planning to turn her into his whore, and after that he expected her to prostitute herself. She would kill him. She had to kill him, nothing else could satisfy her honor and the honor of the Tura tribe.

She'll come around, St. Pal told himself, as his self-satisfaction returned. Oh, he knew how to treat women, no question of that.

Chapter VI

THAT NIGHT MARKED the start of the pitched battle between Chokolade Tura and Sandor St. Pal. The Captain kept Chokolade restricted to his rooms. When he went out, Kemeny was set on guard over her. She had no clothes other than the Captain's robes, but St. Pal no longer had any illusions that lack of proper clothing would keep Chokolade confined to his rooms.

The Hussar troop under St. Pal's command knew that their Captain was not having a happy time with the Gypsy girl. They noticed the fresh scars on his face in the morning, and he took away their leaves for the slightest infraction of rules.

"Karoly," he would shout at morning inspection, "the hilt of your sword is filthy. You can spend the next three days polishing it in the guard house. Feher, you're out of regulation uniform, your pocket flap is unbuttoned! Restricted to barracks for three days..."

And so it went. The men spoke to Kemeny about the Captain's bad humor, and he confirmed what they had guessed.

"It's that Gypsy bitch. She doesn't give the Captain a moment's peace. I'd be afraid to go to bed with a woman like that. One night she'll knife him as he sleeps."

"But he has her," one of the men said, "what more does he want?"

Kemeny shrugged. "He wants more."

Kemeny didn't understand it, and neither did the Captain, but St. Pal did want more. He wanted to conquer Chokolade. He wanted to feel her throb with pleasure, to hear her moan of surrender when her body reached such a peak of ecstasy that she could no longer withhold herself from him.

St. Pal knew that Chokolade would never say, "Take me, I want you." But he didn't need to hear the words, her body could act out her feelings, and that's what he wanted. He knew that a woman at the height of passion was without will, her body ruled head and heart, and it was this feeling St. Pal was determined to arouse in Chokolade. Tenderness, he decided, tenderness was the way. He couldn't conquer a girl with her spirit by force. Sweet words, kindness—that was the way.

But Chokolade responded to his warmth with even greater fury, and finally with sullen silence. She would never reveal to him that he did arouse her. At first, she knew nothing but rage and anger, but then she blamed her willful body for betraying her. St. Pal's touch was electric. She hated those times when he picked her up in his arms and took her into his bed—hated it, because she wanted to throw her arms around his neck, and abandon her body to him. She wanted to say, "Take me, do what you want to me." Those words would never pass her lips, but she couldn't stop her heart from pounding when his mouth came down on hers, and she wanted to moan when his hands searched out the hidden corners of her flesh in a knowing caress.

She would never give in to him, never! She would never forgive him for treating her like a slave girl in a Turkish sultan's harem, but while her mind resisted him, her body cried out for him.

The worst of it was that she didn't know how to guard against her growing feelings for this man. He was holding her against her will, she reminded herself over and over again. But was it completely against her will? Would she fly away if he opened the door of her cage, or was she beginning to enjoy her captivity? She was afraid of the answer.

St. Pal was too skilled, and Chokolade too inexperienced to cope with him. Sometimes he would kiss her so brutally that her mouth was bruised, but at the same time his hands were so tender, so knowledgeable, that she yearned to relax under his caress.

"Say it," he would whisper, "say you want me. Say you like this—and this—and this."

"No," she was barely able to gasp out. "No—never."

But even as she said those words, her body went out of control, and St. Pal knew it. "You want me—I know." He stared down greedily at her erect nipples. "This tells me." His hands searched out the secret core of her. "And this—at last," he breathed. "You do want me—you do! I've won."

It was the words *I've won* which gave Chokolade

the strength to act. If he hadn't said that, she might have been his willing whore forever.

His eyes were closed as he kissed her, but hers were open, and stealthily she reached over to the night table for the brass candlestick that sat there. She would have brought the candlestick crashing down on his head, except that St. Pal, alerted by her unexpected movement, turned quickly.

"Damn!" He tore the candlestick from her hand, and it went crashing to the floor.

Once again his hands pinned Chokolade's hands above her head, and once again his knee forced her thighs open, and he took her with such brutality that it wrested a scream from her lips.

After that night St. Pal was glad when he was called away from the garrison to lead a reconnaissance through the neighboring villages. Before he left, he gave Kemeny strict orders about Chokolade.

"I'll be gone for about four days," he said. "You're responsible for the girl. If she escapes— well, if she escapes, first I'll give you the beating of your life, and then I'll see that you're posted to Galicia as a stablehand."

Kemeny groaned, "I'd rather go with you Captain, sir, and fight Kossuth's New Army, than stay here with her."

The Captain looked at his orderly with a frown. That remark was impertinent, but he said nothing, because he couldn't blame the man. Fighting Kossuth's New Army was easier than fighting Chokolade.

Kossuth's New Army—a brave name for a troop

of visionaries who had teamed up with local brigands to harass the government. Revolutionaries, they had named themselves after the great Kossuth, who had proclaimed Hungary an independent republic in 1849, after a year of revolution against Austria and Emperor Franz Josef.

Captain St. Pal would never admit his true feelings about that earlier Kossuth and his men, but he secretly admired the great patriot of 1849. As a Hungarian, he could understand another Hungarian who wanted to be free of Austrian domination, but as a Captain who led a troop of His Majesty's crack Hussars, he knew that such feelings were treason.

He had read and heard about Kossuth, and he was impressed by a man who could defeat a professional army with a few troops of idealistic cavalry. Kossuth and the Hungarians had been defeated at the last, but not by the Austrians. Oh, no, the Emperor had to ask his cousin, the Russian Czar, for help in conquering that small band of Hungarians. And the Russians had acted with such brutality, slaying the women and children of the men they were fighting, that eventually Kossuth and his men had surrendered, and Hungary was still under the domination of Austria.

No one who loved Hungary had ever forgotten Kossuth, and now, here it was, 1887, thirty-nine years later, and another group of Hungarians had joined together and called themselves Kossuth's New Army. The Emperor and his network of ministers knew that this New Army was only a small group of men, loosely organized, and not rich in supplies or ammunition. But they were also wise enough, after their earlier experience, to want these revolutionaries captured and killed before they became too powerful.

It was for this reason that St. Pal, and other men like him, were sent to small towns and cities close to provincial borders. The Emperor wanted the insurgents destroyed or controlled, he didn't want the embarrassment of having to call for help for a second time from a nation outside of his own.

Very often, the Hussars were able to get information from the local peasants, by claiming that the men in Kossuth's New Army were nothing more than a band of criminals, thieves, and highwaymen. The peasants who believed this would gladly turn the hiding rebels over to the Army for a few *pengö*, or even for a bottle of brandy.

But in those places where the men of Kossuth's New Army were known, they were hidden and protected. The peasants knew that the men of Kossuth's New Army fought for them against the coalition of Austrians and Hungarian aristocrats that wanted to keep them forever poor, and in their power.

It was Captain St. Pal's duty to ferret out the rebels and to have them hanged or jailed for treason. He personally felt that as long as the rebels knew the Hussars were in the area, they could be controlled without having to execute them.

This was the first time he was actually glad to go out on reconnaissance. Maybe after a few days absence, Chokolade would have softened toward him. And maybe while he was away he could think more clearly about why the girl meant so much to him.

Kemeny watched St. Pal leave with a sinking heart. If the Captain couldn't make the Gypsy witch come to heel, what could he do? Chokolade was relieved at the Captain's departure. He was getting too close—too close to her. She had to escape before he conquered her completely. She wasn't worried about Kemeny. She could see that the orderly was afraid of her; it wouldn't take much to outwit him and to make her escape.

She needed two things: clothes and a fast horse. Where would she go after she obtained both these things? She wasn't sure, but she would ride across the Puszta, and head toward Austria. Hopefully, she would catch up with the Turas. They were a few days ahead of her, but they were moving in slower caravans.

Chokolade watched Kemeny closely. She wanted to pace the Captain's apartment like a caged animal, but she forced herself to stretch out on the chaise, and to act the part of a lazy, languid woman content to wait for her man to return. Her actions didn't fool Kemeny. He knew that his master hadn't been able to conquer the girl, and he was sure she was just waiting for an opportunity to escape. No one was allowed into the apartment other than Kemeny and Ilonka. With the Captain away, Kemeny didn't see why he should have to wait on the Gypsy girl; let Ilonka bring her meals and then let Ilonka take the dirty dishes away. Kemeny was a Hussar, not a Gypsy's servant.

And besides, Ilonka was really sweet to him since

the Captain had thrown her over for Chokolade.
She smiled at the orderly, and he was beginning to
think that he might be able to follow his master's
path. True, he was no officer, but he was a Hussar.

"Do you want to go to the *csarda* for a drink?"
Ilonka asked him the third day after the Captain
had ridden away. "I'll stay with her and wait for the
dishes. You must be so tired of having to stay in
these rooms day after day with this Gypsy bitch."

Kemeny was tired, and bored. He wanted to go to
the *csarda* and have a few drinks, and sit down
among men. But what would the Captain say?

"He won't be back until tomorrow—at the
earliest," Ilonka assured him. "Go ahead—take an
hour for yourself."

"But if she tries to get away?"

Ilonka laughed. She was taller and heavier than
the Gypsy girl. "Just let her try."

"You're kind, Ilonka." Kemeny's hand yearned
to pinch the peasant girl's bottom, but he was
cautious about poaching on his master's preserves.
Besides, he reasoned, he'd probably get no more
than a handful of petticoat and a slap for his pains.
And if she were to mention such an incident to the
Captain...

But Ilonka gave him a smile and a little wink.
"Go ahead, Hussar Kemeny, a drink will make you
feel better—not as good, of course, as other things
could make you feel—but we can talk about that
later."

Kemeny left the apartment dizzied by what
Ilonka had said to him. The invitation was plain

enough, he would just have to find the time to be able to take advantage of it. His Captain's woman! He had never dared look that high.

Ilonka waited until she was sure that Kemeny was no longer in hearing distance before she approached the table where Chokolade was poking at the food that Ilonka had brought her. The very way Chokolade pushed at the bits of pork in the plate of *szekely gulyas* irritated Ilonka.

"Isn't our food good enough for you, Gypsy?"

Chokolade looked up warily. What did this stupid peasant cow want from her? Chokolade had been hoping that with Kemeny away she might be able to make her escape. If she only had a few coins with her she was sure that she could bribe Ilonka. Unfortunately, her clothes were locked up, and she couldn't get to the *pengö* and the one gold piece that were sewn into the lining of her sheepskin vest.

Chokolade tried a brief smile. "The food is fine. But being in jail doesn't give me much of an appetite."

"Jail! You call this a jail!" Ilonka was in a rage. Chokolade held the very position which she yearned for. God, if only the Captain had kept her locked up in his rooms without a stitch of clothes, she would have been so happy. Happy and grateful, because that would have meant he wanted her so much that he would have taken her to Budapest with him. Instead, he was probably planning to take this Gypsy whore. Only she would spoil his plans—the Gypsy wouldn't live to see Budapest!

Chokolade saw the flash of the knife, and she

moved quickly as the blade came toward her.

"I'll kill you before I let you have my Captain," Ilonka shrieked.

Chokolade moved quickly to one side. "I don't want your Captain," she said, "I never wanted him. Help me—help me to escape and he'll be yours again."

But Ilonka didn't believe that. As long as Chokolade was alive the Captain would never pay attention to her, she knew that.

"You'll escape all right,"—she chased after Chokolade, the knife blade gleaming—"you'll escape from this world all together."

"Listen—listen to me. Set me free—I only need a horse—and you stay here. I'm sure the Captain likes you better than he does me."

"That's a lie," Ilonka sobbed, maddened and beyond reason, "it's you—it's only you he cares about."

It was true that Ilonka was both taller and heavier than Chokolade. But the Gypsy girl had a dancer's body, and a dancer's ability to move quickly. Besides, years of riding and living out in the open had made her more muscular than the softer peasant girl. The next time Ilonka tried to drive her knife into Chokolade's heart, the Gypsy dancer grabbed her wrist with both hands, twisted hard, and the knife went skittering across the floor.

"You!" Ilonka shrieked, and with her hands in Chokolade's hair, she pulled her down to the floor.

Chokolade lashed out with her feet, and the two girls rolled about on the floor. Ilonka was using her fists, and Chokolade was clawing for Ilonka's face, when they both heard the sound of polite hand-clapping.

The girls stopped fighting, frozen as though they were statues, when they heard the amused voice of Captain St. Pal.

"Very good, ladies. It does my heart good to see two women fighting over me. Please—continue."

Chokolade felt ashamed. She wasn't fighting for the Captain, but he would never believe that. And what a spectacle she made. Lying on the rug, with his robe half-ripped off her nude body. She tried to pull the robe more closely about her, while Ilonka got to her feet, screaming.

"You—you—" The peasant girl attacked the Captain with her fists. "You're the one I should have killed. You cared nothing for me—I never meant anything to you."

The Captain shrugged, he didn't care for screaming women. He pinned Ilonka's wrists behind her back and propelled her to the door of his rooms. Then, still holding her, he raised one foot, and planted a booted kick on her backside that sent her careening down the corridor. Chokolade could hear the girl's screams all through the apartment, but louder still, she could hear the Captain's shout: "Kemeny! Where the devil are you?"

Chokolade could see the Captain standing at the doorway, his back to her. Obviously, Kemeny was hurrying down the hall, because St. Pal said, "It's about time. How dare you disobey my orders?"

He left the door open, and came back into the room where he had left Chokolade. He was facing her, and Chokolade could see the man in the

Hussar's uniform come up behind him. She gave a slight gasp when she saw who it was, but the Captain was too furious to notice.

The Hussar standing directly behind the Captain was holding a pistol. Quickly he raised it, and the butt end came crashing down on St. Pal's skull. The Captain toppled to the floor.

"Gyuri," Chokolade ran to her brother. "Gyuri— my God, I think you've killed him."

"I hope so," Gyuri said grimly. "That's what the bastard deserves. Come on, Chokolade, we've got to get out of here."

Chokolade looked down at the man who had kept her a captive, now lying on the floor, blood matting his dark hair. "Wait," she said, "my clothes—and—is he dead—?"

"Never mind that now. Who cares? He humiliated you—humiliated every Tura. What do you care whether he's dead or alive? I have a horse for you, and clothes. We have to ride—and fast. If he is dead, we can't afford to be captured."

Gyuri actually pulled his sister out of the room. Just a short while before, she had been plotting her escape, but now she looked back, hoping to see some sign of life from the man fallen and still on the floor.

Chapter VII

IT FELT GOOD to be on a horse again, to be riding fast and free. Chokolade followed her brother as they rode toward the great Erdely Forest. They were riding too fast to talk, but Chokolade's thoughts were consumed with Sandor St. Pal. She saw his face as he lay unconscious on the Turkish carpet. His eyes shut, the blood matting his dark hair. Was he dead? She shivered, even though she had changed to the warm clothes Gyuri had brought for her. She was in a whirl of confusion. She wanted him dead. She had said so often enough to the Captain himself. Why, then, was she suddenly so concerned about him?

I won't think about him, she kept telling herself, I won't think about him. I'll forget all those things he did to me in that bed. I'll forget how he made me feel.

Brother and sister rode until they reached the outskirts of the forest. It was only then that Gyuri reined his horse to a halt, and Chokolade stopped beside him.

"How?" she wanted to know. "How did you manage to get to me?"

"I had help." Gyuri was more serious than Chokolade had ever seen him. "Good help, and lots of it."

Gyuri and Chokolade moved slowly through the ancient forest, and as they rode, Gyuri told his sister what had happened to the Turas since she had last seen them.

After the Hussars had destroyed their camp, the tribe had packed up quickly, and ridden away from Gorshö, with Landowner Balog shouting curses after them. They were afraid to return to the open Puszta, and Gyuri had led them toward Erdely Forest. They hadn't gone far down the dark, tree-shaded, and well-worn paths, when they were stopped by a ragged-looking bunch of men.

"*Betyar*—highwaymen," Gyuri told his sister. "I was sure that's what they were. You should have heard Haradi Neni! That old woman, she started to whine and whimper and plead. If they had been highwaymen they would have known from the way she was carrying on that we were carrying something of value."

Chokolade thought immediately of the remainder of the Meleki jewels, and she knew then that Gyuri still had a share of them.

"But they weren't a troop of highwaymen," Gyuri continued. "Have you heard of Kossuth's New Army?"

If she hadn't spent those days in the Captain's rooms, the term would have meant nothing to her, but she heard the Captain and his second-in-

140

command talk about the very men Gyuri was describing, and she also knew that the Captain had left her to hunt down the same men.

"Yes, I know, but why do you say they're not *betyar*? They rob—steal—"

"No!" Gyuri shouted. "That's what the Emperor and his precious Hussars say, but that's not the truth. They're Hungarians—patriots—and they want to free Hungary from Austrian domination."

Chokolade looked at her brother with surprise. She had never heard him talk about *gajos* with such passion. Hungarians or Austrians, what did it matter as long as they weren't Gypsies?

"They're good men," Gyuri was saying, "you'll see."

Chokolade shrugged. They were *gajos*, and *gajos* were never good for Gypsies. They rode along silently for awhile, and Chokolade had the uneasy sensation that they were being followed. She looked behind her, but she could see no one. She tried peering through the trees on either side of the worn, dirt path, but it was like trying to see through a dark green curtain that moved and rippled with each whisper of wind.

"Gyuri," she called to her brother softly, wondering why she felt it necessary to whisper if there was no one around. "Gyuri, how much longer do we have to ride through Erdely? It's daytime, but in this forest it's dark as night. I feel as though I'm choking."

Before Gyuri could answer, Chokolade heard a whistle. Soft, melodic, it came from behind her. She turned in her saddle and saw—nothing. A bird, she decided, but what kind of a bird? And then the whistle was picked up and answered, only now the sound seemed to come from in front of them. Chokolade shivered as they rounded a turn in the path. What did she expect to see? The devil, a vampire? She smiled at her own childish fear; there was no one there, just the continuation of the forest. The same forest that had been ridden through by Huns, and Mongols, and Turks. Ghosts, Chokolade thought, ghosts of all the people who had settled this old land and thought it would be theirs forever, that's what I'm afraid of—ghosts.

But was it a ghost that whistled once again? And again?

"Gyuri," Chokolade called, but before her brother could answer, the whistle was replaced by a song. A few notes softly sung from a bird song written by a Gypsy violinist so famous that every Romany knew his name. Remenyi, someone was whistling and singing a bird song of Remenyi's.

Chokolade was in a confusion. But as long as she heard a Remenyi song, perhaps it was another tribe of Gypsies. That wasn't a signal of the Turas, they didn't go around romantically whistling in the woods like a bunch of schoolchildren, but maybe this was a group of Roumanian Gypsy musicians traveling to Austria from Cluj.

"Gyuri," Chokolade said once again, and her brother turned in his saddle, but before he could say anything, they were surrounded by a group of men who seemed to come through the trees as though they were the spirits guarding the old forest.

Just a minute ago she had seen no one, and now

there were strange men all around them. Where had they come from? Chokolade didn't wait to find out, she dug her heels into her horse's sides, and leaned over the animal's neck. But before she could move forward, a man riding beside her reached out, wrested the reins from her, and pulled them taut. The horse reared at this confusion of signals, and Chokolade would have been thrown out of the saddle if it hadn't been for a strong arm curved around her back.

"Hold it, hold it," the man said soothingly, talking, it seemed, to both the animal and the girl. "It's all right. Nothing to be afraid of here."

Chokolade pulled the reins from him, and patted her horse's neck. She glared at the man. He may have been whistling a song by Remenyi, but this was no Gypsy. This was another damn *gajo*!

The man laughed softly. "Gyuri, tell your sister who we are, before she kills me with a flash of fire from those green eyes."

Gyuri rode up beside her. "It's all right, Chokolade. These are the men I was telling you about. They're with Kossuth's New Army."

But what did that mean? Chokolade had been through too much to trust anyone.

"They're *gajos*," she said.

The man beside her laughed again. "I don't blame you, pretty little lady. Don't trust most *gajos*—that's a good rule. We follow it ourselves."

"Chokolade," Gyuri protested, "these are the men who helped me rescue you. Some of them even led the rest of our tribe through the forest toward Austria. They're friends."

"Chokolade," the man said, "a sweet name for a sweet girl." He swept off his hat, a gallant gesture by a man in rags. "Permit me"—his lips brushed her hand—"I am Fekete Andras."

Black Andrew—Chokolade couldn't help shivering. The man didn't look fearsome, but according to the talk she had heard at Hussar headquarters, he was the leader of Kossuth's New Army, leader of men known to steal and rape.

Fekete Andras seemed to read her thoughts. "Just remember who it was that said all those terrible things about me."

Chokolade relaxed a little. Could these men with their old clothes and hungry faces possibly have committed all the crimes the Hussars accused them of? And could any one of them be more brutal than Captain St. Pal himself?

"I—I'm sorry," Chokolade stammered, "I didn't know who you were—and I thought—I should thank you. You've helped my brother—and you've helped me."

"We would have come sooner, but we had to wait for the Hussars to ride out."

Fekete Andras signaled his men, and they rode on until they reached a small clearing. A few more horses grazed there. A man tended a large pot of *gulyas* that was suspended over a campfire, and a small, cold stream trickled nearby.

"Our camp," Fekete Andras said, and he helped Chokolade dismount.

The guerrilla leader showed Chokolade around the small campsite, and she reflected that he couldn't have been more gallant if he had been showing her through a large country estate. She was amused at first, and then frightened.

"But we're so close," she said, "so close—"

"To Sárospatak? To the Hussars?"

Chokolade nodded.

"The towns belong to the Emperor," Fekete Andras said, "but the land—especially the forests—they belong to us. Remember, you didn't see us until we wanted you to see us. Not even the Hussars come after us in Erdely. We know every path, every hiding place, and they don't. Don't be afraid, I won't let anyone harm you here."

"Believe him," Gyuri said, putting his arm around his sister's shoulders. "You're all right now, truly. I've never known men like these—and neither have you."

Chokolade's eyes widened, and Gyuri could read her feelings in them. *But they're gajos. From the beginning, we are taught not to trust gajos.*

"I know," Gyuri said, "I know—but you'll see. These men are different."

All men were the same, Chokolade thought. They all want women, and money, and the power to do what they wished to other people.

"When do we ride for Austria?" Chokolade asked her brother.

"In a few days," he said. "We'll camp here quietly. I have no wish to run into a troop of Hussars when we ride out of Erdely. The Captain—I'm not sure how hard I hit him."

"Stay here?" Chokolade looked around her with dismay. It wasn't the idea of camping once again under the stars that bothered her, but to be among a group of *gajo* men, to be at their mercy.

"Sari," Fekete Andras called, and a woman came toward them.

But what a strange-looking woman! Chokolade had never seen a woman who looked like this. Her hair was cropped short and hidden beneath a man's cap. She was dressed in cast-off clothes, and men's clothes at that.

"Sari," Fekete Andras was saying, "see if you can make Chokolade comfortable. Her brother just freed her from the Hussars."

"Hussars—murderers," Sari said, "everybody should be freed from them—from them and that bastard of an Emperor who rules our lives from Vienna."

"Sari"—Chokolade was surprised to hear such gentle tones from such a rough-looking man. "Please."

The woman sighed. "Come with me," and she led Chokolade to a side of the clearing that was partially screened by the low-bending branches of willow trees.

The next few days were the strangest that Chokolade had ever spent. She had never known people like the members of Kossuth's New Army. They were different, her brother was right. All her life Chokolade had known people who were interested in acquiring material things for their own use. *Gajos* wanted land and money, while Gypsies wanted food and a place to stay, but all wanted something for themselves. The people who rode in Kossuth's New Army seemed to have a larger dream, they wanted freedom not only for themselves, but for their entire country. And they talked about it constantly.

"But what difference would it make to you?" Chokolade asked. "What good would it do you?"

"To be free—to feel free—this is a marvelous thing," they told her.

She shrugged. "I am free already—when I keep clear of *gajos*," she said.

"You're right," Fekete Andras said, "of all the people in Hungary—maybe in the world—the Gypsies are the freest. You go, you come, you make your own rules—lead your own life. Maybe that's why we feel that you and your brother are one of us."

Chokolade didn't answer him. He seemed to be a kind man, but how could she explain to him that Gypsies could never be one with *gajos*? It was impossible. But Fekete Andras and his people were kind, she could see that. They didn't have much, but what they did have, they shared. If someone had luck hunting, there was a pot of rabbit stew that was ladled out equally among all of them. If there was no rabbit, they all ate their share of potatoes cooked in that same stew pot, and seasoned with salt and paprika.

They didn't stay long camped in Erdely. Fekete Andras and his men led them through the forest until they arrived close to the town of Eger.

"This is home for us," the revolutionary leader said to Chokolade and Gyuri.

"Home." Chokolade looked at the sandy soil, the towering pines that loomed menacingly around

them. The open land of the Puszta seemed more
homelike to her.

"You'll see," Fekete Andras said.

They were riding toward the base of a small hill.
Another night of camping out in the open,
Chokolade thought, without even a caravan or a
feather quilt. Kossuth's New Army was even more
rugged than a tribe of Gypsies.

But when they got to the hill, Chokolade saw that
a pile of brush hid an entrance—but an entrance to
what? She dismounted, and Fekete Andras led her
inside.

"A cave," Chokolade said. "At least it will be a
little warmer."

The revolutionaries lit pine torches, and as the fat
wood burned and smoked, Fekete Andras led her
forward.

"Not just one cave," he explained, "the whole
town of Eger is honeycombed with connecting
caves. Almost one hundred and fifty kilometers of
them. This is why we call it home; no one can find us
here."

"But if they follow you—"

"If they follow us we can lose them in one of the
tunnels. We know every turn, every entrance, every
way out."

Chokolade looked around in wonderment. The
caves were vaulted and arched in many parts,
almost as though a human hand had carved out the
limestone with thought and deliberation.

"It's centuries old," Fekete Andras was saying.
"No one knows who built it, but we do know that
the caves go right through the town—right under

Eger Castle. I wonder how the Count of Eger would feel if he knew we were just a few feet from his wine cellar."

Gyuri looked apprehensively toward the ceiling of the cave. "Can't they hear you?"

"No need to whisper," Fekete Andras said. "Hungarians hid here in the thirteenth century during the Tartar invasion, and the caves helped Istvan Dobo beat back the Turks in the sixteenth century."

"How?"

"Dobo and his men hid in the caves," Fekete Andras explained, "and at the entrance to each cave they placed a large drum. On top of each drum they threw a few handfuls of dried beans. As the Turks moved from cave to cave, the beans would rattle, and send echoing sounds all through the caves. The Hungarians were always able to keep one or two rooms ahead of the Turks, and when the Turks had gotten completely confused and lost wandering around the caves, the Hungarians came out and slaughtered them."

But Kossuth's New Army used the Eger caves not for slaughtering their enemies, but as a perfect hiding place. They emerged to make occasional forays against the Hussars, and to raid the rich estates all around them for money and food— especially for food.

One night they were stretched out in a cave, all of them lying as close to the flickering fire as possible, hoping to dispel the gloom of the damp cave, and trying to forget their hunger.

Their shared dinner that night had been one

helping each of potato paprikas. The large iron pot held a meager amount of potatoes with one onion, a little lard, and a lot of paprika and salt to add flavor.

"What I wouldn't give for a piece of *paprikas szalonna,*" Gyuri groaned.

"Only a Gypsy would wish for that," one of the other men scoffed. "If you're wishing, why not wish that the pot fills up with *szekely gulyas*? Lots of pork, and sauerkraut, stirred around with plenty of sour cream, caraway seeds, and paprika. That's something to wish for!"

"And a big loaf of potato bread to wipe up the sauce," another voice chimed in.

"And for dessert—apple *retes*—"

"Not apple—cheese—"

"You're both crazy," a man roared. "The only decent *retes* is made with poppy seeds. Everyone knows that. Where do you two come from, Roumania?"

"Roumania?" The man who had wanted the apple cake was on his feet, his hand reaching for the knife in his belt. "Who are you calling a Roumanian—you—you Moscow peasant, you!"

The ultimate insult was to even hint that a Hungarian might be related to the hated Russians who had conquered Lajos Kossuth in 1849.

"What did you call me?" The second man also had a knife in his hand.

Chokolade drew back against the wall of the cave. She felt both pity and contempt for these men. They were behaving like children—hungry children. Were these the men who were going to save Hungary from the Austrians?

Fekete Andras seemed to know what she was thinking.

"We've been fighting a long time," he said to Chokolade. "We seldom have enough to eat, and the warmest beds we know are in these caves. We have been together for more than a year, and there is little joy in our lives. But still"—he had separated the two men, and each had sat down scowling and shamefaced before the fire—"this is no way to act when we have guests."

The courtliness of the ragged revolutionary touched Chokolade, and she wanted to do something for him—for all of them.

"Do you remember the song you were whistling when we met in Erdely?" she asked.

"Remenyi's Song of the Lark," Fekete Andras said. "A fine song by a Gypsy composer and patriot."

"Could you whistle it again?" Chokolade asked, "and could everyone keep time to the music by clapping?"

Gyuri was on his feet before the puzzled Fekete Andras had time to answer.

"Yes," Gyuri said, "yes! We will dance for you. And when Gypsies dance there is no need for food. You know the saying? Show a Hungarian a Gypsy dancing, and give him a glass of water, and he will get drunk!"

Fekete Andras laughed, and the others gathered around eagerly. Again Chokolade was reminded of children—sad, tired children, yearning for gaiety and distraction.

The sweet sound of Remenyi's music echoed

through the cave. The clapping was soft, almost diffident. Chokolade threw off her sheepskin coat, and went to meet her brother, who joined her in the firelight. Brother and sister looked small and fragile in the looming cave, but they threw immense shadows on the ancient limestone walls. Gyuri and Chokolade danced as they had never quite danced before. There was no lust, no passion in their dance this night. Instead, there was sadness and longing. As she moved toward her brother, and then stepped away from him, Chokolade expressed the loneliness of a Gypsy child who has been left on the immense Hungarian plain by herself.

She was a child again, as was her brother. They were alone in the world, without anyone to protect or comfort them. Their bodies swayed with tenderness, with loneliness, and every member of Kossuth's New Army felt that the Gypsy pair was dancing the story of his life—the life of each lonely soul who sat by the fire that night.

The whistling grew softer, the hand-clapping slower and more muted. One of the women began to weep silently, and some of the men drew their heavy coats more closely about them, as though that could help them find their way home.

Chokolade's body swayed, and her hand reached out to her brother, expressing her deepest longing. He clasped her hand in return, before he released it, and stepped away from her, saying without words that all through life one is alone, no matter how many people are about.

"Enough," Fekete Andras called out. His voice sounded hoarse, broken. "Enough—no more. This is more than dancing. You tell the stories of our lives. It is too much."

Chokolade and Gyuri stopped. It took Chokolade a minute to remember where she was, and whom she had been dancing for. Her mind was filled with images of her own childhood: the mother she had never known and had yearned for, her father who had adored her, and who had died, leaving her alone and unprotected. She had danced the life of a Gypsy: rootless, traveling, alone, with a gay veneer to hide a sad soul.

Chokolade felt her brother's hands gripping her shoulders. He shook her gently.

"Enough," he said, "enough of this sadness. We must do something to cheer our friends, not to make them feel more melancholy."

With that, he took Chokolade's hands and put them firmly on his shoulders. His own hands gripped either side of her slim waist firmly. The heels of his boots came down hard on the stone floor, sending thunderclaps reverberating through the cave. He threw his head back, and started to sing a fast *csardas*. It took only seconds for Chokolade's feet to follow his in the rhythm of the gayest of all Hungarian folk dances. Soon her own voice joined his in singing.

Brother and sister stamped their feet, moved two steps to the right, two steps to the left. Then Gyuri pulled his sister close to him and whirled her about; they both spun and balanced on their feet placed closely together.

"Let's see it again," the members of Kossuth's Army called out, "again!"

"Yes," Gyuri agreed, "but some of you must dance, too. Here—" He pushed Chokolade toward Fekete Andras, while he reached for Sari, and pulled her to him.

"The Eger caves have seen many things," Fekete Andras laughed, "but nothing like this!"

The hungry, tired men and women had been inspired by Chokolade and Gyuri. Now they stood up and danced and whirled, sang and clapped their hands. The wild, strange, sudden burst of dancing stopped only when Fekete Andras called out, "Enough! That's enough!"

Chokolade stood before him. "You don't like to see me dance?"

He shook his head and took her arm. He led Chokolade back to the fire and wrapped her in a warm coat. He could see that the clothes were clinging to her slim, curved body with perspiration.

"I like it too much. It reminds me of many things I have taught myself not to think about."

"What things?"

"Home, and a woman. Having one special woman waiting, living a normal life with her, having children—"

"Are these things so bad to think about?"

"Very bad," Fekete Andras said emphatically, "if you know you will never have them. It was like that foolish talk of food. It maddens a man to think about what he can never have."

He stared at Chokolade, the firelight awakening gleams of auburn in her dark hair.

"A woman like you can make a man forget what he must do. It makes him want other things."

Chokolade leaned away from the fire, and propped her chin up on one hand.

"What would you like to do, Andras, if you could?"

"I would like to take you away with me," he said, "far away—to Venice or Paris. I would like to make you my woman, I would like to live with you—"

"Happily ever after," Chokolade said dreamily, "as in the fairy tales Haradi Neni told me when I was a child."

"Exactly like that," Fekete Andras said, "only that cannot be. I have my work, and that's why I must get you and your brother to Budapest. You're too tempting to have about."

Chokolade had never known a man like this. A man who would sacrifice pleasure for an ideal. Until she had met Fekete Andras and spoken to him, she had no knowledge of the political battles that swirled about her. All she knew was that Gypsies and *gajos* used each other, cheated each other, and tried to conquer each other with slyness and stealth. But this man wanted something more. And he wanted it not only for himself, but for everyone.

"Someday, perhaps," she said seriously, "someday I will be able to help you—as you have helped us."

Fekete Andras looked at the Gypsy girl, and his eyes were as serious and as solemn as hers. What could the little dancer do to help him? Gypsies were more powerless than any other group in Hungary. It would have been easy to laugh at the girl's solemnity, but Fekete Andras took Chokolade's hand in his, and his lips barely touched the surface of her hand. He was kissing her hand with the respect shown great ladies.

"I thank you," and his seriousness matched her own. "Someday I might be very grateful for your help."

And as though they were living in a fine house rather than a bare cave, he escorted her to a quiet corner, brought her some blankets, and wished her a good night and a good night's sleep. He returned to the fire, and sat with his back toward her. Before Chokolade fell asleep, she reflected that Fekete Andras's manner assured her of more safety and privacy than if she had been behind a closed door.

When Chokolade woke the next day, Fekete Andras and his men were deep in plans. Chokolade watched as Fekete Andras drew pathways in the dirt floor.

"They will come this way," he said, "once they get past this grove, they will be too deep in Erdely Forest to turn back. They will also be too far from the town of Eger for help. That's where we will take them."

"What is it?" Chokolade pushed past the men, and sat down on the dirt floor beside Fekete Andras. "What are you doing?" There was a sense of excitement, and she wanted to be part of it.

Fekete Andras grinned at her. Gone was the solemn and sad man of the night before. Now he showed her that he was a man who could act, who could be strong, and even brutal if he had to.

"It is a coach," he explained, "a coach coming through Erdely Forest. Those fools—they've planned their trip for five at night. A good time for us—a bad time for them. Erdely is almost completely dark by five. They won't see us because of the trees—but we'll see them."

Chokolade laughed. "Then what they say is true—you are *betyar*—a highwayman."

Fekete Andras laughed with her. "It's hard to be a patriot on an empty stomach. We need money. Besides, this coach belongs to Jeno Nagy, the man who owns the most land in the whole district. All that money, and it's never enough for him. He starves the peasants who work for him, and he'd beat them to death if it weren't against the law. He needs a lesson, and we'll give it to him."

"Let me ride with you," Chokolade said.

"You! You better stay here in the cave with the rest of the women."

"No, I want to go with you!"

Fekete Andras stared at the girl. He wanted her—God, how he wanted her. It couldn't be—he knew that. But riding with her beside him on a fast horse, letting her see him take the coach, letting her see him as a man! It was crazy, but he was going to do it. It wasn't as good as sleeping with her, but it was as close to it as he could allow himself to come.

Chokolade was breathing fast. She didn't understand it, but the idea of going with Fekete Andras gave her a feeling she had experienced only once—the one time she had let Captain St. Pal conquer her in bed. It was the same feeling, only better, because this time there was no need to be ashamed of what she felt.

"Please—"

Fekete Andras remembered when other women

had begged him. Begged him when they were in bed together. That was really the sort of pleading he wanted to hear from Chokolade. But if that wasn't to be, at least he would have something—something to remember after she had left him.

"All right! You will ride with us."

There was a murmur among the men but Fekete Andras ignored it. He looked at Chokolade's clothes. "But you can't ride like that. If you want to ride like a *betyar*, you must dress like one."

"Juncsi," he called out to one of his men. "You're the smallest one among us, and you've got an extra pair of pants, too. Ernö—lend Chokolade a shirt and your cape." He looked at Chokolade's small feet. "Boots—"

"I have my own."

"Fine, and you shall wear my hat. Just make sure your hair is tucked under it."

It didn't take long for Chokolade to dress in the borrowed clothes. Fekete Andras clenched his fists when he looked at the girl. In men's clothes she looked even more desirable then before. The voluminous white shirt was open at the neck, and he could see the cleft between her breasts. She had tucked the shirt into the tight black pants, but the shirt still billowed up, and the pants accentuated every curve of her body. Her own boots came up high, and outlined her calves.

Fekete Andras draped his long black cape over her shoulders, and pulled his black, wide-brimmed hat over her forehead.

"Your hair—"

Chokolade twisted her hair around her hand,

and then tucked it up under the hat.

"A fine time to think of it," Fekete Andras asked, "but can you ride?"

"As well as you," Chokolade challenged.

Fekete Andras knew that Gypsy girls were never taught to ride. That was left to the daughters of the gentry. Oh, he knew that the girl could manage to sit on a horse without falling off, but riding through the forest, and managing a horse that got excited while guns were drawn and women screamed, was something else. But he admired Chokolade's spirit.

"We'll see," he said. "You'll ride beside me."

"It's where I want to be," Chokolade replied.

Damn those green eyes, Fekete Andras thought, they were even more exciting than her words. He couldn't have her in his bed, but at least they would share this adventure.

The men of Kossuth's New Army rode toward Erdely Forest. Chokolade was beside Fekete Andras when the path was wide enough, and she was behind him when the path narrowed. It was early, but in the forest it seemed like night. The riders took their positions behind a grove of trees.

"What do I do when the coach comes?" Chokolade asked in a whisper.

"When the coach comes you better stay here," Fekete Andras said softly. "You'll be able to see everything."

"No," Chokolade said, "I ride with you—beside you—all the way. It's what we promised each other. I think it is all that we will have, you and I. Isn't that why you let me come with you?"

Fekete Andras took a deep breath. "You know."

"I know. That's why we must share this moment completely."

Fekete Andras looked at Chokolade in the twilight. What a woman! The women who rode side by side with their Mongol men must have been women like this.

"All right," he agreed. "just follow me, do what I do. There isn't much. We rush the coach, and count on their excitement and fear to make them give in to us. That—and our guns."

Chokolade held out her hand. "You wear two guns in your belt. Give me one."

Fekete Andras didn't hesitate. He pulled a pistol from his belt and held it out, butt end, to Chokolade.

"It's loaded," he said, "but you have to cock it—"

"I know," she said, "I've used a gun before."

Amazing, Fekete Andras thought, a Gypsy girl who could ride, and who could shoot. God, if only he could have her riding by his side every day, and sleeping by his side after the day's riding was finished.

His horse moved restively, and Fekete Andras could hear the sound of heavy coach wheels rolling through the forest. He nodded to Chokolade and to the men around him. The men pulled their guns from their belts. They held their horses on short reins. The horses snorted and moved. Chokolade readied her pistol, her heart pounding. She tried to wipe the sweat off her forehead before it reached her eyes, and she brushed at her face with the back of the hand that held the pistol. The coach was coming closer. The noise made by the wheels and the horses' hooves was so loud that to Chokolade it sounded like an explosion. And then the coach was there—in front of them.

"Now!" Fekete Andras shouted. His spurs were in his horse's flanks, and he burst through the trees with a shout. His pistol was pointed toward the sky, and a shot rang out.

His men rode after him. Chokolade was the last, she had become confused by the noise, the pistol shots, the shouts. But once through the trees, she spurred her horse forward until she was beside Fekete Andras.

"Out," he shouted, "everyone out. You," he yelled at the coachman, "get down from there."

Four people hurried from the coach and stood outside, their backs against the side of the coach, as though it were a protective wall. The coachman moved so quickly that he fell rather than climbed down from the box.

"Money," Fekete Andras said, "hurry. Ladies, your purses—that watch. That ring—very nice—and that pin, if you please." He turned quickly, anticipating the movement that one of the men made for a small pistol hidden in a waistcoat pocket. The small pistol went flying, as Fekete Andras brought the muzzle of his own pistol crashing down heavily on the man's fingers.

"None of that," he roared. "No guns—just wallets."

He looked at Chokolade sitting on her horse, and his eyes gleamed. "You—get down from there," he ordered, "help me search the women."

Chokolade dismounted, and the women

161

screamed at the idea of being searched by this *betyar*, even though he seemed to be only a boy.

"Don't want to be searched?" Fekete Andras asked. "Fine! Then let's have your jewelry—money—double-quick."

With Chokolade walking behind him, gun drawn, Fekete Andras went from one passenger to another quickly collecting the booty. When he was satisfied that he had gotten most of their valuables, he told the coachman to get back on his box, and he hurried the passengers into the lumbering vehicle.

"Move," he shouted, "get out of Erdely Forest—it doesn't belong to you."

The coachman and his passengers were happy at being allowed to ride away. They were poorer, yes, but they were alive. The coachman whipped up his horses, and the four passengers clung to each other as the coach rocked and jolted along the path.

"Do you hear that?" one of the women whispered to her male companion. "Do you hear that?"

The four passengers were silent, and they looked at each other round-eyed and amazed. They all heard it—ringing, pealing laughter—laughter that followed and mocked them. And there was no mistaking it—it was the high, silvery laugh of a woman that followed them as they rode out of the Forest of Erdely.

Fekete Andras, Chokolade, and the others rode back to their hiding place in the caves feeling gleeful and satisfied. They had some money now, and some jewels, but more than that, they had bested some of the people they were fighting.

"Did you see that Jeno Nagy?" they asked each

other as they sat by the fire. "He was shaking more than the women."

Fekete Andras hefted a small leather pouch. "He had more to lose. Though some of the jewelry seemed to be worth as much as these gold *pengö*."

He opened a large handkerchief, and poured a scant handful of jewels on the ground. There were rings, and one pair of earrings, a fine pearl necklace, a diamond broach. The best piece of all was a gold ring that held a large fire opal clasped between a setting of small golden hands.

"This is for you," Fekete Andras said to Chokolade when he and she had moved away from the fire and from the others.

Chokolade took the ring from him and held it up. Even though they were not close to the fire, the opal managed to pick up wandering rays of light, and it seemed to capture the fire and add it to its own warm heart.

"No," she said, "you must keep this ring."

"I want you to have it," he said, "a remembrance—from me."

"I will never forget you," Chokolade said, "never. But understand—I am a Gypsy. I see something in this ring—something that tells me you will need it. Keep it—keep it for both of us. If you have it, I have it, too. And someday—someday if you should ever need me—send me this ring—and I will come."

Fekete Andras took the girl's hands, and his own closed tightly about them. The ring was now hidden in Chokolade's palm. This little Gypsy girl—what could she ever do to help him? But she was so sweet, so sweet, her hands were so warm. He knew she wanted him just as much as he wanted her. He couldn't have her, because if he slept with Chokolade just once, he would give up everything that he had been fighting for. He knew that one time with Chokolade would create an enchantment that would last a lifetime. He could do nothing—except take the ring.

He brought her hands to his mouth, and he kissed them. Chokolade's hand opened, and she held out the opal ring.

"Remember, if you're ever in trouble, send me this ring, and I will come to you. Will you remember?"

Fekete Andras took the ring, and he held it up between them. "I will remember. But are you so sure that you will be able to help me?"

He was a *gajo,* Chokolade thought, and there were some things that no *gajo* could ever understand. But he was willing to accept what she knew to be true, and that was enough.

"I am sure," she said. "The ring has told me so."

Fekete Andras did not question her further. Instead, he slipped the ring into the small inside pocket sewn within his jacket. The pocket that lay directly over his heart. Perhaps it was his imagination, but he believed he could feel the warmth of Chokolade's hand against his heart. Her warmth would always be there for him, that was enough for him to know.

Tomorrow he and his people would escort Chokolade and Gyuri as far as they dared through Erdely Forest. They would take them close to Budapest. It wouldn't be safe for them to enter the city, but he was sure that Chokolade and Gyuri would have no trouble in the glittering capital.

The people who would applaud them in the cafés and the restaurants and the theaters wouldn't question them about their past. Their talent was the only passport they would need. Fekete Andras touched the pocket of his jacket once again. Yes, Chokolade would be safe and fine, and he would never see her again. But he had the ring, and he had his memory of her, and that would have to be enough for the rest of his life.

PART TWO:

Budapest and Vienna

Chapter VIII

BUDAPEST WAS GOOD to Chokolade and Gyuri. The glittering city asked no questions. It was the second most important city in the Austro-Hungarian Empire, though Chokolade knew that most Hungarians bristled at the idea of being second best in any way.

Vienna was the home of the Austrian Court, but the Hungarians claimed that for gaiety and wit and an amusing life, Budapest was the place. And even the most royal members of the royal court were willing to admit it was true. When Empress Elizabeth wanted to be free of her stuffy husband, Emperor Franz Josef, she came to Budapest, and then headed for the Puszta where she rode across the Plain with the best of the *csikos*.

Other court members took the overnight train ride from Vienna to Budapest to attend a gala fete, or to see the new Gypsy dancer who was the toast of Budapest.

Chokolade and Gyuri did nothing to correct the rumors swirling about them. Were they truly brother and sister? And if they were related, were

169

they also lovers? Who was Chokolade sleeping with? Was it true that the aging Emperor himself had sent for her, and that she had said that as a good Hungarian she would never do anything to hurt the Empress, who was beloved in Hungary? And what about Gyuri? Wasn't the Gypsy dancer once a lover of some little provincial Countess? And wasn't a far more sophisticated Baroness interested in him now?

At first, brother and sister feared the avid curiosity that surrounded them. How long would it take, they wondered, before the truth was known? Daily they expected the Hussar Captain to arrive in Budapest and to have them arrested.

It took them a little while to realize that the wealthy people of Budapest, whose lives were filled with parties, theaters, and evenings spent in red-carpeted cafés and velvet-walled restaurants, didn't care about unpleasant truths.

If Sandor St. Pal didn't come riding into Budapest to accuse Gyuri and Chokolade of theft and assault, it was because he would have been laughed at. After a few months in the city that gleamed so enticingly beside the Danube, Chokolade knew that St. Pal would never want his world to know that the only way he could keep a Gypsy girl in his bed was to make her his prisoner.

Once they understood that they were safe from reprisal, Chokolade and Gyuri began to enjoy themselves. They had started out dancing in a small café on the outskirts of Buda. But one night they were discovered by a group of people who had been wandering about the city looking for something new, something different to entertain them.

"She's wonderful," a man in dinner clothes had gasped when he had seen Chokolade's sinuous movements on the small dance floor.

The woman with him fluffed the ruffles of the Worth gown that she had bought in Paris just a short month before on her honeymoon. She barely glanced at Chokolade. Her eyes were on the girl's partner. How that man moved! She thought of her elderly husband, and how much she hated him—almost as much as she loved his money.

"Not bad," she had said huskily, "not bad. But it is a shame that they're stuck here in old Buda. Wouldn't you think that old Kalman would get them for his Café Royale. So much more interesting than those boring French Apache dancers he has there now."

The "boring French Apache" had been the toast of Budapest just a few short weeks before. But audiences were notably fickle in Budapest. The people who frequented the cafés, theaters, and restaurants were used to traveling to Vienna and Paris and Venice for their amusements, and nothing could keep their attention too long. It didn't take long for Zsigismund Kalman to hear about the Gypsies dancing at the little café in Old Buda, and it took him even less time to go there to see them.

He agreed with everything he had heard about them. They were wonderful, especially the girl. She did the traditional Hungarian dances—but yet—yet—there was something more there. After they had finished performing, Chokolade and Gyuri were brought an engraved card by an impressed waiter.

"It is Zsigismund Kalman," he said in awe.

"And who is Zsigismund Kalman?" Chokolade asked.

The waiter sputtered at her ignorance. "He only owns the biggest—most beautiful café in all of Pest—the Royale. Everyone goes there—everyone. Even Prince Rudolf—incognito, of course. The food, the wine, the women, and their jewels! And the terraces of the café face the Danube, and you can see St. Margaret's Island. It's only the most beautiful place in all Budapest—maybe in the whole world!"

The man was actually indignant at their lack of knowledge.

"Fine," Gyuri said, "and what does the owner of the world's most beautiful café want with us?"

"How do I know what he wants with a pair of Gypsy dancers?" the waiter asked sourly. "He wants to see you—that's all I know."

"Well, bring him in, my good man," Gyuri said expansively, "don't keep the impresario waiting."

The waiter scowled at being called "my good man," but he went out to fetch Zsigismund Kalman. The café owner had been figuring rapidly ever since he had sent his card to the Gypsy dancers. They were new to the city. Surely they wouldn't demand too much. Whatever he offered would be more than they were getting now. By the time he got to Chokolade and Gyuri's dressing room, he had a figure fixed firmly in his mind.

But that was before he looked into Chokolade's green eyes, and before she had smiled at him. It was also before he saw the way Gyuri looked at his sister.

172

God, the two of them were wonderful! Of course, they would have all of Budapest talking about them in a few days, and Chokolade would have every man of wealth at her feet.

Zsigismund knew that he was pudgy and no longer young, but he wished that he, too, could lay himself at this girl's feet. Let her walk all over him, he wouldn't care. She made him think of deep-red, musky flowers, Flowers—but at the same time she also reminded him of sparkling streams—the water of his childhood that to his memory was more heady than champagne.

Champagne! That was it. The girl was named after sweet chocolate, but she should have been named after the finest of French bubbling wines.

The amount of money that he had planned to offer them was gone from his mind. All the *pengö* in Hungary would be worthless to him if he couldn't capture this bright bird of a girl for his Café Royale. The café was his whole life, but he would close it down in an instant if she and her brother didn't come dance for him.

He told Chokolade and Gyuri as much in a few stammered sentences, and he was almost pathetically grateful when they agreed to leave the little cafe in old Buda, for his brilliant Café Royale in Pest.

Zsigismund Kalman's mind whirled, and he offered them five times—no—he cursed his own cupidity, ten times the amount of money he had originally planned on offering them. He was overwhelmed at the gracious way Gyuri accepted the sum. Chokolade didn't speak, because she, too, was overwhelmed—overwhelmed at the money Kalman was offering—it seemed like a princely sum.

Brother and sister had remained calm until Kalman left their dressing room, after receiving their repeated assurances that they would appear at his café in less than a week's time.

Once they were sure Kalman was gone, the two hugged each other with joy, and in disbelief. No Gypsy dancers that they knew of had ever been given so much money.

"Not even Miklos Barna, the greatest Tzigany *primas* of all time got that much," Gyuri said.

"But Barna played his violin for kings," Chokolade reminded him.

"And we shall dance for kings," Gyuri said joyfully, "I am sure of it."

If Chokolade and Gyuri didn't dance for kings, they did dance for the people who knew kings. Fashionable members of the aristocracy flocked to the Café Royale.

"It's just the *csardas* they're dancing, and the *bokasz*, but yet when they dance—"

"When they dance, it's more like the Spanish flamenco."

"Not at all like the flamenco," another expert argued, "it is like something from the east—the Orient—or maybe Turkey."

"Turkey." Another man leaned across the table to whisper to a friend. "That would explain it. I hear the girl was a Pasha's favorite in Constantinople. And her brother—if he is her brother—got her out of the harem by killing two eunuchs. They say the

Pasha sent his men after them as far as St. Petersburg. The Czar's own secret police turned them back after she had danced for Alexander."

Budapest thrived on rumor, gossip, and stories. And Chokolade and Gyuri did well because everyone loved their dancing, and loved equally the fanciful stories about the pair.

In addition to dancing at the Café Royale, they were also asked to private parties, where they were treated like honored guests, and given quite honorable sums of money. Everyone in the small city knew of them, but unfortunately, not everyone could afford the Café Royale, or could give large private balls and parties in their honor.

After they had been in Budapest only six months, an impresario arranged for them to give a special performance at the Budapest Opera House. It was unheard of; hitherto, the opera house was considered the sacred haven of opera. Never before had a pair of dancers been so honored. Not even the greatest Russian ballet dancers had been given their own night at the Opera House.

The city thronged the box office to buy tickets, and at the same time, they continued gossiping wildly about Chokolade and Gyuri Tura. Why was the young pair so honored? Was Chokolade sleeping with Baron Windishgraetz, and had he bribed the manager of the opera company to allow his protégé to dance there? No, it was most likely the highly positioned woman who was Gyuri's secret benefactress—she was the one who had arranged the whole thing.

After Chokolade's and Gyuri's performance at

the Opera House, no one questioned the arrangements. The way the Gypsies danced dazzled the audience. People claimed that the roaring applause could be heard as far as the Fisherman's Bastion— the old castle that sat perched on the cliffs above the Danube, and that had served as a fortress during the fifteenth century.

Gyuri, more than his sister, was wild with excitement after their triumph at the Opera House. He looked at their dressing room, which was so filled with flowers that they could hardly move. He knew that many of the bouquets held diamond earrings and emerald rings in their flowery hearts. He had received no flowers, but a velvet jeweler's box had been left on his dressing table, and nestled in its white-satin depths were sapphire studs and matching cuff links.

"Chokolade," he fairly shouted, "we're rich! We can have anything we want. The first thing tomorrow—we will buy a villa on St. Margaret's Island."

Chokolade shrugged. "If you wish. But I'm just as happy at the Hotel Duna. It seems more convenient. We just have to ring, and people come running."

"What do you think will happen in our own house"—and now Gyuri was shouting—"we'll have servants—and they'll come running." Gyuri's shout turned into laughter. "These *gajos*—they're crazy! We may as well take what we can get while it's being offered to us. These people are fickle. They love us today, but tomorrow they're liable to remember that we're only a pair of dirty Gypsies, and run us out of town."

Chokolade joined in his laughter. Her brother was right. They would use the *gajos*, just as the *gajos* used them when they could. She thought back to Count Meleki, and then to Sandor St. Pal. Oh, that arrogant Hussar who had treated her like a slave girl—she just wished he could see her now! She would like him to know that she had the men of Budapest at her feet. She could use them as so many carpets, and step all over them if she wished. The thought of the Hussar Captain made her furious once again. She would like to get even with him, she would like to make him suffer the humiliation she had known at his hands. And if there was no way to revenge herself on Sandor St. Pal, she would exact payment from every man she met in Budapest.

No matter how capriciously she treated her admirers, they still clustered around. Chokolade was the guest of honor at intimate midnight suppers given for her in Gundel's Restaurant.

Janos Gundel was so impressed by the beautiful Gypsy dancer, that he created a dish just for her, and added it to his dessert menu. Palacsinta Chokolade it was called—and the thin *palacsinta* or pancakes were rolled around freshly crushed raspberries, and then topped with hot, bittersweet chocolate sauce.

"Bittersweet chocolate," Janos Gundel had heard one of the men who had entertained Chokolade lavishly complain. "She's chocolate, all right—but not sweet chocolate—oh no. There's nothing sweet or obliging about this girl. She's more like chocolate of the bittersweet variety—with a bite to it."

Chokolade laughed when the story was repeated to her. Sweet, she thought. I'll be just as sweet to them as Sandor St. Pal was to me; they don't deserve any better treatment than I received at his hands.

But it amused her to go around Budapest in an open coach, with eager men sitting at either side. Budapest was a wonderful city. There was Gundel's in the evening after her performance, and the best place to be seen in the afternoon was Gerbeaud's Coffee House. The most elegant and popular place for afternoon coffee and pastry in all of Budapest, it became even more popular once Chokolade was seen there.

She enjoyed sitting at the little tables, beautifully covered in white damask, with a tiny silk-shaded lamp on each table. She enjoyed the admiring looks of the men sitting with her, and the raised buzz of voices when she came into a room. Often, as she would sip tiny cups of inky black coffee topped with spoonfuls of freshly whipped cream, she would think of her Gypsy life, and the meals she had eaten beside a campfire. One day she took only one forkful of a large Indianer—a caramel glazed cream puff filled with whipped cream—and then she pushed it away from her.

Suddenly, the overly sweet dessert sickened her, just as she was occasionally sickened by the cloying manners of the men who surrounded her.

"God and Saint Sara," she burst out, "what I

wouldn't give for a slice of *szalonna* and a piece of potato bread!"

The men who were doing their best to entertain her, were amused by what they took to be a witty remark.

"Right!" one of them roared. "Enough of this sweet stuff—come, everyone—we go to old Buda to find some *paprikas szalonna* for Chokolade."

"And don't forget the potato bread," another man chimed in, also eager to please.

By nighttime, all of fashionable Budapest had heard of Chokolade's remark at Gerbeaud's—and *szalonna*, the favorite rude dish of peasants and Gypsies, was soon being served in the large private homes that lined Andrassy Utca—the street that contained the wealthiest homes in all of Budapest.

"I could say I want to eat the grass from Gellert Hill," Chokolade told her brother, "and everyone would rush off to pick some for me."

"You could say far worse than that, sweet sister, and they'd all be happy to oblige."

Chokolade's taste in fashion soon became the taste of an entire city. She decided one night that she didn't like the way her hair fell in her face when she danced, and taking a diamond pin in the shape of a crescent moon, she clipped her hair back. It only took a few days for jewelers all over the city to receive requests for pins in the shape of crescent moons, and soon women all over the city were wearing pins just like Chokolade's. But when Chokolade discovered it, she gave her pin to her maid.

The little Gypsy girl had come a long way from the days she had spent on the Puszta. She knew now how to entice men, and how to keep them running after her, and she also knew how to make sure that none of them caught her, unless she wanted to be caught. She wanted no more of the days and nights she had experienced with the Hussar captain.

Instead of being one man's slave, she would make all men her slaves. All of Budapest speculated as to who was Chokolade's favorite lover. Naturally, none of the men she kept dangling would admit to anyone that they had never received her favors. Chokolade's sexual reputation was prodigious, but only her brother knew the truth—Chokolade went to bed alone each night, and she did nothing more than dine in the private rooms of the fashionable restaurants where she was served midnight suppers.

Gyuri worried about his sister. A frank sensualist who enjoyed the attentions of all the women who threw themselves at him, he couldn't understand his sister's coldness.

"Is there no one—no one you fancy?" he once asked her.

She looked at him mockingly. "You forget the *leis prala,* my brother."

"The *leis prala.*" Gyuri laughed. "We're way past the *leis prala*—besides—"

"Besides, it no longer applies to me," Chokolade said bitterly, "not after those days and nights I spent with the Hussar captain."

So that was it, Gyuri realized. That damn Hussar had treated his sister so brutally that she had turned against all men. They had no way of knowing what had happened to the Captain after Gyuri had hit him with the butt of his gun, but as far as he was concerned, he hoped the Captain was dead—he deserved death for ruining his sister's life this way.

Gyuri gave his sister an especially gentle kiss when he parted from her that night, and Chokolade realized that he had completely misunderstood her—and that was fine, because she wanted no one to know how she really felt.

The truth was that no man had been able to arouse her the way the Hussar captain had. She had felt a little something for Fekete Andras, but that wasn't comparable to the way the Captain had made her feel. And these ridiculous fops in Budapest—their damp kisses, their soft hands reaching for her, trying to touch her—she felt nothing, nothing.

But no one who observed Chokolade had any idea of her true feelings. Seeing her ride in an open barouche, or watching her walk down wide Andrassy Boulevard was enough to start everyone whispering, conjecturing.

One night Gröf Bela von Bruck and two other admirers asked Chokolade to attend the opera with them. As was fashionable, they arrived at the opera house quite late, and the three men escorted Chokolade into a box that held six gilt chairs covered in blue velvet. It was not the royal box, but the one just to the right of it, and when the bejeweled audience, all in evening dress, heard the flurry above and around them, all turned to see who had entered the hitherto empty box.

"It is the Gypsy dancer," the whisper swept the opera house.

"It is Chokolade, with von Bruck."

All voices were kept low, but the mass of sound was enough to stop the opera from continuing. The orchestra leader, too, had turned at the sound that challenged his music, and the orchestra members stopped playing in a confusion and a clash of sound.

Chokolade knew that everyone was watching her, and she settled down slowly and regally into a chair placed at the front of the box. Von Bruck reached over to remove her black velvet cape, and as he draped it over the back of her chair, women turned their opera glasses on the sight, and nodded to each other as they saw the ermine lining.

The men in the audience were more interested in the sight of Chokolade's perfect shoulders as they were revealed and outlined by her cream satin gown, and while the women admired the ruby-and-gold lace necklace, the men yearned for the perfect throat and bosom it adorned.

Meanwhile, Erno Edy, Budapest's most famous opera singer, who was singing the lead in *Lohengrin* that night, was left standing on the stage, experiencing a mixture of anger and some amusement. The footlights were so bright that he couldn't see what was happening, but the whispers of "Chokolade, Chokolade" were loud enough to reach him.

He smiled at the other singers on the stage, and signaled them to wait as calmly as they could. Finally, Chokolade and her group were seated, and they looked expectantly toward the stage.

The orchestra leader tapped his baton, and signaled the orchestra. He nodded to Erno Edy, who nodded back, ready to continue. However, while the music had stopped, the stagehands, who never listened to the music at any time, had gone on with the stage business, and the boat in the background of the stage—*Lohengrin*'s famous boat pulled by a swan—had already appeared, and disappeared into the wings.

The music began, Erno Edy started to sing the great aria of farewell, and with a sweeping gesture to the heroine, he turned, and prepared to leave the scene in his swan boat. Only when he turned stage right, he saw that the boat was not there. It was not possible to repeat the aria—the orchestra had swept way past it. Erno Edy realized what had happened; his swan had come and gone while the Gypsy dancer was getting settled in her box.

He shrugged, and moved toward center stage. He raised his right hand, signaling the orchestra to stop playing. The audience and the singers and musicians stared in silence.

Erno Edy stepped forward, and in a voice that was famous whether it was heard singing or speaking, he asked, "When is the next swan due?"

The audience roared with laughter, and no one laughed more loudly than Chokolade and her friends. Many stood to applaud the witty opera singer, and he answered with a bow, and a signal to bring the curtains down. The finale of *Lohengrin* was not heard that night, but everyone in the audience agreed that Erno Edy's wit was far more interesting than Wagner.

"We must go backstage and apologize," Chokolade said, as the laughing and murmuring audience left the opera house.

But when she arrived at Edy's dressing room, the singer wouldn't permit one word of apology.

"*Lohengrin* is not that interesting an opera," he said, "but because of it I met the famous Chokolade." He lifted her hand to his lips, "Now I will think of it as my most favorite piece of music."

Chokolade smiled at the great singer, and agreed to join him for supper the following evening.

"But, please," Erno Edy said, "let us meet after my performance. I'm afraid I couldn't stand the competition two nights in a row."

After that, Budapest had more interesting stories to whisper about. Chokolade dined with Erno Edy three nights in a row. The fourth, he hired a boat, complete with captain and crew, and took her sailing up the Danube until dawn. They had a supper of chilled champagne and quails in pastry in the sailing ship's small, but exquisite, dining room. The next day Erno Edy and the entire opera company were leaving Budapest for a tour of the other European capitals.

"A very small remembrance," Edy said, placing a black velvet box beside Chokolade's tulip-shaped champagne goblet.

She pressed the spring on the jewel box, and a perfect jade swan stared up at her with one unwinking diamond eye.

"It is perfect," Chokolade murmured.

"Not as perfect as you," Erno Edy whispered. His dark eyes stared into her green ones—a more perfect green than the green jade of the swan. This girl—this wonderful girl—she was as dizzying as fine wine. One word from her, just one word, and he would happily give up his European tour, give up his entire career, to sit at her feet. But she never said that word to him—never said any word that indicated he did anything more than amuse and entertain her. Erno Edy sighed, the one girl he wanted, and she didn't want him.

Chokolade's smile was tinged with sadness as she looked at the great singer. Why couldn't she feel something for this man? He was kind and warm and a fine artist. She cursed herself, and she cursed the Hussar captain.

At dawn, when she was back in her villa, she tossed restlessly in bed. Was she doomed to feel something only for that one man?

It infuriated her that he had made her feel something for him. She tried to tell herself that she hated him—that she hoped he was dead. But yet—yet—while one part of her mind did hate him—she knew that her willful body did not. She would close her eyes sometimes before falling asleep, and remember that one time—that one time when he had made her body feel the way it never felt before—or might never feel again.

She was tortured with the thought that they had actually killed St. Pal. Once she had even suggested to Gyuri that they ask one of their powerful friends to find out if the Captain was dead or alive, but she was stopped by the look of fear in her brother's eyes.

"Are you crazy? You do that, and they'll find out about us. If he's dead, it means I've killed him while you stood by, and what do you think they'll do to us once they find that out?"

Chokolade never talked about St. Pal after that,

but she couldn't help thinking about him.

"You're the gayest, most wonderful woman in Budapest," Gröf Bela von Bruck said, as he greeted her in her dressing room after a performance. "There's no one like you." He took Chokolade's hand, and pressed an ardent kiss upon it.

Chokolade removed her hand gently. "I'm hot and tired, Gröf. I'm afraid I must go home tonight without being able to join you for supper."

The Gröf stiffened. "Are you dining with someone else?"

Chokolade smiled. "I am dining alone. I am going home."

"Home," Von Bruck said, "but who is waiting for you at home?"

"My maid," Chokolade said calmly, "she always waits up for me."

"Your maid," Von Bruck jeered.

Chokolade looked at him coolly. "You may take me home, if you wish, and you may even come in for one glass of champagne. And then you will leave me, because I am very tired tonight."

Von Bruck looked at the Gypsy girl, and he knew that she was telling him the truth. My God, he thought, she has the icy poise of Empress Elizabeth. These few months in Budapest have certainly changed her.

He bowed slightly. "If beautiful Chokolade will accept my profound apologies for my foolish questions, I will be delighted to escort her home."

Chokolade's smile was a bit warmer. "There are no apologies necessary."

The Gröf took Chokolade home to the gray stone

villa she shared with her brother on St. Margaret's Island. As she promised, she had the Count served one glass of champagne, and then as she had further promised, he was politely shown to the door. And then as she had promised herself, she went wearily to bed—alone.

Chapter IX

CHOKOLADE WAS SURPRISED WHEN, the following morning, Gröf Bela von Bruck sent his card up to her bedroom.

"At this hour of the morning, what could he want? Perhaps he thinks he'll surprise me at breakfast with a man." Chokolade was annoyed. The Gröf had no claims upon her; he had no right to come to her villa without an invitation.

"Tell Gröf Bela I will see him in the morning room," she told her servant, "if he cares to wait."

The servant came back a few minutes later. Gröf Bela would be pleased to wait. Chokolade took her time in getting out of bed. She brushed her hair until it was burnished and touched with auburn highlights. She donned a dark green velvet robe trimmed at the neck and at the hem in an almost-black Russian sable. And then, in her most leisurely manner, she descended the stairs to where the Count waited for her.

His eyes gleamed in appreciation at what he saw, and again he thought how much Chokolade had changed during her stay in Budapest. When she first came to the capital he very much wondered if she had been accustomed to wearing shoes, and now she went about dressed as though she were a member of royalty—and not a minor member at that.

He took her hand respectfully, and kissed it. "Chokolade, as beautiful in sunlight as in moonlight."

But Chokolade was not to be appeased. She was irritated at the Gröf's presence in her home at the scandalously early hour of half-past eleven. Why had he come? She still believed it was to check on her activities. "He has no right," she thought, "no right! I've given no man that right over me!"

She was cold and polite. "Coffee, Gröf Bela? Chocolate?"

Gröf Bela could tell that the girl was annoyed with him, but he had no idea why. Damn! And it was so important that he get her to do him a very special favor.

Chokolade sipped her cup of frothy morning chocolate, while the Gröf held a small cup of inky black coffee. Well, he decided, no use just sitting here, he would have to tell her the purpose of his visit.

"Chokolade, I've come to ask you a great favor."

I knew it, Chokolade thought, I knew it. "Yes?"

"I am giving a gala a week from Monday night. Everyone will be there. At least, everyone wants to be there if you will come. Because, you see, my dear, I have told my friends that the gala is to be in your honor. You will be the only woman there."

Chokolade put down her cup. "The only woman?

And I suppose you want me to come just as a guest. Is that right?"

The Gröf colored slightly. "As a guest, of course, an honored guest. But what would an evening with Chokolade be if she didn't dance?"

"I see. In other words, you want me to come and perform at your fete. That's really it, isn't it?"

"Chokolade, I will send my carriage for you, at whatever hour you wish—"

"For me alone? And what of my brother—my dancing partner?"

"This very special night—this night in your honor," the Gröf said softly, "we would be doubly honored if you would perform a solo for us. Please—Chokolade."

"I have my own carriage," Chokolade reminded him. "Besides, I do enough dancing at the Royale. I am tired, and bored with the whole idea. I think I may run down to Abazzia for a few days. I hear the Adriatic is beautiful at this time of the year. Or perhaps I will go to Baden Baden and take the waters. Count Szecheny told me that they're very refreshing."

"Chokolade"—he reached out for her hand—"I know it would be foolish for me to try and tempt you with money or jewels. You're a great artist, and all of Budapest is at your feet. You're entitled to do just as you wish. But I want you to know that just to see you—to be in your presence—all my guests are willing to forgo the company of any other woman. You will be the only woman present—"

"The only woman? If I am to be the only woman

it is because you and your friends, Gröf Bela, expect me to do one of our special Gypsy dances. The one my brother so foolishly told you about. The dance that a Gypsy bride performs in the nude for her husband on their wedding night."

Gröf Bela's color deepened. "There is no question that we would throw ourselves at your feet with gratitude if you would do such a dance for us, Chokolade, but nude or clothed, I beg you to come and dance for us."

Chokolade got up and started to walk about the room. "My brother was a fool to tell you about that dance. I hear about it every evening at the Royale."

"Gyuri did say that it arouses a man to a height of passion that he has never known."

"It's meant to arouse a bridegroom," Chokolade said, "one man—not a roomful of savages!"

"Savages!" That made Gröf Bela laugh. "Come, my dear, we're not exactly that. Besides, none of us would dare ask you to perform that dance. We're too afraid of angering our Chokolade. However, there is one man who is coming to the gala, and you might be willing to perform that famous dance for him."

"For no one!"

"This man," Gröf Bela continued, "is one of the most important men in the entire Austro-Hungarian Empire. I have no doubt that someday he will be the most important. And this man—he is coming all the way from Vienna, just to attend my gala and to see Chokolade dance."

"This man—this man—who is *this man?*"

Gröf Bela shook his head. "I may not tell you. No one but myself knows of his plans at this moment. But if you want to meet him, come to the gala in your honor."

"There will really be no other women there?"

"Where there is Chokolade, other women are not only unnecessary, they are actually in the way."

"And this man—"

"He comes from Vienna, just to see the fabulous Chokolade dance. And I know that once he does so, he will be at your feet with the rest of your worshipers."

Chokolade was intrigued. Who could this very special man be? She had told the Gröf the truth when she said she was bored. Perhaps this strange man would add a bit of spice to her life.

"Just one thing," she said. "I want to be sure that it is understood that if I come, and if I dance for you—it will be in costume. I prefer to keep my nude dances for the bedroom."

The Gröf sighed. His friends all believed that Chokolade had long admitted him to her bed. It had never happened, and he doubted that it ever would, but he was willing to accept as much as she would give. Just now, all he wanted from her was a promise that she would come dance for him and his friends, and for his one, very special guest.

The Gröf looked at Chokolade questioningly.

"Very well," she said at last, "I will come. After all, it is in my honor, is it not?"

"It certainly is." Gröf Bela took Chokolade's hand once again, and his dark mustache brushed the back of her hand. "I am most grateful." And with another bow, he left Chokolade to her morning chocolate.

The night of the gala, Chokolade dressed with special care. She knew that Gröf Bela's guests from Vienna were expecting to see a Gypsy dancer, but it pleased her to come in her most fashionable Paris gown. Created by the House of Worth just for her, it was made of black taffeta that rustled with the slightest movement of her body.

The sleeves were elbow length, and then puffed out enormously. The dress was cut low over the bust, the bodice was tight, and so cleverly tucked that it raised Chokolade's bosom even higher. The dress was provocative, but so well-made, and so fashionable, that a lady of the French court would have appeared in it. So said Monsieur Farroux, the representative of Worth who had come to Budapest to fit the dress properly on Chokolade.

"Mind, I said the French court," he explained. "The Viennese Court is a little stuffier about such things. Teutonic background, I suppose."

As usual, Chokolade went to the gala in her own carriage. It was a throwback to the days when she and Gyuri rode their own horses to the castles where they were to perform. Chokolade still thought of these people as *gajos*, and with *gajos* she preferred always to have a way of making a fast escape.

"That's silly," Gyuri had said when she had told him about her feelings.

"I suppose," Chokolade said, but she still used her own carriage, and her servants were instructed to wait at the ready, even though it might mean sitting on the coach's box until dawn.

Gröf Bela's palace was on the summit of Gellert Hill, and from that vantage point, the Danube with its boats and bridges and lights were visible, as was the rest of the city which lay spread at the bottom of the hill, as though this were a medieval kingdom, ruled by the palace and its owners.

"It was something like that back in the fourteenth century," Gröf Bela had once told Chokolade. "Much of old Buda belonged to my family. There's nothing left of that, of course, nothing but this old palace."

The old palace was magnificently constructed of heavy blocks of graystone. Chokolade remembered how once she had been impressed with Meleki Castle. She now realized that was a provincial country home compared to the von Bruck Palace on the top of Gellert Hill.

When Chokolade arrived at eleven at night, all the other guests were already assembled. The men in their evening clothes had worn their decorations. Some had red sashes stretched across the bosoms of their shirts, while others had ribbons and medals and decorations pinned to their jackets.

A hush fell over the large party of men when Chokolade was ushered into the salon. Gröf Bela came forward immediately.

He raised her hand to his lips. "Now that you have arrived, my dear, I can present my two guests of honor to each other."

Chokolade took Gröf Bela's arm, and the guests parted, forming an aisle, down which Chokolade walked with the Gröf. A tall, brown-haired man waited at the other end. He was slim, with a small mustache, and the only thing that particularly distinguished him was his dark brown eyes. Chokolade thought she had never seen eyes quite that penetrating. She knew that this man's mood could be gauged by looking into his eyes. Right now they looked at her coolly. It was an appraising look, and it piqued Chokolade. She was used to men who looked at her with instant adoration.

Compared to the other guests, this man was simply garbed. He wore the usual evening clothes, but he sported no red sashes across his white shirt front, nor did he wear a bevy of medals or ribbons. There was one large eight-pointed gold star pinned to his jacket with a bit of red, white, and green ribbon above it—nothing more.

Gröf Bela released Chokolade's arm, and bowed deeply. "Your Highness, if I may be permitted to present to you our great Hungarian Gypsy dancer, Chokolade Tura."

Chokolade took her cue from Gröf Bela, and she offered the Gröf's guest a curtsy that sent her taffeta skirts rustling to the floor.

When she was standing once again, Gröf Bela continued, "Chokolade, our special guest who honors us all, and especially you, Crown Prince Rudolf."

Chokolade's heart began to pound. She had met many people of noble birth since coming to Budapest, but Crown Prince Rudolf—the only son of Emperor Franz Josef, and Empress Elizabeth— the man who would one day rule all of the Austro-Hungarian Empire. It was despite herself that

Chokolade was impressed; she had long boasted to her brother that no *gajo*—not even a king—could impress her. But there she was, faced with a future king and emperor, and she was quite impressed.

The Crown Prince was quite used to the effect he had on most people—especially women—and the smile on his face was just a little bored, and more than a little patronizing as he said, "I am sure that once I see this lovely young lady dance it will have been quite worth my trip here from Vienna."

His bow was so slight as to be almost nonexistent, and he moved forward into the throng of men followed by his two close companions, Count Joseph Hoyòs and Prince Phillip von Coburg.

Gröf Bela hurried after the Prince, while a bevy of admirers surrounded Chokolade. She laughed and talked, and took a glass of champagne at the bottom of which were crushed three raspberries, but her green eyes followed the slim form of the Crown Prince. She had been snubbed! No, not even snubbed. A snub indicates importance, but the Crown Prince hadn't even given her that much attention. She could see Rudolf in conversation with Gröf Bela, and while the Gröf did look her way occasionally, Rudolf never so much as turned his head.

"She's lovely, of course," Crown Prince Rudolf was saying, "but my dear Gröf, I think we have as pretty faces, and bodies perhaps even a trifle more interesting, in Vienna."

Gröf Bela smiled. "Ah, yes, perhaps. But, sir, you haven't seen Chokolade dance."

Rudolf shrugged. "Of course, I haven't. But I've

had a very special version of the cancan performed for me in Paris—privately, of course. And there was a Moroccan dancer—what was her name, Hoyòs?—who paid us a brief visit at my hunting lodge in Mayerling. She moved—oh, you can't believe how that woman could move!"

Gröf Bela smiled slightly. "Wonderful, I'm sure, sir—but until you see Chokolade—"

It was now the Gröf's turn to be piqued by the glaze of boredom in Rudolf's eyes as he looked about the room. "Is she truly going to be the only woman here?" the Crown Prince asked.

"Any other woman would pale beside Chokolade," Gröf Bela maintained, "after one sees her dance."

Now the Crown Prince's smile was clearly patronizing. "I'm sure, my dear Gröf, I'm sure."

His attitude clearly said, *Here in the provinces I'm sure she's considered to be quite good, but back in Vienna!*

Gröf Bela could feel the heat rise around his neck, and he was sure even the tips of his ears were reddening. Later, he would tell close friends that he would never know what possessed him to make his wild offer, but make it he did.

"I would be willing to wager anything," he said to the Crown Prince, "that once his Highness sees Chokolade dance, he will agree that there is no finer dancer on earth. I will further wager anything that Chokolade will arouse feelings that the Crown Prince was not aware existed."

Once he made that outrageous statement, the red faded from his face and neck, and he paled. What had possessed him? Had he gone too far? After all, he was talking to the Crown Prince. But the boredom had left Rudolf's eyes, and now his smile was genuine. This evening was finally beginning to amuse him.

"Anything?" he asked Gröf Bela. "Did you truly mean it when you said you would be willing to wager *anything* on this little dancer's performance?"

Gröf Bela's eyes met his. "Anything."

"Fine." The Crown Prince grew even more amused. "But I don't suppose, my dear Gröf, that *anything* includes this delightful palace?"

Now it was Gröf Bela's heart that began to pound, but his hand never trembled as he took a glass of raspberry-scented champagne.

"Anything would, of course, include the von Bruck Palace, sir. I repeat, if Chokolade does not enchant and fascinate you—the palace is yours."

Rudolf's bow was one of genuine admiration for his host. Quite a man, this, who would wager his ancestral home on the few steps and twirls of a little Gypsy dancer.

"And what would you like me to wager in turn?" he asked Gröf Bela.

"Absolutely nothing," Gröf Bela assured him quickly. "I wish only to see the Prince pleased and happy. If I see that, I will feel that I have won a great wager."

The man was gallant, Rudolf thought. These Hungarians—they were nothing at all like the more prudent Viennese. He couldn't imagine one of them wagering a magnificent palace upon a dancer's performance.

"If your Highness will excuse me," Gröf Bela said, and bowing again, he went off to ask Chokolade to dance. She left the drawing room, and went upstairs to change into her costume.

The Gypsy musicians tuned their instruments in the parquet-floored ballroom, and the news of the Gröf's wager swept around the salon like wildfire.

The two maids who were helping Chokolade change her clothes knew of the bet, and were eager to tell her about it. Chokolade was amused. Gröf Bela certainly had a lot of confidence in her dancing. Not that she was worried—everyone adored her when she danced. She had seen a rapt look on men's faces over and over again.

But still, she was annoyed at the way the Crown Prince had looked at her—looked through her was more like it. Oh, he had been polite enough, she couldn't say anything about that. Polite, but not one bit impressed, and after her months in Budapest she had grown used to making an impression on the most important of men.

Well, he would see, she told herself. He would see! She was standing before the large pier glass completely naked, when Gröf Bela walked into the room without knocking. The maids gave little shrieks, but Chokolade turned and faced him calmly. She wouldn't demean herself by reaching for a petticoat to hide her body.

No, she stood before him, her skin gleaming as though it had been brushed by a thousand pearls. His eyes widened as he saw the broad shoulders, the high, proud breasts, the hips that curved down to splendid thighs, and the long, shapely legs.

Chokolade stood straight and tall, but he could tell the way her belly moved from her breathing that she was not as calm as she looked.

Wonderful, he thought, as imperious as a queen, and every bit as haughty. He moved forward and raised her hand to kiss it. He behaved as respectfully as though she were completely clothed, even though she had nothing on but one wide gold bracelet on her right wrist, and high-heeled black-satin slippers on her feet.

"Well, Gröf Bela?" Chokolade's voice was cold.

"My dear, I have wagered my palace on your performance this evening."

Chokolade still made no move to get dressed. "So your servants have told me."

Gröf Bela smiled slightly. "And seeing you this way—well, even if I lose—it will have been worth it."

"I will win your wager for you, Gröf Bela, have no fear."

Gröf Bela nodded. "Go down like this, and I am sure of it."

"I will win your wager dressed. My dancing will win for you—and I dance with my clothes on. Now, if you will permit me, I should like to get ready."

The Gröf raised her hand to his lips once more. "May I escort you downstairs once you are dressed?"

"If you will return in half an hour."

The Gröf bowed and withdrew.

Chokolade had chosen her simplest costume for her performance. There were no spangles, ruffles, or lace on her outfit. She wanted nothing to distract from her essential self as a woman, and a dancer.

She wore a white blouse with a neckline cut wide to the tips of her shoulders. The blouse was held together by a simple string tie. The sleeves were long, loose, and full, and were buttoned tightly about her small wrists. It was the same blouse worn by Gypsy dancers through the centuries, but the fabric was the sheerest, finest voile cotton, and Chokolade disdained to wear a camisole beneath it.

Her skirt was a scarlet shaft of crimson silk. It fell like a column around her slim body, but she was able to move with a dancer's ease, because the skirt was slashed on both sides almost as high as her hips.

Beneath her skirt she wore brief underwear of the same red silk as her skirt. Her legs were encased in the new gossamer silk stockings imported from France, and her shoes were a matching crimson velvet. Both heels and toes of each shoe had small, sliver-thin metal taps affixed to them.

Gröf Bela tapped on the door in precisely thirty minutes. The maid who had been helping Chokolade dress opened the door, and she swept out into the corridor. Gröf Bela gasped. There was something about this girl, the moment she appeared she affected him like a heady wine. She was a picture in scarlet and white, with no other color adorning her except for the rich, burnished hair cascading down her back. Here was a woman, thought Gröf Bela, who needed no additional adornments. Jewelry, flowers, they all paled by comparison to the intrinsic sensuality of this amazing girl.

The Gröf bowed to Chokolade; he bowed to her, and to her beauty, and to the vitality and eroticism she was able to project by merely moving across the floor. Chokolade made a sign that she was ready, and he bowed once more and preceded her down the stairs.

The men assembled in the ballroom knew she was approaching when they heard the clicks made by the heel and toe taps of her crimson velvet shoes. They grew silent, and every head turned toward the door. The cimbalom player took his mallets and began to keep musical time with Chokolade's steps.

The Gröf stepped back when they reached the entrance to the ballroom. And Chokolade swept past him with a whirl that sent the slim panels of her skirt swirling high above her hips, as though they were petals of the scarlet Imperial Tulip—the flower symbol of Hungary. The men moved back quickly from the center of the floor, and Chokolade spun past them, as though they didn't exist.

Kovacs Karoly, the *primas* of the finest Gypsy band in Budapest, tucked his violin under his chin. Chokolade didn't dance in time to the music; the musicians played in time to her dancing.

The men in the Gypsy band were as mesmerized as the men in the audience, and their music was one with the Gypsy dancer's very soul. At first, Chokolade moved slowly, and every man there was reminded of his own childhood as she seemed to dance the story of her early years. There was innocence in those first steps, a sad innocence, as everyone realized that innocence can never last.

Chokolade moved into a gayer dance after that; the dance of a young girl who is just beginning to discover life. Again, the audience was reminded of their own years as young men.

But then, suddenly, abruptly, the dance changed. Chokolade's body swayed back and forth provocatively. There was no question that she was demonstrating a woman's feelings when she first experiences a man. At first there is pain, possibly even brutality, and then there is passion, and at last there is the acceptance by the body of a man's will even as the spirit rebels. Chokolade was able to express all that with her dancing, and the men in the room felt the blood behind their eyes. Every man wanted to be alone with her—every man wanted to take her—to have her—each man wanted to throw her down on the hard wooden floor and possess her.

"Because it's really what she wants," Gröf Bela thought.

"It's what she wants, and only I can satisfy her," Crown Prince Rudolf exulted silently, "and I will satisfy her. I have never known a woman like this—but she has never experienced love with a man like me."

The dance ended abruptly. The sheer blouse clung to Chokolade's body, outlining her breasts, and the slim skirt fell once again in straight lines, but it revealed flashing legs as she moved, now quite quietly, across the floor.

There was no applause; only stunned silence greeted this supreme offering of a great dancer's art. It was Crown Prince Rudolf who broke the silence. He raised his glass, first to Chokolade; when he bowed to her this time, it was the bow of a Crown Prince to the woman who is to be his Queen. She acknowledged his offer with a slight nod of her graceful head.

After that, Rudolf raised his glass once again, this time to Gröf Bela. "I want to thank you for this most wonderful evening. I hope I may be invited to spend many more of them here in your splendid palace and in your fine company." He smiled slightly. "It is only as an invited guest that I can hope to be here, because, my dear Gröf, you have more than won your wager."

With that, the other guests finally broke into applause. The tremendous sexual tension that Chokolade had created was broken, and the men once again began to talk and drink.

"To Chokolade," Gröf Bela said, and all glasses were raised to the beautiful dancer.

Chokolade smiled, and started to leave the ballroom.

"You are not leaving us," Gröf Bela cried.

"I must change," she said. "I will return."

"If you will permit me to escort you." Rudolf, Crown Prince of Austria, stood beside her.

Rudolf and Chokolade walked slowly up the curving staircase, while Count Hoyòs and Prince von Coburg nodded to each other.

"Our Rudi doesn't waste much time."

"I wouldn't either, with a girl like that."

Once in the bedroom above, the Prince stretched out on a white brocade chaise, and Chokolade, without any demur, allowed the maid to help her out of her dancing costume, while the Prince watched. The maid dried Chokolade's perspired body with a large, white swansdown puff. Not even bothering to slip on a robe, Chokolade sat down before the dressing-table mirror and began to take off her makeup. She knew the effect she was having on the Prince, and it amused her. This was the man who had snubbed her just a short time before—but that was before he had seen her dance. Well, now she could act the coquette, knowing that while it caused him pleasure, it also caused him pain.

"I would like to see you dance again," the Prince said.

"Yes? I dance many evenings at the Royale."

"I would like to have you dance for me alone." The Prince's voice sounded strangely husky.

"At a gala perhaps? At the Hofburg or at Schönbrunn?" Chokolade named the Prince's residence in Vienna, and his summer palace just outside the city.

"Neither. I meant at Mayerling. It's only twenty miles from Vienna, but for me it's another world. It is my true home—I go there only with good friends. I am happiest there, and I would like you to share that happiness with me."

"Share it—how? By dancing for you?"

"Dancing a special dance—a dance done just for me, without costumes, without pretense. A dance done as I see you now, where you would reveal yourself to me completely, not only as a dancer—but as a woman."

Rudolf's words caressed Chokolade. She could see his image reflected in the mirror. He hadn't touched her, but he didn't have to. She turned to look at him. She saw a man who interested her—a man who made her pulse beat more quickly. The first man who had made her feel anything since the Hussar captain, Sandor St. Pal. And he saw a nude woman, her body open, inviting, girlish and yet evoking memories of women of magic: Cleopatra, Circe, women who bent men to their wills. Except that he would bend her to his will—that was what he intended to do.

"There is a special dance"—she spoke so softly that he had to lean forward to hear her—"a very special dance—and I would like to dance it for you."

"At Mayerling?"

"At Mayerling."

The Prince stood up. "We will start as soon as you are dressed."

Chokolade smiled. "I must go home first—to pack."

The Prince smiled. "You won't need clothes at Mayerling."

Chapter X

IN THE PRIVATE railroad train that took them first to Vienna, and then to Mayerling, Count Hoyòs and Prince von Coburg treated Chokolade with the grave respect due a princess. When they bowed their way out of the car, the bow seemed to be meant equally for the Crown Prince and for Chokolade.

But when they were alone in the lounge of another car, Hoyòs groaned, "Another one. How are we going to get rid of this one when the time comes?"

Prince von Coburg shrugged. "I know she's a dancer, and a Gypsy at that, but this girl doesn't have a hardness about her. Not like that Polish actress—"

"Or the Italian opera singer—"

"Or the Russian ballerina."

The two men grinned at each other.

"You can't blame him," Count Hoyòs said. "When I saw her dance—"

"Yes," Prince von Coburg said, "and besides, you can't blame him when you think of his wife."

The Prince agreed. "Stephanie, the royal

209

Princess of the Belgians. No one likes her at court, not even Rudi's mother."

"It is too bad Rudi had to marry her," the Count said.

The Prince shrugged. "A marriage of state, dear fellow, it happens all the time. How many heads of state marry for love? Rudi knew that."

"True. But poor Rudi did nothing to deserve Stephanie. She's a narrow-minded, pompous little bigot."

The Prince laughed. "And a bony bigot at that. Thin body, thin lips. There's nothing to enjoy in bed with that one. You can't blame Rudi."

"I wouldn't blame my Crown Prince even if Stephanie were as plump as a partridge."

The two men continued discussing Rudolf's wife, and went on to compare her—unfavorably, always—to the many women in Rudolf's life.

In the next car Chokolade and Rudolf talked quietly. Rudolf could have taken the girl as the train rattled through the Hungarian and Austrian countryside. His private car was luxuriously paneled in dark mahogany, and fitted out with more comfort than the bedrooms of many large homes. But he enjoyed the wait, it added a certain piquancy to the situation, and the hours went quickly as Chokolade told him something about her life on the Puszta, and what it was like traveling about in a Gypsy caravan.

"I would like to try that someday," Rudolf said, "living out in the open, cooking meals over a campfire. It sounds like a gay life."

Chokolade smiled, and looked down at the Bokhara carpet at her feet. Oh yes, she thought, quite gay. Especially when a sudden rain puts out the campfire, and the food remains uncooked. And there are other times when it gets so cold that even sleeping under a goosefeather *dunyha* isn't warming enough.

But she wouldn't tell the Crown Prince anything about that. Looking at him she guessed that he was ten or twelve years older than she was, but somehow he seemed years younger. If she didn't tell him the truth about life among the Gypsies, she also left out other interesting facts about her past. No point in telling him about the Hussar captain, or about Fekete Andras. It hadn't taken Chokolade long to learn that there were certain interesting details about her past that were best omitted.

Though she spoke to no one about Sandor St. Pal, he remained in her mind, a defiant, clinging memory. She looked appraisingly at the Prince, and thought that he might be the man to exorcize him from her heart. She bit her lips in anger at her own thoughts. If the Hussar captain had no place in her life, why must she persist in remembering him? She smiled warmly at Rudolf, and her eyes met his boldly. This was the man, this was the man who would make her forget the Captain, she was sure of it.

The train arrived early in the morning at Mayerling, the Crown Prince's retreat and hunting lodge in the Viennese woods. Two coaches were waiting for the Crown Prince's party, and the horses set off at a smart trot. Looking out of a coach

window Chokolade saw the gates with the royal
crest swing wide, and the horses, without slackening
their pace, trotted through. Chokolade saw that
they were now riding through the park that
surrounded the hunting lodge.

The coachmen brought the carriages to a smart
halt before the entrance to the lodge, and a footman
rushed forward to open the carriage doors. Rudolf
insisted on helping Chokolade down. The well-
trained servants who lined the steps looked straight
ahead; not an eyelid flickered, as Chokolade, with
Rudi's arm about her waist, walked up the steps and
into the lodge.

Mayerling, from the outside, looked like a large
comfortable hunting lodge—the kind that was
popular all through Austria and Switzerland. But
once within, it was clear that the lodge was built
with an eye to creating as much comfort as existed
for the Prince in Vienna. True, there were no silk
walls or cream-damask upholstered furniture, but
the highly polished wooden floors were decorated
with thick carpets that had been hand-woven by
Bedouin tribes in Morocco, and fine Gobelin
tapestries illustrating the hunt of the unicorn
adorned the walls.

Chokolade had little time to examine the rooms
of the hunting lodge, because with Rudolf's arm
firmly about her, she was whisked into a suite of
rooms at the far end of a wide corridor.

"Loschek," Rudolf shouted to his personal
servant, "champagne—quickly! Hurry, man."

Loschek permitted himself a smile only after he
had bowed, and turned away from his Imperial

master. It had been a long time since he had seen the Crown Prince so enthusiastic about a woman. True, plenty of women were brought to Mayerling, but Rudolf, while charming to all of them, behaved in an amused, but disinterested, manner. The women he chose would come for a day or two, at the most three—and then he, Loschek, would bundle them back in the carriage, and see that they were taken to the train that would once again deposit them in Vienna. They all left with a jeweled memento from the Prince—a bracelet, a brooch, and if they especially pleased the young Prince, they might even receive an intricate, expensive necklace. None of them were ever asked to come back, that Loschek also knew. This one—he thought—something about her—she seemed different. More exciting than the ladies Rudolf usually invited to Mayerling.

Chokolade was trembling beneath Rudolf's stare. She wanted to look away, but she was also determined not to let him make her lose her poise so easily. She was no shy peasant from some little Austrian village, who looks downward when a prince gazes at her. But she was also glad when Loschek finally returned with a tall bottle of champagne icing in a silver bucket, and two tulip-shaped crystal glasses on a silver tray.

"Leave it," Rudolf ordered abruptly. "I will open the wine myself. Just get out."

Loschek bowed, and started to back out of the room.

"And don't come until I call for you," Rudolf called after him. "Don't even knock."

The door closed behind Loschek, and Chokolade

felt her heart racing. *Now,* she wanted to cry out, *now. Don't make me wait.*

It was Rudolf who said the word that she would not permit herself to say out loud, "Now!"

The two of them were on the bed short seconds after that, and neither of them bothered undressing completely for the first time that they made love. Chokolade felt Rudolf's lips nibbling her earlobe, and then she felt his hands ripping at the buttons of her tightly fitted black velvet jacket.

"Yes"—she tossed beneath his fingers, and her body arched upward to meet the lips that searched for the hard nipples of her breasts—"yes."

Her acquiescence and her eagerness inflamed Rudolf, just as much as her struggling had once excited the Hussar captain. She wanted him as a man, Rudolf understood, she didn't give a damn whether or not he was a Crown Prince. He could have been a corporal in his father's army for all this girl cared. No, she wanted *him,* the *man.* She wasn't one to brag that she had slept with a prince, and he knew that no gift of money or jewelry could have brought her to his bed if she hadn't wanted to be there.

For the first time in her life, Chokolade let her body speak to a man. His hand cupped her breasts, glided over the slight curve of her belly, and then searched for the triangle between her legs. She moaned, and relaxed beneath his touch. His hands ripped her elegant undergarments downward, and Chokolade raised her hips to make his task easier. When he finally touched her, she came alive in a flame of feeling.

"Anything," she gasped, "anything—only now, now—please!"

Rudolf felt her body throbbing beneath his. Of all the women he had had, of all the women he had taken to his bed, he had never had a woman respond to him in this way. He moved, and she moved with him. He thrust and her body opened welcomingly to receive his thrust. She seemed to melt into him, and he yanked impatiently at the fabric of her skirt that came between them.

When his lips left her mouth he heard her moan, her arms clasped him to her, and her thighs tightened around his body. Chokolade was trembling. What was this, what was this? She wanted to control her body, her fine, dancer's body that had always responded so easily to her directions. But now her body was writhing in a wholly different way—it was moving in response to what this man was doing to her—and she could in no way control it. She just knew that she never wanted him to stop, she didn't want this feeling to end.

She didn't know that she spoke, but Rudolf heard her, and gloried in her words. "Don't stop," she begged, "please, please, don't stop."

Her words were followed by a cry—a cry, as she tried to clutch him even more tightly to her. Her cry moved Rudolf to an intensity of feeling that he had never known. He couldn't see, he couldn't think, he could only feel, and soon his own cries had joined Chokolade's. The two of them lay joined for a few more seconds, and when Rudolf moved away from Chokolade, she gave a little gasp.

"Oh—no—" she said softly.

"No?"

"I don't want you to leave me."

Rudolf turned on his back, and gently he took Chokolade in his arms. He cradled her head against his chest. His lips caressed the damp hair that lay against her forehead.

"I won't leave you," he murmured, "not for a long, long time."

That first time in Rudolf's bed was Chokolade's true initiation to the pleasures of lovemaking. She realized that she had come close to experiencing such feelings with the Hussar captain, but she hadn't allowed herself to respond fully to a man who had used her like a slave.

She had no trouble responding to Rudolf, because in bed with him, she was his equal. It didn't matter that he was the heir to the throne, and she was a Gypsy dancer, their bodies were equal partners enjoying the art of love—so Rudolf said.

"Love?" Chokolade questioned. "Is this love, then?"

Rudolf looked at her closely, for a moment he was afraid she was laughing at him. But there was no laughter in those beautiful deep-green eyes.

"I don't know," he answered. "This is as close as I have come to feeling something for someone. Can there be more? I don't know."

Chokolade looked at him. "This is as close as I have come, too."

"Truly? A beautiful girl like you, has there been no one in your life—no one you wanted to love— live with—"

The image of the Hussar captain flashed into

Chokolade's mind, and she closed her eyes tightly, hoping to shut out his image as well. "No one," she said.

But Rudolf had seen the look of pain just before her eyes shut. Of course there had been someone. What had happened between them? He didn't want to know. He was happy to take these few days, hidden with Chokolade at Mayerling. He didn't want to know about the past, and he certainly didn't want to think about the bleak future which stretched before him, filled with duties and obligations.

Chokolade spent a week with Rudolf; a week that she would remember for the rest of her life. She had been in many palaces and elegant homes since she had left the Puszta, but she had never seen anything like the bedroom in which she spent her days and nights.

Rudolf was right. She didn't need any clothes in Mayerling, simply because he refused to let her leave the huge bedroom. Chokolade's ripped and shredded clothing were taken away by Loschek, and the only time Rudolf allowed her to put something on was when the servants came in to bring their meals or more champagne. She would then slip on Rudolf's dark brown brocade robe that was trimmed with sable fur.

Were there other people in the outside world? Was there even an outside world? Chokolade no longer knew or cared. She was happy to be in this one room with this one man. Was she now the slave that the Hussar captain had once wanted her to be? No, because she was doing exactly as she pleased.

Rudolf wasn't trying to break her spirit, and she was happy to accede to every demand that he made.

One day she sat curled up on the chinchilla throw that lay across the huge bed, and her fingers gently traced Rudolf's spine as he lay on his stomach beside her.

"I feel like a happy, contented cat," she said, enjoying the feeling of his skin against her fingers, and the fur against the rest of her body.

He turned over and looked up at her. "You look contented—like a contented woman." He reached up and pulled her down beside him. "Do I please you, my little Gypsy?"

She snuggled close to him. "Oh, so much; and you, my Prince, do I please you?"

"As no woman has ever pleased me," he said huskily. "It's as though you were taught all the arts of love—as though you were made for love." He stroked her velvety skin. "A woman like you, Chokolade, you were made to please a man, and that's all you should be allowed to do. You should be kept in bed, always ready for lovemaking—like a favorite in a Turkish pasha's harem."

Chokolade laughed. "That was one of the rumors about me in Budapest—that I came from a Turkish harem. Why does that idea keep coming up so often?"

Rudolf kissed her. "The Turks ruled Hungary for a hundred and fifty years, and the only good idea they left behind them was the harem."

Chokolade tried to sit up. "You think that was a good idea?"

But Rudolf wouldn't let her move away from

him. "Of course," he murmured. "Think about it. Let's say that I'm that infamous Turkish pasha, and you're my favorite. But you won't remain my favorite unless you do everything to please me. I'm a man—and fickle—and if you bore me, or displease me—back you go to the harem where you have no one to amuse you—"

Chokolade laughed. "You mean—no men."

"Only eunuchs. And a warm girl like you wouldn't find that very interesting. That's why you would want to remain my favorite."

"Because you have a choice among many—and I have none."

"Exactly." Rudolf's bantering tone was gone. "Now, knowing that—what would you do to please me?"

Chokolade entered into Rudolf's fantasy easily. This man made her feel things she had never felt before. She would be his willing slave—his eager harem favorite, if that was what he wanted.

She sat up, moving slowly and sinuously. "I would do this," she said softly, and her fingers roamed over his body, "and then I would do this."

In just a few days, Rudolf had taught her well. He had taught her how to use her hands, her lips, her entire body. He had taught her how to move him to passion, and he had taught her to do it slowly. He wanted the passion to build up, and up, until he could stand it no more.

Rudolf leaned back against the four soft pillows. He never touched Chokolade, but he knew by the way she caressed him that she, too, was becoming more and more excited.

When Chokolade was sure that neither of them could stand waiting another minute, she adjusted her body to Rudolf's. Her eyes were half-closed, and she no longer had any sense of self—she belonged to this man—she had been created to please him, and in doing so she was experiencing pleasure greater than she had ever known.

"Yes," he said hoarsely, finally taking her in his arms, "yes . . ."

What was fantasy, what was reality? Rudolf was a Turkish pasha, and this girl had to please him or suffer for it. Thinking of herself as a harem favorite titillated Chokolade: she wanted this man to enjoy her, she wanted to feel his body move beneath her lips and hands, and then she wanted him to take her, take her and still the hunger her body felt for his.

It was later—much later—when Chokolade was able to speak to Rudolf.

"I—I fell asleep."

He was lying beside her, and she could see the glow as he inhaled deeply on his cheroot.

"Yes," he answered, "I—too—for a little while. The French call it 'the little death,' the sleep after lovemaking."

Chokolade gave an involuntary shudder. She had a Gypsy's instinctive distaste toward any discussion of death.

"That's wrong," she said, "wrong—bad. To associate love with death."

"Why? If this is death, it's not such a fearful thing. Perhaps death is preferable to life."

But Chokolade couldn't stand to listen to such talk, and she quickly turned, and her fingers moved teasingly across Rudolf's chest.

"Well?" she asked. "Did I please my Turkish pasha? Am I still his favorite?"

Rudolf laughed, and turned on his side. He flipped the covers back, so that he could enjoy the sight of Chokolade's nude body. Perfect, he had never seen such a perfect woman. She was both slim and curved, and probably because of her dancer's training, she could do things with her body that no other woman could do.

"Umm"—and now it was his turn to tease her— "yes, I suppose you're my favorite—for the moment, anyway. But don't you think you should think of other ways to amuse me?"

Chokolade sat up in bed, and she let her toes play with the chinchilla fur. "Other ways?" She looked at him with frank interest. If there were other ways to give and receive pleasure, she was eager to know about them. "What other ways?"

Rudolf leaned back comfortably against the pillows. "You might dance for me. That famous dance—the one a Gypsy bride performs only for her man."

Chokolade laughed. "But that is a dance performed by a virgin. That's what makes it so enticing. It's a young girl's first act of sensuality. I think we're past that, you and I."

Rudolf smiled. "A virgin's dance? Very good. I do believe that by now you'll be able to add something special to it."

Chokolade caught the look of challenge in the Prince's eyes. Very well, she would dance for him. She knew the effect her dancing had on men, and she knew the dance of the Gypsy bride. Just a short while before, her own passion had made her Rudolf's slave, maybe her dancing would have him lying at her feet.

Chokolade swung her long legs off the bed. She kicked aside the heavy, red fox rug that partially covered the gleaming teakwood floor.

"There is no music," she said.

"There is no need for music when you dance, Chokolade."

The Bride's Dance was traditionally done very slowly, and Chokolade, fully conscious of what she was doing, moved even more slowly than before. She had never danced in the nude for any man, and as she extended one leg outward, she could see her body reflected in the large mirrors that covered one entire wall of the bedroom. The sight of her own image startled her. She had never seen herself so open, so vulnerable. Performing without clothes, she was beginning to understand the true meaning of the Bride's Dance. It was meant to be the dance of a young girl, offering herself up freely to the man she has just married; but she couldn't help herself—she was young, but she wasn't inexperienced, and the way her body moved took any sense of innocence from the dance.

Comfortably stretched out on the bed behind her, Rudolf laughed. He could see the blush that spread over the girl's olive skin; her sudden shyness, after her wanton behavior in bed just a short while before, amused him.

Chokolade tossed her head, and her heavy, dark

hair flew behind her. It was ridiculous, she decided, angry that her emotions should be so obvious. Did she care that she was no longer a virgin? What was happening? Was her body being taken over by the spirit of a young Gypsy bride, long since dead? She shivered at the thought, and she was both glad and angry when Rudolf told her to stop dancing.

"That's enough," he commanded, "come over here."

No one had ever interrupted her dancing before. She took pride in the fact that she could mesmerize men into complete silence and obedience when she danced for them. She moved sullenly toward the bed. She had just started the Bride's Dance, but perhaps it had so affected Rudolf that he wanted to make love to her at once.

She stood before him, and he reached up and pulled her back down on the bed, but it was not to make love to her.

"Let me see your right foot," he said.

"What?"

"Your right foot. Stretch your leg out—quickly."

The Prince has gone crazy, Chokolade thought. What strange desire did he wish to have fulfilled now? But Rudolf was examining her right foot with strange interest. He had even taken a monocle from the table beside the bed, and he was looking at the birthmark on her instep through the glass.

"What is this?" he asked her.

Chokolade tried to pull her foot away, but he wouldn't release it.

"It's nothing—a birthmark. What of it?"

"Have you ever noticed the shape of your birthmark? It's shaped like a tulipan—the Hungarian tulip—"

Chokolade stared down at her foot. He was making her feel most uncomfortable.

"I don't know," she said. "I never paid much attention to it."

"The tulipan," Rudolf persisted, "it's a symbol of Hungary. You must have seen it before—the Turks used it—the Hungarians use it today—this stylized tulip is visible in every bit of Hungarian folk art."

"Well, what of it?" And this time she succeeded in pulling her foot away. "Who cares?"

Rudolf stretched out his own right leg. He showed Chokolade the mark on his own instep. It was another tulipan, quite similar to hers.

"That's funny," she said. "What a strange similarity."

"Not so strange." Rudolf got out of bed, and putting on a robe, he tossed another one to Chokolade.

The Prince was suddenly serious. Chokolade hadn't seen him behave so formally since he had brought her to Mayerling, and she was sure that his actions were just the prelude to another sexual fantasy.

"It's a family birthmark," Rudolf said.

"Of course." Chokolade laughed. "We're related."

"That's just what I'm trying to explain to you. Now be a good girl, and listen."

"Very well." Chokolade put the Prince's robe on and closed it tightly about her. She sat down demurely on the bed, tucking her legs beneath her as though she were a little girl about to hear a lecture. *If that was what he wanted.*

It took her a few minutes to realize that Rudolf was not fantasizing and not trying to amuse her with a child's fairy tale. He was very serious when he told her that the birthmark that both she and he bore was one that was inherited from one generation to another.

"Chokolade—we are related—"

"Impossible." She laughed again. "That's crazy. Besides—all that fancy story about the symbol of Hungary—"

"I grant you the resemblance of the birthmark to the symbol of Hungary—that is a coincidence. But the fact that both you and I bear the same mark— that is not. You don't look all Gypsy, Chokolade, surely you've heard that before. Perhaps from other Gypsies."

Chokolade listened to him in silence. She was remembering Haradi Neni, and her words many months ago—it seemed like a million years now. The old woman had taunted Chokolade, she had said that the girl was no true Gypsy—she had even called her a *beng's chave*—a devil's brat.

"Think, little Gypsy, who was your mother?"

"I—I don't know," Chokolade faltered, "she died when I was born. My father never said much about her—he only told me that she was very beautiful."

Rudolf looked at the girl sitting so seriously on his bed. There was something special about her. Her skin, her hair, and eyes—they were all of a lighter color than a true Gypsy's. And the way she danced and moved, there was a manner to her, a haughtiness, that was not seen in most Gypsies.

"We must find your father—ask him—"

Chokolade shook her head. "My father is dead."

"Your brother, then, he might know."

Chokolade shrugged. "He has never said anything." Suddenly she laughed. "Rudi—this is too silly."

But Rudolf didn't join in her laughter. "Not so silly. A long time ago I heard a story—I was just a boy, and it was a story I wasn't supposed to know. But there was a woman—I suppose she would have been my third, or maybe fourth cousin—she was quite young—seventeen or so—and she ran off with a Gypsy fiddler.

"Of course, the family disowned her, but they did learn that she had died in childbirth. She was a baroness, Chokolade—Baroness Pavonyi—and supposedly very beautiful."

Chokolade's eyes widened. "But who was the Gypsy she ran off with? Doesn't anybody know?"

Rudolf shook his head. "They just cut her out of their lives, Chokolade. Nobody wanted to know. Even if she hadn't died, they would have thought of her as dead. She had done something so unforgivable—"

"Unforgivable—to love a Gypsy?"

Rudolf sighed. "Unforgivable to love anyone you're not supposed to love. Most marriages in royal families are arranged—for better or worse. Love has little to do with it."

Chokolade shook her head. "I still don't believe it."

"I do," Rudolf said. "The more I look at you—the more I can believe it. I'm sure of it, You're the daughter of Baroness Pavonyi—it would explain many things about you. It also means that you and I are related, Chokolade—distantly, but still related." He laughed at the irony of it. "And you're not just related to me, but to the entire family—the family that rules the Empire, Chokolade."

Chokolade shook her head. It was all too impossible. She was still waiting for the Prince to tell her that the whole story was a joke, but Rudolf was doing no such thing. He was sitting thoughtfully by the bed, trying to remember details of past family history.

". . . Now that would mean that your grandfather would have been the old Baron Arpad Pavonyi—no, maybe it was Baron Albrecht Pavonyi—I'm not sure—"

His musings were interrupted by Chokolade's wild laughter. She had thrown herself face down on the bed, and she was laughing and laughing.

"Chokolade—"

But she couldn't stop. It was too wild—too unbelievable—and once again the image of the Hussar captain came to her mind. Damn, she thought she was well rid of all memories of him. Certainly Rudolf had made her forget him during their days and nights in bed, but now, here he was again. What would he say, Sandor St. Pal, if he knew who she really was? He had thought that he could rule her, but if what Rudolf said was true, she might well hold a position higher than his. Her fists clenched. If she was truly a baroness's daughter, she would have him thrown in jail! Yes, that's what she would do.

At first, when Rudolf had told her of the possibility that her mother might have been a baroness, she wanted to tell him to forget the whole matter; she saw it as nothing but an added and unwanted complication in her life. But now, suddenly she saw that being even partially of royal birth might have its advantages. Certainly no man could come along to use her and abuse her the way the Captain had.

"Chokolade." Rudolf sat beside her on the bed, gently stroking her hair. He could sense that her laughter was mixed with tears, and he wondered if he had done the right thing telling her of his discovery. "It's over, our little idyll—it must end. I want to take you to Vienna—you're entitled to a new life."

"A new life." Chokolade sat up in bed. "Each of us is only given one life, Rudolf. Whether you're a Prince or a Gypsy, no one gets more than that."

"A different life," Rudolf amended. "Why shouldn't you be treated with the honor due a daughter of Baroness Pavonyi?"

"The daughter of Baroness Pavonyi and Bela Tura," Chokolade reminded him. "Tell me, Rudi, do you know—were my parents properly married?"

"No priest in Hungary would have dared marry them, but Gypsies have their own wedding ceremonies, haven't they?"

"They do." Chokolade smiled once again. "And I was just about to show you part of it, the Bride's Dance, when you interrupted me—"

Rudolf bent over her, and unloosened the sash of the robe that covered her. "I'll never see the Bride's Dance now, it's too late for that. But at least let me enjoy what would have followed it—for the last time."

"For the last time," Chokolade whispered, as her arms went up around his neck, and this time their lovemaking was sweeter than it had been during the whole week that they had known each other. Sweeter, but tinged with a sad note of farewell.

Chapter XI

VIENNA WAS NOT like Budapest, Chokolade decided. On the surface, everything in the city reminded her of decorated pastries. The buildings were elaborately ornamented with rococco angels and baroque carved stone flowers. The homes, the castles all looked as though they were huge layer cakes rather than busily worked gray stone.

And the people, too, resembled the pastry dolls that stand on top of wedding and anniversary cakes. The women were heavier than the women in Budapest. And the men started on little paunches when they were only in their thirties.

"It's all the good Viennese cooking," Rudolf laughingly told her, "all the *knodle* and *kaiserschmarren* and Sachar *torte*. Sweet food for sweet people."

But Chokolade didn't find the people so sweet. They were pleasant enough on the surface as they bowed over her hand, and murmured polite words. And they looked open and friendly—blonde, blue-eyed, and rosy-cheeked, as most of them were—but it didn't take long for Chokolade to see that the smiles and seeming openness were only a facade for a pompous, haughty attitude toward anyone who was not Austrian.

And Chokolade was emphatically not Austrian. She was part Hungarian, and if that wasn't bad enough, she was also part Gypsy. The Viennese court went into shock when Rudolf appeared with Chokolade at the Hofburg Castle.

"My dear boy," his usually gentle and kind mother told him, "you must understand that I can't receive this girl—at least, not in public."

"But she's the daughter of a distant cousin—Baroness Pavonyi."

"That may be so, though as yet you have no proof. But even if that is so, she is still the illegitimate daughter of the Baroness and a Gypsy fiddler."

The Empress looked wistful. "Don't think I wouldn't like to greet this girl—but you know how they speak of me in Vienna."

Rudolf brought his mother's hand to his lips and kissed it. It was true, he could understand why his mother couldn't befriend Chokolade openly. All of Vienna, and especially the court, had always been critical of Empress Elizabeth. They couldn't understand why she spent so little time in Austria. It had all started when the Empress had discovered that her husband was a philanderer. She had boarded her yacht and set out for the Greek Islands, where she stayed for months at a time.

Ever since, she spent very little time in Austria, preferring to stay in her castle, Gödöllö, on the Puszta. If that behavior wasn't strange enough, word filtered back to the stuffy Viennese that the Empress actually befriended and rode with the *csikos*, the cowboys of the Hungarian plains. Elizabeth was always doing something to shock the Viennese. A court that was used to secrets and constant intrigues didn't approve of the Empress's open manner. If she did something as innocent as sending her fifty favorite hunting horses to a shooting box in Ireland, so that she could enjoy riding in that country, all of Austria buzzed about a probable secret lover living in Ireland.

"I am constantly watched," Elizabeth told her son. "As far as the Austrians are concerned, I can do nothing right, while your father can do nothing wrong. I don't think it would be of any help to this girl if I were to befriend her. People would resent me still more, and they would hate her."

Rudolf sighed, but he had to agree with his mother. "Someday, perhaps, I could arrange a secret meeting between the two of you. You would like her, Mama."

Elizabeth smiled at her only son. He was tall, lean, and brown-haired—she was grateful that he resembled her more than he did the Emperor.

"I would like that, Rudi."

Though neither the Empress nor the Emperor could openly receive Chokolade, this did not mean that she did not enter the whirl of court life. There was a big difference between formally appearing at the court levees, or attending the balls and parties at the Schönbrunn and Hofburg palaces.

"Rudolf's newest is coming," the whispers went around the court the night Rudolf was to introduce

Chokolade at a large ball. "He has courage bringing her here. Crown Princess Stephanie will kill him."

"Or her."

But the whispering stopped when Rudolf entered the grand ballroom of the Schönbrunn Palace with Chokolade on his arm. Chokolade's eyes widened as she looked about her. The ballroom was ablaze with lights from the many suspended crystal chandeliers.

The royal family's favorite orchestra leader, Joseph Strauss, brother of the famous Johann, stood on the podium, alertly awaiting the signal to begin. When the guests had gathered, the chief footman pounded on the floor three times with his gold-topped cane. Joseph Strauss raised his baton, and the orchestra played the salute to the Hapsburgs: *Gott Erhalte*.

As the music began, Rudolf and Chokolade stepped forward. They came slowly down crimson carpeted staircase. Two footmen stood stiffly at attention on either side of each step. When the Crown Prince and Chokolade stepped down from the last step, the guests in the ballroom stepped back, forming an aisle down which the couple walked. Rudolf nodded, and as they passed, the men bowed, and the women curtseyed.

Chokolade looked straight ahead, but she could sense, rather than see, the avid stares that followed her every movement. She was wearing a royal blue, cut-velvet gown that Rudolf had chosen for her.

"Royal blue?" she had questioned. "It's not one of my usual colors. Most of my gowns are in cream, black, or red."

"*Royal* blue," he emphasized the first word. "I want everyone to understand who you are."

But while no one dared be openly critical to the Crown Prince, Chokolade could sense antagonism when Rudolf insisted upon introducing her as "My cousin, the Baroness Pavonyi."

"Cousin," and the whispers started again. "How dare she claim a relationship to the Hapsburgs?"

The first time Count Hoyòs heard that, he made a quick answer. "It is not she who claims the relationship—not at all—it is the Prince who insists upon it."

No one wanted to openly incur the Prince's displeasure, and if the more conservative members of the court drew back when Rudolf led Chokolade out on the shining floor to open the ball, in time the younger people gathered more closely about her.

Soon, Chokolade was the center of her own circle—her own clique. Princess Stephanie could rail at her husband, and weepingly claim that he was embarrassing her before all of Austria, but Rudolf calmly replied, "If you don't like what I do in Vienna, Stephanie, perhaps you should spend a little more time with your dear parents in Belgium."

This was a challenge Stephanie could not ignore, and she wired her parents telling them that she wished to leave Rudi and return to Belgium. But King Leopold would rather have his daughter unhappy than risk a scandal and a schism with the head of the Austro-Hungarian Empire, and he wired back: "Stephanie: It is your duty to remain at the side of your husband, the Crown Prince."

Stephanie stayed in Vienna, and so did Chokolade, but it was Chokolade who was amazed at what went on in court circles.

"These people," she said to Rudolf, "they lead

wilder lives than the entertainers I knew in Budapest. The other evening I saw Count Hoyòs in the conservatory with Countess Barisch. They were just kissing, but—"

"But," Rudolf finished for her, "you were sure that the kissing was just a prelude to other, more interesting matters, and you are right. You can do anything in Vienna, Chokolade. The key word is discretion."

Chokolade looked at Rudolf with her clear, green-eyed gaze. "But you, Rudi—can you do anything here—even if you do it with discretion? It doesn't seem so."

Rudolf looked at her regretfully. "There's very little discretion possible for me in Vienna, Chokolade. My every move is watched, that's why I go to Mayerling."

Impulsively, Chokolade sat down at Rudolf's feet, and she rested her chin on his knees. "Let's go back to Mayerling, Rudolf, let's go back to playing our games. You're not the same here."

Rudolf stroked Chokolade's hair, but he allowed himself nothing more. "I want more than that for you, Chokolade, much more. I want you to be more than my playmate at Mayerling. I've introduced you at court, and I want you to make a good marriage—"

"A good marriage." Chokolade picked her head up. "You think I could have a good marriage with one of these pompous, stuffy Viennese? Rudolf, I am going back to Budapest."

"Chokolade"—Rudolf pulled the girl to her feet—"please—stay a little longer. You'll see—

you'll like it here after awhile—"

"You've been here all your life," Chokolade said. "Do you like it here? I don't think so."

Rudolf looked at her sadly. "No, I don't like it, but I must stay—I have no choice."

"But I have."

"Stay for me—because you are my friend. I am very lonely, Chokolade—stay and be my friend—if only for a little while."

He held his hand out to her, and Chokolade extended her own. She had never known a man like this. A man who had made passionate love to her for an entire week, and who now wanted nothing more from her than friendship.

"Very well," she said, "I will stay—for a little while."

Rudolf smiled. "That's all I ask. Sometimes I think I will only be here for a little while as well."

Chokolade didn't ask the Prince what he meant, but from conversations she had heard she decided that Rudolf was worried that the monarchy might one day be toppled.

"Perhaps that is why they're all so gay—or pretend to be," Chokolade thought, "they are afraid that they won't rule forever."

The talk swirled about Chokolade at even the gayest of parties, the most colorful of balls and it didn't take long before she was introduced to the Viennese habit of dining in the private rooms provided by the great restaurants. At first, these private dinners surprised Chokolade. Budapest had a few intimate dining rooms, too, but the gregarious Hungarians preferred to see and be seen, especially when they were escorting a beautiful woman. The Viennese liked to be seen at the great balls and at the opera, but they liked private dinners, hoping that seduction would follow dessert.

One Viennese gentleman who frequented the private dining rooms was asked if the after-dinner hours always lived up to his expectations.

"Not always," he replied, "but I have the consolation of a good dinner, and the knowledge that I am still capable of the effort."

The men that Chokolade dined with were more than capable of the effort, and she was frequently asked to dine in one of the small, jewel-like rooms above The Grinzing Restaurant.

The first time she was taken there by a Viennese state minister, Doctor Loewe, she was amazed to be led away from the crowded dining room and into a small room that contained a wide chaise longue in addition to a small, round table that was set with an embroidered cloth, and lavishly embellished with a centerpiece of voluptuous white and pink peonies.

Chokolade knew that most men liked to be seen with her; they liked the world to know that they were dining with and possibly enjoying the favors of a Gypsy dancer who had caught the eye of the Crown Prince.

She looked around the room, and her eyebrows went up questioningly. "Are we dining alone?"

Gunter Loewe seized her hand and covered it lavishly with kisses. "Ah, my dear Baroness Pavonyi, this is not by choice, I assure you. I wish that I could dine with you below, in full view of all Vienna, but a minister has to be so careful."

His voice faded away, and Chokolade was sure that they were both thinking the same thing: why did a minister have to be more careful than a Crown Prince?

Chokolade was angry—angry enough to walk out of the small dining room and leave Doctor Loewe alone with his intentions. But she decided to hide her anger, and use this time alone with Doctor Loewe to find out as much as she could about the Austrian government's plans regarding Kossuth's New Army. Doctor Loewe was not as powerful as von Weis, the head of Austria's State Police, but he would do until she could get just a little closer to von Weis.

With that in mind, Chokolade flashed her most dazzling smile. "It is much better this way," she said, "I, too, prefer privacy—sometimes."

Again her hand was in Doctor Loewe's grasp, and if possible, his kisses were even more lavish; Chokolade managed to pull her hand away when she felt his mustache brushing the inside of her wrist.

"Doctor Loewe, so impetuous! But first, surely, I may have a little wine?"

Those words *but first* drove Gunter Loewe crazy. They offered a promise of everything he hoped for. He pressed the buzzer that summoned the waiter, and when the man arrived, he said, "Champagne, the best! And caviar, yes, yes, beluga, of course. And then? What do you mean—then?" He turned distractedly to Chokolade, who did her best to hide her amusement by answering seriously.

"A pheasant in pastry," she said, as though she

was making an important decision. "And asparagus—do you have them? Good, definitely asparagus, and a side order of truffles, but only if you have the white ones, of course. No white truffles?" She made a little face of disappointment. "Forget them, then. But perhaps, if you have the Ribier grapes from Spain, I may be tempted with one or two of those, if they're quite, quite fresh."

Doctor Loewe looked stunned as he heard Chokolade order. All that food! A meal like that would be sure to put him to sleep, and sleep was not on his agenda. And it wasn't just the quantity of food that bothered him, it was also the amount of the eventual bill. Though a man of wealth, Doctor Loewe was well known through all of Vienna as a miser. Chokolade knew this too, and her lavish order of a dinner she didn't want, and wouldn't eat, was meant to put Doctor Loewe in his place. He didn't want to be seen with her in public? Very well, then.

Course after course of the dinner was brought in by two waiters, who knocked softly before they entered the velvet-walled dining room. But no matter how discreet the waiters were, they were *there*, bringing in large-grained beluga caviar, serving it with what looked like a ladle to Doctor Loewe's eyes, and then removing it to return with another course.

After Chokolade had taken exactly one mouthful of pheasant in pastry, she moved languorously to the chaise. Her black gown, with its overlay of rose chiffon, spread about her like so many sleepy flower petals. The waiter who entered with the commanded

bowl of Ribier grapes did his best to look away from
the vision she made—he was one of the Grinzing's
best waiters—but even he had to stare at the
sculpted bosom above the neckline of the dress, and
at the slim ankle that dangled over the edge of the
chaise.

"My God," the waiter reported when he arrived
in the steamy kitchen, "if old Doctor Loewe can't
make it with her he's a dead man!"

Doctor Loewe had every intention of getting
Chokolade to welcome him warmly on the chaise
wide enough for two, or even for three, if necessary.
But Chokolade moved gracefully away from him
whenever he came too close. She reminded the
Doctor of some elusive substance—mercury, yes
that was it—she seemed so willing, so available, yet
she was never quite there.

But first, that was what she had said, *but first*,
when she had asked for wine. What had she meant
by that, he wondered with frenzy. What had the
little bitch meant?

And now, now, she was actually talking politics,
politics! Unbelievable, who wanted a woman to
discuss affairs of state? Especially this woman.
What was she saying? He tried to listen, and then
Chokolade raised her champagne glass, looked at
him over the glass's rim, and he was mesmerized and
drowning in the green of her eyes.

"I am so afraid, dear Doctor, so afraid. But
then—then I comfort myself with the thought that
an important man like you can protect me."

"Afraid?" He looked at her distractedly. What
had she been saying? "Afraid of what?"

"I hear these terrible stories, these frightening stories. Surely you must hear them, too—all of Vienna knows. Is it true?"

"True? Is what true?"

"That Vienna is going to be besieged by the Hungarians led by Fekete Andras and the New Kossuth Army. Is that what it's called?"

"Kossuth's New Army. But that's nonsense, where do you hear such stories, my dear Baroness?"

"But everyone hears them. I am thinking of moving to Switzerland." She fixed the Doctor with another gaze. "Unless, of course, if you could assure me that it's all right to stay. You're such a strong man, so powerful."

Her words worked even better than the champagne Chokolade had been pouring for Gunter Loewe. He sat back expansively, and without even realizing it, he told her all the plans that the government had made for controlling the rebel Hungarians. Doctor Loewe didn't know everything, he was not that highly placed, but he knew enough. Chokolade realized that she had to return to Hungary and see Fekete Andras. But first she had to get rid of this stupid little man, and get out of The Grinzing Restaurant. She looked at Gunter Loewe, and with the understanding that had come from dancing in the cafés, she estimated that two—at the most, three—brandies would put him to sleep.

She reached behind her, and pressed the buzzer. "A little kirsch," she told the waiter, "but only if you have the kirsch from the Black Forest. Do you have that? Good."

She then turned to Doctor Loewe, and he

thought he had never seen anything quite as wonderful as Chokolade's smile.

"You have made me feel so much better, so relaxed. Now that I know all is well, I can take pleasure in life once again. And after a brandy, I know I will feel completely relaxed."

Just as she had thought, it was Doctor Loewe who relaxed completely after two thimble-size glasses of cherry kirsch brandy, and Chokolade left him asleep, and quite alone, on the comfortably wide chaise.

The waiter grinned as he saw her walking calmly downstairs, enveloped in a froth of rose-trimmed black chiffon. He ran to open the door for her, elbowing the man at the door out of the way in his zeal to serve her.

"A carriage, Baroness?" the waiter asked.

Chokolade was startled to see the waiter out of the dining room, but she nodded yes, she did want a carriage. It was only when he opened the door, and helped her in, that she understood.

"I'm a Magyar, too," he said softly, speaking in Hungarian, and then, though he had no glass in his hand, he offered her the traditional Hungarian toast, "We'll never die!"

Chokolade bent down from the carriage step and kissed the man full on the mouth, "That's right," she answered, just as softly, "we'll never die."

The waiter watched the carriage drive off, and then returned to The Grinzing. For one night, at least, he was the hero of the restaurant staff. The legendary Chokolade had kissed him on the mouth, even the doorman swore to it, he was a better man they they had ever given him credit for, that was sure.

For the next few weeks Vienna wondered about Baroness Pavonyi. Where was she? Everyone had ideas, and many people insisted that they *knew* Chokolade's whereabouts. She was seen taking the waters in Baden-Baden; no, she was visiting that Count in Venice, and he had even offered her his family's pink *palazzo* that fronted on the Grand Canal. That was pure nonsense, someone else insisted, Chokolade had been seen just the other night dancing at Maxim's in Paris.

The talk eddied and swirled, but no one knew or guessed that Chokolade was with her good friend Fekete Andras and his troop from Kossuth's New Army.

Traveling incognito between Vienna and Budapest, Chokolade had time to ask herself just why she was so involved with the men of Kossuth's New Army. She was a patriot, yes, but only in a small way, and she had to admit to herself that her liaison with Fekete Andras and his people came about because she had nothing—nothing else in her life.

Chokolade knew that to the rest of the world it seemed as though she had everything that any woman could want. She had fame, and money, and jewels, and even the notoriety imposed on her because of her affair with Rudolf, but to her, it was nothing. She loved no one, and no one loved her. Sandor St. Pal had ruined her in a way that he could never have imagined; because of him, no man could arouse her to deep feelings, or to true passion. If the world thought she had everything, Chokolade thought of herself as an empty shell. A beautiful, decorative, hollow shell, and it was only when she knew the excitement of riding with Fekete Andras that she felt whole again. Whole, but not complete, because deep in her heart she admitted that it was only love that could make her complete—a love that she was doomed never to know.

"Chokolade," Fekete Andras warned her more than once, "you shouldn't come to Eger so often. Send me word instead. You know I have men I can trust in Budapest. I've told you—just go to the Tulipan—it's a little tavern in old Buda—they'll get word to me. The police, the Hussars, and von Weis's Secret Police—they're just one hot breath behind me. And if they should capture you—"

"And if they should capture you?" Chokolade asked.

"They'll hang me," Fekete Andras said, "but they'll put you in jail—perhaps for the rest of your life."

Chokolade shuddered at that. Better death than being locked up, she was still Gypsy enough to feel that to the very marrow of her bones, but even her fear of capture, her terror of iron bars caging her in for the rest of her life, couldn't keep her away from Fekete Andras and Kossuth's New Army. She came to them as often as she heard news that could help them. And she rode with them as often as Fekete Andras permitted her to do so; it was the only time she felt truly alive.

Back in Vienna there was rage and frustration at von Weis's headquarters.

"How do they know? How do they know?" von

Weis asked over and over again. "They seem to know our plans even before we've completed them." A spy, he brooded, could it be a spy? The thought nagged at him from time to time, but he knew the men he worked with, and he couldn't believe that any one of them would be brave enough to test his power this way. A spy? Not possible! But the men around von Weis felt his piercing glare chilling them more than once.

Kossuth's New Army was a constant embarrassment to von Weis; they evaded his smartest men and the Emperor's highly trained Hussars with equal ease, and if that wasn't bad enough, they did the sort of things that made the stupid Hungarians proud of them, and that caused even the Viennese to laugh and snicker—laugh at his expense. The matter of the Emperor's Tokay wine was one of those small, but irritating matters, that seemed to rankle most.

Every year a small quantity of very special Tokay wine—Tokay Hegyaljai Aszu—was laid aside and bottled especially for the Emperor. The wine was sealed in hand-blown crystal bottles, and then laid gently in a specially made box of the finest Herend porcelain. The box and the wine were presented to the Emperor at a court ceremony from his "loyal Hungarian subjects."

This was traditional and expected, but what was most unexpected was the appearance of a band of highwaymen who surrounded the coach carrying the wine, and made off with it before the startled escort could react quickly enough to do anything about it.

A few days later, the announcement appeared in

the court newspaper that the wine-offering ceremony would be cancelled that year because the Emperor had taken to his bed with a cold and a slight fever. That was what the newspaper said, but all of Vienna knew, and most of Vienna laughed—laughed at von Weis.

Damn! The head of the Secret Police was furious, and he took his anger out at the idiots who had composed the escort, and who could give him no concrete information about the highwaymen other than that they were probably members of Kossuth's New Army, and that a woman seemed to be riding with them.

"A woman? What woman?" Von Weis knew that there were women with the men of the Army, but he had never heard of one of them riding along on a raid. "Damn you, what woman? What did she look like?"

But no one could give him a decent description, other than to say she wore man's clothes, and had a hat pulled low over her forehead hiding her face.

"And she laughed," one of the men offered eagerly. "Yes—I remember—she laughed."

"Of course she laughed," von Weis roared, "just as all of Vienna is laughing. How can I find a woman by her laughter?"

But the man persisted, "It was so musical—so lilting—I—I think I would know it if I heard it again."

"Get out of here," von Weis shouted, "get out! You see if you can find her—idiot!"

The woman who rode with Fekete Andras haunted von Weis. He was to hear of her again and again—why, she had even dared interrupt the Saint Stephen's Day Parade that was held every year in Hungary. Saint Stephen was Hungary's most revered saint, and it was believed that as long as his crown was kept safely under the supervision of the Crown Guard, monarchy and royalty would be safe in Hungary. This Holy Crown of Hungary was removed from safekeeping only for coronations and on Saint Stephen's Day, when it was carried solemnly in to Saint Stephen's Church, and held aloft so that everyone could see the three bent bands of gold surmounted by a cross.

But this year—this year—in the middle of the Saint Stephen's Day parade in Budapest a group of masked riders had actually dared to ride in to the parade carrying banners that proclaimed "Kossuth Still Lives." The signs—the riders—so startled the solemn escort that they almost rode into the crowds lining both sides of the street. The people screamed and shouted, some fell; horses reared—and in all the excitement a slim figure dressed in black and riding a bay mare had actually ridden up to the coach that held the sacred crown.

The soldiers guarding the coach had turned for just a minute—or so they said at the official investigation—to try and quiet the crowd. In that short minute the rider in black took the crown from the pillow on which it was resting and rode off with it through the milling crowd.

"Wait—wait," the driver of the coach had called out, and he insisted that it was a woman's voice who had answered him.

"Don't worry, friend," the rider in black had said,

"I, too, am a Hungarian; I won't let anything happen to Saint Stephen's Crown," and then she had disappeared into the crowd.

"She," von Weis questioned, "she?"

The coachman stood at attention. He could feel the sweat rolling down his forehead and into his eyes, but he didn't dare reach up to wipe his face.

"Yes, sir, a woman—I'm sure it was, sir!"

Again—a damned woman. But this one time von Weis considered himself lucky. He had managed to surpress all stories about the theft of Saint Stephen's Crown in the newspapers of both Budapest and Vienna, and though many people had seen—or thought they had—the theft, the whole matter was hushed up. This was easier to do than he had hoped, because the thieves had returned the crown with a written plea for freedom to Budapest's leading newspaper. What they couldn't have known was that von Weis would not permit the story or their plea, to appear in print.

"Never mind," Fekete Andras had said to Chokolade, "we had to return it. As I know the Austrians, they would have called in the Russians against us if we had dared to keep the Holy Crown.

"We must walk softly, Chokolade. If we go too far, they will concentrate all their efforts on exterminating us. We are in enough danger without that—you, most of all."

Chokolade knew he was right. The biggest danger of all came from herself. She was too tempted to speak out when she was with members of the Viennese Court—too tempted to tell them what she really thought, how she really felt.

One night she went to the Spanish Riding School with the Prince, Count Hoyòs, and others. The Count and the Crown Prince sat on either side of her in the royal box explaining the fine points of dressage, and telling her about the great, pearl gray Lippizaner stallions that made up the mounts of the Spanish Riding School.

"You see how these horses move, Chokolade? They don't step—they prance."

"And look—look—you will see—they will move in time to the music."

Chokolade was entranced by the sight of the muscled, deep-chested animals. These horses were far different from the slight, almost Arabian, mounts she was used to from the Puszta. The Puszta—she thought of it with longing, and she smiled as she looked down at the sleek, curried animals, and pictured what it would be like riding one of these great horses across the open plain.

Only I wouldn't care if the horse could prance, she thought. I would just like to see how fast it would gallop.

The men sitting in the box were pleased to see that Chokolade was enjoying the horses being put through their gaits and paces, and they talked among themselves about the political unrest in the country.

"Have you heard," Count Hoyòs was saying, "the Secret Police raided the *Viennese Morning Paper,* and closed it down—they claimed the paper was also printing revolutionary material."

"Foolish." Rudolf was speaking softly, but

Chokolade could hear him. "All this repression just makes the people angrier—"

Prince von Coburg was laughing. "Closing the paper was nothing, but yesterday the secret police raided the Café Roma near the Prater. The place is supposedly filled with radicals. Well, they arrested everyone there, including Count Stru, who had come there to meet that pretty little singer he's been having an affair with.

"He was furious, but at the same time he didn't want to let everyone on the street know who he really was, so he actually went to jail. I hear he stayed there for three hours before he could get anyone to listen to him."

The men laughed, and Chokolade smiled, but the men, seeing how intent she was upon the high-stepping horses were sure she wasn't listening to them, and they went on in a more serious vein.

"The trouble is," Count Hoyòs was saying, "that von Weis sees a radical at every corner or under every bed. The slightest remark criticizing anyone in the government, and von Weis makes arrests."

"You can't blame him," Phillip of Coburg replied. "Some of these groups appear mild enough, but how is von Weis to know whether or not they're affiliated with that damn Kossuth's Army group."

"They're in Hungary—"

"What does that mean?" Prince von Coburg scoffed. "It would be easy enough for them to infiltrate Austria. You never know where that bloody Fekete Andras and his Magyars are going to turn up next."

When Chokolade heard that familiar name, she sat up a little straighter on the thin gilt chair, but she didn't turn her head. Let them think she wasn't listening, that was the best way to hear something about her friend.

"You're just as frightened of your shadow as the eminent head of our Secret Police, von Weis," Count Hoyòs said. "Did you know that last week the fool arrested ten members of the Christian Socialist Party because they wrote a letter to the *Neue Presse* suggesting that it was time the people of Austria were given the vote?"

"A vote?" Prince von Coburg exploded. "Next they will be wanting a democracy, like those damn thieves who follow Kossuth, and who follow Fekete Andras—a bunch of wild Mongols, that's what all those Magyars are."

"Maybe we should give them the vote," Rudolf said quietly. "It may be the only way to save the monarchy. I know that is what my mother thinks."

The men exchanged glances. That was just another example of the Empress's madness, though not a man there would have dared to say so to her son.

Chokolade always listened carefully to the political discussions that went on around her. Sometimes Rudolf was with her, but often he wasn't, and when the Crown Prince was absent, the men talked openly about the dangerous thinking of Empress Elizabeth; they were sure it was a symptom of mental illness.

"Pray to God that Rudolf does not inherit this sickness from his mother," Chokolade heard one of

Rudi's friends say. "Do you know what the Empress actually said yesterday? It was at lunch, and Count Larisch swears that he heard it. It seems Her Majesty actually said that she didn't know why the Hapsburgs expect the people to love them, when the people are in rags while the Hapsburgs are in silks and laces."

"Mad," they all agreed.

"No wonder the Hungarians love Elizabeth," someone else commented. "She's as democratic as their worst radical."

"The Queen of Hungary," another man jeered, using the Empress's other title. "They can have her and keep her—she's not true Austrian."

Chokolade wanted to get up and raise her glass with a cheer to the Empress. Instead, she took a sip from her glass of champagne, and said a silent "*Eljen*—live" under her breath.

Discretion, that was what Rudolf had advised her from the very first, and now Chokolade was more discreet than ever. She listened to every word, and made no comment.

It was clear that the men of Vienna thought of her as a pretty, empty-headed doll who didn't understand one word they were saying. It was hard, but only by keeping quiet could she hope to escape detection by von Weis and his Secret Police, and she knew that her silence didn't buy her safety forever. One day she would ride with Fekete Andras, and one day she would be caught. She shivered at the thought, shivered at the thought of capture and jail. But not even her fear could stop her from riding with Kossuth's New Army. Even as she smiled and flirted and danced with the men about her, she would think of the Hungarian forest, and the bay mare that Fekete Andras kept just for her, and she would long to be riding among her own people.

"Good for dancing, and good for bed," that was the opinion of the men of the Austrian nobility about Chokolade. They were also sure that her affair with Rudolf was continuing, and that meant none of them could do more than flirt with her—not until their Prince gave the signal that he had gotten bored with the Gypsy dancer. But Rudolf gave no signal, and though he still continued to see Chokolade, they hadn't been to bed together since they left Mayerling.

"Why?" Chokolade asked him one evening, his coldness upsetting her.

"Because we were becoming too close. And I can't allow myself to become close to anyone. I think I could love you, Chokolade, perhaps I do already, and love would cause me nothing but pain. I can't risk it."

Chokolade looked at this strange man. He was the only man in her life who treated her like a thinking, feeling, being. To Rudolf she was good for more than the bed and the dance floor. She looked away from him, afraid he could read her thoughts if he looked in her eyes; she didn't want him to know that while she enjoyed talking to him, she missed going to bed with him.

"This Fekete Andras," Chokolade asked, "I hear talk about him all the time. Is he really such a terrible scoundrel?"

"Scoundrel! The man's no scoundrel—he's a Hungarian patriot. These fools don't realize that if they don't give Hungary some measure of freedom, the whole monarchy will be destroyed. Chokolade,"—he looked at her narrowly—"it's clear that you pay a lot more attention to what is going on than most people realize. You must tell me what is being said when I'm not around. Most of those men won't talk openly before me—they think of me as a radical, too."

After that, Chokolade repeated every conversation to Prince Rudolf. She was a faithful reporter, until the night she learned of the plans made by von Weis to capture Fekete Andras. The Secret Police Chief had managed to infiltrate Fekete Andras's group with one of his own men, and with this man's help, he was able to devise a plan to capture the rebel chief.

Chokolade's heart was pounding as she listened to the brutal plans they had for Fekete Andras. Some wanted to hang him, others advocated shooting, still others recommended life imprisonment as the worst punishment of all.

Chokolade smiled and nodded through the conversation, but all the time she knew that she had to get back to Hungary—she had to warn Fekete Andras. Her hands clenched beneath the table, and her nails cut deep grooves into her palms. This was her most dangerous expedition of all; she would actually be racing against von Weis's men—racing against them to get to Fekete Andras first.

"And once he's caught," Chokolade heard one officer say, "we won't have any trouble with the others. Not even a snake can function without his head."

Chokolade knew that if she told Rudolf of

von Weis's plans he might do something to thwart it, and if he did, the Crown Prince would be in danger. Many monarchists felt that a Crown Prince should be nothing more than a figurehead, a role Rudolf despised. Chokolade made her own plans, and the first thing she did was to ask Rudolf to dine in her house near the Hofburg.

Rudolf came willingly. As usual, when he wanted to move about Vienna with some measure of privacy, he hired Bratfisch, who owned and drove a coach for hire. Chokolade laughed when she saw Bratfisch pull up in front of her house. The Prince stepped from the ordinary black coach and hurried up the steps to where she was waiting for him.

"What will you do when people learn that Bratfisch is really your very personal coachman?"

The Prince smiled. "I'll find another Bratfisch. But for the time being, the man is invaluable."

Rudolf followed Chokolade into the house, and he looked about him with some surprise. No servant leaped forward to take his hat or cane, no one opened the door to the salon for them. Chokolade performed all those duties herself, and then she said, "I've sent them all away. There is no one here but us, Rudolf."

She led him into the salon, and Rudolf saw that a cold supper was laid out before the récamier chaise, and a bottle of champagne was chilling in a silver holder.

Rudolf sat back, sighed, and relaxed. "Is it true? Is there no one here but you and me?"

"No one," Chokolade assured him. "I wanted us to have this last evening all to ourselves."

Rudolf sat upright. "Last evening?"

"I must go back to Budapest, it's been so long since I've seen my brother—my other friends. And—I want to be among Hungarians once again."

Rudolf nodded. "I understand. But you will be back?"

"Of course. Very soon—but something tells me that things will not be the same between us ever again."

Rudolf smiled. "A little Gypsy fortune-telling, perhaps?"

"Don't laugh, there is more to *dukkering* than you *gajos* ever realize."

"*Gajos*." Rudolf smiled sadly. "Is that all I am to you, Chokolade? Just another *gajo?*"

"The best *gajo*—one of the best men I have ever known." Her lips brushed his gently. "A man who cares about other people."

"That is not how the world thinks of me."

"The world doesn't know you, but I do. You're a warm man, my Prince, and a romantic."

Rudolf leaned over, and put his finger to Chokolade's lips. "Don't let anyone hear you say that—that's not the way the future Emperor is supposed to act. I'm supposed to be stern, and cold; hard like my father, and just a little bit mad like my mother."

Chokolade laughed. "And very bad, because you're a prince and entitled to be so."

Rudolf laughed with her. "Exactly. Luckily there's no one else here, or the real story about Crown Prince Rudolf would be in tomorrow morning's *Neue Presse.*"

"There are other reasons why I'm glad there's no one here," Chokolade said softly, "very glad."

She moved closer to Rudolf, and her fingers undid the high stiff collar of the jacket of his uniform. The Prince was an honorary officer in every crack regiment of the Empire, and as such he was usually dressed in uniform. Chokolade's fingers moved adroitly among the heavily embroidered frog closings of his Hussar's uniform. *Another Hussar*, her heart reminded her, while her mind did its best to dismiss that unbidden thought.

Rudolf sighed, and leaned back against the couch. His eyes closed, and he gave himself over to the enjoyment of feeling Chokolade's hands roam over his body once again. His jacket was off, and his shirt was unbuttoned, and he felt her lips against his collarbone and the base of his throat. He only opened his eyes when he felt her move away from him.

And then he gave himself up to the pleasure of watching Chokolade slowly undress, the firelight casting rosy reflections on the marble sheen of her body. Chokolade had been wearing a gown of beige moire taffeta. The bodice was cut in a low heart-shape, and the tight tucks forced her breasts into high, arched mounds.

Now as Rudolf watched, Chokolade slowly undid the tiny pearl buttons one by one. She moved with tantalizing slowness. And when the gown was open to the waist, she sat down beside Rudolf once again, her back to him. He kissed the back of her neck while his hands moved around to cup and caress her breasts. If she had tantalized him before, he now chose to do the same to her. She moved languorously from side to side, her eyes half-closed, while his hands and lips made her body long for him.

It was a game between them—a game they both played as experts, and this time Chokolade was the first to give in, to acknowledge that he had won.

"Please," she said, "please—undress me—now."

Rudolf pulled the gown from her shoulders, and then he made Chokolade stand before him while he continued unbuttoning the gown, tugging slowly at the tiny buttons that went all the way down the front of the gown, hidden under a froth of cream lace. The gown was soon at her feet.

Chokolade stood before him, clad in nothing more than shimmeringly sheer stockings that were held up by black lace garters attached to a narrow, black corselet. She had never looked more provocative than she did at that moment—the corselet hid nothing, but it emphasized the curves of her breasts and her buttocks.

Tonight Chokolade longed to play the wanton for him; Rudolf could see that. She continued standing there, and he knew that she was waiting for him to tell her what he wanted her to do.

"Over there," he said, pointing to the silver-fox rug that lay before the fireplace. "Lie down."

She moved slowly, not because she was reluctant to obey him, but because she knew that slowness made her even more enticing. Chokolade stretched out, the rich fur caressing her, and she held one leg straight up and started to unfasten a garter.

"No," Rudolf commanded, "leave them on."

She lay there for another minute, still clad in corselet, stockings, and absurdly high-heeled shoes, and then she moved slowly and voluptuously from side to side. She reminded Rudolf of a large cat, sensually enjoying the caress of the thick fur against her skin. Rudolf heard the soft sounds that came deep from within Chokolade's throat, and again he was reminded of a cat, purring. Chokolade rolled over on the rug, and he could see the lovely back, slimming to her waist, and then arching out again in a curve of hips. Finally, she turned over one more time. There was nothing coy about her. Her green eyes were wide open now, she stared at Rudolf, and her body arched toward him, frank with invitation. With a cry, Rudolf was on the fur rug beside Chokolade, and his last thought, before he surrendered himself to her, was that he would never again know another woman like this, never.

Later—much later—when Chokolade and Rudolf were wrapped in robes, and eating their cold supper, he asked her, "Why? Why tonight?"

Chokolade's white teeth bit into a small drumstick. "Lovemaking makes me hungry," she said, and then, to answer his question, "because—as I told you—I think that after tonight things may be different between us."

"How different?"

Chokolade shrugged. "I don't know—just different—and no more jokes about my Gypsy *dukkering*."

"No more jokes." Rudolf grinned at her. This girl was wonderful. She made love as frankly and as openly as a young animal with a healthy appetite, and now she was eating the same way. None of the damn coyness he had known in most of the bedrooms he had visited. If he could only keep this girl with him forever—a girl who openly admitted to enjoying her appetites. This wasn't the first time that Rudolf had cursed fate for making him a prince, but he had never meant it more.

It was close to three in the morning when Rudolf decided that he had to leave Chokolade.

"Poor Bratfisch," Chokolade said, remembering the coachman who had been sitting patiently before her door for better than five hours.

But when Chokolade walked to the door with Rudolf, neither Bratfisch nor his worn black fiacre were there. Instead, a coach from the Royal household was waiting.

"What are you doing here?" Rudolf asked furiously. "Who told you you could come here? And where is Bratfisch?"

The coachman saluted, and his voice was shaking. "It was the Crown Princess, Your Highness, she told me to drive here, and then she drove away in your coach, sir."

"Damn Stephanie," Rudolf said angrily, "she has no right—"

But he was interrupted by peals of laughter from Chokolade.

"It's not funny," he roared.

"Oh yes it is," she said. "Admit it Rudi—it is funny."

Rudolf managed a weak smile, and the Princess's

coachman breathed a sigh of relief. The Gypsy dancer, he decided, had probably saved him from a horsewhipping.

After Rudolf had ridden off in the Royal coach, Chokolade went back into the house to take a long warm bath. She stretched out in the green travertine tub and enjoyed the feeling of the warm water against her pleasantly bruised body. *Why tonight*, Rudolf had asked. She was off to Budapest in the morning, that was as much as she had told the Prince. What she could never tell him was that she planned to rescue Fekete Andras from the Emperor's Secret Police. She was sure that with Gyuri's help she could do it, but she also knew that to tell Rudolf about her plans would be to put him in a precarious position. She had heard enough to know that many people in the Empire didn't approve of him, or of his open admiration for the Hungarian cause. If she should be captured, she didn't want Rudolf to be involved in any way.

But all that was for tomorrow. She closed her eyes, and gave herself up completely to the pleasures of her bath. She smiled, as she remembered some of the people who had told her how wonderful it must be to live the life of a Gypsy. Wonderful! Especially taking baths in cold streams, or not bathing at all if the weather was too cold.

Chokolade stepped from the long rectangle of marble onto a thick rug. She wrapped herself in a robe of heavy toweling, and through the steam-clouded floor-to-ceiling mirror she glimpsed her face. She felt warm, satisfied, the way she always felt after making love with Rudi. She smiled at her own image: this is the way St. Pal wanted to make me feel. *He should see me now*. The smile in the mirror disappeared, and she threw a bar of pure rose soap at the now frowning face in the mirror. Damn, must she always remember *him?* Even after coming from bed with another man?

Barefoot, Chokolade padded into her bedroom. The wide bed, the large pillows plumped up against the brass rails of the headboard suddenly looked less inviting than they should have. Chokolade climbed into bed, and pulled the covers about her shoulders. Maybe the life of a Gypsy was better after all. It certainly seemed less complicated than the life of a *gajo*.

Chapter XII

THE NEXT DAY, Chokolade embarked on the morning train that left Vienna at eight and arrived in Budapest twelve hours later. She knew that if she had wished it, the Prince would have ordered his private train to take her from one city to the other, but she didn't want to travel quite so conspicuously.

A few days earlier she had sent her maid to the railroad station to reserve a first-class compartment.

"And I want the entire compartment to myself," Chokolade had instructed the girl, "all six seats. Remember."

"Yes, Baroness Chokolade." The girl had curtseyed. "I understand."

Baroness. Chokolade smiled after the girl left the room. Rudi had insisted that she be called that at every ball and fete she had attended, but Chokolade felt she had no right to the title. Perhaps Rudolf was right, and her mother had been a Hungarian baroness, but she had given up all right to that title when she had run off with Chokolade's father.

"That doesn't matter," Rudi had assured her.

"Titles can be conferred at the will of the Emperor, you know that."

"Really? And do you think your father would be interested in conferring a title upon me?"

But Rudolf took the entire matter of titles far more seriously than Chokolade. "My mother could name you Lady-of-the-Palace, if she wished. And then, once you made a good marriage, you would have a title of your own—"

Good marriage. Chokolade found those words hateful. She knew that it meant marrying a man with money, a respected family, and a title. One more prison. She didn't want to offend Rudi, but she longed to ask him what difference it made whether a woman sold herself into marriage or merely for money. She knew that she could never live that way. Better to be a Gypsy dancer than to give herself to a man simply for money and a title.

Traveling alone to Budapest, she breathed deeply. She experienced a sense of freedom she hadn't known since the night she had left Budapest and the von Bruck Palace. As the train neared the Hungarian border the landscape changed. On the Austrian side, the land was parceled out into neat checkerboard squares, each square carefully fenced, and indicating the ownership of each small farmer.

On the Hungarian side, the land was more hilly, the train traveled through deep, dark green forests, and the borders between the farms were not so clearly marked. Waves of wheatfields and cornfields merged one into the other, with a few houses in between.

Every now and then a ragged child, riding a horse

magnificently, tried to race the train for a few kilometers. The horse would be without a saddle, and the children were usually barefoot, but to Chokolade, they rode as well as anyone she had seen at the Spanish Riding School in Vienna.

The conductor knocked respectfully on the door of Chokolade's compartment. He had no idea who she was, but a pretty woman, so well-dressed, and rich enough to pay for the entire compartment had to be someone important. He informed her that dinner would be served in the dining car at one o'clock, unless the lady preferred to have her meal sent to her compartment.

"Thank you. I'll go to the dining car."

The dining car was even more elaborate than Chokolade's wood-paneled and red-plush compartment. The tables were set with the finest of white linen, and gleamed with hand-cut crystal from Prague and heavy silver flatware from Germany.

The Captain of the dining car sat her respectfully at a large, comfortable table for four, and informed her that the train was well-stocked with crayfish and oysters from Fiume, asparagus from Belgium, and, of course, fresh pastries baked especially by Sachar's of Vienna.

Chokolade thought longingly of *szalonna* roasted over an open fire, fresh potato bread, and slices of green pepper—all to be eaten with the fingers. She compromised with a soufflé of fish and dry white wine. The Captain was crestfallen that he couldn't tempt her with something more exotic, but at least he was able to offer her outsize hothouse peaches and pale green grapes for dessert.

Back in her compartment, Chokolade reviewed everything she had heard about von Weis's plans to capture Fekete Andras. The man who was posing as a loyal member of Kossuth's New Army would inform the Secret Police Chief when Fekete Andras would be in a particularly vulnerable position. The Rebel Chief couldn't remain in the caves of Eger forever. He had to forage, and to speak of his cause to the peasants in the countryside. Von Weis planned to capture him at one of the supposedly secret underground meetings—secret no longer thanks to the Judas who rode with Fekete Andras.

As the train neared Budapest, Chokolade grew restless. She hoped to get to Fekete Andras before he was captured, but if she couldn't do that, she had another plan to free him. She knew that von Weis was planning to take Fekete Andras through the forests of Erdely to a prison fortress in Transylvania, and remembering the men of Kossuth's New Army, she felt sure they would be invincible in Erdely Forest. They knew every path, every byway, while the soldiers and police of the Austrian Emperor would be traveling through foreign territory.

Chokolade was the first person off the train as it pulled into Budapest Station.

"If you please—" The conductor held his hand out to her, but she moved down the train steps quickly, and the porter who piled her luggage on the handcart had to trot to keep up with her. Chokolade signaled a carriage, and the luggage was placed at the coachman's feet while Chokolade gave the driver the name of her villa on St. Margaret's Island.

The coachman touched the brim of his hat respectfully, and he snapped his whip above his horse's bony flanks. *The Gypsy dancer, she was back.* Everyone in Budapest knew about her romance with Crown Prince Rudolf, but he was the first person to know of her return to Hungary. He could think of quite a few fine gentlemen who would be happy to pay him for that information with two or three *pengö*.

"Gyuri"—Chokolade burst into the Kerman carpeted hallway of her villa—"Gyuri, where are you? I need you!"

"Miss Chokolade." A maid came running up the back steps, while the butler hurriedly shrugged into his jacket. "Miss Chokolade—we weren't expecting you."

"My brother? Where is he?"

"At—at the Café—the Café Royale."

"Of course. I must change, and order my coach. Hurry, Juliska—help me."

Chokolade was running up the stairs, the maid panting after her. God, Chokolade thought, she hadn't been able to move this freely since she left Budapest. This was her own home. If she wanted to hike her skirts up, and take the stairs two at a time there was no one to look at her disapprovingly the way those Viennese had looked at her if she had done anything that they felt was improper.

Chokolade's entrance into the Café Royale that night caused a sensation. The *primas* had been playing a slow, plaintive melody when he saw her walk in. He immediately signaled the musicians behind him to stop, and then he swung into a fast, foot-stamping *csardas*. Chokolade laughed with joy when she heard the music—her music—and her brother came running from a back dressing room when he heard the sound of what had once been their entrance song.

"Chokolade." He hugged her right there in the café. "You're back—God—I've missed you."

"We've all missed her." Zsigismund Kalman fairly jumped up and down in glee. "The Royale wasn't the same. You've come back to dance for us, yes?"

"No, no." Chokolade shook her head, but at the same time she couldn't stop her feet from tapping an answering rhythm to the music.

"Come on." Gyuri tried to pull her out on the dance floor.

"No—no, I'm not even dressed for dancing—my dress—my shoes—"

"What does that matter?" Gyuri shouted at her. "You never cared about things like that before. Come on."

Chokolade let her brother lead her out on the floor, and the patrons of the Café Royale were treated to the sight of a booted Gypsy dancer whirling about with a beautiful woman dressed in a formal, black, lace-trimmed gown. The music grew wilder, and the applause caught the rhythm of Chokolade and Gyuri's flying feet.

"Wait," Chokolade said, "wait." And she pulled away from her brother for a second to kick off her black satin slippers, and to step out of the constraining and heavy skirt. And then Chokolade danced: barefoot, and in a full white petticoat that stopped just above her ankles, she danced. She danced her joy at being home once more, and she danced her happiness at being free.

The audience went wild, and then just as quickly as she had come, Chokolade snatched up her skirt and her shoes and ran from the Café Royale. Gyuri followed her, and the two of them leaped into their waiting coach, which started out quickly for their house on St. Margaret's Island. Half the guests had boiled out of the Café Royale after them, shouting, "Chokolade—we want Chokolade," and Zsigismund Kalman was only able to get them to return by promising them that Chokolade would surely return the following night to dance once again at the Café Royale.

By midnight all of Budapest was babbling with the news that Chokolade was back. She had left the Prince, some said, because she had tired of him. No, he had tired of her, and had found another one of those opera singers he seemed so fond of. No, no, it was nothing like that, the rumors went on, it was the Princess Stephanie who had threatened her husband with a divorce if he continued seeing Chokolade. That last was greeted by laughter; everyone knew that the Prince would be happy to divorce his Belgian wife if only his duties as a Crown Prince didn't keep him bound to her.

But by the next day, Budapest was as mystified as ever about Chokolade, because she had once again disappeared from the city.

"Completely disappeared." Zsigismund Kalman was tearful as he kept repeating the news to Bela von Bruck and Chokolade's other admirers. "She was here last night, and by this morning she's gone." He wrung his fat hands. "Like a snowstorm in spring. Here one night, and then gone in the morning. Terrible! And I promised half the city that they could see her dance at the Café tonight. I don't know what to do."

"Her brother?" Gröf von Bruck asked. "Where is he?"

"Gone, too," Kalman practically wailed. "Gone—both of them—like a spring snowstorm."

"Yes, yes," Gröf von Bruck said impatiently, "you've said that. But gone where?"

But Zsigismund Kalman didn't know the answer to that, and neither did anyone else in Budapest, which was just as Chokolade had hoped things would be.

The next morning Chokolade and Gyuri were on a train, second-class compartment, that was bound eventually for the town of Eger, with two changes at Miskolc and Debreczen. Chokolade had borrowed a skirt, blouse, and coat from her maid, and she had pinned her heavy hair into a severe bun and then placed a wide-brimmed black straw hat on top of it.

The compartment was crowded with four other travelers, and brother and sister spoke little to each other.

"The less we say," Chokolade had told Gyuri, "the more likely that we won't be recognized."

Gyuri had agreed to a trip of almost absolute silence, just as he had agreed that the two of them had to do their best to free Fekete Andras.

Chokolade didn't dare tell Gyuri that this was

not her first trip back to Hungary—not the first time she had ridden with Fekete Andras. He didn't know that she had been passing information to the rebel leader on a regular basis, and she would never tell him. He would be in a rage that she had put herself in such desperate danger, and she wanted her brother to be calm. She needed him if she were to succeed with her plan.

"He saved us when we needed his help," Gyuri said, "and now it's our turn to help him. But if only you had gotten to Hungary before they captured him—if only we could have warned him.

"Now, I don't know. They'll probably have half the army as an escort taking him to that prison in Transylvania."

But remembering the conversations she had overheard in Vienna, Chokolade didn't think so.

"You don't know the Austrians," she had told her brother. "They have such contempt for Fekete Andras—for all Hungarians—that they won't think they'll need many soldiers to take care of someone from Kossuth's New Army."

"I hope you're right." But Gyuri felt pessimistic about the entire expedition. He wanted to help Fekete Andras, he felt committed to do so, but he just wasn't sure how effective they could be against both soldiers and police.

Brother and sister waited half an hour on the Miskolc platform, and then another forty minutes at the Debreczen station. It was night when they arrived at Eger.

"Now what?" Gyuri asked.

"We can't do anything tonight. We'll have to stay at a *csarda*, and ride out to the caves tomorrow morning."

The innkeeper at the small *csarda* smirked when they came in and asked for two rooms. He pushed their keys across the counter, and waited until they had started up the stairs before he said to his daughter, "Two rooms. Society folks from Debreczen trying to pretend they're not lovers. Fine! Let them have the two rooms. It means twice as much money for me, even though I know they'll only be using one room."

"Society folk? In these clothes?"

"Never mind the clothes. Did you see their hands? They've never done any work. At least she hasn't." He looked thoughtful. "If I know anything at all, though, he's a Gypsy, and she's probably some fine lady who's run off with him." He bent over the counter, and licked his lips. "Not that I care what they do, mind. Let them dirty themselves all they please."

His daughter looked toward the stairs. "He's a good-looking man, all right."

She was startled into a sharp scream when her father reached across the counter and dealt her a slap full across her face.

"No bastard of a Gypsy is good-looking to a decent girl. Remember that."

The girl sobbed, and her hand went to her face. Later, when she took supper upstairs for Chokolade and Gyuri, she didn't dare look up from the floor. Brother and sister just saw the bent blonde head and heard a murmured, "Will there be anything else, kind sir, will there be anything else, kind lady?"

"Nothing, thank you," Gyuri said, and the girl bobbed a curtsey and practically ran out of the room.

Gyuri looked at his sister and shrugged. "What was all that about?"

"Who knows? Her father probably told her you were the devil. Let's talk about tomorrow, Gyuri. Do you think we can hire horses from the livery stable?"

Gyuri grinned. "Why should we hire horses? It's been awhile, but I bet I could still go out to a meadow, and cast the glamor over a couple of good horses."

"None of that," Chokolade said sharply. "We're here to free Fekete Andras. You steal two horses, and the whole town will be after us."

"Hiring horses," Gyuri said gloomily. "I just hope no one in the Tura Tribe ever hears of it."

Chokolade laughed. "I promise not to tell. Now, let's eat some supper and go to bed. We have to be up early tomorrow."

Gyuri poked around with his fork in his plate of veal *pörkölt*.

"They don't know how to cook in these small towns, I can hardly wait to get back to Budapest."

But Chokolade, who had long gotten sick of the heavy and rich food of Vienna, was eating the stew with great enjoyment. "It's better than that everlasting *knodle* and *kaiserschmarren*."

"What?"

"Never mind. Just eat, and then go to bed."

The next morning Gyuri went out to the livery

stable to see about hiring two horses. The stable owner was happy for the business, but he was curious as to why Gyuri needed the horses.

"Can you keep a secret?" Gyuri asked the stableman in a whisper.

The man nodded eagerly.

"Well, I'm here with a very rich lady. She doesn't want anyone to know who she is, but she's inherited a nice piece of property around Egar, and if she likes it here, she plans to build a big house—a villa. It would mean a lot of work for everyone in town. Of course, it all depends if the area pleases her, and if she thinks the people are kind. So, if you want to make a good impression, give me your two best horses, none of your old fiacre horses that are ready for the glue factory."

"Toth," the stableman called out, "Joszi—bring me that bay gelding and the chestnut mare. Hurry."

The horses were led out, and the stableman helped with the saddling.

"Fine horses, sir. You can see—fine horses—eager to go for a bit of exercise."

One had a swollen fetlock, Gyuri noticed immediately, while the other could use a treatment of oil and ash leaves for his breathing. But Gyuri said nothing. The man would know he was a Gypsy immediately if he revealed his very specialized knowledge of his animals.

"We may be back this evening," he told the astonished stableman, "but my lady may decide she wishes to keep the horses for a few days longer, so let me pay you for the whole week. Is that all right?"

The man bobbed his head, and insisted on

holding the horse as Gyuri mounted.

"Careful there, sir, you can see that he's a bit skittish. Eager—ready for a fast gallop."

Gyuri mounted the placid animal, and just hoped that the horse would be capable of a fast canter if need be.

"Gyuri." Chokolade was dismayed when she saw the horses that Gyuri brought over to the *csarda*. "They look half-dead."

"They move as if they're all dead," Gyuri said sourly. "Well, it's your doing—you wouldn't let me borrow a couple of good horses, and this was the best I could do."

"No borrowing," Chokolade said. "Come on, let's go."

"Just a minute. Everyone in this town is curious about us, and they'll be watching where we go. We can't go riding into Erdely Forest just like that. First, we'll head up into the hills above the caves— pretend to be looking at a piece of land. Then, we'll ride to the forest."

Chokolade sighed with impatience, but she knew her brother was right. The two of them made a big pretense of riding about the countryside as though they were looking for the perfect vantage point on which to build a villa.

After an hour or so, when they felt reasonably sure that most everyone's curiosity was satisfied, they rode off into Erdely and the caves of Eger.

"I hope we're in time," Chokolade said, and she tried to spur her horse with a quick nip of her heels.

The horse quickened its pace for a few feet and then returned to its normal slow gait.

"Gyuri, these horses." Chokolade groaned.

"I know. Let's hope that there are some better ones at the caves."

But the caves were dark and silent when they got there. There was no sign of anyone from Kossuth's New Army, no sign that anyone had ever been there.

"Chokolade—they're gone—what shall we do?"

"Wait a minute, don't you remember?" And softly, Chokolade began whistling Remenyi's Bird Song. The song she had heard Fekete Andras and his men whistle in the forest. But this time, there was no answering whistle, no one picked up the trilling melody.

"I told you—they're gone."

"Wait. Remember the story of the drum, the beans and Istvan Dobo?"

Chokolade saw a large dried gourd lying at the entrance of the cave, and she also saw the pebbles that were tossed on top of the hollow vessel. It was no accident, she was sure of it. She stood quite close to the gourd, and with her boots gave a dancer's rat-a-tat-tat on the cave floor. The pebbles danced on top of the gourd, causing a noise that echoed from the first room of the cave toward the dark chambers that honeycombed the entire hill. Almost in a frenzy, she continued the tapping noise, followed once again by the whistled song.

Softly, so softly that Gyuri thought at first it was imagination, they heard an answering bit of music. Chokolade repeated her signal, and the answering whistle seemed to grow louder.

"It's coming from in there." Gyuri pointed to the dark caves.

"No, it's from behind us," Chokolade insisted.

In another minute, they realized that they were both right, as they found themselves surrounded by the men of Kossuth's New Army, who had crept up quietly with guns and knives drawn.

"Wait!" Chokolade turned from one to the other. "It's me—Chokolade—"

"And Gyuri Tura."

Silently, the freedom fighters drew closer and just as silently they circled the brother and sister.

"It is—"

"By God, it is!"

"What are you doing here?"

"Why did you come?"

It was one thing, they reasoned, for the Gypsy dancer to ride with them when Fekete Andras rode at their head, but now that he was gone, they were lost—lost. Without a leader they didn't know where to turn. It was just as von Weis had predicted, they felt helpless and sure that their cause was as lost as they were. Why had Chokolade come to them now? Didn't she realize the danger.?

Quickly she dismissed their questions, and insisted that they concentrate on freeing Fekete Andras.

"How? It's not possible."

"It is," Chokolade insisted. "They'll bring him right through Erdely on their way to Transylvania—if they haven't done so already—"

"They haven't done so," Fekete Andras's lieutenant, Tomas Ban, emphatically assured Chokolade. "If they had done so, we would have seen them pass. Besides, they'd never do anything so foolish. They know we'd never let them take Fekete Andras through this forest."

"That's just it. They're so sure of themselves that they are planning to bring him this way—right under your noses. I heard von Weis himself say that there's nothing you could do against a troop of soldiers!"

"You heard him say that?"

"Yes, and I also know who it was that betrayed you to von Weis. Have you a man riding with you called Imre Kovacs? He's a member of the Secret Police."

"We *had* a man riding with us called Imre Kovacs, but he disappeared just at the time they captured Andras. We thought the police had killed or captured him, too."

Chokolade shook her head. "He was the informer."

"And you know this—"

"And other things besides. I know that Fekete Andras will be brought through this forest—close to these caves. Do you want to save him?"

"Of course, but how?"

Chokolade smiled. "Such accomplished highwaymen as yourselves should know the answer."

"Hold up the Army? The Secret Police? As though they were ordinary people? These aren't civilians, you know."

Chokolade remembered the men she had known in Vienna. "They are more ordinary than you know."

She had to persuade them that what they were afraid of was the reputation of the Secret Police, the reputation of the Army.

"They are not gods, they're just ordinary men—like the Turks who were defeated by Istvan Dobo in these very caves."

Gyuri watched his sister with amazement and admiration, watched as the men rallied around her. He could see that Fekete Andras's men would follow her, follow this slim girl who once again donned the outfit of a highwayman: a man's boots, shirt, cape, and black-brimmed hat that shielded her face.

"Horses," Chokolade asked, "do you have horses that Gyuri and I can ride? We won't be able to keep up without good horses."

The one thing that Fekete Andras and his men were proud of were their horses. Often they did without food, but their mounts lacked for nothing. It was the only way they could be sure of escaping their pursuers.

"They'll have Andras in a coach," Chokolade told the men before they left the cave. "There will be just one member of the Secret Police in the coach with him, and another riding with the coachman. There will only be a small escort of soldiers. Von Weis decided this is the best way. He doesn't want to attract attention, and he thinks his plans are completely secret."

Fekete Andras's lieutenant stared at her again. "But how do you know—how—"

"Never mind that now," Chokolade said impatiently. "Do we ride?"

"We ride!"

Gyuri was just as curious as the others about how his sister had obtained the secret information she was now using so well. He knew that she had gone to

Austria with the Crown Prince. Budapest had been buzzing with that news for months. And now she was back, and without a word about her romance, she was leading a group of highwaymen— patriots—whatever you wanted to call them, against the Secret Police and the Army of the Austro-Hungarian Empire. She was his sister, but sometimes he remembered Haradi Neni's words, and decided the old woman was right. Only a devil's child could know so much—do so much—and get into as much trouble as Chokolade.

Once again, Chokolade was caught up in the excitement of riding through the forest, a group of men behind her, about to commit what others would call a crime against the Emperor—a crime punishable by death. But she wouldn't let her mind wander to those thoughts; they would have to catch her before they could execute her, and she had no intention of getting caught.

Chokolade, with the men riding closely behind her, rode to where the forest path narrowed. They dispersed on either side, well-hidden by trees and heavy brush. According to von Weis's timetable, the coach bearing Fekete Andras would arrive in Erdely Forest sometime in the early afternoon. They would stop for the night in Eger, and then ride out again the following morning. But early afternoon passed, and soon it was three, four, and five o'clock. In the forest it seemed even later, because once the sun went down, it was dark as night.

Tomas Ban looked at Chokolade suspiciously. He must have been crazy! Why had he listened to this woman, what was she up to? They made a fine sight, waiting in the forest like a bunch of fools—

waiting for what? Who knew what her real plan was; if she was a friend of von Weis's she could have easily told him about their hiding place in the caves, and his men would be waiting for them once they rode back there. Maybe she was the one who had betrayed them.

With Fekete Andras captured, he was in charge, but he wasn't at all sure if he was doing the right thing, following this girl—this dancer. Who was she? How much did any of them really know about her?

But it was too late—too late to turn back—too late to worry about what he had done. He had made a decision, and they would all have to live with it, even if it meant jail and hanging for most of them. He heard the soft thud-thud made by horses' feet riding through the hard-packed dirt trails of the forest. A second later he could distinguish the sound of the rolling wheels of a coach—moving fast, and scattering rocks and pebbles as it traveled.

He raised his hand, and the men behind him grouped closer. Chokolade's eyebrows went up, and Gyuri said "What?" before Tomas Ban put a quick finger to his lips.

Let it be the right coach, Ban thought, *and let it not be surrounded by a troop of crack Hussars.*

He had no illusion about the ability of the ragged men around him to stop a whole troop of trained professional soldiers. They could hold up a coach of unarmed travelers, and moving fast, get away with a little money and a few jewels, but now they were coming up against soldiers, and this was another matter.

God! He licked his dry lips. How could he have

listened to this girl? She must have bewitched him. Retreat—that was it! Maybe it wasn't too late, maybe he could signal retreat. They could disappear into the forest all around them, and no one would be the wiser.

But it was too late. The thud-thud sound was louder, and the rumble of the coach was almost upon them. Usually, the sound of horses' hooves told him how many men were riding, but this time his ears were filled with a strange pounding sound— the sound of his own hammering heart. *Too late,* the beating rhythm of his own heart told him, *too late, too late.*

He couldn't find the words, he couldn't find the strength to signal, and it was the girl—that damn girl—who raised her hand in a fair imitation of Fekete Andras ordering his men forward. It was the girl who shouted, "Now! Ride!"

Chokolade's horse was the first to plunge out of the brush, and the men could do nothing but follow her. It was a mess, Ban decided, a terrible mess. Chokolade just rode forward like a mad fool, she knew nothing about strategy, nothing about tactics, she just rode forward as though she were in a race.

This was crazy, Chokolade thought, as she urged her horse forward, crazy! She was afraid—she had never known such fear. But surging through her was another feeling—a feeling of exultation—of excitement that most women only experience with a man they love. Chokolade felt all that as she rode to free Fekete Andras. *I'm alive,* she thought, *I'm alive. I'm more alive at this moment—the moment when I may die—than at any other time in my life.*

She behaved like a woman gone wild when she reached the coach. It was she who opened the door of the coach, she who yelled for the men riding behind her to bring a horse for Fekete Andras. And it was she who gave the shouted command, "We ride!"

The men behind Chokolade were surprised to find themselves riding hard after her, and the men in the coach, and the five Hussars riding escort, were just as surprised to see the men emerge from the forest.

Men—and was there a girl among them? Later, when they had to make their report to von Weis they were never able to tell him clearly what had happened.

"There were men," was all they were able to say. "Men—dressed in rags—but on splendid horses."

"How many men?" Von Weis had barked. "How many?"

But they weren't sure. It had happened too fast—and then there was a girl, or at least they thought it was a girl.

"A girl? What girl? What do you mean—you *think* it was a girl—was it, or wasn't it?"

It might have been, but then it might not have been. And if it was a girl, she was dressed in men's clothing.

Von Weis was furious with the lot of them. One soldier had been killed, and von Weis regretted that the rest of them hadn't met the same fate.

"Secret Police," he jeered, "Hussars. And you let Fekete Andras get taken by a group of peasants and a girl!"

Most of the men were standing silently at attention, but one of them was unwise enough to speak.

"Maybe it wasn't a girl, maybe it was a *delibab* come all the way from the Puszta. That's how she looked."

The moment he said that, the man knew that his career was finished in the Army. He looked down at the floor. Von Weis didn't speak, but his look indicated that he knew what to do with a soldier who blamed a mirage for losing the Crown's most important political prisoner. Transfer from the Hussars to the infantry, and posted to the Polish border for the rest of his military life. He was lucky at that; if von Weis could have had his way, he would have court-martialed and shot the whole lot of them for failing to obey orders, and for general idiocy.

Von Weis was unreasonable, because while the afternoon that Fekete Andras was saved from the Hussars became a legend in Hungary, neither Chokolade nor the men who followed her could ever give an accurate account of what had happened.

"You were fantastic," Fekete Andras said to Chokolade when they were back in the caves of Eger. "The way you rode forward—my God—I've never seen anything like that! And what were you shouting?"

"Me? Shouting? I wasn't shouting?"

"But you were," Gyuri told her.

"What? What was I shouting?"

"*Ap i mulende*—by death. You can travel far, my

sister, but you'll always be a Gypsy."

"I've never wanted to be anything else," she told him, and in her heart, she knew that she spoke the truth. Rudolf could tell her that her mother was nobility and she was part *gajo*, but how had living in the *gajo* world helped her? It had never brought her true happiness. From those first few moments with the Hussar captain until this moment when she actually led an attack against other Hussars, she had known little deep happiness, little heart-felt joy.

Fekete Andras watched her slow smile, and he wondered what had pleased her, but Chokolade couldn't explain that it was the idea of fighting against the Hussars that gave her pleasure. She had actually conquered some of the men whose leader had so brutally conquered her.

"What contempt they have for us," Fekete Andras said, "to send such a small armed escort. They were so sure of themselves, so damned sure."

"That's what will beat them in the end," Chokolade said. "They're too stupid, too smug. You will win," she told the rebel leader, and he gave a shiver as she said that. She seemed to know, she seemed to see into the future. But how could she? He shook himself. He didn't believe in Gypsy *dukkering*.

But while he didn't believe in fortune-telling, he did believe they would win, and if anyone had asked him why his belief was so strong, he would have answered, "Because we are right."

"We will win," he said to Chokolade as they sat before the fire in the Eger caves, "and when we do, all of Hungary will know what you have done,

Chokolade. You'll be another Csinka Panna—another Gypsy heroine."

Chokolade leaned back on her elbows, and looked up at Fekete Andras. "But Csinka Panna loved Rakoczi, and she followed him for years while he fought to liberate Hungary from the Turks. While you and I—"

"While you and I met at the wrong time, and the wrong place, and are comrades, not lovers. Chokolade, I am a simple man. So simple that there is no room in my heart for two loves. And if I were to give in to my love for you, I would have to forget my country. And that is why—"

"And this is why we are comrades," Chokolade finished for him. "And that makes me happy. There are few people I can think of as friends."

"Think of me that way. Here—" He reached for the cord around his neck, and she saw, once again, the opal ring. "Do you remember this?"

"The ring I asked you to keep. I told you to send it to me if you were ever in trouble."

"But when I was in trouble, I had no way of getting the ring to you, but yet you came anyway. I still remember what you said. 'Keep this ring for both of us. If you have it, I have it, too.'

"Now I want you to take it. I'm not a Gypsy, and I can't see into the future, but sometimes I think I can see into the heart of this fire opal, and I want you to have it. You have always come to us, and I want you to remember, if ever you're in trouble, send me the ring, and I'll come to you—even if I have to travel from the other side of the Blue Lake that separates the living from the dead."

The firelight glanced off the heart of the fire opal, and the light in the dark cave seemed multiplied because of it.

Chokolade took the ring from Fekete Andras's hand. "Yes," she said slowly, "it is my turn to have the ring. The center of the ring is cloudy, but it tells me that I may need it."

Fekete Andras looked at the ring lying in Chokolade's palm, and his hand closed about her hand and the ring.

"If you need the ring, you will also need me. The ring is the pledge between us. Don't forget. If ever you're in trouble—"

Chokolade looked up at him, and gave a small shiver. "I don't know why, but I think trouble may be coming into my life. And I won't forget."

PART THREE:

Meetings...and Farewells

Chapter XIII

"WE'LL BE SAFE in Budapest," Gyuri had told his sister when they returned to their house in the capital city of Hungary.

"We'll be safer in Vienna," Chokolade said, thinking of Rudolf, but she knew that not even the Prince could help her, if von Weis came to suspect that she was involved in freeing Fekete Andras.

"Vienna," Gyuri smiled. "I would like to go to Vienna with you, Chokolade. Do you think my talents would be appreciated there?"

"Which talent? Your talent as a dancer, or your talent as a lover?"

"Both." Gyuri's voice was a mocking drawl. "All your talents seem to have been appreciated, Chokolade. Or would you be ashamed to admit to the Viennese society that I'm your brother?"

"Ashamed? Why should I be ashamed?"

Gyuri shrugged. "Budapest isn't a million miles from Vienna. I heard that the Crown Prince introduced you as Baroness."

"Gyuri"—Chokolade leaned forward—"that's what Rudolf thinks. But I'm not sure that isn't his imagination. Or maybe it's a joke that he wanted to play on that stuffy court in Vienna."

"It's no joke. I always knew—at least, I always thought—that we were only half brother and sister." He pulled Chokolade to her feet, and led her to the large, gold-framed mirror that decorated one end of their salon. "Look at us. I'm all Gypsy—but you, with those light eyes, and dark brown hair, and olive skin, it's clear you're not all Gypsy. That's why Haradi Neni called you a devil's child."

"But I feel all Gypsy."

"Of course. That's because your father—and mine—was all Gypsy. But your mother—"

"Who was she? What do you know about her? Do you remember her?"

"I remember very little. Don't forget, I was only three when you were born and your mother died. But the little I remember tells me that she wasn't my mother."

"How can you remember? How?"

"Because—because somehow I remember that once there was someone else—my mother, I suppose. I even remember our father telling me something about her. But then—then she wasn't there anymore. And there was this other lady, a nice lady, and then there was you—and the nice lady was gone. I remember, but it's like seeing things through a fog."

"I'll never know." Chokolade sighed. "I'll never know for sure."

"Wait," and Gyuri dashed out of the room, and Chokolade could hear him running up the stairs.

When he came back down, he held something in

his hand, and he opened his palm and held it out to her. It was a small, round locket, no more than an inch or so in diameter, and Chokolade took it from him, and turned it over and over, wondering.

"What is it?"

"I found it after father died. He had it carefully put away. There's a picture inside, open it up."

Chokolade opened the locket slowly, and a young girl's sweet face looked out of a picture. Was there a resemblance? Or did she only imagine it, because of a desire to find the elusive woman who had given her birth.

"My mother?"

"I think so. But look on the other side. There's a coat of arms etched in the gold. Are those the arms of the Baroness's family who was supposed to have run off with a Gypsy musician?"

"I don't know, but Rudolf would know. Perhaps if I showed him this locket, he could tell me."

Gyuri gave his sister a mocking little bow. "And suppose you find out you're the daughter of a Baroness. What will I have to call you? Your Highness? Madame Baroness? What?"

Chokolade laughed. "Don't be a fool, Gyuri. I am still Chokolade, that's what I'll always be. Chokolade, the finest Gypsy dancer in Europe, and that's all I want to be."

"You may not find it so easy to stay Chokolade, the Gypsy dancer, once you find out who you really are. Maybe it would be better not to know."

"Nonsense, nothing will change. Come with me to Vienna. I'll always be your *prala*—you'll see."

"Yes, I'll see."

Chokolade felt much happier about the trip to Vienna than she had about the trip to Budapest she had made a short time before. Fekete Andras was free, and soon she might find out the truth about her mother and about herself.

She opened her house in Vienna, and then tried to send word to the Crown Prince that she had returned.

"Things have changed," Count Hoyòs told her when she asked him to let Rudolf know that she was back in Vienna. "I'm not saying the Crown Prince is a prisoner in his own palace, but the Emperor is very angry with him. There have been too many scandals, too much gossip about the Crown Prince and Stephanie divorcing."

"Divorce! But Rudolf told me that such things were impossible. Has he fallen in love with an opera singer, this time, or is it a ballet dancer?"

"Neither," Count Hoyòs said evasively. "But I shall tell him that you have returned. He talks of you frequently, Chokolade. I know he'll be happy to see you again."

That night the discreet coachman Bratfisch pulled up before Chokolade's house once again, and Prince Rudolf walked quickly into the house.

"Bratfisch again! I thought by now the Crown Princess would have sent him to exile somewhere— where do you exile people who displease you, Rudolf? Siberia? Or is that reserved for Russians?"

Rudolf frowned. "Stephanie won't do that again. I can't force her to return to Belgium, but she can't force me to live with her."

Chokolade sighed. The same sad foolishness.

Count Hoyòs was wrong. Nothing had changed at the Viennese Court, and nothing ever would. Chokolade served the Crown Prince a very special Tokay wine she had brought back from Hungary.

"No champagne tonight?"

"This is the champagne of my country," Chokolade said. "Please try it."

Rudolf took a few slow sips. The wine was golden in color and seemed to be heavier than most wines, but it wasn't sweet or cloying.

"Golden in color, and golden in taste," he murmured. "What is it?"

"A wine so special that only a few bottles of it are made each year. I understand that the Empress Maria Theresa once sent some bottles to the Pope, and he responded by rewarding her with a very important order given only to a few people who do great things for the Church."

Rudolf laughed and took another sip. "The Pope was right. This wine deserves a medal, and so do you for bringing it to me." He looked at her over the rim of his glass. "Is that what you were doing in Budapest? Searching for fine wine?"

Chokolade longed to tell him the truth, but she knew that in this case, danger shared was not danger halved.

"Not exactly. I was searching for something else—my mother." Chokolade unfastened the locket from around her neck. "My brother gave this to me. Does it mean anything to you?"

Rudolf took the delicate locket from Chokolade and held it up to the light. "It's the coat of arms of the Pavonyi family. I don't think there can be any

297

doubt now, Chokolade. It was a young Baroness Pavonyi who ran off with a Gypsy. The family tried to hush up the story, and they said that she died. It didn't take long for the true story to get around Vienna. You know how everyone loves to gossip in this city."

"Oh, yes."

"Well, they had a marvelous time with that story. Baroness Pavonyi—convent-raised—and then right after her debut at court she meets a Gypsy, a musician, and she runs off with him. Naturally, the family disowned her."

"Naturally," Chokolade said coldly. "How old was she when she ran off?"

Rudolf shrugged. "Seventeen, eighteen at the most."

Chokolade bit her lips, and she was more surprised than Rudolf to find herself crying. "That poor girl, that poor girl."

"Yes," Rudolf said, "that poor girl. That's the way I would look at it, too. But these people," he said bitterly, "you don't know these people."

"These people?"

"The people of the court. They care for nothing but keeping up appearances. They don't care about love—about happiness."

Who was he talking about, Chokolade wondered? About a seventeen-year-old girl, abandoned by her family because she did something they could never approve of, or about himself?

"I hope she was happy," Chokolade murmured, "if only for a little while."

Rudolf's hand covered hers. "I hope so, too. As

you say, if only for a little while. And Chokolade, a little bit of happiness is worth everything—everything! It's worth any sacrifice. Better that drop of happiness than a life dry and dusty without love."

Chokolade took the locket from Rudolf. She stared at the picture again. "I wonder—I wonder."

"I think you can stop wondering," Rudolf told her. "I'm sure that you're Baroness Pavonyi's daughter. This locket proves it. And you can see how it changes your life."

"No, I don't see that at all. Why should it? Do you think the Pavonyi family is suddenly going to claim me as long-lost kin?"

"The Pavonyis are dead," Rudolf informed her. "But you are still part of an old, distinguished family. You're entitled to a good life—a good marriage."

"A good marriage? You mean to someone with money? Someone who also comes from a distinguished family? You say this to me?" Her voice rose sharply. "And what about love?"

Rudolf looked tired. "We have to live in the world as it is. You can't go back to being a Gypsy dancer, it wouldn't be right."

"I'll go back to dancing if I wish."

"Yes? And who do you think will come to see you? People who care about you as a dancer, an artist? No, they'll come because they want to see the illegitimate daughter of Baroness Pavonyi, because they'll be excited by your story. They won't care about you—they'll only care about the scandal in your past."

"That wasn't my scandal," Chokolade cried out.

"It won't matter to the people who love to talk and live on gossip. I tell you, Chokolade, you won't be a dancer to those people, you'll be a freak, like someone in a circus sideshow."

Chokolade cried out, his words had stabbed her. She had always been so sure of herself as a dancer, so proud of her talent, proud of what she could make people feel, the emotions she created in her audience. If the discovery about her parentage was to take that away from her, it would have been better if she had never learned the truth about her mother.

"I will dance again," she said stubbornly, "I will," but her voice broke, and Rudolf put his arms about her and held her just as he would have held a small, hurt child.

"It is not always necessary to make big decisions," he said soothingly. "You might fall madly in love with someone you meet at court, and then the decision will be made for you."

Chokolade looked up at him. Yes! To fall in love, truly in love. To love someone so much that all past memories would be wiped out, the memories of the Hussar captain, and even the memories of the week she spent with Rudolf at Mayerling. She wasn't ashamed of those days with Rudolf, but yet—yet—if she were to love someone she would like it to be with a new feeling, with a heart so whole that the past would be gone from her.

She took the handkerchief that Rudolf offered, and she wiped her eyes.

"Do you think so? Do you think it's possible to fall in love like that?"

"Yes," Rudolf said. "I think it is possible. I know it is."

Before he left that evening Rudolf told Chokolade that he would have Count Hoyòs bring her an invitation for a ball that was to be held the following week.

"It's the biggest ball of the season," he said, "the ball before Lent. Who knows? You may meet your Prince Charming there."

Chokolade smiled. She could have told Rudolf that he was her Prince Charming—she knew that most women would have said that—but she and Rudolf were beyond courtly gestures and polite flirtations. They were beyond lies; it was as though the week they had spent together in deep sensuality had stripped away all facades.

"I will come," she said.

"I have to open the ball with Stephanie"— Rudolf grimaced—"but I trust you will save a dance for me."

The night of the ball Chokolade dressed with special care. Her ball gown was made of silver tissue fabric, and the neckline continued off the shoulder into tiny sleeves. Her eighteen-inch waist was accentuated by a full skirt that ended in a small, but definite, rounded train.

"A train." Gyuri was stretched out on her bed, the heels of his boots making indelible indentations in the white satin coverlet. "I thought it was incorrect for anyone but the Empress and the Crown Princess to wear a train. Are you sure you know what you're doing?"

Chokolade whirled before the mirror, her green

eyes sparkling. "So they say, but this isn't really a train. Not really. It's just—"

"Just a rather long dress that wasn't hemmed properly."

Chokolade laughed with him, and then she looked guiltily at his long, lounging figure stretched out so casually on her bed.

"I'm sorry Rudolf didn't send an invitation for both of us."

"Don't think of it," Gyuri said. "I wouldn't be happy at a court ball, and I have plenty of opportunity to meet the interesting ladies of the court."

"You do? How? Where?"

Gyuri shrugged. "Do you think they're always bowing and scraping at court? The Viennese Court is a pretty dull place from all I hear, and after everyone makes a command appearance, they go on to other places. The restaurants, the cafés. I've had three offers to appear as a dancer this very week. Of course, I must say that being your half brother was some help."

It is just the way Rudolf said it would be, Chokolade thought with a pang, they're not interested in Gyuri's dancing. They want to see him because he's my half brother—another freak— someone to gossip about. But Gyuri seemed so pleased at the many offers that he had received that she said none of that to him.

"And have you met many charming, titled ladies in these cafés and restaurants?" she asked him.

Gyuri shrugged. "I've met many, yes. But, you know—since Magda Meleki, there have been lots of women, but they're not—not—"

"I know," Chokolade murmured, "I know."

"You do?" Gyuri looked surprised. "You have felt that way, too? But who was there for you—I mean—"

Chokolade didn't answer him. Never for the world would she tell him about Sandor St. Pal. She would go to her grave with that secret buried with her. She merely shrugged, and looked at her silvery image in the mirror once again.

"Of course," Gyuri said, and his voice was filled with pity. "Of course—the Prince—"

Chokolade started to say that it wasn't the Prince—that it had never been the Prince, but then she remained silent. It was better for her brother to think that her heart was broken over the impossibility of Prince Rudolf than he should know the shameful truth.

"I'm sorry Chokolade," Gyuri said with a new gentleness, "but maybe someday there will be someone else."

Chokolade smiled at her brother, and said nothing. She took a necklace of pear-shaped diamonds and clasped it around her throat. She wore no other jewelry, and carried in her hand a glittering silver mask that would cover the upper part of her face. She held the mask up, and turned to her brother. Her green eyes sparkled, surrounded by the silver mask.

She was semi-masked, true, Gyuri thought, but with those cat eyes and with that supple body that was accentuated rather than hidden by her gown, everyone at the ball would know that this was Chokolade.

He studied the silver-and-diamond-jeweled

figure for another moment.

"The Ice Queen," he said with a little smile, "but you weren't like ice to everyone, were you, Chokolade?"

Oh, yes, that was the brother she recognized. "Not to everyone. I can be warm enough. Just like you, my *pral*. Just like you."

Gyuri licked his full lips. *Pral*—brother. True, he was her brother—half brother, anyway. And that was a fact he had regretted more than once. What a pair they would have made if they hadn't been related. Oh well, there were plenty of other women in the world, and he was sure to meet one or two interesting—and interested—ones after the ball. Gyuri had learned that an elaborate court function where everyone had to be on their best behavior brought out exciting emotions in many women.

They could touch at a ball, and be touched, but the touching was limited to the formalities of the dance, and most women were eager for more than that—especially after they had been excited by the heat and the flirtations of many dancing partners. Gyuri had satisfied that eagerness more than once. He would go to the Café Luxus after Chokolade left for Schönbrunn, and he knew that in a little while he wouldn't lack for company.

Rudolf had sent Count Hoyòs to escort Chokolade to the ball, but she wasn't the center of interest the way she had been when Rudolf had first introduced her to court. The Crown Princess was also present, and the shrewd members of the Viennese court understood that they would fall out of favor with the Princess if they made too much of a fuss over a girl who was still only a Gypsy dancer, even though her mother had been a baroness.

Then, too, Rudolf was not constantly at Chokolade's side as he had been in the past. The Court was accustomed to the fickleness of their Prince, and if this meant that Rudolf was no longer interested in Chokolade, well then, neither were they. None of them could know, or understand, that Rudolf feared it was his interest that prevented Chokolade from entering the life he wanted for her.

Rudolf wanted Chokolade to be regarded as more than his temporary bed partner. He wanted the girl to be treated with respect, and he believed that the only way he could accomplish this was by acting with courtesy rather than with sexual interest.

"I expect you to dance with Chokolade," Rudolf instructed Prince von Coburg and Count Hoyòs.

The men bowed their acquiescence, and helped fill out Chokolade's dance card.

"How many times have we been through this before?" Count Hoyòs asked Phillip of Coburg, meaning that this was far from the first time they had to deflect the interest of a lady from their fickle Prince.

"I know," Prince Phillip agreed, "but this girl—I didn't think Rudolf would ever tire of this one." He stared at Chokolade across the ballroom floor. She looked like a silvery dream, her diamonds sparkling even more as they were reflected by the hundreds of chandeliers and wall sconces that dripped crystal tears around the ballroom. "I don't think she would bore me—no, not at all."

"Be careful," Joseph Hoyòs warned, and when Phillip turned, they both bowed to Crown Princess Stephanie.

"That girl"—she had noticed the woman they had been staring at—"who is she?"

Count Hoyòs coughed and murmured, "A daughter of the late Baroness Pavonyi, I believe, Your Highness."

Stephanie's thin lips became even thinner. *How dare Rudolf invite that woman to a ball she was attending?* But then she remembered her father's constant and cold refusals to allow her to return to Belgium. There were other ways she could cope with this situation, and in her heart she experienced one wonderful and secret pleasure: if she was miserable in her marriage, she knew that Rudolf was even more miserable. They could never divorce, but someday she would be the Empress, and then she would run this dissolute Viennese Court with a firm hand, and Rudolf would have to rule beside her for the rest of his life. That would be his punishment; it was the only thing that made her happy.

Chokolade had been dancing; as one partner bowed, and thanked her for the honor of the dance, the next partner appeared at her side, with a small bow of his own. It was all too planned and perfect, too automatic, and Chokolade thought with longing of the cafés where she could kick her shoes off and dance to wilder music.

It was too much, too polite, too cold, and leaving her partner in the middle of the dance floor and before her next partner could claim her, she picked up her skirts, and moved quickly across the gleaming ballroom floor. Her destination was the French doors that opened outward into the garden.

Air, she thought, I must have some fresh air. And she wondered if she could reach her coach by way of the garden. If so, she would go home, or try to find her brother. Anything was better than remaining at the palace.

As Chokolade moved across the floor, her reflection was repeated a hundred times in the floor-to-ceiling mirrors that covered the walls of the ballroom. She flashed across the room like a streak of silver.

There was one man who had been talking to his dancing partner and laughing happily; or at least he had thought he was happy until he had seen that reflection in the mirror. And it wasn't just one reflection, it was a reflection repeated over and over again.

Once would have been quite bad enough, but to see that face, that figure over and over again made him gasp. For a moment he thought he was dreaming, because that same face and body had appeared in his dreams so many times over the past months. His nights had been haunted by this very reflection. He pulled himself erect and remembered where he was. This was no dream created to mock him.

"Please excuse me." Sandor St. Pal bowed to the girl he had been talking to and walked off. She responded with a small gasp of fury.

Unheard of! A man didn't abandon a girl in this fashion; he stayed until her next partner came to claim her. But there was this fool of a captain of the

Hussars practically racing for the garden as though he had seen a ghost. No wonder he had been stationed at some small outpost of the Empire! With manners like that, they should never have allowed him to return to Vienna. She ruffled the feathers around the neckline of her white gown, and looked after St. Pal like an angry swan. But Sandor St. Pal wasn't aware of her look or her anger. He only knew that he had seen a girl who looked remarkably like Chokolade, and he had to find her.

Outside, Chokolade paused at the edge of the wide, flagstone terrace, and looked down at the garden laid out in formal tiers at her feet, the hedges trimmed into topiary shapes. Silly, to cut those bushes into neat shapes. Perfectly fine growing things were cut into pyramids, cubes, and round balls, and one hedge was even shaped into the form of an unbelievably large peacock, its fan of a tail spread out in a mass of green privet leaves. *Gajos*— why couldn't they leave things and people as God had meant them to be?

"It is you, my God, it is." She felt a rough hand on her shoulder, and she was spun about to face a tall man in the dark-blue-and-gold dress uniform of His Emperor's Royal Hussars.

Chokolade's hand flew to her mouth, but she couldn't quite stifle one small scream. Each of them took one step forward—a step that placed them that much closer to each other; it was a step taken out of desire, but the next step was based on thought and both Chokolade and Sandor St. Pal took a quick step back.

"What are you doing here?" St. Pal demanded. "Are you crazy? How did you get in? If anyone finds out, they'll arrest you—throw you in jail—not that you don't deserve it! You and that other damn Gypsy almost killed me."

Damn him, damn him, Chokolade thought. He always aroused conflicting emotions in her. His first words told her that he was concerned about her, and that he didn't know anything of what had happened to her since that time in his barracks. But immediately afterward, she was furious with him for even suggesting that she belonged in jail. He was the one who should go to jail! He was the one who had raped her, and kidnapped her, and now he had the audacity to accuse her of a crime.

She wanted to blurt out, "Are you all right? I was so worried," but the words that came out were, "How dare you talk to me that way? You don't know who I am!"

"Oh, I know who you are, all right," St. Pal said. "A little Gypsy witch who gave me this." He touched his hand to the streak of white that now ran through his dark hair. "And I know why you're here, too. Lots of jewels around here tonight. But you're crazy if you think you can actually rob the guests of the Royal Family. And where did you get that?" His fingers flicked her diamond necklace.

Chokolade retreated even further as she felt his fingers against her skin.

"How dare you!" It had been a long time since anyone had spoken to Chokolade except with respect. And now—and now this oaf dared to talk to her as though she were a girl of the streets! Not even Prince Rudolf would presume so. "I want you to apologize to me—"

"Apologize—"

"Yes! And if I wanted to, I could make you do it on bended knees. I know the people to make you do just that."

The Captain threw his head back and roared with laughter. The audacity of this girl. She truly was wonderful. Here he had caught her in a situation that could result in a jail sentence for her, and she tried to carry it off by acting like an indignant princess.

"Apologize! To a little Gypsy bitch?" He reached out for her. "There are still many things I want to do to you, many lessons I want to teach you, but apologize—" He pulled her to him, and once again Chokolade felt his strong arms around her.

"No." She struggled, even though she knew that a part of her wanted to give in, a shameful part wanted to be his slave once more. But she was more than just a little Gypsy dancing girl—much more— and knowing that she could never make him believe it if she didn't believe it herself, her struggles intensified. She turned her head as his mouth came close to hers, but she knew that if he hadn't been gripping her tightly by the shoulders, she might have fallen to the ground, so strongly did his physical presence affect her.

"No"—*she must never give in to this man*—"no!" And her voice rose to a scream.

"Chokolade, what is this? Captain!"

Sandor St. Pal turned, and his eyes met those of Crown Prince Rudolf, the heir to the throne, and the next Emperor of Austro-Hungary.

Sandor St. Pal released Chokolade so quickly that she stumbled, but it was Rudolf who moved quickly to her side, it was Rudolf who offered her his arm, and it was Rudolf who glared at the Hussar captain.

"Disgraceful," Rudolf said quietly, but with unmistakable fury. "This is not the time to ask how you dare behave this way at the Schönbrunn Palace, but you can be sure your superior will hear of this. Chokolade, my dear, are you all right?"

And Sandor St. Pal was treated to the sight of the Crown Prince holding Chokolade tenderly.

"I'm quite all right, Your Highness," Chokolade said, and at that moment she understood what would be the finest revenge of all. "You will pardon this—this man," she said, looking up at the Prince. "Too much champagne, I imagine; it led him to believe I was someone he once knew."

Rudolf frowned. "Hussar officers are not supposed to get drunk and make such mistakes."

"Please?" Chokolade smiled up at him. "Won't you forget the whole incident? For me?"

Rudolf returned her smile. "For you, of course." But he turned around and glared once more at Sandor St. Pal. "Lucky for you the Baroness Pavonyi has asked me to forgive you."

Baroness. Sandor St. Pal felt his face go hot, and he bowed.

"Well?" Rudolf's voice was sharp once again. "No words of thanks for the Baroness? I must say, we are letting strange men serve in the Royal Hussars."

"Baroness"—and St. Pal felt the words stick in his throat—"my humble apologies."

St. Pal saw the look of triumph on Chokolade's

face as she swept back into the ballroom on Rudolf's arm. *On your knees,* she had said, and she had just about done that to him, the Gypsy witch. He was still on his feet, but in every other way she had certainly brought him to his knees.

Rudolf was angrier than Chokolade as they entered the ballroom again.

"Who was that fellow? Do you know him?"

Rudolf felt Chokolade tremble slightly as she answered, "Yes, a long time ago—before I arrived in Budapest. I danced at the Meleki Palace in Sárospatak, and he was there."

"Infernal nerve," Rudolf said. "This is just the sort of thing I was worried about, Chokolade. I'm afraid you've become too famous to return to the life you knew before we met.

"You must get married. You must have a man who will give you his protection, and his name."

Sandor St. Pal's words were still ringing in Chokolade's ears: *Gypsy bitch,* he had called her, and told her there were other lessons that he wanted to teach her. He felt nothing for her. Oh, he would be happy enough to have her in his bed once again, that was clear. In his bed to use and abuse as he had done once before. She had to forget this man, get him out of her mind. She had to destroy the weakness that made her whole body feel fevered when he touched her.

She looked up at Rudolf standing so straight and tall beside her. He was the only other man she had felt something for, the only man who seemed truly caring. She knew they couldn't marry, but why was marriage so important? As long as she had Rudolf as a protector she would be all right.

"My Prince"—her arm entwined within his pressed closer—"must I marry? As long as I have you?"

Coldly and deliberately, Rudolf loosened Chokolade's arm.

"Have you heard that saying, 'Never put your trust in princes'? You mustn't trust me too much, Chokolade, because before I am a man I must play the part of a prince."

Chokolade felt her face flush. First Sandor St. Pal had called her a bitch, and now Rudolf was clearly indicating that he was getting tired of her. She was beginning to understand the battle of life just a little bit better; men and women both used each other, although in different ways. Very well, if that was the way life was meant to be, she wouldn't be the one to try and change it.

She looked up at the Prince. "What would you suggest I do?" And her voice was every bit as cold as his.

"Princes do not make suggestions, they give orders."

Chokolade bit her lips. "And you expect me to follow your orders?"

"Yes. Especially when I tell you that my orders are for your own good."

Chokolade looked away from Rudolf and out at the sea of dancers. It wouldn't do for him to see that her eyes were filling with tears. She would never want him to know that he could make her cry. She blinked and the dancers moved and whirled before her. The womens' gowns made patterns of color across the floor, highlighted by the black-and-white evening clothes of the men, and accentuated by the dress uniforms of the officers and the scarlet sashes displayed proudly across white-linen shirt fronts. It took a few more seconds for Chokolade's eyes to clear, until she felt that she could see everything clearly—quite clearly.

"Very well, Your Highness." Her cold formality almost made Rudolf wince. "And your orders are?"

Rudolf didn't enjoy Chokolade's tone or words, but he was determined to do what was best for her, even though she was slow to recognize it. He raised his eyebrows, and gave a slight nod. In seconds both Count Hoyòs and Prince Phillip von Coburg were at his side.

"Your Highness?"

"Count Friedrich von Kaplow, didn't I see him tonight?"

"Yes, Your Highness. He's just returned from Galicia and grateful to be back in Vienna."

"Perhaps we can make him feel more grateful still," Rudolf said. "You may bring him to me."

The Count and the Prince moved swiftly around the ballroom, and it was Count Hoyòs who returned first with Count Friedrich von Kaplow at his side.

"Your Highness"—Count Friedrich's bow was low and respectful—"you do me the honor of asking to see me."

"Count Von Kaplow." Rudolf's smile was warm. "I am pleased to see you here tonight. It has been a long time—too long for a man such as yourself to have been posted away from Vienna."

The Count smiled. "A week away from Vienna is too long, Your Highness."

"I especially wanted you to meet the Baroness Pavonyi," Rudolf continued. "Baroness, may I present Count Friedrich von Kaplow, better known to many friends as Fritzl, isn't that right?"

The Count bowed once again and he raised Chokolade's hand and brushed it very lightly with his lips.

"Now that I have met the Baroness, may I say that even a day away from Vienna would be too long."

Chokolade smiled at Count Fritzl. So this was the man that Rudolf had chosen for her. Well, why not? In his favor were his shock of blond hair and his Delft-blue eyes. Her life had been filled with dark-haired men: Sandor St. Pal, Prince Rudolf, even Fekete Andras. Maybe Count Fritzl was the change she so badly needed in her life.

"With Your Highness's permission"—Von Kaplow bowed again—"if I may ask the Baroness to leave your side for a short time, to honor me with a dance?"

Rudolf smiled his acquiescence, and Chokolade found herself on the ballroom floor in the arms of Fritzl von Kaplow. The Count was a fine dancer, though he held Chokolade more tightly than was usual at a formal ball.

He likes me, she thought, and it was quite apparent that he did. His blue eyes looked down into her green ones, and gradually but quite unmistakably, his arm tightened around her waist. Chokolade could feel the warmth of his hands right through his white gloves and the fabric of her dress. Chokolade, quite aware of what the Count was doing, didn't resist the increased pressure of his hands. Was this the man Rudolf had chosen for her? Very well. What did it matter, this or another, it was all the same to her. The Count's manner was formal, but the pressure of his body against hers wasn't. After the waltz, he quite properly bowed and led her back to where Prince Rudolf was standing.

"It was a great pleasure," he murmured, and once again Chokolade felt his lips brush her hand, "and a great honor," he said to Rudolf, before he retreated with yet another bow.

"Well?" Rudolf asked Chokolade.

"As Your Highness said," Chokolade bit down on the words, "princes give orders and the rest of us must obey them."

Across the room, and only when he was sure he was far from Rudolf's gaze, Count Friedrich von Kaplow was making his own inquiries.

"Baroness Pavonyi?" one of his Viennese friends said with a little smile. "You mean you don't know who she really is? Let us take a walk on the terrace. It's a delicious story."

The two men strolled on the stone terrace that stretched out before the windows of the ballroom, and Fritzl von Kaplow listened with great interest. It didn't bother him that the girl was half Gypsy, and not a real baroness, or even a legitimate member of the family of Pavonyi. Nor did it bother him that she was obviously still another woman whom Rudolf had used and was looking to pass along to one of his friends. If anything, that made matters more interesting; with Rudolf's reputation, this girl had to be something worthwhile in bed, and it could only help his career if he could do his Prince a favor.

He smiled, and nodded to the friend who walked beside him regaling him with juicy bits of gossip, mostly invented, about Chokolade.

"Yes," Fritzl von Kaplow said, "I shall call on the Baroness Pavonyi tomorrow."

"Baroness! After all that I just told you?"

"Because of all that you have just told me."

Chapter XIV

"Yes, yes, he seems nice enough," Chokolade was saying to Count Hoyòs, who had come one afternoon to take coffee with her. "But what of it?"

Count Hoyòs took the small cup of white Meissen porcelain filled with inky black coffee, and waved away the minuscule silver sugar tongs.

"His Highness is very interested in your opinion of our Fritzl."

"His Highness has known Count von Kaplow far longer than I," Chokolade replied. "I don't see why my opinion should matter at all."

"Ah, but it does." Count Hoyòs stirred his coffee slowly. "Your opinion of Fritzl will greatly affect the man's future army career."

"I didn't realize that I was all that important. Does Rudolf regard me as some sort of military objective?"

God, she's beautiful, Hoyòs thought, *all fire.* He could understand a man's desire to get her into bed, to see what she was really like flat on her back with her legs spread wide, and her body open and welcoming. He would have liked to have known her that way, too, but the price was too high. He had willingly followed Prince Rudolf into other beds, but this time the Prince demanded that the next man to enjoy Chokolade also marry her. He took a sip of the strong coffee and looked at Chokolade over the rim of his cup. Diamonds, yes, a pair of matched Arabian horses, a small villa in Fiume, all that he would willingly give to bed the girl, but marriage to a Gypsy bastard—because that's what she really was—no, he put his cup down regretfully, the price was definitely too high.

"Well?" Chokolade was looking at him, and he realized he hadn't answered her.

"Prince Rudolf feels that if you are really interested in Fritzl von Kaplow he would do all in his power to make things easier for both of you. Fritzl is on leave, and he is due to go back to Galicia quite soon. But the Prince would certainly not want anything to disturb the course of true love, and if you do care for him—even a little bit—he will be happy to have Fritzl's orders countermanded, and arrange to have him posted in Vienna."

The man was so smooth he was disgusting, Chokolade decided. It was all a game to him, a game that he obviously enjoyed playing.

"Is this usual?" she asked sweetly. "Does the Prince generally countermand orders for lovesick officers?"

Count Hoyòs was suddenly serious. "The Prince cares about your welfare, Baroness Pavonyi, and he wishes to do all he can to insure your happiness. He knows you have no family, and he is acting in the capacity of one. Let us say that changing Fritzl's orders would be his dowry to you."

"Dowry!" Chokolade was pacing the salon, the sweep of her long, mauve skirt almost sending the coffee table crashing to the floor. "I need no dowry—I need nothing. There is no need for me to marry, if I don't wish to do so. I have made my way as a dancer, and I can do so once again."

"The Prince doesn't think that would be advisable."

"I don't think it's advisable that everyone try to tell me what to do with my life—not even the Prince!"

"Then you wish me to tell the Prince—"

"I wish you to tell the Prince that I am not a foreign province to be conquered by the invincible Austrian Army. I am a person—a woman—with feelings, and I must be given time to explore those feelings."

"Feelings?" Count Hoyòs shrugged. "But we are talking about practical matters."

"My marriage must be based on something more than practical matters."

Count Hoyòs gave up, and went back to the Hofburg to report to Crown Prince Rudolf. "Perhaps if you were to talk to her," he suggested. "She has some romantic notions about marriage. I don't understand that at all. An experienced girl like Chokolade, one would think she would be more of a realist."

"Experienced." Rudolf turned on his aide. "What do you know of her experience?"

"Nothing, sir," Count Hoyòs said hastily. He was constantly forgetting that the Crown Prince wanted

everyone to regard Chokolade as a young girl who
had just made her debut. A young, sheltered girl
from a good family. But it was a little hard to forget
the week that Chokolade had spent locked in a
room at Mayerling with Rudolf. Especially when he
had been there.

"I shall talk to her," Rudolf said.

That was just the trouble, Chokolade felt,
everyone was talking to her—and at her. Everyone
but Friedrich von Kaplow himself. He had made his
proposal of marriage, and then he seemed quite
willing to let everyone else do the courting for him.
First it was Count Hoyòs, and then Rudolf himself
came calling.

"What do you mean, you'll go back to Budapest
and a dancing career?" he demanded. "You're
Baroness Pavonyi now, and you may not do such a
thing."

"May not?"

"May not, must not. And that's a command!"

"You Austrians," Chokolade said angrily, "that's
all you ever want to do—command Hungarians on
how they should live their lives."

Rudolf was startled. "What has that to do with it?
Where did you hear such talk?"

Chokolade was silent. She had heard it during
the short time she had spent with Fekete Andras,
but she had no wish to tell Rudolf about that.

"You sound like one of those Hungarian
revolutionaries," Rudolf said.

Chokolade didn't answer him, and Rudolf had
the terrible feeling that Chokolade might indeed be
mixed up in some revolutionary activity of the

Hungarians. Secretly he sympathized with them, and there was more than one rumor in Vienna that emissaries from Kossuth's new army had come to Rudolf, and asked him to become the ruler of Hungary—a Hungary that would be separated once and for all from Austria.

But they were just rumors; Rudolf would never have received such an emissary, no matter how he felt. His loyalties remained with his family—with the ruling house of the Austro-Hungarian Empire. Now he truly feared for Chokolade; he could protect her against almost everything, but he could never save her once she was involved with Kossuth's new army. More than ever, he knew that she had to marry Count von Kaplow.

"What have you got against von Kaplow?" Rudolf asked, wondering where he could find another aristocrat who would be willing to marry the illegitimate daughter of a runaway baroness and a Gypsy fiddler.

"I have nothing against him. I hardly know him."

Rudolf was relieved at her answer. "You can get to know each other once you marry. When can I tell Fritzl that he may announce your engagement?"

"I don't know," Chokolade cried out. "Why all this rush? Why can't I wait before I make such a big decision?"

Rudolf sighed. "Because I would like to see you married, settled. Can't you do this as a personal favor to me?"

"But why is it so important to you?"

"I won't always be around to protect you, Chokolade," Rudolf said. "And without me, or a husband, Vienna might not be a comfortable place for you."

"But why won't you be around? Where will you be? Can't I go with you?" Chokolade thought with longing of Mayerling. Life seemed so much simpler there than it was in Vienna.

"No," Rudolf answered sharply. "I may be taking a long trip quite soon, and you absolutely cannot come with me."

"You have a new love," Chokolade said bitterly, "someone else to take to Mayerling."

Rudolf said nothing, and Chokolade decided bitterly that he was no different from Captain St. Pal. They both used women as long as it pleased them, and then they went on to still other women with a casualness that made it quite clear that their feelings were not involved. Why should she expect anything more from Friedrich von Kaplow? He made very little effort to know her, even though he had asked her to be his wife.

But when she related her thoughts to Gyuri, he disagreed with her.

"That's how these aristocrats are, they're formal with a woman if they intend to marry her. You should be pleased that he's treating you this way. It shows that his intentions are the very best."

Chokolade laughed at that. "What can you know about good intentions?"

But Gyuri, too, had changed. He was also urging her to marry von Kaplow.

"It's time you settled down, Chokolade, had a regular life—a respectable home."

Chokolade gestured at the salon in which they

sat: there were Oriental rugs on the floor, and elaborately carved French furniture covered in rich silks graced every wall and corner.

"You don't think this home is respectable enough for me?"

"You know that's not what I mean. A woman alone—an unmarried woman—well, she's not considered to be quite nice, here in Vienna. Unless, of course, she's still living with her parents. That's what people say."

"Since when do we care about what people say? Gyuri, let's leave here, let's go back to Budapest. Let's dance together again."

But Gyuri evaded her eyes. "I don't want to leave Vienna. Not right now."

No one understood her, Chokolade decided, not even her brother. Suddenly she remembered that he was really her half brother. That had never mattered to her, but it suddenly seemed to be of great importance to him. She didn't care, she tossed her mane of dark hair away from her face. She would do as she pleased, not Rudolf, or Gyuri, or Fritzl von Kaplow could make her change her way of life.

It was Gyuri who reported the comments he heard in the cafés and restaurants about von Kaplow's proposal of marriage to Chokolade.

"You better say yes soon," he said gloomily, "or von Kaplow might change his mind."

"Why should he? What are you talking about?"

"His fellow officers are giving him a fine ribbing. Especially that St. Pal. He says why should von Kaplow marry you when he can have you in bed without marriage. What went on between the two of you, Chokolade? Of course, I knew some of it—but you never told me the whole story."

"Because there was nothing to tell. How dare that barbarian Hussar speak that way about me? I shall tell Rudolf."

But Rudolf was strangely unsympathetic. "Not even I have the power to stop every man in Vienna from talking about you, Chokolade. Marry von Kaplow. He's known to be an excellent hand with a rapier, and a dead shot with a pistol. Marry him, and no one will dare say another word."

But Chokolade was still not persuaded, and to escape from all the unwelcome urgings of marriage, she went riding one day in the woods near Vienna. It was only there that she felt a little freer. She was riding sidesaddle—a sop to Viennese proprieties— but as she felt the well-muscled horse stretching out beneath her, she could forget for a little while the restricted life that everyone insisted she accept.

There were other riders in the Viennese woods, but Chokolade never did more than nod to anyone as she rode along the pine-scented paths. That afternoon she heard the hooves of another horse approaching from behind, but she didn't turn, only guided her horse to the edge of the path so that the rider who seemed to be coming at a fast gallop could pass. Her horse's ears went back at the sound of the approaching horse, but Chokolade held the reins firmly with one hand, while with the other, she patted the horse's neck soothingly. It was while she was leaning forward, calming her horse, that the other rider drew abreast. Chokolade still didn't look up, she was so sure that the stranger was in a hurry to pass. But instead of doing so, the man reached out, gripped the reins of her horse, and pulled her animal up so short that Chokolade was almost thrown from the saddle. She was saved by leaning forward, and by gripping the horse's mane.

"You fool"—she turned in fury to the man who had ridden up beside her—"what are you trying to do?"

When she saw who it was, her throat tightened, and her heart started to pound. It was Sandor St. Pal. She was reminded of that night—it seemed a lifetime ago—when he had ridden after her on the Puszta, pulled her off her horse, and raped her. She felt a quiver of fear, but she knew instinctively that she must never let him see it. She swallowed, and forced herself to speak calmly.

"I repeat: what are you trying to do?"

Sandor St. Pal's face reddened. She hadn't reacted as he had expected. She had come a long way from the Gypsy girl he had once known; she had changed, and he didn't much like it. The memory of the way she had humiliated him in front of the Crown Prince was still strong, and he had ridden after her, planning revenge. But the girl he wanted was a Gypsy girl, wearing men's riding clothes, and letting her hair fly free behind her; this woman was dressed in an elegant sidesaddle habit, her black skirt covering the tops of her neat, highly polished, black leather boots. There was a white stock at her throat, and a ridiculous, but quite correct, top hat on her head. The wonderful long hair was tucked into a neat roll at the nape of her neck, and even though he held the reins of her horse, she looked at him like an abused princess who was still quite ready to command, and who expected to be obeyed.

"Yes?" she said.

Damn, he longed to pull her off her horse, and have her right there on the ground, just as he had taken her that first time. It was only the thought that she was under Rudolf's protection that stopped him.

St. Pal released the reins of her horse, and touched two fingers to his officer's peaked hat in a mock salute.

"It has been so long, I thought it would be pleasant to renew an old acquaintance—a warm, old acquaintance."

Chokolade shivered. His voice was enough to make a thousand memories flood into her mind.

"It was not an acquaintance that I desired," she said frostily, "and therefore not one that I would want to renew."

The Gypsy had even learned to speak like a lady, but underneath those fine words and those fine clothes, St. Pal was sure she was still a bitch whom he could warm in bed. He remembered her that one time when she hadn't been able to control herself, that one time when he had heard her moans, felt her body respond to his. He knew he was risking everything. She could report his words to Rudolf, and the Crown Prince would have him cashiered from the Hussars, but he didn't care, she was worth any risk.

"I think you're lying," he said softly but quite clearly. "I think you desire an acquaintance, all right—I think you desire much more. I don't care how many beds you've been in since I've last seen you, but I'll wager my commission that it's my bed, and what I did to you in it, that you remember, no matter who you go to bed with now."

Chokolade tried to urge her horse forward, but the Captain was blocking her path. "Oh, I remember—I remember being treated like a slave girl—made to do your every bidding—"

"Exactly," Sandor St. Pal said, "and that's exactly the way I'd treat you now, if I could. And do you know why?" He leaned forward, his face so close to Chokolade's that she trembled at his nearness. "I'd treat you the very same way because it's what you want—what you really want. Admit it, and come with me now. I still remember my promise to you, and I'm willing to keep it."

"What promise? I remember no promise."

"The promise that I would bring you to the capital and make you my mistress. Come with me now, and it's done."

The audacity of the man! That was the way he still saw her—his mistress—a woman to be kept for his pleasure in bed. Nothing had changed, nothing. She raised her leather riding crop, and would have brought it slashing across his face, if he hadn't captured her wrist, and closed his fingers so tightly about it that she cried out in pain.

"Still the same." He was actually grinning, amused at her anger. "That's what I thought. Still the little wildcat who needs to be tamed, and I'm the only man who can do it."

"You! You'll never have me in your bed,"

Chokolade spat at him. "I'm going to be married. Married—do you hear? To Count Friedrich von Kaplow."

Sandor St. Pal exploded with laughter. "I've heard that story, it's the dirty joke of every barracks between here and Budapest, but I don't believe it—I don't believe that von Kaplow could be fool enough to actually marry a little Gypsy dancer who's whored her way through the beds of the Empire. Some of the best beds, to be sure, but still."

His words cut through Chokolade's rage, and she became cold and determined. Rudolf had been right, after all. She would have to get married. Count von Kaplow would let no one speak about his Countess in such an ugly way.

"Let me pass, Captain," Chokolade said, and he was taken aback by her new and strange manner. He was accustomed to her anger, but he didn't know what to make of this quiet dignity.

"Chokolade." His manner changed to match hers. Perhaps he had gone too far—said too much.

"Let me pass."

The Captain's hand went to his cap, and this time there was nothing mocking in the salute he offered Chokolade. He reined his horse back, and she rode past him without a backward glance.

Look how she sits that horse, St. Pal thought. *Baroness Pavonyi! She rides like a baroness, that's for certain.*

No one ever knew that it was thanks to Sandor St. Pal that Chokolade agreed to marry Count von Kaplow.

* * *

"I'm glad she finally decided to take my advice," Rudolf said to Count Hoyòs.

"I'm glad you finally decided to take my advice," Gyuri said to his sister.

"I am pleased that you have consented to marry me," Fritzl said to Chokolade.

She smiled and nodded to all who congratulated her, but all the time she was thinking, *I'll show him, I'll show him. And once I'm married, I'll be able to forget him. Fritzl will destroy my memories of Sandor St. Pal forever, I'm sure he will.*

Everyone seemed pleased at Chokolade's decision—everyone except the von Kaplow family.

"Are you insane?" Frizl's father asked him. "A woman like that, a woman who is no better than one of those painted beings a man can buy on the street for a night's use."

"Father," Fritzl said, "you're talking about my future wife."

"I know what I'm talking about. Do you want this woman so much that you're willing to give her the von Kaplow name? That's what I can't understand. If you must have her, set her up in a private villa on the outskirts of the city. Keep her as long as you wish, and then get rid of her. But once you marry her, it's forever, don't you know that?"

Fritzl smiled slowly. "I do know that. It's the word *forever* that appeals to me. A man can do so much more with a wife than he can with a mistress, isn't that so, Father?"

His father stared at him. "I don't understand you, Fritzl."

For a moment Fritzl had been afraid that he had

said too much, but his father's words reassured him, and to placate the old man Fritzl reminded him that he was really acting to obey the Crown Prince's request.

This was the one factor that Fritzl's father could understand and sympathize with. This hadn't been the first time that the von Kaplow family had been asked to do something unsavory for the ruling family. He could remember some romantic errands that he had to run for the Emperor himself, but whatever he was asked to do, it certainly never included marriage to a cast-off mistress. Even the Emperor wouldn't have gone that far. The old Count sighed; times had changed, and not for the better.

"Very well," he said, "if you say it was the Crown Prince himself—"

"It was."

"You must obey, I suppose it will be worth it to your career. But Fritzl, even though you will always be my son, despite this disastrous marriage, you cannot expect anyone in our family to receive this woman. Of course, you will always be welcome."

Fritzl nodded. He understood that his father was making a great concession. He had been afraid that the old man would disown him completely. As long as the von Kaplow family still recognized him as a member of the clan, he didn't really care whether or not they accepted Chokolade.

"I understand, Father, and I'm grateful."

The old Count accepted his son's dutiful kiss on the cheek. This was not the way he had thought his son would marry, certainly not; but then, in time much could happen even to a marrage. He had good friends at the Papal Court, and besides, perhaps Rudolf was planning to give Fritzl the command of the Viennese barracks. That would make this marital sacrifice quite worthwhile.

"Father," Fritzl said hesitantly, "about the wedding—"

"I don't wish to hear about it," his father replied. "I would not want all of Vienna to think that I approve of what you're doing—for whatever reason you're doing it."

"I understand."

Fritzl understood his father's motives, but Chokolade did not. Deep in her heart, she had been longing for a large, elaborate wedding. This would be the one and only time in her life that she would get married, and she wanted a glittering ceremony, an elegant reception, and the whole world to know that she was the Countess von Kaplow and expected the respect due that old name. Most of all, she wanted *him* to know—to acknowledge that, now, he could have no claim over her.

But none of this was to be. The wedding was held quietly—almost secretly—in a small church on the outskirts of Vienna. Gyuri was there, and Count Hoyòs appeared, bearing Rudolf's apologies at his inability to attend.

It was his idea, and now he's deserting me, was Chokolade's thought.

But Fritzl understood—or thought he did— Rudolf's decision. *He doesn't want a scene with this girl. I'm grateful that he sent Hoyòs, that shows he intends to do something for me in the future. I'm sure of it.*

Compared to the many gay and glittering fetes

that had been given in Chokolade's honor, the wedding was sadly disappointing. There was no one to raise glasses of champagne to the bride and groom, and there were only Gyuri and Count Hoyòs to wish them well.

Count Hoyòs nóticed that the new Countess von Kaplow seemed strangely pensive; she didn't show any of the joy or excitement generally seen in a new bride, but that was probably because it had been Rudolf she had been hoping to marry. Women get crazy ideas. But as for Fritzl, he seemed happy enough for the two of them. Hoyòs couldn't understand von Kaplow. He, too, wanted Chokolade in bed, but not at the price of marrying her.

"Where will you be honeymooning?" Hoyòs asked Fritzl as they left the church. "Abbazia is nice this time of year, but then, so is Monte Carlo."

Fritzl smiled. "I was not planning on a trip at all. My villa near Vienna is quite comfortable. Less tiring for my bride than a long journey, I should think."

My God, Hoyòs thought, *he's talking about Chokolade as though she were some delicate virgin. I hope he won't be too shocked.*

Chapter XV

BUT CHOKOLADE APPRECIATED Fritzl's tender care of her. The very way he handed her into his carriage, the manner in which he escorted her into the villa that was to be her new home showed his regard for her.

The servants were standing in a double row in the center hall of the house when Fritzl and Chokolade arrived. Their bows were respectful enough, but Chokolade caught the avid glances that followed her. Of course they would be curious, curious about their new mistress.

A maid stepped forward. "If I may help the Countess unpack?"

"Not now." Fritzl was strangely brusque. Chokolade hoped that he didn't make a practice of speaking so abruptly to his servants. "There will be plenty of time to unpack later on. Right now all we will want is some champagne."

"It is already upstairs," the butler said, stepping forward.

Count von Kaplow merely nodded his thanks, and with his hand firmly beneath Chokolade's elbow, he led her upstairs. The servants exchanged glances, but only when they were safely below stairs did they dare speak openly.

"He's really eager to get that one into bed," the seemingly demure maid said.

"They say she was a great dancer," the butler commented, "and those dancers—they know how to move in and out of bed."

Fritzl's valet, who had traveled with him from one outpost to another, and who knew his master better than anyone, grinned. "He'll teach her a few moves she never thought of, I can tell you that."

The suite of rooms that Fritzl took Chokolade to was strangely bare, the furniture dark and Germanic. Chokolade, who was accustomed to the French furniture that was in fashion in both Budapest and Vienna, was surprised at the lack of comfort in her husband's villa. It was nothing she couldn't change after awhile. Fritzl had probably inherited the dreary furnishings, and because he had lived away from Vienna for so long, he hadn't cared about making the villa a comfortable home.

"Come." Fritzl held his hand out to her from a doorway, and she followed him into the bedroom.

If anything, this room was even grimmer than the preceding salon. A massive bed dominated the center of the room, and a canopy of dark, maroon velvet dominated the bed. The drapes were dark, and the remainder of the furniture was black and highly polished; when Chokolade drew closer, she could see that the wood was carved with leering gargoyles and grinning devils.

"Fritzl," Chokolade said with a little laugh, "this

furniture—it looks as though it came from one of those terrible castles in Transylvania. Where did you get it?"

But Fritzl had closed the door behind him, and now he was staring at Chokolade. The slow smile she had seen so often on his face was not there. Suddenly, he seemed as serious—almost as grim— as the furniture.

"I didn't bring you here to discuss furniture," he said, "nor did I marry you to talk about castles in Transylvania."

He crossed the room and sat down on a plush-covered couch.

"Now," he said, "get undressed. Slowly. Let me see the merchandise that I have bought with my name and title."

"Fritzl"—Chokolade's heart started to pound— "have you gone mad? Why are you talking to me this way?"

"How did you think I would talk to you? As to some great lady? Is that how you see yourself? Well, that's not how I see you. I see you as the Prince's whore, a whore who was able with the clever use of her body to get herself named a baroness. And now you're a countess—a real one, this time. I want to see you use your body with cleverness once again. I want payment for making you Countess von Kaplow."

Chokolade ran to the door. She tried the knob, and discovered that Fritzl hadn't only closed the door, he had locked it. She stood there, her back against the door, while her husband looked at her calmly.

"Open this door—open it, or I'll scream the house down."

"This is an old house. Scream if you wish, I doubt that anyone would hear you. But even if they should, they would know better than to come running. Dumma, my valet, wouldn't let them. Undress"—his voice had sunk to a whisper—"now."

"No," Chokolade said, her back still against the door, "no."

To her surprise, her refusal didn't enrage her husband.

"Good," he said, "I'm glad to see you have spirit. It will give me more pleasure to break you." He stood up, and held his hand out toward Chokolade. "Will you come willingly? No? Very well, then."

He moved toward her slowly. Chokolade wanted to run, but where? The door was locked, and both the bed and Count von Kaplow were between her and the tall locked and draped windows. For the first time in her life, fear paralyzed her. This was no Hussar captain who had kidnapped and taken her, and he was no Rudolf, who liked to play out his sexual fantasies with a willing partner. This was the man she had married, and in doing so, she had placed herself in deeper bondage than she had ever known before.

And then Fritzl was standing before her. With one hand he pressed her back against the door, and with the other he gripped the neckline of her gown and ripped downward. For a few seconds he merely stared at her half-nude body, at the breasts that seemed to offer themselves to him, free as they now were of the confinements of her dress.

And then he did more than stare, his hands formed themselves into claws and curved painfully around her breasts. Chokolade tried to wrench her body away from him, but he released her breasts only to press his entire body against hers. His mouth came down hard, and she felt his teeth biting her lips.

Fritzl was strong—for all his slim, blond boyish looks he was a stronger man than Chokolade would have thought. He removed his mouth from hers, and when Chokolade touched her tongue to her lips, she could taste the blood.

"Now," he asked, his arm pressing back against her throat so that she could hardly breathe, "will you do just as I say?"

"No," she choked out.

"Good. This gets better and better."

He stepped away from Chokolade, and gave her a back-handed slap across the face which sent her reeling to the floor. She tried to rise, but when she got as far as her knees he came up behind her and pulled her head back with a painful yank of her hair.

"On your knees, that's right, that's the way I want to see you."

Chokolade tried to get up again, but this time Fritzl pinioned her wrists together, and his booted right foot kicked at her bent knees so that Chokolade was flat on the floor. Grasping her wrists, her husband pulled her to the bed.

"No," Chokolade gasped, "please, no." She was sure that the bed would be a torture rack for her.

"I like that." Fritzl laughed with delight. "I like that 'please.' Oh, but this is just the beginning. Soon

I'll have you begging me."

"Never," Chokolade managed to choke the word out, "never."

For that Fritzl buffeted her face with two more slaps that brought tears to her eyes, and set her head ringing. While she was still dazed from the blows he pulled her upright, and then threw her on the bed. She tried to crawl away from him, but it was easy enough for him to pull her back by the ankles, just as it was easy enough for him to rip her clothes from her body. Her clothes came off in shreds, while Chokolade struggled beneath his hands.

He looked down at her nude body. "And the next time, when I tell you to undress for me, what will your answer be?"

"No," she screamed out, "no."

Fritzl roared with laughter, and Chokolade shuddered. It was the laughter of an insane man. Fritzl picked her up by the shoulders, and flung her back against the pillows.

"Now, I'm going to step away from this bed for just a moment. But don't move," he warned. "I can assure you it will be worse for you if you do. Your punishment will be even harder if you disobey."

Punishment! Of course Chokolade was not going to lie in bed meekly and wait for Fritzl. She had to get out—out of this room, out of this house, away from this man—she watched as he walked to a large wardrobe at one side of the room, and then wrapping the red velvet throw from the bed around her, she stepped off the bed and ran toward the windows. The windows, she discovered, were bolted with heavy iron latches, and as she struggled fruitlessly with a heavy iron bar, Fritzl came up behind her.

He grabbed at the velvet throw and wrenched it from her. "I warned you. Please remember, I did warn you."

That was when she saw the whip in his hand, and she was just able to throw her arm up to protect her face when he struck.

"Now," he said, "you will crawl, quite slowly, back into bed."

Chokolade didn't speak—she couldn't speak—but she was able to shake her head. Again she heard her husband's manic laugh, and again his whip came down on her naked body. Her back arched with pain, and the sight of that drove him to apply the whip again.

"Now," he said with slow relish, "crawl back to bed."

This time Chokolade obeyed him. She had no doubt that if she didn't, he would continue beating her until he killed her. But crawling on her hands and knees toward that bed of torture was not enough for Fritzl. He applied the whip to her back even as she moved painfully across the floor. When she reached the bed, Chokolade climbed onto it. She huddled there lying on her side, her knees pulled up against her chest, her arms crossed protectively over her breasts.

"Oh, no," Fritzl said, "that won't do. That won't do at all. On your back, that's how I want to see you. Flat on your back, and spread-eagled, open and waiting for me. Go ahead, do it!"

But that was too much. Even though Chokolade

knew that her refusal would cost her dearly, there was no way she could obey that humiliating order. She remained as she was, her arms gripped more tightly in front of her, her knees clamped together.

"Wonderful," Fritzl whispered, his eyes glowing insanely, "wonderful."

And then he struck, and struck again. Chokolade screamed and tried to roll away from the madman wielding the whip, but wherever she turned, he was there waiting, waiting to cut into her flesh with his whip.

It was only when she was exhausted from the pain, and no longer completely conscious, that her body relaxed. Only then could Fritzl place her body in the position he had demanded. Chokolade was partially aware that her legs were spread wide, and she tried to move her limbs together, but a blow from Fritzl's whip, applied to the inside of her thighs, made her moan, and weep with pain. She lay still after that, there was nothing else to do, and Fritzl took her as brutally as he knew how. He entered her, and moved in quick, sharp thrusts. It was a new kind of pain—a different pain—but a more terrible and intimate pain than he had inflicted on her with his whip.

"Nice," he gasped, "nice. This is how I like you, my wife, nice and quiet and obedient. Yes. This is the way."

Chokolade lay without moving during the long hours of the night. She would awake and be aware of the pain of her lacerated and abused body. She longed to get up, to run from this man she had married, but he had one arm and a leg flung across her body, and she was afraid to stir for waking him. She would snatch a few minutes of sleep, only to be awakened by the pain.

Next morning she looked with fear at Fritzl, but he bounded out of bed, pulled a dark silk robe about him, went to his bath, and afterward to his dressing room. Chokolade lay back dully on the heap of pillows. Obviously, he restricted his perverted performances to the night. She took a deep breath; she would spend no second night with her husband. She was only waiting for him to dress and leave the house, and then she would flee.

Fritzl came back into the bedroom once again. He was fully and elegantly dressed. By the light of day, he looked normal, ordinary, and quite like an elegant Austrian officer.

"Well?" he said, looking down at Chokolade. "No words for me this morning, my bride? No good-morning kiss?"

Chokolade turned her head on the pillow as his mouth came down toward hers, but he did nothing to force a kiss from her.

"That's all right," he murmured, pretending the solicitude of a bridegroom. "Last night tired you. I quite understand."

Chokolade opened her eyes wide and stared up at him. "You're mad," she whispered, "quite mad."

"Other women have said that to me before. Words do not bother me."

"Don't they? Perhaps words will bother you when I leave you and tell everyone just why I have done so."

Fritzl laughed. "Who do you think will care

about what happens in the privacy of our bedroom?
How do you think most of Viennese society enjoy
themselves? There are those little evenings at
Countess Marton's house where five men and five
women have the best of times enjoying each other's
wives and husbands. And then there's the old
general—you know the one I mean—he needs two
young girls to warm him up, and he always insists
that they be girls from some of our best families."

Fritzl stared down at Chokolade. He could see
that she was trembling beneath the sheet that was
drawn up closely beneath her chin, and the fear he
had caused pleased him.

"I'm a mild-mannered man—practically an old-
fashioned gallant—when you compare me to other
men and the little games they play in other fine
bedrooms in this city."

"I don't care, I don't care what anyone else does. I
won't live with you—not another day or night."

Fritzl shrugged. "You're the Countess von
Kaplow now. Where will you go? No one will be
interested in hearing your ravings about me, my
dear. The Viennese don't care what you do, as long
as you do it with discretion. They won't listen to
you, because almost everyone will have been guilty
of far worse actions than mine, and they know that I
know it.

"Oh, no, you have no place to run. You'll try to
expose me, but they'll be afraid that I might expose
them. Besides, I'm the Count von Kaplow, and,
when it comes down to it, they'll have to stand
solidly behind me. That's the way it always is," he
confided in a confidential manner. "The aristocrats

stand together, it's the only way we can survive. And what will your word be worth against mine? The word of a little Gypsy-bitch dancer against a von Kaplow. Ridiculous."

Trapped. He was telling her that she was trapped. The one thing that Gypsies feared more than anything else was prison, and she had been maneuvered into a prison, without her even realizing that it was one, until she had heard the gates clang shut behind her.

Fritzl sat down on the edge of the bed, while Chokolade cringed away from him. "But you don't have to worry too much. I like variety. Not even the effort of taming you can amuse me every night. There will be others." Again she saw that open, boyish smile. "Many others. Of course, you will have your turn. Oh, don't fear, I won't neglect you."

Chokolade had never been so frightened. It was probably best not to answer the man; she didn't yet know what could provoke him into a rage—but yet, she had to know. "Why did you marry me?"

"Why?" his eyebrows went up. "Because it amused me to do so. That's reason enough for doing something. I'm finding it harder and harder to find women who entertain me. I get tired of doing the same things. And you—you with your reputation— after all, you were Rudolf's mistress. I thought, how amusing to take her, to make her do whatever I want her to do!"

Chokolade bit her bruised lips hard. She wouldn't answer Fritzl, but he guessed her thoughts.

"Oh, I know. You think you *won't*. But I can make you do my will. Breaking a spirited woman is the best thing for taking the boredom out of life.

"And once I force you into doing exactly what I want, I'll make you do it with others. Other men, other women, in my bed, with me watching and directing every move. Oh yes, that should be quite entertaining."

He got up from the side of the bed, and actually took Chokolade's limp hand and raised it to his lips. He gave a little bow, again playing the part of the gallant, solicitous husband.

"I will leave you for today, my dear. I fear that last night might have fatigued you, and I don't want to weary my little bride."

Chokolade could hear his laughter as he left her room, closing the door quietly. The obscene sound floated back to her as he walked down the stairs and out of the villa. Only when she was sure he was gone did Chokolade ring for the maid. She would have the girl draw her bath, and then she would ask her to pack a few things. Once she was bathed and dressed she would leave the villa—leave Count Friedrich von Kaplow—forever.

But to her surprise, it was Fritzl's valet who answered her ring.

"Madame rang?" Dumma stood at the door, his grin slick and knowing.

"I rang for the maid," Chokolade said brusquely. "Where is she?"

"The Count suggested I attend to the Countess today." Dumma's words were as oily as his smile. "The Count feels that I may be of more assistance. I have had experience in these matters before."

This obscene man, Chokolade raged. It was plain

that her husband wouldn't mind if she entertained his valet in her bed—it was probably one of the amusements he had planned for her.

"Get out," Chokolade said, "get out!"

"But, madame." Dumma took another step into the room.

"Out," Chokolade shouted, "out!"

Dumma did not have the courage of his master. He bowed, and backed out. It didn't matter, he told himself as he went below stairs once again. He would have her yet, he was sure of that. The Count always gave him his women for at least one night after he was through with them. He had to. It was Dumma's payment for his silence. Not all of the Count's women had survived his assaults, but Dumma had never told anyone of the serving girls, the pretty peasants, who had disappeared from the various small towns where the Count had been stationed. He was silent, he was discreet, and the Count properly showed his gratitude.

Chokolade didn't ring again. She got out of bed, and moving painfully, she locked the bedroom door. She ran the water for a hot bath, but no matter how long she stayed in the tub, she felt she could never scrub herself clean. The hot water stung her lacerated flesh, but she didn't care, she wanted the water to cleanse her through and through. How else could she rid herself of the signs and marks that Fritzl had put on her body—the signs that showed she belonged to him.

For the rest of the day, Chokolade stayed huddled in the bedroom. She was sure that Fritzl would have instructed Dumma not to let her leave, and she was terrified of what he might do if she tried to run away. She had to think—to think—but she felt feverish. One moment she would be hot and burning, the next she was shivering with cold. She had to get out of this—out of the house, out of her marriage. She would run—run to Gyuri—run to Rudolf—they would protect her. She was sure that Fritzl was wrong—crazy—when he said that no one would listen to her. Everyone would listen, sympathize, but first she had to get away—get away before this madman killed her.

For the rest of that day, Chokolade remained behind a locked door. She wanted to run, but she also knew that her bruised body wouldn't let her run far.

Dumma brought her meals to her, but she refused to open the door to him. "Leave the tray at the door," she called out, trying to make her voice sound as imperious and as unafraid as possible, but she didn't open the door until she heard Dumma's retreating steps.

That night she half-slept behind her locked bedroom door. Half-slept because every sound brought her awake, shivering and frightened, huddled like a small child beneath the covers.

When she awoke the next day, some of her courage had returned. Fritzl hadn't returned, and that helped her. She was Chokolade, she kept telling herself. She was the Baroness Pavonyi, she was the girl who had been toasted and praised by half of Europe, and she would leave this house of pain and degradation.

Chokolade took the breakfast tray Dumma, or

someone, left by the door, and ate ravenously. She had hardly touched the food they had brought the day before, and she realized she was hungry. Besides, she knew that the food would give her strength. She had a large cup of strong, black Viennese breakfast coffee with frothy hot milk. Then she ate two small crescent rolls which she spread liberally with sweet butter and apricot jam. Her appetite amazed her, but anger was slowly replacing fear, demanding extra energy.

After breakfast Chokolade dressed quickly. She would take nothing with her, she decided. She would be able to move more quickly if she carried nothing, and if any of the servants saw her, it would seem as though she were just leaving to pay a morning call. What would she do if she ran into Dumma, and if he tried to stop her from leaving the house? Chokolade didn't know, but she would face that menace if it happened. And as her courage returned, so did her faith in herself. She must never forget who she was, and whether people called her a Gypsy dancer or a baroness, she had enough pride and bearing to cope with a cowering servant.

The one thing she hadn't planned on, however, was having to face Fritzl that same morning. Her courage had come from the fact that he had been gone a day and a night, and she believed that she would be able to leave the house without seeing him again.

It was when Chokolade was adjusting her small maroon hat with the coq feathers that she had heard someone try the knob of the bedroom door. That man Dumma, she thought, he's impertinent!

"Yes?" And she was pleased that her voice sounded firm and unafraid. "Yes? What is it?"

"Open this door, Chokolade, open this door." But it was Fritzl's voice, not Dumma's she heard, and his voice was slurred and thick.

Once again Chokolade felt the tightening in her throat, the spasm of fear.

"Come on." His booted feet kicked at the door panel. "Let me in. Dumma, bring me the keys!"

Chokolade sat down on the bed, trying to stop trembling. There was no way she could stay barricaded in the bedroom. Dumma would bring Fritzl the keys; besides, she could never get out until she opened the door, passed Fritzl, walked down the stairs, and out the front door. She would have to do it, and she would have to do it in such a way that he never realized how deeply afraid she was.

Chokolade took a deep breath and stood up. Her shoulders went back, her head was high. She walked slowly to the door, and just as slowly, she unbolted the lock.

"Yes?" she said. "What do you want?"

But it was one thing to feel brave behind a closed door. It was another to face the man who had brutalized her—the man who now stood at the door, his arm thrown around the shoulders of a young army officer.

"You don't lock doors in this house," Fritzl said, and he gave Chokolade a backward push into the room. "You are not permitted to lock a door against me, do you understand?"

Thank God he isn't alone, Chokolade thought. He wouldn't dare abuse her in front of another man and a fellow officer. Hadn't he spoken about discretion to her just yesterday morning?

"What do you want?"

Fritzl stumbled past her, and threw himself on the bed. He was very drunk, had probably been drinking since he had left her yesterday morning.

"First I want slivovitz. Dumma, some slivovitz!" He tried to focus his eyes on the young officer who had come into the bedroom with him. Chokolade could see that he was just as drunk as her husband; the man had thrown himself on a maroon, plush-covered chaise longue, and his voice was even more slurred than Fritzl's.

"Slivovitz? What's slivovitz?" He tried to focus on Chokolade. "Is her name slivovitz?"

Fritzl roared with laughter as though he had heard a very funny joke.

"No, she's Chokolade. Slivovitz—plum brandy—learned to drink it in Galicia. Good stuff. Dumma!"

The Count's personal servant came running, a bunch of no-longer-needed keys in his hand. "Yes—yes, sir?"

"Slivovitz," Fritzl demanded. "But first—my boots—take boots off."

Fritzl's eyes were almost shut as Dumma bent over to take off his boots, but then they opened again. "His—his, too. My good friend Horst—his boots, too."

Dumma bent to this task, too, and then he was racing down the stairs for the slivovitz. He arrived panting, bearing a tray and a crystal decanter filled with a colorless liquid. Chokolade noticed that the man's hands were trembling as he filled two brandy glasses almost to the brim. It wasn't just women Fritzl terrorized, Chokolade realized. His servant was just as afraid of him as she was. While her husband took a large swallow from his glass and held it up to be refilled, she edged slowly toward the door.

"No you don't." Fritzl had seen her careful movements. "How dare you leave this room? Did I give you permission to do so? Don't you see we have a guest—a guest has to be entertained."

Chokolade looked over at the guest. The young officer was so drunk that the glass of slivovitz had fallen from his fingers, and there was a dark spot where the liquor had stained the carpet. Dumma put down the slivovitz decanter and ran from the room. But Chokolade looked at Fritzl with a cool and appraising eye. He was drunk, so drunk that she felt sure she had nothing to fear.

"My guest." Fritzl waved vaguely at the half-asleep Horst. "I want you to entertain him."

"Entertain him? How?"

"Dance for him, one of your filthy Gypsy dances. That'll wake him up. And after that, I want you to really entertain him—in bed."

Chokolade felt her face burn. "You want me—your wife—to go to bed with another man?"

"My wife?" She heard his terrible laugh again. "My paid-for whore, you mean. That's right—that's what I want. Exactly. And I want you to do it now. Get undressed!"

"No—"

"I told you—I showed you what would happen if you said no to me—"

Fritzl sat up, and tried to move from the bed, but he was so drunk that his stockinged feet couldn't find the floor. Chokolade backed away, and she didn't wait for Fritzl to try and get off the bed again. She ran—ran from the room—ran down the stairs and out of the house. She ran down the broad, tree-lined avenue that led to the iron gate. She managed to push it open, and then she continued running until she reached a small railroad station. Even as she ran she kept looking behind her in fear, but Fritzl had been too drunk to follow her or to send anyone after her.

Only when she was seated in a first-class compartment of the small train did she take a truly deep breath. She was free—free from Fritzl and through with her disastrous marriage. Her tense body was still trembling, but when the train arrived in Vienna she felt safer. She hired the first public fiacre she saw outside of the railroad station, and instructed it to take her to Count Hoyòs's apartments. She would be safe there until Rudolf could come to her.

"Ask Prince Rudolf to come here?" Count Hoyòs sounded as though Chokolade had just woken him from a deep sleep. He kept repeating her phrases. "Come here? Now?"

"Yes!" Chokolade just about stamped her feet at the infuriating man. "Here and now. Right now. I must see him. Why is that so hard to understand?" What was wrong with the man? She had come to the Prince's equerry before with similar requests, and he had never acted so befuddled.

"Well, it's just that—now—now—the Prince has many things on his mind."

"I'm sure that the Prince would want to see me," Chokolade said.

Count Hoyòs sighed, but one more time, and he hoped it would be the last time he did Chokolade's bidding. The girl was really getting far above herself, he decided. Here Rudolf had thought he was getting her out of his hair by marrying her off to Count von Kaplow, and now she was on his doorstep once again.

Count Hoyòs expected the Crown Prince to send him back to Chokolade with a curt message, and he was surprised when Rudolf said, "I'll come. Immediately. I may not be able to come to do this again, but this one time—"

The two men rode back to Count Hoyòs's apartments, where Chokolade waited. She could hardly wait until Count Hoyòs bowed himself out of the room. She wanted to talk to Rudolf alone; after all, all of Vienna did not have to know that she was married to a pervert and a sadist.

"Oh, Rudolf," she began, but before she could continue, she burst into tears.

The Crown Prince sighed, and sat down on the couch. He looked patient and possibly a little bored, but he didn't look really concerned. She had expected him to take her into his arms, to comfort her, and now he just sat there.

She was finally able to control herself enough to tell Rudolf about the horrors of her wedding night—and the further horror of what Fritzl expected their life together to be. To her surprise the Crown Prince didn't look particularly shocked.

"Chokolade, there's not much I can do—you're married to the man. I'm sure in time you'll learn to manage him—"

"Manage him! I don't want to live with him—"

"Not live with him?" Once again Rudolf's face held a look of puzzlement. It was almost as though he hadn't really been listening. "But my dear girl, you're married to him. Once you marry someone you have to live with them. There's no way out of that. Believe me, I know."

"But there has to be a way out—you must help me."

Rudolf shrugged. "Help you? I can't even help myself, how can I help you?"

Chokolade sank down on the couch, bitterly disappointed. He was a *gajo* after all, just another *gajo,* and no *gajo* could ever care about what happened to a Gypsy. It just wasn't in them to care. She had grown up with the saying, "In the warmest *gajo* heart, a Gypsy will find an enemy." But not Rudolf, she thought, not Rudolf. She had thought he was the one person she could turn to and trust.

Now he was talking to her, rambling on about some girl or other that he was interested in. But Chokolade and Rudolf shared the same problem. Both were so enmeshed in their own worries that neither of them could listen properly to anyone else's.

"There is this girl, Chokolade, such a lovely girl, only seventeen . . ."

So, Rudolf had gotten himself another girl, Chokolade thought. Well, what was new about that? All he did was flit from one woman to another.

"...She's so lovely, so fresh. I wish you could meet her. So innocent..."

Innocent. Well, she wouldn't stay innocent very long around Rudolf.

"...And I love her, really love her. She's a baroness. Her family is Greek, originally. Maybe you've heard of them—she's a Baltazzi on her mother's side—"

A Greek family. That was probably more acceptable to the damned Viennese than a Gypsy family.

"And her father is Baron Vetsera. I met her at the Polish Ball. There were all the Polish nobles—you know most of them—dressed in that fancy Polish dress. God, I'm so bored with fur and more fur, and gold-embroidered velvets. That's how I noticed her at first. She looked so lovely, sitting to one side, an angel in simple white—"

Another one of Rudolf's angels, but this one did sound different. From what she remembered of Rudolf, he preferred his women to be more on the devilish side.

"...Her name is Maria. Maria Vetsera. I do understand what you're going through, Chokolade, I do. I even went to my father to see if he could intervene for me with His Holiness—see if I could get a divorce. He said it was impossible, impossible—"

But what did it matter if the Emperor said that Rudolf was not permitted to divorce? He could have this girl—Maria What's-Her-Name—as his mistress until he got tired of her. He could do what he wanted with his life. It wasn't quite the same as being trapped in a marriage with an insane husband who might kill her. She had to make him see that, had to make him pay attention to her!

"Rudolf, please, I am sorry if you're upset, but—"

"Upset! I am something more than upset—"

"Yes, yes, I know. But, please, please do listen!"

The Prince was silent as Chokolade went into her recital about Fritzl once again. He was listening to her this time, Chokolade realized, but he also had a look of disappointment on his face, as if somehow she had let him down. Because of Fritzl? Not possibly. No, obviously he wanted to rave on about his new love, and Chokolade hadn't given him her full attention.

Rudolf sighed. "All right, Chokolade, there is one thing I can do. I can arrange to have Fritzl's orders changed. It's true I promised him a permanent posting in Vienna, but after what you've just told me, I'll see that he gets sent to Kolosvar. Is that far enough?"

"But he'll come back," Chokolade cried out. "Come back to me. Can't you do more? Can't you help me to get my marriage annulled?"

"I'm sorry," Rudolf said heavily, "I told you before. Annulments—divorces—they are not so easily come by."

Chokolade took a deep breath but she said no more. Rudolf was obviously so besotted with this Maria that he had no time to pay attention to her. Well, never mind, at least this would get Fritzl out of Vienna temporarily, and once Rudolf got over his

357

latest infatuation, she would be able to talk to him again.

The Crown Prince rose from the couch, and Chokolade stood, too.

"Chokolade, I am glad that we were able to meet once again."

He was so serious that he made her smile despite herself. "Once again? I trust we will meet many times again."

The Crown Prince shook his head. "I told you once before. I am thinking of taking a journey—"

"To Mayerling?"

"To Mayerling, first, and then onward from there."

"I will see you when you get back, then," Chokolade said.

Rudolf took Chokolade's hand, and kissed it. Strange, she had expected him to give her a warmer kiss than that. Was Rudolf suddenly practicing fidelity to his latest love? That was a change. Chokolade responded to Rudolf's new formality by dropping him a deep curtsey. She felt his lips brush the top of her bent head, and then he was gone from the room.

Count Hoyòs came into the salon a few minutes later. "The Crown Prince suggests that you stay here for a few days—until he arranges things about Count von Kaplow—"

"I have my own house in Vienna."

The airs of this girl were really wearying. "I know that quite well. It's just that you might be safer here. I am going to Mayerling with the Crown Prince, but my servants will take care of you."

Chokolade was ashamed of her brusqueness.

"Thank you," she said, "I do appreciate your kindness."

He was kind, Chokolade thought, watching him bow and leave the room, and Rudolf was kind, too, though she still felt that he didn't do as much for her as she would have wished. But she would talk to him again. Long after he had forgotten Maria, they would still be good friends.

Chokolade knew that when Rudolf went to Mayerling, Count Hoyòs and Prince Phillip of Coburg attended him. She could imagine the gay times the Prince was having at his hunting lodge. Chokolade was happy to stay indoors at Count Hoyòs's home. It was cold—the coldest January that the Viennese could remember. The Austrians grumbled about the weather. Their superstitions told them that when a new year started out with such bitter cold, it meant bad luck for the entire year.

Chokolade sat before the fire in a small drawing room, and she felt as contented as a cat. She was warm, and even if only temporarily, she was safe from her husband. For the first time in her life she enjoyed being alone—alone, without anyone to worry her or demand anything from her. She was irritated when the peace was shattered by the cry of a servant running down the corridor.

"Madame, oh, madame." Chokolade decided that Kurt, Count Hoyòs's normally calm and discreet butler, had gone mad. The man rushed into the room and thrust the official paper of the Viennese court at her. Kurt was actually weeping.

Chokolade took *Die Offizielle Wiener Zeitung,* dated January thirty-first, 1889, from his trembling fingers. The unaccustomed black border around the first page of the paper startled her—the Emperor—it must be the Emperor! She read the announcement quickly: "His Royal and Imperial Highness, Crown Prince Archduke Rudolf, died yesterday, January 30th, at his hunting lodge of Mayerling, near Baden...."

The paper dropped from Chokolade's fingers, and she threw herself face down on the couch weeping. Rudolf—Rudolf was dead. There were more words in the paper, but Chokolade paid no attention to them. The official statement claimed that Rudolf had died of a heart attack, but Chokolade knew that it was no heart attack that had claimed him. She remembered his words during their last meeting, and her heart broke. He had been trying to talk to her, trying to reach her, and she had been so selfishly involved with her own woes that she had paid scant attention to him. If only she had listened, if only she had tried to help him.

It was from a gray-faced and exhausted Joseph Hoyòs that she heard the truth a day later, and by that time the entire Empire knew that the Prince had killed himself after the suicide of his young love, Maria Vetsera.

"We found them together," a broken Count Hoyòs told Chokolade. "Together, the way they always wanted to be. She had his violets close to her, and he was leaning against her shoulder. They were together in death, the way they couldn't be in life. They both left notes. That young girl—she wrote to her mother—'We are wondering what the Great Beyond looks like,' and Rudolf—my Prince—'Give my most affectionate remembrance to all my friends.' Rudolf, there will never be another like him."

Count Hoyòs buried his head in his hands and wept, and so did Chokolade.

"The papers," she said finally. "Why did they make up that story about the heart attack?"

"At first—at first—they thought it would be better that way, to hide the truth—"

"The truth," Chokolade interrupted bitterly, "the truth is that Rudolf died—not of a heart attack—but of a broken heart. That is the truth that the world should know."

Joseph Hoyòs sat up and looked at her. "I will leave Vienna," he said finally. "Without Rudolf, there is nothing for me here—nothing."

Nothing, Chokolade's heart echoed, *nothing.*

Chapter XVI

"YOU'RE CRAZY!"

"What?"

"I say that you're crazy—you're behaving like a crazy person."

"Who are you to criticize my behavior?" Chokolade asked Gyuri angrily. "Are you such a model of virtue? Everywhere I go, people greet me with the latest gossip about your amours."

"That's different," Gyuri said stubbornly.

"Why? Because I'm a woman?"

"Yes, that, and also because the Crown Prince did his best to give you a name—a position. You're supposed to be more than I am—more than just another wild Gypsy dancer."

Chokolade was silent for a moment. "I wish I could go back to that time—I wish I could be a wild Gypsy dancer once again."

"You can't," Gyuri insisted. "Besides, you're a married woman."

Chokolade's face was grim. "Married—to a sadist. I would give anything—anything—not to be the Countess von Kaplow."

She waited, sure that her brother was going to give her an argument, but he surprised her by saying, "I understand. I do understand. Viennese society is sick. There are many women in bondage to terrible men—men who are perverted. But yet, they may not divorce—they dare not. Divorce is considered worse than murder, worse than cruelty. Keeping up appearances, that's all they care about."

"Really? Then why were you lecturing me before? Why were you telling me that my behavior is crazy?"

"Because it is. I'm not saying you should continue living with von Kaplow. All I'm saying is that you don't have to make yourself the centerpiece of every dirty story, every bit of gossip that goes around in Vienna."

"They are just stories," Chokolade insisted, "for the most part, anyhow. Which is more than you can say."

"You're wrong. I can say the same thing, Chokolade." He hesitated, suddenly as shy as an inexperienced boy. "I'm in love."

Chokolade laughed. "Again?"

"No, not again! This is not like anything else that has ever happened to me before. This is not *again*—this is for the first time."

Chokolade stopped laughing. "You're serious. Who is she?"

Gyuri hesitated, and then finally he spoke. "Princess Telmeny."

"Princess Telmeny? Are you crazy? A princess? Besides, she's married."

"Well," Gyuri reminded her, "Rudolf was Crown Prince, and he was certainly married. I didn't notice those little facts stopping you."

Chokolade could have said that was different. But just how different was it? She was many things, but she was no hypocrite. Besides, this was no time to lecture her brother; it would be far better to help him get out of a very dangerous situation.

"How did you ever meet Princess Telmeny?"

"I told you once before that after the palace balls and fetes are over, people come in droves to the cafés and the restaurants. I was dancing at the Restaurant Roma. You haven't seen me dance lately, Chokolade, I've worked up a flamenco solo that's fantastic—well, the Prince and the Princess came in one night for a midnight supper.

"Chokolade, I couldn't help myself—I looked at this woman, and for the first time in my life I felt something that I have never felt before—"

"Now, Gyuri—"

"Don't laugh at me!"

"I'm not laughing. I was just wondering, with all the women you've known—"

"This was different," Gyuri was almost shouting. You've known enough men, but tell me, wasn't there one—just one—that made you feel differently from any of the others?"

Chokolade was silent, and then she said, "Go on, Gyuri, that's how you felt, but what about her?"

Gyuri sat down beside his sister. "It was the same with her. We looked at each other, and we knew. Isn't that amazing? And wonderful? We felt it at the same moment. She told me there's some kind of fancy French saying for when love hits two people at the same moment—"

"*Coup de foudre*," Chokolade supplied. "Being hit by a thunderbolt."

"That's it! Exactly. It was a thunderbolt. I danced that night the way I've never danced before. I danced for her, and she knew it. Look, before she left the restaurant, she gave me this."

Gyuri held out something to her, and Chokolade gasped when she saw it. "That's the largest sapphire I've ever seen. She just handed you that?"

Gyuri nodded. "She slipped the ring off her finger, and pressed it into my hand. That's how it started."

Chokolade groaned. "You mean there was more than that? The two of you have been seeing each other? Do you know that the Prince is one of the best shots in Austria? He's fought more than one duel, and he's the one who's walked away from all of them.

"He looks for opportunities to challenge men to duels. Someone told me that he said to a waiter at his favorite café, 'Ferenc, this morning it will be pistols for two, and coffee for one,' and he was the one who came back to calmly drink his coffee."

"I've heard that story about almost every man in Vienna," Gyuri said impatiently. "Besides, I don't care how good a shot the Prince is—I love Dita, and she loves me. Don't worry," he assured Chokolade, "we meet very secretly."

"There are no secrets in Vienna," Chokolade said, "and if for some reason the Prince shouldn't learn about you and the Princess, her two brothers will. If the Prince doesn't kill you, her brothers will see to it. Gyuri, what have you gotten yourself into?"

"I thought you would understand," he answered reproachfully. "If anyone would understand, I was sure it was you. After what you've gone through with von Kaplow—well, Prince Telmeny isn't very different."

Chokolade sighed. "Gyuri, how long do you think the two of you can go on this way? Someone is bound to talk. A servant, a coachman, a girl in a flower shop, a waiter who sees the two of you at the Roma and notices the way she looks at you. Gyuri, for God's sake—"

"Don't worry, we're not fools. We have plans. We won't stay in Vienna, we're going to run away."

"Run? Where? There's no place in the entire Empire where you'd be safe from Prince Telmeny or the Princess's brothers."

Gyuri smiled, and again Chokolade noticed that it was the smile of a boy rather than that of a worldly, cynical man. "We know that. That's why we're planning to leave the Empire entirely, Chokolade. We're going to America! People are free in America, no one cares there whether you're a princess or a Gypsy dancer. They accept you for what you are, without asking questions about the past."

"Very nice! America. You may as well tell me that you're planning to go to the moon. Before you can go to America, you have to get out of Austria. And just how do you plan to do that?"

"We're leaving for Budapest in a few days," Gyuri told her. "We'll be safer there. The Hungarians aren't all that crazy about the Austrians, and we can hide in Hungary until the excitement dies down."

But the excitement wouldn't die down, Chokolade well knew. The Prince wouldn't let it die down, not until he had killed her brother. She had to help them, help these two loving people get away. There was little enough love in the world, and she would regret to her dying day that she wasn't sympathetic when Rudolf tried to tell her how he felt about Maria Vetsera. It was too late—too late—to do anything about that; she couldn't help the dead, but she could try and help the living.

"Listen to me," she said, "you must listen to me. There's only one man who can get you out of the Empire and away from the Prince. Fekete Andras, he's the only one. Gyuri, you must do exactly as I say."

"Chokolade," he protested. "I don't want you involved in this."

"Listen, *pral,* I am involved. Aren't you my brother? This is what we'll do: you and I will leave for Budapest in the morning, and I'll get a message to Fekete Andras—"

"How?"

"Never mind, I will."

"I can't go with you, Chokolade, I can't leave Dita here in Vienna."

"Dita will follow us in three days. Don't you see, Gyuri? It's much safer if the two of you don't travel together. We'll go to Budapest first, and then Dita will meet you there. By the time she arrives I will have gotten word to Fekete Andras, and he'll slip you out of the country. It's the only way. And be sure and tell the Princess that she must travel very lightly—as though she were only going to Budapest for a few days. Be sure to tell her that."

"Do we have to leave tomorrow?"

"Can you get word to the Princess today?"

"Yes."

"Then the sooner the better." Chokolade shuddered when she thought of Prince Telmeny and his beautiful and deadly ivory-handled pistols. "The sooner we do this, the sooner the two of you will be on your way to America."

Gyuri brightened. "That's true."

The following morning brother and sister were once again on the express train that ran between the two capital cities. Chokolade ordered their meals sent into their private compartment. There were no secrets in Vienna, but she felt that the longer the news of their departure took to reach the Prince, the better off they would be. Fritzl was still posted out of the city, and Chokolade didn't have to worry about him interfering with her plans. She was sure, however, that now that Rudolf was dead, Fritzl would once again manage to get his orders changed, and he would return to Vienna. But she would worry about that once she had seen Gyuri and his Princess safely on their way.

"Why are we staying here?" Gyuri demanded after they had arrived in Budapest, and Chokolade had hired a coach to take them to a small *csarda* on the outskirts of the city. "Why an inn? Why don't we check in at the Gellert Hotel?"

Chokolade sighed. "I've told you. The fewer people who know where we are, the better off we'll be."

After they had been shown their two small rooms at the inn, Chokolade told her brother that she had to go out for awhile.

"Hadn't I better go with you? If you're going to try and contact Fekete Andras—"

"You stay here," Chokolade said shortly. She was reasonably sure that she could move more quickly and quietly without her brother at her side.

As Gyuri watched from a window, Chokolade once again got into a coach. "Take me to the Tulipan," she instructed the driver. "It's in old Buda."

The coachman looked at her with surprise. "I know where it is. But isn't the lady mistaken? That's just a tavern—and not in the best part of town, either. Wouldn't the lady rather go to Gerbeaud's for some nice coffee and cake?"

"The lady wants to go to the Tulipan," Chokolade said, "and the lady wants you to take her there now."

The coachman looked at her sourly. "If that's what the lady wants," and he clicked his tongue at his sorry-looking horse.

Half an hour later the coach pulled up before an old tavern on a narrow street. The coachman looked at the place doubtfully. A place like that, and such a well-dressed woman, too. He thought about asking her if she wanted him to go in with her, but then he thought better of it. The Tulipan had a reputation for drawn knives and split skulls, he had his family to think about. But after Chokolade paid him, he did ask, "Shall I wait? The lady may find it hard getting another coach to take her back in this neighborhood. That is, if the lady is going back?"

Chokolade nodded. "The lady will be going back

in a few minutes. You may wait."

The coachman watched as she swept into the tavern. A real aristocrat, he could tell. Just by the way she moved and spoke, oh yes, he could always tell when he was carrying a titled person to some secret rendezvous. They had an air about them.

Luckily, the tavern was fairly empty, and only a few heads turned when Chokolade walked in, only a few people eyed her with both interest and hostile curiosity.

"The patron?" she demanded of a black-aproned girl. "Where is he?"

"Who?" The girl stared at her. "Who do you want?"

"The patron of the Tulipan," Chokolade said impatiently. "The man who owns this place."

The girl laughed derisively. "Patron! That's a fancy name for it. I suppose you mean old Lajos. Just now he's in the kitchen cooking the veal *pörkölt* for tonight's supper. You want me to get him for you?"

"No," Chokolade said, "I'll go to him."

The girl pointed the way, and Chokolade entered a blackened kitchen and saw a small gnome of a man standing over a wood-burning stove, stirring the contents of a huge black iron pot.

"Yes?" he squinted up at her. "Who are you? And what the hell are you doing in my kitchen?"

"I'm looking for Lajos Vajda."

"What do you want with him?"

"Are you Lajos Vajda?"

"And what if I am?"

Chokolade moved closer to him. He looked up at

her through the clouds of steam that came from the veal stew, and he reminded Chokolade of an elf from a fairy tale heard long ago.

She pulled a glove off, and quickly slipped a ring—a fire opal—from her finger. She took the man's hand, and pressed the ring into it. "Please give this ring to my friend," she said softly.

"Friend? What friend? How would I come to know a friend of yours?"

"My friend is your friend," Chokolade said, "he's the friend of all true Hungarians."

The opal ring disappeared quickly into the man's deep apron pocket. "All right," he nodded, "where are you staying?"

Chokolade told him the name of the small inn, and he nodded again. "In two days," he said, "maybe sooner. Better get out of here now."

Chokolade left the kitchen and the tavern quickly. She stepped into the waiting coach and told the driver to take her back to the inn. For half the distance of the ride, the coachman wondered about the errand that took the fine lady to such a disreputable tavern, but by the time they arrived at the inn, he had stopped wondering. Gentry had strange ways, it wasn't his business to worry about it. He had troubles enough of his own.

"Where were you?" Gyuri asked. "What were you doing?"

"You'll know soon enough," Chokolade said. "In a day or two, it will all be arranged."

She smiled at her brother, but she didn't feel half as sure as she acted. What if the man she had given the ring to was a thief? Or worse, a police spy? Or, possibly, he didn't even know Fekete Andras, and he had just taken the ring because she had insisted he do so.

She tossed in her bed. Had she done the right thing, trying to contact Fekete Andras? What if she had been followed? What if von Weis suspected her? By bringing Fekete Andras into Budapest she could be costing him his life—and if his life ended, so did the entire Kossuth movement.

And what of Gyuri and Princess Dita? They might have been better off trying to get out of the country without the help of a rebel leader. Now they would have two sets of people on their trail: the Secret Police, and their families.

Chokolade wondered if she would ever be able to enjoy a simple life again, a life free of intrigue. She no longer asked for love—she knew that was impossible for her to attain—but she longed for a small amount of peace. She finally fell into an uneasy sleep, and she didn't feel much better the next day when Gyuri kept harrying her with questions.

"Be patient," she said. "It will work out."

"Patient! Dita will be here in a few days. What are we supposed to do? Where are we to go?"

Chokolade didn't answer, and that in itself calmed him. His sister seemed so relaxed, so sure, she must have contacted Fekete Andras and worked out a plan. Well, he had never claimed to be as smart as she was; she would probably tell him the details when the time was right.

It was during the second night, while Chokolade dozed fitfully, that she was awakened by a sound—a strange sound. Rain against the windows, she thought drowsily, or hail. But no, the sound was not quite like either rain or hail. She sat up in bed, suddenly wide-awake. Slipping on a warm, silk-lined peignoir, she hurried to the window, and pushed the casements open. She blinked at the apparition she saw beneath her window.

It was a Gypsy—but she had never seen such a Gypsy! He was gorgeous, wearing every sash, every piece of jewelry that a Gypsy could possibly own. There was a scarf around the man's throat, and a fancy sheathed knife thrust into an even fancier gold-buckled belt. Chokolade knew that no true Gypsy ever dressed that way unless he was planning to perform for the *gajos* and wanted to conform to their idea of how Gyspies dressed. This was no Gypsy, this was her friend, and she ran down quickly and opened the door for him. Fekete Andras listened glumly to her laughter once she had managed to get him safely to her room.

"You think this is funny? Well, you should see yourself dressed as a highwayman. That's pretty funny, too."

"I suppose so. But for the next time—just remember that a Gypsy doesn't wear every piece of jewelry he owns at one time, and when he carries a knife, it's tucked into his boot, never in his belt where everyone can see it."

Fekete Andras smiled. "Good to know. Just in case I have to appear as a Gypsy again. Now, my lady dancer, you sent for me. Why?"

Chokolade told him in a few swift sentences of her brother's romance with Princess Telmeny.

"Gyuri must get out of the country, quickly, before the Princess's husband or brothers decide that they want him dead."

"And the Princess?"

Chokolade nodded. "She wants to go with him—to America."

Fekete Andras whistled. "That's a long way."

"Can you get them out of Austria-Hungary? That's the first step."

"I think so. Look, here's what we'll have to do."

He spoke quietly to Chokolade, and she nodded, understanding that his plan just might work—if they were lucky.

"And remember," he cautioned, "the less you tell your brother, the better. I remember him. He gets nervous, and then he likes to talk a lot. It will be enough for him to think that the three of you are going for a ride in the country."

"That's all he will know," Chokolade assured him.

Fekete Andras grinned, and gave her a kiss on the tip of her nose. "Good night, highwayman," he said.

Chokolade responded by giving him a light kiss on the mouth. "Good night, Gypsy."

"Well?" Gyuri asked her the next morning. "The walls are thin in this place, you know. I heard someone in your room. Was it—"

"Never mind," Chokolade said quickly. "Princess Dita arrives today, doesn't she? I'll go to the train to meet her."

"I'll go with you."

"You'll stay here."

"But she'll be expecting me," Gyuri insisted. "Besides, I want to see her."

"If you listen to me, you'll be seeing her for the rest of your life. Now, stay here, I'll go to the train station myself."

The same coachman who had taken Chokolade to the *csarda* was available to take her to the train station. Business was slow in Budapest just then. Many people didn't go out on cold days, and he reasoned that the rich lady staying at the out-of-the-way inn would have errands to run. Whenever he didn't have a call, he stationed himself close to the inn. Now she was going to the railroad station, but she didn't have luggage, so she wasn't taking a trip. Probably going to meet someone.

"Shall I wait?" he asked when they arrived at the railroad station.

"Yes, yes, you may wait," Chokolade said shortly, as she got out of the coach.

Sure enough, the driver was pleased at his own understanding of the habits of the wealthy. The driver smiled as she came out of the railroad station, another pretty lady with her. Oh, yes, he knew how these people thought. *Wait for me, money is not as important to me as convenience.* That's why he could make a living driving a coach. He knew what to expect of people, and what they expected of him. He did notice that the two women hardly spoke inside the coach. But what did he care about that? The lady always paid him well, that was what mattered.

Chokolade led Dita, Princess Telmeny, up the back stairs of the inn, and to her small bedroom.

Gyuri came in seconds later, and the two of them clung to each other as though it had been three years since they had seen each other rather than three days.

Once she was in her lover's arms, the Princess began to weep. "I was so frightened. I was sure he would stop me—or try to."

"It's all right now," Gyuri said soothingly, "it's all right. You'll see. We have a good friend—and he has plans for us." He looked toward Chokolade, and she nodded. "Definite plans. You'll see, we'll be out of this country very soon."

"But how?" Dita wanted to know. "How?"

Again Gyuri looked toward his sister. They're like children, she thought, like young, lovesick children. Well, perhaps that wasn't such a bad way to be, after all.

"I'll leave the two of you alone," Chokolade said. "I must see about renting some horses for us, for our morning's ride."

"Ride?" Gyuri asked.

"Yes, I'm tired of being cooped up in this place, aren't you? I thought it would be pleasant if we went riding tomorrow morning. Nice and early, when the air is crisp. Perhaps we could ride toward Lake Balaton."

"Riding?" Gyuri exploded. "You want to go riding at a time like this?"

Chokolade nodded. "Yes. Just riding, that's all. We'll all go riding, because we have nothing else to do and what could be pleasanter than going riding with a few friends? Naturally," she continued in the same casual, conversational tone, "when one goes

377

riding, one does not carry baggage. Except, of course, if the Princess has any jewels, or if you have any money, Gyuri, I suggest you bring it with you." She looked at the round-eyed Princess Dita. "Simply because it's best not to leave anything valuable in a place such as this. You understand?"

Gyuri looked at his sister. "I understand."

Chokolade nodded, and left the room. Once they were alone, Dita started to cry. "I'm so afraid," she said, "so afraid."

Gyuri took her into his arms again, and led her gently to the bed. She leaned back against his shoulder like a tired child, and he held her and stroked her.

"There's nothing to be afraid of," he said gently, kissing the top of her golden head, "nothing."

"You'll take care of me"—the Princess snuggled close and comfortably into his chest—"always?"

"Always," Gyuri said, "always and forever," and with his arms about her, and his murmured assurances soothing her, the Princess slept happily in his arms.

The next morning the coachman who had driven Chokolade about was disappointed to see a groom from a nearby stable lead three horses into the yard of the inn. Why would anyone ride horseback, he wondered, when they could ride far more comfortably inside his coach? And he was even more disappointed when he saw who the three riders were. One was the lady he had taken to the railroad station, the other was her delicate-looking friend; they were escorted by a dark-haired man who looked for all the world like a Gypsy, except that the coachman knew that ladies of quality did not go riding with Gypsies, so perhaps he was some kind of Italian nobility. Well, it was no affair of his, and he clicked to his horse, and set out for the center of town again.

"Breakfast?" The innkeeper ran out into the yard when he saw that his three distinguished-looking guests were about to go riding. "Ladies, sir, perhaps a little breakfast? The fresh poppy-seed crescent rolls have just now arrived from the bakery, and there is good strong coffee made with plenty of chicory, I assure you."

"Sounds lovely," Chokolade said. "Please be sure to put at least a dozen of the poppy-seed rolls away for us. We'll be even hungrier when we return from our ride in about an hour or so. Will you keep the rolls for us until then?"

"Certainly, certainly." The innkeeper bowed and smiled and stood in the yard as the three of them rode off. Riding before breakfast, that was the gentry for you. Now for himself, he would rather have stayed in bed than gone riding on a cold morning without even a cup of coffee in his belly.

For a short while the horses hooves clop-clopped slowly on pavement. Then they were on a dirt road leading out of the city and toward Bakony Forest.

"Now," Chokolade said to Gyuri and Dita, "now we ride."

There was no one about at that hour of the morning, no one to see the three riders who urged their horses from a canter to a fast gallop. If anyone had seen them, they would have known that here were three people who rode not for pleasure but with a definite purpose in mind.

Princess Dita rode calmly beside Gyuri Tura. She didn't ask him where he was taking her. She loved him, she trusted him, and she was willing to follow wherever he led. In the same way, Gyuri followed Chokolade's lead. She hadn't offered him any details and he had stopped asking her for them. Once they reached Bakony Forest, he looked around him as they rode, and he wasn't surprised to see two men on horses waiting for them at a forest crossroad. The three reined their horses to a halt, and Gyuri saw that one of the men was Fekete Andras.

"I am grateful," Gyuri began, but the leader of Kossuth's New Army cut him short.

"We shouldn't tarry here," he said, "my men have seen uniformed riders in the area."

Princess Dita gasped, but Fekete Andras reassured her. "Soldiers, madame, searching for me, not for you. But it's best that we ride toward Fiume, we'll take you as far as we can. And in Fiume you'll be able to get a boat for Italy. You'll be safer there than here."

"You're right," Chokolade said, "let's not remain here." Her horse had been cropping the grass, and now she pulled his head up. "Let's ride."

But Fekete Andras put his hand upon her gloved ones. "We ride," he said, "but it would be better if you went back."

Chokolade paled. "I'll ride along for a little while, not the whole way, of course, just a few more kilometers."

Fekete Andras shook his head. "You'll be

endangering all of us if you do that. There will be no one to ride back with you, and if you should run into a troop of cavalry, what will you say? What are you doing deep in Bakony Forest all by yourself?

"Perhaps you are staying at Lake Balaton? No, you have ridden out from Budapest. No one rides this far from Budapest just for a day; you know that, and so will they. They'll be suspicious, and they'll start out after us, not knowing what they're looking for, you understand, just looking. I'm sorry," he said gently, "better to say good-bye here."

Chokolade swallowed and turned to her brother. "Andras is right. Let us say good-bye here."

Brother and sister got off their horses, and Gyuri took his sister in his arms. They held onto each other tightly.

"You will let me know where you are," Chokolade said.

"Of course." Gyuri's voice was husky. "I will write to you—to our house in Budapest. I think that will be best, don't you?"

Chokolade nodded, unable to speak.

"Chokolade." Gyuri stepped back and looked at his sister. "What will happen to you—you and that von Kaplow?"

"Don't worry about me, I'll be fine. Just fine. Fritzl is far from Vienna right now. Who knows? He may never come back."

Gyuri gripped her arms and gave her another strong hug. "We will meet again. It won't be long. We will be together once again."

Chokolade did her best to smile, but Gyuri's face blurred through her tears. "Of course. America is part of this world, not the next. One doesn't have to cross the Blue Lake to see it. Many people visit America these days. I should like to see it myself, one day."

Gyuri nodded and climbed into the saddle once again. He knew that if he tried to say another word, he would weep. It was Fekete Andras who helped Chokolade onto her horse.

"Will you be all right?" he asked. "It's a long ride back."

"I'll be all right. Please—go now—now."

Fekete Andras looked at her, brought her hand to his lips for a swift kiss, and then moved quickly to his horse. Chokolade didn't move until she saw her brother and the rest disappear among the trees. Gyuri was sitting stolidly in his saddle, and he rode out of her line of vision without once looking back. She could understand that. If he had looked back and seen his sister alone, he might never have left. It was the little Princess Dita who had turned just before the road curved, and it was her small gloved hand that gave a final wave. That was the last Chokolade saw of them, and then she wheeled her horse about and set out once more for Budapest.

As she rode, she prayed that she had done the right thing. If only she could be sure that she hadn't endangered the lives of the people she most cared for by putting her brother and his Princess in the hands of the most wanted man in the entire Empire. Worst of all, she was facing a time of uncertainty. There was no one who could get word to her about Gyuri and Dita; trying to contact her would only create more danger. She would have to wait, wait and rely on the gossip that would eventually filter back to Vienna—gossip that was usually based on truth.

And while she waited, she would be alone, completely alone.

She no longer had Gyuri, and Rudolf, the only other man she could have turned to, was gone, too. Alone, alone, that was the message her horse's galloping hooves hammered out along the lonely road that led back to the city.

Chapter XVII

CHOKOLADE RETURNED TO Vienna as quietly as she had left that city. She felt sure that if her absence was noted at all, it was probably attributed to a period of mourning for Rudolf. Vienna was certainly not the same after the death of the Crown Prince. People still spoke of it in the dazed manner of the unbelieving. Many of the people Chokolade had known were gone. Count Hoyòs and Prince Phillip of Coburg left the Empire; they no longer wished to live there now that Rudolf was gone, and the Emperor blamed them, in part, for what had happened to his beloved son.

The one touch of lightness in the entire city was the whispers about Gyuri Tura and Princess Dita Telmeny. The Viennese loved to gossip, and the romantic story of the Princess who ran off with the Gypsy dancer distracted them from their sadness over the death of their Crown Prince.

When the stories about her brother reached Chokolade, she breathed a sigh of relief. She knew that Gyuri and Dita were safe, and that Fekete Andras hadn't been captured while helping them.

One day more of freedom for Andras was the way she thought of it, because she knew that any member of Kossuth's New Army had to count his life and his safety in days.

Chokolade was amazed one day to receive a delegation from the Frosch Patisserie of Vienna.

"It is Herr Frosch himself," her butler announced, "and two other gentlemen."

"Herr Frosch? Here? I can't imagine—very well, show him in."

The dean of the Viennese pastry and confectionmakers bowed himself into Chokolade's salon. He was formally dressed in striped pants, a tailcoat, and a top hat, and as Chokolade asked him to take a seat she wondered why he had come.

"It is about your brother," Herr Frosch said very seriously.

"My brother? What about my brother?"

"One of my pastry chefs has created a new cake." He snapped his fingers, and a man standing behind Herr Frosch produced a high, white box. "If the Countess will permit?"

"Certainly," Chokolade said, not at all sure what she was permitting.

With great ceremony, the box was opened, and a small plate of Rosenthal china was carefully lifted out. On the plate was an exquisite slice of cream-and-beige pastry.

"If the Countess would do us the honor of tasting?" Herr Frosch asked.

"Taste the cake?" Chokolade's bewilderment grew. "Now?"

"If you please."

Chokolade swallowed down the laughter bubbling up in her throat, and she did her best to match Herr Frosch's serious manner. "Certainly."

A white linen napkin was laid across her lap, the plate and a large silver fork were presented to her. Very slowly, Chokolade cut a forkful of cake, and slowly, seriously, ate it.

"Delicious," she said, "absolutely delicious. What is it made of?"

"It is an almond torte, the layers separated by almond-flavored whipped cream. If the Countess noticed, there is almond icing on top, and a macaroon crust at the bottom."

"Yes, well. It certainly is delicious. And what do you call this wonderful pastry? I don't think I've ever had it before."

"Certainly not. It is brand new, created in honor of the occasion. And with the Countess's permission, I would like to call it the Gyuri Tura Torte."

Chokolade managed to control her laughter, and she hoped that Herr Frosch would take her smile to be an indication of pleasure rather than amusement. She knew of the Viennese practice of naming pastries after famous entertainers, and Gundel's in Budapest had named a dessert after her, too. She wondered, though, how her brother would feel if he learned of this pastry named for him—not because of his excellence as a dancer—but because he had seduced a princess.

"It is a great honor," she said gravely. "I have no way of telling my brother of this wonderful news—"

"I understand."

"But I am sure he will hear of it in time, and be just as pleased as I am."

Herr Frosch nodded. He knew he had done an

important thing for the Tura family. Next to having a statue erected, having a pastry named after one was the best honor. Herr Frosch snapped his fingers, and fork, plate, and napkin were removed from Chokolade's lap. Chokolade rang for her butler, and Herr Frosch and company were led out of the salon, after many more bows and flowery phrases of thanks on both sides.

It was only after the famed pastry-shop owner was safely out of her house that Chokolade allowed herself to give in to peals of laughter. She controlled herself after a while, and thought how amused Rudolf would be when she told him the story of Herr Frosch's visit.

Rudolf. She would never again tell this, or any story, to Rudolf. He was gone, and she didn't know how to reach Gyuri, who might have enjoyed the news of his fame. She was alone—so alone.

Chokolade was feeling absolutely friendless when she received a visit a few days later from a court equerry. The man arrived in a private unmarked coach, with as little ceremony as possible. Again, Chokolade thought of Rudolf, and reminded herself with a pang that Rudolf was no longer alive to send messages to her.

"I come from the Empress Elizabeth," the equerry said. "Her Royal Highness would be very pleased if the Countess von Kaplow would visit her tomorrow afternoon at four at the Schloss Lainz."

Chokolade nodded, too stunned to speak. The Empress had always avoided her. Rudolf had explained to Chokolade that his mother would not be able to receive her, it wouldn't be proper.

Chokolade had understood—understood far more than she did this sudden summons.

"Tomorrow, at four, then?" the equerry repeated. "Her Majesty prefers that the Countess come in a coach that will be sent for her. It will be more discreet."

It was a dream, Chokolade decided, a *delibab*. She had imagined the entire episode. She couldn't believe that the Empress would send for her, or invite her to Schloss Lainz, a small castle, close to Schöbrunn, but kept very private for the comfort of the Hapsburg family. Outsiders, guests, not even heads of state were invited to Schloss Lainz.

The next day Chokolade dressed, undressed, and changed her outfit five times. She finally settled on a dove-gray skirt of wool challis, topped with a matching gray jacket that buttoned high and severely beneath her chin. A small, black hat perched forward on her forehead, and white, *glacé* kid gloves came up over the sleeves of her jacket.

The coach came for her promptly at two, and at ten to four it entered the large gates of walled Schloss Lainz. From the coach window the grounds looked to Chokolade like something out of a fairy tale. There was formality, yes, but not the cold formality of the Schönbrunn or Hofburg castles. Chokolade had long heard that the Empress was a woman of exquisite taste, and as she looked out at the masses of flowers, the beds of peonies, she knew whose touch had created this bower of flowers.

The castle itself, Chokolade discovered, was more Greek than German or Austrian. There were no rococo angels flying about the ceilings, no baroque, overly carved flowers, dripping from urns. The design of the castle was beautiful, elegant, and simple—as beautiful, elegant, and simple as Elizabeth herself, Chokolade thought as she curtseyed deeply to the Empress of Austria, and the Queen of Hungary.

Elizabeth held out both hands to Chokolade. "Sit by me, my child, I have heard so much about you—mostly from my son."

The Empress's voice was low and musical, but Chokolade could see the tears in the sapphire-blue eyes when she spoke of her son.

"Your Majesty," Chokolade said, sitting tentatively on the edge of the white silk Louis Quinze loveseat.

Elizabeth shook her head. "Don't be afraid of me, and please don't be shy. I wanted you to come here, to Lainz, because we can be alone—away from prying eyes. These Viennese—they would make a great story of this, if they knew you were here."

"I knew they would. That's what Rudolf said—" Chokolade stopped in mid-sentence.

"Yes? Go on. *Rudolf said.* Please tell me everything you can remember about him. Memories, they're all I have now. Do you understand?"

"Oh yes," the words burst out of Chokolade. "I do understand. It's awful—I think of him so often—think of different things I want to tell him—just the other day when Herr Frosch came to see me—I thought, this will make Rudolf laugh." Chokolade stopped again in some confusion. Was she saying too much? She was talking about the Crown Prince. Was she being impertinent? Too informal?

"Please, please go on." One of Elizabeth's hands covered hers. "I am so grateful to you, my dear. You were one of the few people able to make my Rudi happy—if only for a little while. He spoke often of you, of your love of freedom, your gaiety, your wonderful dancing. Talk to me about him, tell me what you can remember."

For the next hour Chokolade regaled Empress Elizabeth with some of the escapades she shared with Rudolf. "... And then, he insisted on dressing like a Gypsy, and going to this tavern with me. Oh, you should have seen him, Your Majesty, he looked so funny, and poor Bratfisch—he was so worried, so solemn driving us to this awful place. But Rudolf loved it—loved the music, the cheap wine, everything. He loved life!"

She stopped then, afraid she had said too much, but now the sapphire eyes looked at her with great understanding.

"Exactly," Elizabeth said, "he did love life. I think you and I are the only two people who really believe that. And even I—I wonder— how could he, loving life so much, do this thing?"

"If only he had been allowed to live with Maria Vetsera," Chokolade said. "Rudolf loved life, but he couldn't bear to live it unhappily. He told me once that a little bit of happiness was worth everything."

Elizabeth looked at her sadly. "There are obligations, especially if we are to rule a country. It is hard to escape, though some people do manage it, like—"

"Like my brother and Princess Telmeny," Chokolade said.

"Exactly. But are they all right, do you know? I understand Prince Telmeny tried to follow them. Do you think they are safe, out of the country?" Again Elizabeth's hands touched Chokolade's. "I hope they are. I would like to think that they, at least, have found happiness."

"I'm sure they're safe," Chokolade said. "They had the help of a friend of mine—a friend of all Hungarians."

"A friend of all Hungarians?" Elizabeth's eyebrows went up questioningly. "And who is this friend of all Hungarians? I am the Queen of Hungary, do I know him?"

Had she said too much? The Hungarians loved Elizabeth, surely she could trust her. In a low voice Chokolade told Elizabeth about Fekete Andras and Kossuth's New Army, she even told the Empress how she had helped him make his escape from the Austrian Secret Police.

"Wonderful," Elizabeth said, her voice also low and conspiratorial. "You did the right thing. I just wish I could have ridden with you. I would have, you know!"

What a marvelous woman! The Hungarians were right in asking her to be their Queen. Knowing she had a sympathetic listener, Chokolade spoke about some of the political prisoners languishing in Austrian jails.

"I know," Elizabeth said. "Rudolf spoke to me often about the same thing, and he tried to speak to the Emperor, too. Now maybe he will listen to me—though it's too late to listen to Rudolf. Perhaps I can persuade him to do something in memory of our son."

An aura of sadness filled the room. Chokolade and the Empress could speak of many things, but neither of them could forget Rudolf, lying now and forever in the crypt of the Capuchin Church.

"And you, my child." Elizabeth turned to Chokolade. "I know you recently married Count Friedrich von Kaplow. Are you happy?"

Chokolade longed to burst out with the truth, but there was no way she could tell the shocking details of her marriage to this gentle woman who sat at her side.

The most she dared to say was, "I am afraid, Your Majesty, that I may have married too hastily."

Elizabeth nodded, and there was no mistaking her look of genuine pity. "I know, my dear. Do believe me, I understand. But you are not alone. Many, many women have experienced suffering in their marriages.

"Perhaps it is our lot. I don't know. I have never understood why these things happen. But I think it is up to us to try and make things better. That is what a woman must do, she is the only one who can have a softening influence on her husband. Perhaps you could try, my dear. You may not succeed all at once, but at least you know you will have done the right thing. Will you try? For me?"

"I will try," Chokolade said, terribly moved by the Empress's words and request. "I promise, I will try."

The Empress sighed and was silent, and Chokolade remembered again all the stories she had heard about the Empress, who, through the years, had stayed away from court, from Vienna, from her marriage bed, as much as she possibly could.

Chokolade bowed her head. The Empress had suffered, yet she was patient. Maybe she could learn something from her. Chokolade had heard that Franz Josef had been a tyrant as an Emperor and a husband, but Elizabeth's sweetness had changed him.

She had no illusions about herself. She knew that she could never be as soft, as forbearing as Elizabeth, but she could try to be a little more patient, a trifle more understanding. Perhaps she could come to terms with Fritzl and save their marriage.

Elizabeth's attitude gave her hope. If Franz Josef could change, why not Fritzl? She had to try, because she had no one, absolutely no one to turn to. She, who had never felt afraid, now felt like a lost and lonely child. She had never tried to talk to her husband, never tried to understand what drove him toward his strange ways. Was Fritzl an evil man, or a sick one? She didn't know, but sitting beside the Empress, she decided to try Elizabeth's way.

At six, the equerry appeared quietly in the salon. Chokolade understood that this was the signal for her departure. She rose, curtseyed, and once again the Empress took her hand.

"I am afraid it will not be possible for us to meet again," Elizabeth said, "but I will always be grateful for the hours of happiness you gave my son, and I shall remember you in my prayers." The gentle Empress looked at the Gypsy dancer. "And may I hope that I will be remembered in yours?"

Impulsively, Chokolade was on her knees, and gripping Elizabeth's hands, she kissed them. The

Empress saw the tears in the girl's eyes.

"Thank you, my dear." And that was the last time Chokolade was to hear the soft, musical voice of the Empress.

The equerry led her swiftly from the room and from the house, and soon Chokolade was being driven away from Schloss Lainz and back to her own home in Vienna.

Chokolade felt that the meeting with the Empress gave her strength to face her marriage and her life with Fritzl. She stayed in her own house, but she was sure that Fritzl would soon return to the capital, and she was prepared to return to his villa, and to try and make a life with him.

For the next few weeks, Chokolade stayed quietly at home. Once again Vienna buzzed. Why wasn't the Countess seen at the opera? What did she do during the long afternoons, when fashionable Vienna was accustomed to seeing her riding in the Prater, or taking coffee at either Sachar's or Frosch's?

No one would believe that Chokolade was by herself, quietly considering the shambles of her life, and trying to think of ways to bring order into it. Everyone was sure that Chokolade was in hiding with yet another lover—a lover so demanding that he didn't want to let Chokolade out of his bed, or out of the house.

It was these rumors that greeted Friedrich von Kaplow when he arrived in Vienna from Kolosvar. Being posted away from the city had put him in a foul mood, especially when he discovered that he

was being sent to a small town in Hungary. He knew
that Rudolf had been responsible for his transfer;
Rudolf, to whom Chokolade had run with her
whining and complaints. He didn't grieve when he
learned of the death of the Crown Prince; instead,
he immediately requested a transfer back to Vienna.
The transfer took some months to be processed, and
with every passing day, Fritzl's rage increased. With
Rudolf dead, his anger was concentrated on his
wife. That bitch! She obviously thought he was a toy
soldier, or a pawn on a chess board to be moved
about at her will. Well, once he got back to Vienna,
he would show her that he was not one to be trifled
with. He thought he had frightened her into
obedience on their wedding night, but obviously the
lesson hadn't yet been learned. But just let him get
back to Vienna, just let him get back—he would
reduce her to an abject, sniveling slave—a slave
happy to do his bidding because of her great fear of
him.

When Fritzl got back to Vienna, he reported to
Baron Goelsh, Commander of the Viennese
barracks. Goelsh, who had no love for Fritzl, was
only too happy to pass on gossip about Chokolade
to her husband.

"Well, von Kaplow," he said, "I am sure you are
glad to be back in Vienna, and happy to come home
to your new bride, isn't that so?"

Fritzl looked at him warily. "I am pleased to be
back, of course, and I will certainly be glad to see the
Countess."

Goelsh smiled. "But you won't surprise her, will
you, my dear fellow? Don't just walk in on her. It's a

bad idea to surprise a wife after one has been away for such a long time—especially a wife as lovely as the Countess Chokolade."

Fritzl wanted to hit the man. Hit him across the face with a glove, and then kill him in a duel, but he controlled himself. A subordinate officer didn't challenge his superior—and the Commander of the entire Viennese garrison at that—to a duel. It just wasn't done. But if Goelsh couldn't be made to pay for that remark, Chokolade would—and he would see to it as soon as he was relieved of his duties.

Before he could leave the garrison, he had to speak to the duty officer, the officer of the day, and the officer in charge of the mess. He had to hand in his report, and arrange for the stabling of his horses. All this took time, and while he would rather have gone immediately to his home, rules were rules, and Fritzl didn't get to be a successful officer by disobeying the rules. But wherever he went in the barracks, he saw sly winks and little smiles.

"Home, Fritzl! Good for you. Do you think we'll be seeing something of you and the lovely Countess now that you're back? She certainly has kept to herself ever since you left."

"Except for that supposedly secret trip to Budapest." Another officer supplied that bit of news. "Well, it was supposed to be secret, but someone saw her get into a private compartment with a young man. Probably your brother, right Fritzl? Escorting your lovely wife to Budapest?"

"I have no brother," Fritzl said stiffly, aware that his fellow officer knew damn well he had no brother.

"Right—of course! I forgot. Well, maybe it was

her brother." And the officer laughed at the absurd idea that the beautiful and wild Chokolade could find no man more interesting to travel with than her own brother.

Fritzl was in a wild fury by the time he left the barracks, and he rode his horse into a lather before he arrived at his villa on the outskirts of Vienna. When he got there, his fury increased.

"The Countess," he shouted, "where is she?"

Most of the servants cowered below the stairs, and it was Dumma who faced Fritzl.

"She's in Vienna, sir," Dumma said, "in her own home, sir."

"This is her home," Fritzl roared. "She should be here. Damn her!"

It had never occurred to Fritzl that Chokolade would have returned to her own house when he was posted out of Vienna. His orders had come through so quickly, thanks to Rudolf's influence, that he had no chance to see Chokolade again—no chance to make sure that she obeyed his orders.

"Get me another horse," he said to Dumma. "Hurry, and have Buckner follow me with the coach."

The servants ran. Dumma hurried to the stables, the groom brought out a skittish bay gelding and threw a saddle across its back. Buckner shrugged quickly into his coachman's uniform, and had two grays put into the coach's traces.

In a very short time, Fritzl was pounding down the road and the avenues toward Chokolade's house. The servants there were startled by the banging of the brass knocker and the shouting.

Chokolade took a deep breath and waited in the small drawing room to receive her husband; she was doing her best to remember the lesson she had learned from Empress Elizabeth.

Fritzl burst in to the room, and she greeted him. There were no words of love, no words of tenderness from Fritzl von Kaplow.

"You," he said, "get your things—you're coming home with me now!"

"Yes, Fritzl," Chokolade said, "whatever you want."

Her quiet demeanor, her agreeableness, stunned him. He was expecting an argument, resistance. This new behavior didn't altogether please him. If Chokolade was so acquiescent, it meant she had been up to something while he was away and she didn't want him to find out about it. Never mind, let him get her to his house, away from her staring servants, and he would find out just what she had been up to while he was away.

Fritzl bustled Chokolade into the carriage that arrived some minutes later. He rode alongside, glancing at her from time to time. Chokolade looked straight ahead, she was doing her best to marshal her strength and to conquer her fear. It would be all right if she did nothing to aggravate Fritzl, he would have no reason to hurt her. She would be obedient, she would do as he asked, and maybe in time he would come to love her, to treat her with gentleness.

Once they arrived at the villa, Fritzl ordered her about just as he had on their wedding night.

"Get upstairs. Dumma—slivovitz and champagne. Cold champagne—hurry."

It was the same dreary suite of rooms, just as dark and forbidding as Chokolade remembered it. She had to stop herself from running out of the room, down the stairs, and flying from this place forever. But she remembered her promise to Empress Elizabeth, and sat quietly by, watching Fritzl alternate glasses of fiery Polish slivovitz with icy French champagne.

"I heard you've been doing a little traveling," Fritzl said, putting his glass down, "taking little trips while I was away. Did you enjoy yourself?"

"Traveling?" Chokolade said faintly. "I don't know what you're talking about."

"Don't lie to me," Fritzl roared. "You were seen—getting on the train to Budapest—with a man."

Gyuri, he was talking about her brother, and the time they went to Budapest, the time she helped him and Princess Dita get out of the Empire. She felt her throat tighten. How could she explain that trip to Fritzl? She didn't dare tell him the truth; she was sure that if he knew that she was involved with Fekete Andras he would torture her until she revealed everything she knew about his hiding place. And torturing her would only be a preliminary to turning her over to von Weis.

"I—I don't know what you mean." But Chokolade was a bad liar, and her faltering words only made him think the worst.

"I'll teach you to lie to me," he whispered, and his whisper was more menacing than his shouting. "Stand over there, and get undressed—slowly."

It was the same command he had given her on their wedding night. She had refused to obey him then, but now she did as he wished. She would do anything to stop his questions. She stood before him, and with stumbling fingers, unfastened the buttons of her dark brown, fitted jacket. She then slipped the jacket off her shoulders, and walking across the room, placed it on a chair.

With slow steps, she stood before her husband again, and slipped out of her long skirt. Once again she walked across the room to place the skirt neatly on the chair.

"Never mind that," Fritzl said with impatience. "Drop your clothes where you stand."

Chokolade did as she was told. She unbuttoned her camisole, and Fritzl stared at the firm breasts, the rose-colored nipples, and the slim rib cage. The camisole fell to the floor, and Chokolade opened the snaps of her petticoat, and this garment fell to her feet in a froth of white lace. She stood before her husband wearing nothing more than the beige boned corselet that began beneath her breasts, ending at her hips, and held up her sheer, beige stockings.

What the devil was wrong with the girl, Fritzl wondered? She didn't excite him at all. There she was, practically nude. She had a fine body, and clothed in a corselet and stockings she presented a lewd picture that should have tantalized him. But he wasn't tantalized at all; if anything, he was a little bored. She was too obedient, that was what was wrong. He liked his women to fight him, he liked to subdue them. But this new Chokolade—she stood before him like some provincial shopkeeper's bourgeois wife, obedient, willing, and altogether dull.

He missed the flash, the fire of the Chokolade he had. married. He was determined to taunt her, to bring her to anger, even to rage. That was the only way he could enjoy her.

"Very well," he said, "nicely done. Now you may undress me. First of all, my boots."

He expected her to throw a champagne glass at him, but instead she obediently grasped one booted leg, and actually tried to pull his boot off.

"Not that way," Fritzl said, "turn around."

She did as he asked, and she even took one of his booted legs between her naked thighs, while he planted his other leg, boot and all, on her rump.

Damn, this was no good at all, Fritzl thought with fury. What had happened to the girl? What had turned her into this spineless, worthless being?

"Never mind," he shouted, "get into bed. I'll take them off myself. You can't do anything right."

Still silent, but still obedient, Chokolade walked slowly to the bed and lay down on top of the red velvet cover. Fritzl followed, though he no longer really wanted her. Who could want such a broken woman? But he had to take her, and he managed to get himself interested by planning what he would do to her the following night. She thought she could get around him by pretending to be completely subservient; well, he would see how subservient she could be. He would test her, and he was sure that he could bring her back to being the fiery creature who interested him. He wanted a fighting bitch in his bed, not a dull cow.

Chokolade lay flat on her back, and let Fritzl take her. She didn't fight him, though his hands, his booted legs, his entire body punished her flesh with his. She restrained herself from making any sound. She wanted to shout, to weep, and to curse this man who used her so brutally, who treated her like an object, not like a flesh-and-blood woman. But she controlled herself, and made not one sound; finally, when he rolled off her and fell immediately to sleep, she told herself that she had done the right thing. At least he hadn't beaten her, and he hadn't questioned her further about her trip to Budapest.

The next morning Fritzl looked at her quizzically. What was she up to? Her behavior wasn't normal; he knew that. But at least she seemed to know her place as his wife, and he would see to it that she continued to know it. They were invited to a dinner at his commanding officer's that night, and while he didn't really like Baron Goelsh, he wanted the man to know that he was in complete control of his wife.

"We are going to Baron and Baroness Goelsh's home this evening," he informed Chokolade, "I want you dressed by eight-forty-five exactly, and I want you to behave decently when we get there. Remember, you're a von Kaplow now."

Chokolade longed to tell him that she always behaved decently, and if she only dared say it, she would rather be a Tura or a Pavonyi than a von Kaplow, but she said nothing, and only looked at her husband warily. She had promised the Empress that she would try and make a go of her marriage, but more important, she was afraid of Fritzl finding out about her meetings with Fekete Andras. He had been brutal toward her in bed, but thank God, he had not mentioned again her trip to Budapest.

She dressed carefully that evening, choosing a dark maroon watered silk gown that was finished with a lace top that went from the neckline of the dress to her throat. The sleeves were long; but while the demure dress covered her completely it also outlined the the curves of her slim body. Chokolade decided to wear no jewelry, since most of her necklaces and earrings had been given to her by men other than her husband. She was dressed and ready by eight-thirty, and when Fritzl came into her boudoir he was obviously disappointed that he couldn't harangue her about lateness.

He eyed her coldly. "That dress makes you look like a whore. Where do you get these outrageous clothes, from a manufacturer of dance costumes?"

Chokolade couldn't stop herself from answering him, though all day long she'd been planning to make only cautious replies to Fritzl's nastiness. "It's from the House of Worth," she said, "from Paris."

"The French! Decadent bastards. From now on you have your clothes made here in Vienna."

Chokolade sighed and said nothing, and the two of them went downstairs to their coach in silence. *I must be quiet,* Chokolade kept saying to herself over and over again. *I must say as little as possible. I must try not to make Fritzl any angrier than he usually is. I must be quiet.*

It wasn't hard to play the part of a quiet woman at the Goelsh's. Chokolade realized the moment she walked into the drawing room that here was the enemy. Every man in the room undressed her with his eyes, and every woman looked at her with hate. It was easy to see what they were thinking: so this was Rudolf's whore ... well, he wasn't around to protect her anymore. She was nothing but a cheap little Gypsy dancer. They would put her in her place, and keep her there.

Realizing that there was not one friendly face in the room overburdened with rococo carved angels and heavy, carved teak furniture, Chokolade did little more than smile and nod, and sip quietly from one glass of champagne. It was hard, though, hard to keep her counsel when she heard the mean little remarks made around the dining table about the Crown Prince and his mother. Rudolf was mad, was the consensus, and it was clear that he inherited this madness from his mother, that foreigner—that Bavarian.

Chokolade sat silently through course after course of heavy food. During a course of pike in aspic, Rudolf was shredded apart. When the consommé was served, Elizabeth had her turn. With the venison came more comments about Rudolf, but the gossip about Elizabeth mounted with every mouthful of partridge, and Chokolade felt her stomach turn as she looked at all the men surrounding her, and watched people devour both the bird and the reputation of the Empress.

"Of course Elizabeth travels a lot," Baroness Goelsh said with a little laugh, "when she went hunting in Ireland, wasn't there some talk about that man who breeds those Irish hunters? And in Hungary—"

"In Hungary," Baron Goelsh interrupted, "it is

said she actually goes out at dawn to ride with the *csikos*. And who knows what else she does beside ride?"

The guests roared with laughter, and Chokolade put her fork down across her plate, wondering if she could manage to escape the table before she threw up the little food she had eaten.

"The Empress and her precious Hungarians," someone else sneered. "Next thing, she'll take up with that murdering Fekete Andras and his bunch."

"That man, he'll murder us all in our beds if we don't watch out. What is wrong with von Weis? You think by now he would have caught the bastard and hanged him from the highest tree—"

"Ssh, ssh—there are ladies—"

"I don't care," the man who called Fekete Andras a bastard roared, "the ladies know about him, too. The man rapes, murders—"

Chokolade could stand no more. "That's not true." And her voice, hardly heard all evening, startled everyone into silence. "He does none of those things. Fekete Andras is a fine man—a Hungarian—a patriot, and with God's help, one day he'll free us from you damned Austrians—"

Chokolade's words were greeted with a roar! The elegant guests at the table suddenly seemed capable of tearing her limb from limb.

"Hungarian bitch."

"Rudolf's whore!"

Men were shouting words at her that had never before been heard at a polite dinner party, and the women were urging their men to say more—and still more. Chokolade had unleashed passions that were usually kept hidden. The people who had been smiling at her so politely—so falsely—all evening suddenly felt free to reveal everything they really felt about her.

It was Fritzl von Kaplow who brought the shouting and screaming to a halt. He was beside Chokolade, his hand clamped tightly about her wrist. But he wasn't there to defend her. His voice rose above the others.

"You will forgive my wife," he said, "she is not used to dining in polite society. Her manners leave much to be desired, I am afraid she has much to learn." His final words came out in a venomous hiss: "And I will teach her."

The other voices subsided, and the guests sat down once again. They reminded Chokolade of snakes retreating to their pit, but even as they sat down, ashamed of what they had revealed, their eyes were bright and hard upon her. But no one's eyes were harder than Fritzl's. Chokolade shuddered as he pulled her from the table and from the room.

My God, she thought, *what have I done? What have I done? He'll kill me.*

Fritzl didn't say a word to Chokolade until they were in his house, and in their own suite of rooms. She saw the ominous set of his shoulders as he carefully doubly locked the bedroom door, and she tried to brace herself for what he would do to her.

"So, you admire Fekete Andras, do you? You dare speak out that way in one of the finest houses in Vienna, you dare to speak well of that Hungarian peasant—that rapist—"

"He's not—" Chokolade began, and then was silent.

Fritzl's hand was at the lace throat of her gown. "How do you know? How do you know so much about him? How?" He pulled her to him, clutching the lace at her throat, and Chokolade was afraid that he was going to choke her.

"I—I don't know—I've heard—that's what all Hungarians say—that he's a patriot—"

"Patriot." The very word, applied to the rebel leader, enraged Fritzl, and with his free hand he struck her hard across the face. Her head went back, and she heard, rather than saw the ripping movement.

Fritzl had torn her gown in half, and she stood before him helplessly, her body exposed to his eyes and his punishing hands.

"So you like the rapist, yes? You like that Hun, that Mongol? Very well, I'll give you what you like."

Her two wrists were clasped in his powerful hand, and he dragged her across the room, but not to the bed. He pulled her over to a marble table on which rested a large vase filled with cream-colored roses. With the side of his hand, Fritzl sent the vase and the flowers crashing to the floor, and then he pressed Chokolade back so that she lay stretched out on the hard surface, her still-slippered feet dangling above the floor.

"Bed is too good for you," he hissed. "I'm going to take you the way your precious Fekete Andras would do it. He wouldn't bother letting you get comfortable first and neither will I."

Fritzl freed her body only of the clothes that

hampered him. He didn't strip her completely, and by leaving her in shreds of clothing he made her feel more nude, more helpless than ever. His booted legs forced her thighs apart, and he plunged into her with such force that her back slammed against the ungiving marble. He took her with one hard, punishing stroke after another.

"Is this what you dream of? And this? Is this the way you think he'd do it to you, tell me—tell me—"

Chokolade bit her lips to keep from crying out the words—the words that would reveal that she knew the real Fekete Andras—knew the gentleness of the man without ever having known his loving.

"Oh, no," she sobbed, "no—" Because after Fritzl had finished with her on the table he threw her on the floor, and standing above her he gave her one obscene command after another.

"No," she said, "I can't—I won't—"

"You will do it," he shouted, "you will do exactly what I tell you to—you will!"

His hands were around her throat and he was shaking her, shaking her, until suddenly he realized that the woman he was shaking so brutally resembled a rag doll, nothing more than a limp rag doll. She had fainted. Fritzl let her body fall to the floor, and for a moment he looked at the still body with fear. A faint—that's all it was—just a faint. Not like that time in Poland, when he had gone a little too far with the peasant girl. He bent down beside Chokolade. No, it was just a faint. He stood up and straightened his clothes. He would leave her alone for a few days. Let her recover. It didn't amuse him to beat a half-senseless woman. He liked his women strong, and struggling. He gave Chokolade only a slight backward glance before he left the room and the house to continue his pleasures elsewhere.

It was close to morning when Chokolade came to her senses. She dragged her bruised body up from the floor, and looked longingly toward the bed. But before she could lie down she had to bathe, had to try and wash the filthiness of Fritzl's acts from her body. She didn't ring for a maid, but ran her own bath water. In the steaming tub she contemplated her body, and she saw that the marks made by Fritzl were turning an ugly black-purple.

She would leave him, she decided, she would leave him. But where could she go? She no longer had friends in Vienna now that Rudolf was dead; last night's dinner party made that crystal clear to her. If she returned to Budapest Fritzl would follow her. He was quite capable of marching into the Café Royale where she would be dancing, and dragging her away.

Chokolade thought of Fekete Andras. She could always run to him, but her presence would make his own precarious life even more dangerous. Not only would von Weis and the Secret Police be after him, but she was sure that Fritzl could marshal an Army troop to hunt her down, and finding her would mean that she had led him straight to Fekete Andras.

No, no that wasn't the answer. She stepped from the tub, and her bruised body was shivering even though the room was warm. She wrapped herself in her warmest challis robe and then climbed wearily into bed. Think, she had to think, but not now, not until she had some rest.

Fritzl didn't return home for close to a week, and though Chokolade knew it wasn't possible, she prayed that he would never return. Her weary mind and body hadn't allowed her to find any solution, and one day looking out of the tall window at the enclosed park below, she thought, my God, this could be my life—the whole rest of my life shared with a madman. I can't live this way.

When Fritzl slammed into the house and into her room one morning he found Chokolade huddled in bed. Her green eyes were wide, frightened. Too frightened to please him. He chose to pretend that nothing had happened at their last night together, and he talked to her in the casual, normal manner of a husband chatting with his wife while sipping his breakfast coffee.

She didn't answer him, and he felt sure she was playing some little game with him. Well, he would bring her out of this silent, obedient, make-believe shell—he knew just how to do it.

"I've been away from Vienna a long time" he told her, "and I've missed my friends, missed decent company. There will be a guest for dinner tonight; be prepared to entertain him after dinner."

"Entertain?" Chokolade looked at him warily. "How do you mean—entertain?"

"We'll discuss it after dinner," Fritzl said smoothly. Let the bitch have something to worry about during the day. She would find out soon enough what he meant by "entertain." "Just be dressed for dinner at eight."

Chokolade nodded. Fritzl pushed his coffee cup away with disgust, and marched out of the room and out of the villa. She was absolutely no use to him if she was going to behave in this limp fashion. He would have to do something quite definite to bring her out of this trancelike behavior.

Chokolade dressed with care that evening; Fritzl was bringing a friend for dinner, she wanted him to be pleased with the way she looked, the way she acted as his wife and the chatelaine of his home. Maybe then he wouldn't abuse her.

But when her husband walked into the dressing room where she sat giving her hair a final brushing, he was not at all pleased with the way she looked.

"What is this?" His fingers flicked at the pleated collar of her georgette crepe green-and-white dress. "I said I wanted you dressed for company—properly dressed."

"But—but—I am properly dressed. This gown comes straight from Paris."

"Another Paris gown! Who wants to see a little Gypsy bitch dancer in a Paris gown?" He strode over to the large mahogany armoire in which her gowns were hung and he began to paw through them. "None of these are right. Where are some of the costumes you used for your dancing?"

"You want me to wear a dancer's costume to entertain your dinner guest?"

"Why not? Let my guest see why I married you. It wasn't because I thought of you as a fine lady, you know. It was because I saw you for what you really are—a little whore."

"I have no dancing costumes here," Chokolade said evenly. "I didn't understand that you wanted me in your home as an entertainer. I thought you wanted me here as your wife."

"Wife! You made me ashamed to have you as a wife when we were at Baron Goelsh's." Fritzl pulled the dresses from the armoire and threw them onto the floor. "Here, this isn't quite what I meant, but it will have to do."

Fritzl had chosen the black ball gown Chokolade had worn long ago to the fete in her honor given by Bela von Bruck. It was a beautiful creation, and the most provocative gown in her collection.

"That gown is meant for a ball. It was never intended to be worn at a dinner party at home."

Fritzl pulled her to him, and with one wrench he ripped the pleated collar from the dress she was wearing.

"You will wear what I tell you to wear, or you will come down in your underclothing. That's your choice."

Chokolade shivered and quickly stepped out of her ruined green-and-white dress, and reached for the black ball gown.

"And put some color on your face," Fritzl commanded. "I don't want to see you whey-faced. Do you understand me?"

Chokolade nodded, and he slammed out of the dressing room. She understood him, all right. She was his wife, but even though he had given her his name, that was not the way he thought of her. He wanted to show his guest that she was a trollop, a woman he had purchased for his bed. No decent woman in Vienna put paint on her face, that practice was strictly for entertainers or women of the streets. But her husband didn't want anyone to think of her as a decent woman, that was quite clear.

Wearily, Chokolade dressed. She redid her hair, piling it high, and decorating it with elaborate tortoiseshell combs from Spain. She rubbed some color into her cheeks and on her lips, and outlined her eyes with the black kohl she normally used only when dancing.

Before she went downstairs she took a long look at herself. She was beautiful, yes, but beautiful as a dancer, ready to perform before an audience.

"I am Baroness Pavonyi," she said out loud to the image staring back at her from the gold-framed mirror. "I am Countess von Kaplow." But the girl in the mirror mocked that statement. "You are Chokolade, Gypsy dancer, and that is all you ever will be."

Very slowly Chokolade walked down the stairs, and into the salon where her husband and his guest waited, standing before the fire, and sipping golden glasses of Tokay.

"Ah, there you are, my dear." Fritzl led her into the salon. His hand was under her elbow, propelling her forward until she stood before Fritzl's guest. "Chokolade, my dear, I would like you to meet our guest, Captain Sandor St. Pal, of the Royal Hussars."

Chokolade swallowed hard, she could say nothing—nothing in the face of the mocking little smile, the mocking little bow tendered to her by the Captain.

"It is a pleasure, Countess," St. Pal said, and he brought her hand to his lips.

Chokolade couldn't speak, but her husband spoke for her.

"Don't be so formal, St. Pal. Call my wife Chokolade, every man in Vienna and Budapest calls her that. There are so many who have gotten to know her well. Chokolade, you have no words for our guest? Never mind, it is not your conversation that we are interested in. You have far more charming qualities."

Before Chokolade could answer him, the butler was at the door announcing dinner, and Chokolade took her husband's arm.

Chokolade had no memory of touching any of the food on her plate as she sat between the two men. The candlelight made her rouged cheeks seem a more vulgar red, contrasted as it was to the rest of her pale face.

Course after course was brought to the table. The men ate, drank countless glasses of wine, and laughed and talked about military matters. Chokolade neither spoke nor ate. She sat at the table and concentrated solely on not weeping.

I must not cry. I must not cry. I must not let either of these men know that I am ready to weep, ready to destroy myself from despair.

At last dinner was over, and a decanter of port and a box of cigars was brought into the room. Chokolade rose. This was the usual signal for women to leave the dining room, and she was only too happy to do so.

"No, no." Fritzl put his hand out, and pulled her back down into the chair. "You must not leave us, my dear. It's only ladies who leave the dining room when the port and cigars are brought in, and you're no lady, are you?"

Chokolade stared at him—stared at the man she had married. He was drunk, she could see that, but he would have spoken this way to her even if he had been sober.

"Besides," Fritzl continued, "you're the star of the evening. Stars don't walk out on their audience. I have brought St. Pal here because I believe it will amuse me to watch you entertain him."

"Entertain?" Chokolade spoke for the first time, and her voice broke just slightly. "What do you mean—entertain—do you mean you want me to dance for the Captain?"

"You can dance if you wish, that's of no interest to me. I mean something far more amusing than that. I mean really entertain him—like the good little whore you are—in bed."

"Von Kaplow!" Sandor St. Pal exploded. "What are you talking about?"

"Just that. Hospitality of my house, St. Pal. I want you to enjoy it all—including my wife."

"Von Kaplow, you're mad!"

"Not at all. Why do you think I married the bitch? Expected her to entertain my friends. She knew that when I married her, she knew she'd have to pay for being made a von Kaplow."

Sandor St. Pal looked at the man sitting beside him with disgust, and then he turned that same gaze on Chokolade. To think he had spent months, months, thinking about her—dreaming about her. He had cursed himself for abusing her, for treating her like a little Gypsy tramp. But that was all she was, after all, and he had wasted his days—and his nights—longing for her. And what had he longed for? Nothing more than a trollop who would fall into anyone's bed, do any man's bidding for a price. He was disgusted with her, and he despised himself for being so caught up in his feelings about her that he hadn't been able to enjoy any other woman.

By Saint Stephen, he was going to leave this sinkhole of a house, he would go to old Buda, get good and drunk, and then he would find himself a whore or two. Honest whores, who admitted that they took money for what they gave, and didn't go around pretending to be fine ladies.

"Sorry to disappoint you, von Kaplow," said Sandor St. Pal. "And you, too, Countess. I choose my own bed partners, and I don't indulge in public exhibitions with them—"

It was Sandor St. Pal's words that finally broke through Chokolade's trancelike state. He thought— he actually thought—that she was a willing partner to Fritzl's obscene suggestions.

What had she been thinking of these past few weeks? Her fear and her loneliness had come close to destroying her sanity. She was afraid no longer. What was the worst that Fritzl could do to her? He could kill her, but death was better than becoming a fearful, sniveling coward who could be treated like a slave. *Ap i mulende*—by death—she had used the Romany oath before, but she had never understood it as well as she did at this moment. Death was not the most terrible thing: dishonor was far worse. She suddenly remembered who she was, and she also remembered old Matyas's words said to her so long ago on the Puszta.

"*And did you win?*" a little girl had asked an old man.

"*No,*" the old man had answered, "*but I would make the fight again.*"

She hadn't understood him then, but she understood him now. It wasn't winning that was important, it was making the fight for what you knew to be right. Fekete Andras had known that all along. Only she had never quite believed it. But she believed it now, and she was sure enough of that belief to face up to Fritzl von Kaplow, and to tell him and this arrogant pig of a Hussar Captain exactly what she thought of them.

"You," she said with contempt, "both of you—conceited, disgusting, rotten—do you think that I would go willingly to bed with either one of you? Never!" She stood up and pushed her chair back so hard that it fell backward on the floor. "Here—" She pulled a gold wedding band from her finger and threw it across the table at Friedrich von Kaplow. "I am not Countess von Kaplow, I am not Baroness Pavonyi, I am Chokolade, Gypsy dancer—and Gypsy dancers are worth more than titled ladies—because we do not sell ourselves."

With that she picked up her skirts, and fled from the room. The two men looked after her, and Fritzl was the first to speak.

"Good, good," he said softly, "now she is worth something. The little hellcat, how I'll enjoy taming her again—after you have her, of course, St. Pal. Then I'll punish her, first for refusing to sleep with you, and then for sleeping with you. Ahh, I'm going to enjoy tonight."

Sandor St. Pal stared at the man. "This was your idea? The whole thing? And your wife—" the words were bitter in his mouth—"Chokolade, she agreed to it?"

"Agreed? Of course not. And I knew she wouldn't, but don't you see, St. Pal, that just makes it more exciting. No fun at all, if she agrees."

Sandor St. Pal had never felt such disgust in his entire life. This perverted man was more than he had expected. He had heard stories about von Kaplow, but this went further than anything he had heard or could have imagined. He was still staring at the sickness that was Friedrich von Kaplow when he heard quick footsteps on the stairs. It was Chokolade, she appeared once more at the door of the dining room. She was dressed in a simple dark traveling suit, and she had taken the time to scrub her face clean of paint. In one gloved hand she carried a small bag.

"I'm leaving you," she said to her husband, "and this time I'm leaving for good. I was mistaken in marrying you, mistaken in thinking that we could ever have a life together. I am gong back to Hungary, and I am going to find my people. Better to be a Gypsy dancer, living in a caravan, and sleeping on the hard ground, than to be something dirty called Countess von Kaplow."

Fritzl walked over to her. "Leave me? Oh no, you'll never leave me. Do you think I'd allow that? Allow a little Gypsy whore of a dancer to walk out on me? Especially after I've given her the von Kaplow name? I'd be laughed at through the streets of Vienna." He pulled her to him by gripping one of her wrists. "I'll kill you first!"

"Von Kaplow!" Sandor St. Pal said. "Let go of her!"

"Stay out of this, St. Pal. I said you could have her in bed, and you still can, but you can't tell me what to do with my wife. I bought her—she belongs to me!"

"I belong to no one! I am not something you can buy—I am a woman, a Gypsy—and I will be free—"

She struggled with her husband. He held her with one hand and slapped her hard across the face with the other. Chokolade gasped, but she didn't stop fighting. It was Sandor St. Pal who brought the matter to a swift conclusion.

"I told you, von Kaplow, to let go of her." And when Fritzl turned toward him, Sandor St. Pal slapped him hard across the face.

Fritzl released Chokolade's wrists, and with a little cry she picked up her bag and ran from the room and the house. Friedrich von Kaplow stared at the Hussar captain. He was thoroughly sober now, and having difficulty believing what had just happened. St. Pal had struck him across the face; that was clearly an invitation to a duel, but a duel because of what, over whom?

"Are you crazy, St. Pal, or just too drunk to know what you are doing?"

"Neither. I know exactly what I am doing."

"You mean you challenge me to a duel? Over a Gypsy tramp?"

420

Sandor St. Pal's hand itched to slap von Kaplow once again, but he controlled himself. Save that for the morning they would meet with pistols.

"That's just it. She's not a Gypsy tramp, never was one, not even when she was traveling with the Gypsies and dancing for a few *pengö*. I was wrong about her—so wrong I would give my life to make it up to her—but you were even more wrong than I, von Kaplow."

"But that's exactly what you will do—give your life." Fritzl von Kaplow looked at him with a little smile. "You are in love with her. A great foolishness, that; you will die for that love, St. Pal."

"We will see. My seconds will call on you in the morning." And he gave Count von Kaplow a small, but thoroughly proper, bow.

Von Kaplow's return bow was equally correct. "My seconds will be here to receive them."

Sandor St. Pal hurried from the house. "The Countess," he asked the footman who was holding his horse, "did she take a carriage?"

The footman shook his head. "She was walking, sir, almost running. Toward the city."

The Captain put his crop to his horse. He knew he would catch up with Chokolade, she couldn't have gotten very far. In a few minutes he saw the slim figure striding alone, walking the deserted road as though she were on a wide city boulevard.

"Countess." He reined up beside her. "If you will permit me—"

She stared up at him. "Don't call me that."

"Sorry, Baroness Pavonyi—"

"Nor that. Chokolade. That's my name, a name

I've never had any reason to be ashamed of." She turned away and walked resolutely on.

"Please." Sandor St. Pal's horse pranced after her. This was ridiculous, and he leaped off his horse to walk beside her. "Won't you let me help you? At least let me take you to Vienna. If you would care to ride my horse—"

"I want nothing from you. Nothing! Including your horse."

God, she was magnificent! After all she had been through, she still had spirit and strength. He looped his horse's reins around his hand. "Very well, then, we will both walk."

"No need to do that. I can walk quite well by myself."

"You must allow me to escort you—"

"I can't stop you," Chokolade said bitterly. "I never could stop you from doing exactly what you wanted to me."

"I know that," St. Pal said. "I see things that I never really understood before. Everything that happened to you since you left Sárospatak was my fault. I—I'm sorry."

"Sorry!" Chokolade threw her head back, and her laughter filled the quiet night air. "Sorry!"

Of course he sounded ridiculous, and he knew he did. "I would give my life to make it up to you—that's what I told your husband."

"Husband—I can imagine how he must have laughed at that."

Sandor St. Pal realized that Chokolade didn't know that he and von Kaplow were to fight a duel. He wouldn't tell her, but if he was victorious, if he managed to free her from that bastard of a husband, then he would come to her. Come to her, and plead with her to allow him to devote his life to her.

The two of them continued walking, with Chokolade continually refusing the Captain's offer of his horse. They were close to Vienna when the Captain saw a solitary coach; he hailed it, and a weary Chokolade was able to ride the rest of the way to her home. St. Pal rode a few feet behind, and didn't leave until he saw Chokolade safely admitted to her own house.

He wanted to talk to her, longed to tell her of the love that he felt for her. If only he could convince her of his feelings, tell her of the empty months since he had last been with her. But there was time for that, time after the duel, after he had gotten von Kaplow out of the way.

If he got von Kaplow out of the way, he reminded himself. He was a good shot, but he knew that von Kaplow was supposed to be a better one. If only they could duel with rapiers, but von Kaplow was the challenged party, and, as such, he was entitled to the choice of weapons. St. Pal had no doubt that his choice would be pistols.

It didn't matter. He wheeled his horse about and went back to his rooms and to Kemeny, who had waited up for him. It was in God's hands now, or as he had once heard Chokolade say, "God's hands, or the devil's." He fell into a deep sleep, and his last thought was that if he died at von Kaplow's hands Chokolade was worth fighting for.

The next morning he instructed two of his friends

who were lieutenants under his command to meet with von Kaplow's second.

"Von Kaplow." One of his friends whistled. "Did you have to challenge such a good shot?"

"Don't be a fool," his other friend snapped. "Sanyi is as good as the best of them."

The first lieutenant reddened. "Of course, Sanyi, forgive me."

"It's all right, Erno," Sandor St. Pal said, "just make the arrangements. For tomorrow morning, if possible. I want to get this over with."

The two men left for the von Kaplow villa, and one of them said, "What does he mean—'get this over with'—is he suicidal?"

The other man looked equally gloomy. "Sanyi is a damn good shot, but still—"

"But still," his friend echoed.

The next morning Sandor St. Pal and Friedrich von Kaplow met on the outskirts of the Vienna woods with only their seconds and a doctor in attendance. It was dawn, the traditional time for duels, and the seconds seemed more nervous than the principals. Franz Josef had recently issued a strict order against dueling; he had been losing too many fine young officers to the custom of pistols or rapiers at dawn. The seconds felt that they would be blamed if the news of the duel became public, and if either man was killed, the news would be all over Vienna before the day was out.

St. Pal and von Kaplow listened to the instructions. They were told how many paces they were to walk, and on what command they could turn and fire.

She's worth it, Sandor St. Pal thought exultantly, *she's worth it. Even if I die, it's a well-deserved penance.*

This is stupid. Von Kaplow shook his head as he stepped out the required number of paces. *Stupid. Two men from fine families fighting over a little Gypsy whore. Insane.*

"Turn. Fire!"

Stupid, von Kaplow thought as he fell, *stupid.* And then he thought no more.

Sandor St. Pal's seconds were at his side examining his arm, which was covered with blood.

"Let the doctor look at your arm," Erno said.

"I don't have time for that now," the Hussar captain said. "Just put my dolman over my shoulders. Hurry."

"Sanyi—you must have that arm looked at."

"Later." One booted foot was already in the stirrup, and his friends saw him wince as he rested his weight on his wounded arm while mounting. "Later."

The two friends watched him ride off, and then turned with serious faces to the men who had come with Friedrich von Kaplow. They all looked down at the staring eyes, the bloody body.

Von Kaplow's seconds bowed to Sandor St. Pal's seconds. "It was all absolutely correct," one of von Kaplow's seconds said.

"Absolutely," St. Pal's seconds repeated.

"We'll tell that to his father. That, at least, will comfort the old man."

"Yes."

Sandor St. Pal was galloping toward Vienna.

With every movement his arm jolted and pained, but that didn't matter—he was going to Chokolade—going to her to offer his apology and his love. If she would only let him, he would willingly spend his life making everything up to her. He would treat her gently—oh, so gently—like a fragile porcelain Sèvres figure; and maybe in time, if God was good to him, she would consent to be his wife.

Chokolade's servants were startled out of their sleep by the pounding of the brass door knocker against the front door. The butler just managed to slip on a robe before he went to the door. His eyes widened when he saw the man in the Hussar uniform, his arm bloody and his dolman slung carelessly over one shoulder.

"Chokolade," the Hussar demanded, "Chokolade."

The butler looked at him severely. The man was probably drunk; he certainly wouldn't explain to him that his mistress had sold the house, and given all the servants a month's pay with permission to stay until the new owners took over. Why should he tell this man his mistress's business? But the look in the Hussar's eyes told the butler that he had better say something.

"Gone, sir," he said, "gone back to Budapest, I believe."

The butler was terrified by the sudden pallor of the man's face, and even more terrified when the Hussar pitched forward and fell unconscious on the doorstep.

It certainly had been exciting working for the

Baroness Pavonyi, or the Countess von Kaplow, or whatever she liked to call herself, but he would be just as glad to find a job with a quiet family where less happened. He looked at the man, bleeding and unconscious at his feet. Well, it was none of his affair; the best thing would be to get the police, let them make of it what they wished.

Chapter XVIII

"YES, YES, SHE'S BACK." Zsigismund Kalman beamed. "Chokolade has come back to the Café Royale, and she will dance here once again."

"Chokolade." The man who had questioned the proprietor of Budapest's most elegant café, snickered. "You mean the Baroness Pavonyi, don't you? Or perhaps I should say Countess von Kaplow—"

"You should say Chokolade," Chokolade said, having overheard the conversation, "just Chokolade."

The man bowed and backed off in confusion. It was just as Rudolf had warned her it would be. People came to see her not because of her dancing, but because of the notoriety that surrounded her. She became even more popular when it was learned that her husband had been killed in a duel. The Captain had killed Fritzl; perhaps she should feel grateful to him, but she wanted to feel nothing—not gratitude, nor love, nor pain. In the past she had felt too much, experienced too much, and now she just wanted to be left alone. She came to the Café Royale to dance, and afterward she stepped into a waiting carriage and went to her villa on St. Margaret's Island. Gröf Bela von Bruck suggested a fete in her honor, but she thanked him and refused. Other admirers begged her to dine with them, to attend the opera, or even to join them at Gerbeaud's for afternoon coffee, but to all of them she had the same answer: "I am tired, too tired—"

"But you're not too tired to dance," they often protested.

"Dancing is my life. It helps me rid myself of my anger and pain and sadness."

Everyone looked properly mystified upon hearing that, and no one understood what Chokolade meant—no one until Sandor St. Pal came to Budapest and heard Chokolade's explanation of her art.

"Of course," he said, "I understand. I know what she means."

He wanted so much to see her, to tell her that he understood, but he didn't want to make declarations of love and understanding at the crowded Café Royale, and instead he waited in front of her villa on St. Margaret's Island. She was startled one night to see a tall figure step forward from the shadows.

"Chokolade—"

That voice, that familiar, hurting voice. She didn't step back, but her chin went up higher. "Yes, Captain St. Pal?"

"Chokolade, please, let me talk to you—please—"

She knew she could insist that he say whatever he had to say on her doorstep. Even if she did that he would be back the next night, and the next. But she no longer had the need to play such games; besides, she didn't want him coming back night after night. She no longer wanted him at all.

"Very well, Captain St. Pal, you may come in."

Once inside the gilt-and-mirrored salon of her villa, St. Pal had trouble speaking to her. She was as beautiful as ever—perhaps even more beautiful, if that was possible—but cold, absolutely cold.

She caused him such confusion that the words burst from him awkwardly, and not at all the way he had planned to say them.

"Chokolade—I love you—I want you—I want you to marry me—"

He had said it all badly—so badly he wasn't surprised at her reaction.

"'Marry a little Gypsy dancer who's whored her way through the beds of the Empire.' Why would you want to do that, Captain St. Pal?"

She was repeating his words to him—the ones he had thrown at her when they had met riding in Vienna. He remembered those words as well as she did, and he cursed himself for ever having said them.

"I was wrong," he said, "terribly, stupidly wrong. Can't you forgive me?"

She shrugged. "It no longer matters."

Her indifference was worse than her anger. He had to break through her shell of ice. Words— words were all wrong between the two of them. He still remembered how she made him feel, and how he made her respond. He had to make her feel something for him once again.

It was desperation that made him move toward her, made him take her in his arms and kiss her. But it was like kissing a statue, a beautiful, impervious statue. She didn't try to fight him off, she didn't even appear to be angry. He was the one who lost his temper.

"What is it? What's wrong with you?"

"Nothing's wrong with me." Chokolade regarded him calmly. "I'm just not interested, that's all."

"I could make you interested," Sandor St. Pal said softly. "You'll see, you could be very interested if you'd only let yourself be."

"I don't think so," Chokolade said, as coldly as if she were inspecting a menu at a restaurant that bored her. "I don't really think so, Captain."

"Damn you," St. Pal exploded, "if I could get you into my bed again, I'd show you!"

Chokolade looked at him without moving, and Sandor St. Pal felt like a fool. "Forgive me, Countess von Kaplow," he said with bitter formality.

"Don't call me that." And it was the first time Chokolade behaved with some of her old fire. "I never want to be called by that name again!"

"Very well, then, Baroness Pavonyi—"

"Nor by that name," Chokolade flashed. "No countess or baroness for me—I am Chokolade, and that's quite good enough."

"Chokolade"—St. Pal had a feeling of hope—"just Chokolade, the Gypsy dancer, is that enough for you?"

"More than enough—for me, and for the whole world."

Sandor St. Pal bowed and took his leave. Better and better! She was Chokolade the Gypsy dancer, that's what she wanted to be, and that's how he could make her come back to life. He remembered with shame the names he had called her: Gypsy bitch, Gypsy tramp, Gypsy whore. She was none of those things, but she was a Gypsy witch, a beguiling Gypsy witch who was in his blood—no, not in his blood alone—in the very marrow of his bones—and it was as a Gypsy that he would win her.

The Captain's horse reared, so abruptly did the Captain handle the reins and the spurs, but the horse's nervous behavior didn't bother St. Pal. *He knew,* by God, *he knew,* and now he would just have to work out a plan.

Chokolade told herself that she wasn't one bit disappointed the next day, or the next, that the Hussar captain was no longer mooning about her door, or even sitting by himself at a corner table at the Royale. Good, she had gotten rid of him at last; she wanted no man around her, not even the Captain, who had now humbly asked her to marry him. With a pang, she remembered Rudolf; the Crown Prince felt that she would be safe and protected if she married. She had tried that with von Kaplow, and she knew that marriage was not for her. She would make her own life, go her own way, and she would depend on no one.

If Chokolade was convinced that living alone was best, St. Pal was not. He had ridden out of Budapest the very night he had left Chokolade at her villa, and he had driven his horse hard, anxious to get to the Lake Balaton region of Hungary. The lake was a rich man's resort during the summer months, but in early spring it was where the Gypsies gathered. The authorities didn't like having them there, but as long as they were gone before the large hotels opened, the local people felt it best not to make a fuss.

When the Captain arrived at the lake, its very expanse both impressed and depressed him. The lake was forty-one miles long and six miles wide, and looked like the sea. He realized he would have to spend days—days searching out the people who could help him win Chokolade.

He stopped at a local tavern, demanded breakfast and a fresh horse, and without snatching a few hours sleep, he started out on his journey around the lake. Everywhere he rode, he saw Gypsy caravans, and everywhere he rode he was faced with the blank, hostile stares of the Gypsies.

"The Tura Tribe? Never heard of them."

"The Turas? They're in the north. No, I don't know where."

"Turas? Are they Gypsies? Strange names for Gypsies. Are you sure they're Gypsies?"

After two days Sandor St. Pal realized that he would never get a straight answer, never hear the truth from these people who so obviously distrusted him. And why wouldn't they, he thought. He had ridden across plenty of Gypsy camps, not caring about the children who scampered to escape his horse's hooves, not caring about the cooking pots, and the caravans overturned in his wake.

He decided that the Turas, if they were camped around Lake Balaton, would have to come to him. He rode out again the next morning, and whenever he saw a Gypsy, he spoke to him.

"Look, if you see the Tura Tribe—"

"Don't know any Tura Tribe."

"Of course not, but just in case you should meet them in your travels, I would appreciate your giving them a message." He took a *pengö* from his pocket, tossed it in the air, and caught it again.

"What message?" The Gypsy eyed both the Hussar and the spinning silver coin warily.

"The message that Chokolade needs help from the Turas, and if they want to know more, tell them to see me at the inn."

Sandor St. Pal didn't wait for an answer, he tossed the coin to the Gypsy. "Will you do that?"

"If I meet some people called Tura—whoever they may be—and if I remember, and if I'm not in too much of a hurry—I will."

"Thank you." St. Pal touched his cap, and clicked to his horse. That day he spoke to eight more Gypsies, and he told each man the same thing. Each time he got a noncommittal answer, but by the end of the day, he felt reasonably sure that if the Turas were anywhere about, they would have received his message.

He waited impatiently at the inn, wondering if the search was hopeless. The second night he was having a supper of pork *szekely gyulas* with sauerkraut when an old Gypsy violinist came into the inn and asked the proprietor if he might play for his guests.

The man who owned the inn shrugged. "It's all right with me. But I haven't got any guests. This isn't the season. He's the only guest." And he pointed to the Hussar captain.

The old man came over to St. Pal's table.

"Perhaps the Captain would like to hear a song?"

St. Pal was about to chase him away, but something about the old man, something familiar, teased his memory, and he said, "I'd like that. A love song, a sad one, that's what I'd like to hear."

The Gypsy tucked his fiddle beneath his chin, and played a sobbing rendition of "There's Only One Girl In The World For Me." St. Pal listened attentively, handed the man a handful of silver *pengö*, and then asked him if he'd care for a glass of wine.

"No—I thank the Captain."

"A glass of *barack,* then. Landlord—" And the man scurried over, bringing a bottle of apricot brandy.

It was only after he finished his drink, and was toying with his glass, that the Gypsy spoke.

"Is it the Captain who has been riding around Lake Balaton looking for the Tura Tribe?"

"It is."

"May I ask the Captain why he's looking for that thieving bunch? The Turas give all Gypsies a bad name, and I don't think the Captain will find them anyway. I hear they're in Spain."

"I don't believe they're a thieving bunch,"— Sandor St. Pal chose his words carefully—"and I hope they're not in Spain. I need their help."

The old Gypsy shrugged. If a *gajo* needed help, that was none of his affair.

"And one of the Turas badly needs help from the tribe, too."

The old man looked up. "One of the Turas? The Captain knows someone from the Tura Tribe?"

Sandor St. Pal nodded, and took a deep breath. "Chokolade, Chokolade Tura, I know Chokolade Tura."

The Gypsy looked more wary than ever. "It is hard to believe that the great dancer, Chokolade, would need help. It has been said that she is a baroness now, or is it a countess? Why should someone like that need help from us—I mean, from the Turas?"

"You are a member of the tribe," Sandor St. Pal exulted. "I thought so, you looked familiar—"

"And so do you, Captain," the old man said dryly, "very familiar. I still remember the day when you rode into our camp at the Balog estate, Gorshö. You took Chokolade away with you that day, as hostage, I believe, for some jewels." The old man paused. "Is the Captain still searching for the same jewels? I hope they may have been found by now."

The Meleki jewels—he had forgotten all about them. Of course, the Turas would think that he was still hounding them for the jewels, when, in truth, the Melekis had been quite happy with the ones he had recovered. Neither they, nor he, cared about the other missing gems.

"I am not here about the jewels," he said. "I hope you will believe me, I am here because I love Chokolade and want to marry her, and I won't be able to unless you—and the Tura Tribe—help me."

"Chokolade has been away for a long time. Why should she listen to us? I'm sure that by now she has quite forgotten all about the *leis prala*."

"The *leis prala?*"

The Gypsy sighed, and launched into an

explanation of Gypsy laws. Sandor St. Pal was stunned. Everything he had thought about Gypsy girls had been wrong. He had forced Chokolade to break one of the most important laws of the Romanys, and more than ever he felt responsible for everything that had happened to her since that night on the river bank.

"You must help me," Sandor St. Pal said, "you must! Chokolade has become so sad, so lonely." He hesitated. "I don't even know your name."

"It is Miklos," the old man said. "Uncle Miklos is what Chokolade called me. I am Miklos Tura."

Sandor St. Pal sat back, poured glasses of *barack* for himself and Uncle Miklos, and launched into the explanation of his plan. Uncle Miklos listened, but shook his head.

"It won't work. If we were to do as you wish, we would be arrested. The police of Budapest would never let us do such a thing. They'd ride us down with their horses, and cart us all off to some jail."

"You can trust me," the Hussar captain said. "I won't let any such thing happen to you. I will arrange everything with the police, and with the commander of the Budapest garrison. You won't be chased, and you won't be arrested—I promise you."

Uncle Miklos looked at the man for another minute. Yes, he might be the right man for Chokolade. He was tall, lean, his body hard from spending time in the saddle. His dark hair had a wavy streak of white across the front, and he looked tired, but despite that, he had a young face. It was a good, strong face, Uncle Miklos decided, the face of a man who could keep a woman happy and satisfied.

Uncle Miklos winked. "All right, *pral,* we'll do it."

"*Pral?*"

"Brother, in Romany, and if you do marry Chokolade, that's what you'll be to every Gypsy—a *pral.*"

"There is no *if* about it," St. Pal said, "I will marry Chokolade." He threw his head back and laughed, and Uncle Miklos saw the tiredness leave his face. "How could she resist such a courtship? Now, this is what I want you to do...."

A few days later Budapest was treated to a sight that had never been seen in that old and sophisticated city. It looked like an invasion, but not a military invasion of Hun or Mongol. No, this was a colorful invasion of Gypsy caravans.

Householders stared out of their windows, strollers stopped to stare, and then waved as they watched caravan after caravan move slowly down the city streets. Five caravans, were there? No, ten! No—more than that—so many that everyone stopped counting, and still the caravans kept coming.

Each caravan was decorated with flowers, and driven by Gypsy women in their best and brightest clothes. Gypsy men rode alongside on proudly prancing horses, their golden earrings catching the sunlight that flashed off the bright metal. But the gold was not any more dazzling than the white satin shirts, the embroidered vests, the polished and scalloped high boots.

And at the head of the caravans, leading the entire tribe of Turas and other Gypsies who had come along for the excitement, was a Hussar captain on a chestnut stallion that had also been polished and curried for the occasion.

If possible, the Captain was even more gorgeous than the Gypsies who followed him. Not satisfied with his elaborate daily uniform, he wore the dress outfit usually donned on the most formal of state occasions. His cream-colored whipcord pants were tucked into mahogany leather boots that came up to his knees. His short blue jacket had every gold-embroidered fastening carefully closed, and his white wool dolman hung with the most carefully designed carelessness from one shoulder. Tipped at just the proper angle over his right eyebrow was the Captain's high golden helmet with the plume of white feathers floating in the front.

"I've never seen a soldier look like that, Mama," said one little boy who watched the parade go by.

"Neither have I," said his mother, "except at the Coronation of the Emperor and Empress. I wonder what is happening?"

All Budapest wondered what was happening, and much of Budapest watched as Sandor St. Pal led the caravan of Gypsies to Chokolade's villa on St. Margaret's Island. At his instructions, the caravans grouped in front of the door, and when he gave the signal, the ten finest violinists of the Tura Tribe massed beneath a balcony and began to play "There's Only One Girl In The World For Me."

Chokolade had heard a commotion outside, but she decided that the servants could attend to it, and she turned over in her bed and tried to go back to sleep. But then—then—the noise grew louder—and it wasn't noise alone—it was music.

She got out of bed, wrapped herself in a pale green cashmere robe, opened the French windows, and stepped out onto a small balcony. She was dreaming! She had to be. Gypsies—every Gypsy she knew from the Tura Tribe, and many others, were on her lawn.

"Chokolade, Chokolade!"

Uncle Miklos, was that Uncle Miklos waving at her? And was that Cousin Laci playing the violin? The violinists saw her, and swept from the song they had been playing to another old favorite of hers, "Acacia Street."

"Wait," she called down to them, "wait. What is this? What are you doing here?"

The Gypsies stopped playing and Cousin Laci stepped forward to answer her, but before he could speak a gorgeous Hussar rode forward and shouted, "No, no—don't stop—keep playing. Chokolade, let me in—let me talk to you, please."

"No," she shouted down to him, "you're crazy, and there's nothing to talk about."

Sandor St. Pal nodded. "All right, if you won't listen. Go on—go on playing," he instructed the violinists, who struck up a loud, fast *csardas*.

Chokolade disappeared from her balcony into her bedroom. He was crazy, they all were! They'd have to stop eventually and go away. But the music continued through the morning, and the noise among the nonmusicians grew more raucous. It was obvious that someone had passed a number of bottles of good *barack* among them. My God, they would all be arrested. She hurried into her clothes, and ran down the stairs and out of the house.

441

"Chokolade, Chokolade." She was surrounded by Turas, who hurried to greet her and hug her as she looked out upon an unbelievable scene. The caravans appeared quite at home on the elegant lawn, and she could see that someone had even built a small fire.

"*Szalonna,*" she said, halfway between laughter and tears, "is someone actually roasting *szalonna* on St. Margaret's Island? You must all stop—go away—you'll be arrested. This is Budapest, not the Puszta."

Uncle Miklos stepped forward. "It's all right, Chokolade—really it is. He says it is." He nodded toward Sandor St. Pal, who was moving from caravan to caravan like some sort of benevolent host. "He seems to be an important man, Chokolade, and in love with you. We came to tell you, we think you ought to marry him."

"Marry him! Do you know who he is? What he has done?"

Uncle Miklos shrugged. "Not even God can undo past mistakes, and only the devil insists on reminding us of them."

He nodded to the Hussar captain, who came over to Chokolade's side.

"How long is this going to go on?" she asked St. Pal.

"Until you say you'll marry me." He took her hands in his and brought them to his lips. "Forgive me, Chokolade, and marry me."

"Marry him, Chokolade." Uncle Miklos had been hovering nearby. "It's true he's only a *gajo*, but he's got the instincts of a good Romany."

With a little cry, Chokolade pulled her hands free

and ran into the house. Uncle Miklos winked at Sandor St. Pal.

"Go ahead, *pral,* go ahead."

Sandor St. Pal followed Chokolade into the house and found her sobbing on a couch in the small salon. He tried to take her into his arms, but she fought herself free of him.

"You're crazy," she said. "It's too late for all this—too late!"

"Is it? Too late for this—and for this?" And then he folded her in his arms, and though she struggled he wouldn't let her go. "Don't talk," he said, his mouth coming down upon hers. "There has been altogether too much talk between us."

She sighed as she felt his lips, and when she knew his kiss and allowed her head to rest against his shoulder she knew that she had come home at last.

Outside, Uncle Miklos was explaining important matters to the Turas. "They will marry in St. Stephen's Church, that is the *gajo* way. But he leaves it to us to arrange a true Romany ceremony as well. He says he wants to be married to Chokolade as completely as possible. And then—"

"And then?" Cousin Laci laughed. "Do you expect to go on their honeymoon, too, old man?"

Uncle Miklos's eyes gleamed. "The Captain has asked us to escort them out of the city to his estate in the north, near the Great Alföld Plains. And he has given his promise, we can camp there as long as we wish."

"Camp in one place?" The Turas were immediately indignant. "Does he think we are farmers, peasants? We are Gypsies!"

"No, no," Uncle Miklos assured them, "no one

can keep us in any one place. But we can camp there in the summer, or the spring—if we wish."

"If we wish," Cousin Laci repeated, and then he picked up his violin and began to play a Gypsy song so old that no one remembered its name, or knew any words that might have been written to its haunting melody. The Romanys said that each pair of lovers wrote their own words to the song.

Chokolade heard the music as it drifted softly into the house, and she raised her head from Sandor's shoulder.

"It is the love song," she said.

"Which love song?"

"*The* love song," she said. "It has no other name."

"We will make it our song—it will be ours forever."

"Forever," Chokolade echoed as she nestled against him again. She shut her eyes and let their song of love transport her. Sad and bad memories disappeared as the sweet music throbbed and melted, telling them both that their love would last forever, even, as the legend said of all true lovers, when they met on the other side of the Blue Lake.